The
ROSE
VARIATIONS

In memory of Linda Jadwin

ACKNOWLEDGMENTS

I am grateful to the many people who responded to this novel in manuscript: Merie Kirby, Lucy Chamberlain, Paulette Alden, Patrice Koelsch, Lois Metzger, Freya Manfred, Cris Anderson, Jon Spayde, Margaret Hasse, Amie Miller, Cheri Collins, and Lee Thomas. Also, my peerless agent, Stephany Evans, and my excellent editor, Katie Herman. For insight into the world of classical composing, thanks to composers Libby Larsen, Randall Davidson, Carol Barnett, Fritz Bergman, Melinda Wagner, and Jennifer Higdon. Thanks to Jan Terrio for her informative discussion of Alzheimer's patients, to Linda Gallant for helpful details about family court, to Brian Mahaffy for explaining piano tuning, and to Anna Meigs and Ruth Weiner for insight into academic tenure. And finally, a particular thanks to Luigi Salerni.

PART ONE

⬦

"... there is a space of life ... in which the soul is in a ferment, the character undecided, the way of life uncertain, the ambition thicksighted. ..."
—John Keats, preface to *Endymion*

Chapter ONE

R ose MacGregor laughed and shouldn't have. Frances, it seemed, was going to cry. Frances Dupre, leaning against the kitchen counter of Rose's sublet in a twisting old neighborhood in St. Paul on a muggy August night, held a full wine glass that she didn't seem to be drinking from, but rather posing with as the tears trickled down her face. She wept because Rose was lucky in love, while she, Frances, was not. This was ridiculous, something Frances had invented out of thin air.

"Look at you," said Frances. "How your clothes drape on you. Your hair. You're one of the lucky ones," she declared through the majesty of her tears.

"Oh, please," said Rose and glanced down at herself, at her lean, unremarkable body in the well-worn T-shirt and jeans, at the unraveling sleeves of the dark green sweater that had gotten her through grad school. Her bones were big, her breasts too small, and her clothes, she knew, hung plainly. People remarked that her eyes were very blue, MacGregor blue, her father's eyes. And she had a good head of hair spilling down her back; but nearly everyone wore their hair long then. Frances did. In her pressed linens, Frances was far better dressed than Rose, and her dark hair was longer than Rose's and thicker, held back from her face by a pair of genuine tortoiseshell combs.

"You just watch. Someone's going to grab you up in a minute," said Frances, pulling the combs out and thrusting them back in again.

Rose supposed the college had grabbed her up; and though this was not exactly love, it was luck of a generic sort. The year was 1975; *Time* magazine's Man of the Year was the American Woman, though no one woman in particular; colleges were hiring women, at least temporarily. Rose was referred to as the Girl Composer behind her back. Frances had told her. In the all-male music department, Frances was the secretary and heard all the gossip. "Girl Composer" was not a term of esteem, Rose knew. In nine months' time, when her teaching appointment ended, she might be waiting tables. She might very well end up a secretary herself, she told Frances.

"No, you won't," said Frances. "You won't have to. You'll meet someone."

"If you say so." Rose had what she considered a pathetic history with boyfriends and had told Frances all about it. Her last affair had been a solemn three-week fling with another music student, a misguided show of how much they thought they'd miss each other after graduation. They hadn't even swapped postcards since then. But none of that seemed to matter to Frances, who gazed into the future as her wine glass wobbled.

"You'll get some new guy within the month," she said.

"Now, there's a prediction," said Rose, who had never felt more alone in her life.

She was twenty-five. She'd arrived in St. Paul only the week before with nothing but a few T-shirts, a couple pairs of jeans, sneakers, a box of books, her bicycle, and her cello. She knew no one there but the people she'd met in the music department, and was on a first-name basis with no one but Frances.

She took the sloshing wineglass, set it down, and slipped her arm around Frances. Did they know each other well enough for this sort of scene? Perhaps they did.

Frances was close to homely: thin as a scarecrow, with piercing eyes. Nonetheless, her attention to details of hair and clothes made her seem born to fascinate. Her focus was on love, on love alone, on some tragic love that she seemed to be working up to revealing. Rose didn't mind hearing about tragic love. Her previous girlfriends, however, had been tomboys—ambitious types who liked dancing, teasing, getting men into arguments and into bed, getting in and out of affairs without any obvious falling to pieces. Rose's mother and her sister, too, were both so peculiarly themselves that their femaleness seemed almost incidental. As for Rose, she was composer first, woman second. It was how she'd survived. So she didn't quite get why Frances saw her as girlfriend material, nor could she imagine how she could reciprocate all the attention, for Frances had been uncannily involved in everything that concerned Rose since she'd first set foot in Minnesota the previous spring.

Just before her grad school commencement back east in Philadelphia, Rose had been invited to the college in St. Paul to interview. She recognized the opportunity, a job in music and a title, but had had to refer to a map to sort Minnesota from Wisconsin and Iowa and all the other blocky states in the middle and had quailed at the warnings that blizzards out there started in October and didn't end till May.

On a day in May, wearing a borrowed wool dress and pumps, the pumps too small, the dress too hot, she'd stepped off the plane in Minnesota, not into snow but into boiling green springtime. From her cab window an old army fort loomed. Then the Mississippi, a wide wetness, turned below a bridge and the freeway emptied into streets that led uphill to the college. It could have been a college anywhere—lush lawns, red brick and ivy, bell tower, library columns with motto above and wide steps below, and a shifting crowd of jabbering young people, wrapped up in themselves as though theirs was the only possible life. Rose appeared to fit in: just another girl in a sacklike garment—the dress she wore which she'd thought flowed nicely was, in fact, too large at the waist. Somebody belched and she smiled, pretending to be one of them. The schedule was firm—interview, guest lecture, reception—but just then, just before she announced herself, the need to utter her name struck her as painful. For no reason she could think of, it seemed a burden to be someone in particular. And then she saw Frances.

At the entrance to the music department, at the center of a glass cubicle—a fishbowl, Frances would say; a glass case for an ornament, Rose would come to think—stood Frances's desk and on it a name plate which read not her name, but *The Beauty*.

"Do you go by *Beauty*," Rose asked, "or *The* for short?"

Their eyes met and Frances chuckled. Then she went still. "Rose Mac-Gregor? Good heavens! Was there no one to meet you at the airport?" Her voice was low and dry like two pieces of cardboard rubbed together. Her hand in Rose's was slim, the fingers exaggeratedly long. Frances was certainly someone in particular.

"The Chairman went to meet you." Frances reached for her phone.

Rose picked up the nameplate. "I've got to get one of these."

"You? You don't need one," Frances had replied.

And Rose had felt her spirits lift. Frances's appraisal, however mistaken, made her feel well-favored. Her shoes eased themselves around her feet and if her dress ballooned as she was conveyed from place to place, at least the hot wool didn't stick to her skin. She felt keen, percussive, a jolt of lightning in a cloud, very possibly a beauty. She found her voice, became loquacious, chatted her way through the interview, waxed eloquent for her lecture, and, during the reception, bantered, prompting small explosions of laughter even from the Department Chair. Chairman and Professor Harold Atkinson, in tweed vest with braided leather buttons, flanked by his small, pale, freckled wife, Doris, occupied the same corner of the faculty lounge the whole of the reception, where people approached him and murmured as if at a shrine. The Chairman was the one due for sabbatical, whose teaching duties Rose would assume. A sabbatical for reasons of health and of family, said Frances, who handled protocol as though with silver tongs. She purred and jingled and ferried Rose from person to person, buoying things up, creating the occasion. And so it was partly Frances's doing that Rose got the job and the borrowed office and the sublet of the Atkinsons' apartment, where Frances now prophesied Rose's future luck.

"Alan likes you."

"Alan?"

"Come on, *Alan*. The good-looking one."

Of course Rose knew Alan, the other junior faculty member in the music department. Why pretend she didn't? She'd seen him up close just an hour before.

Earlier that evening, she'd taken her bicycle for a fast ride through the winding streets around the college. The neighborhood amused her. Informally called Tangletown, the hilly old district had never been leveled or squared. Sidewalks and streets went where footpaths and wagon tracks must have first gone and houses never stood quite side by side. The streets coiled and wandered and intersected, creating islands and extra corners, forcing drivers to stop to ask for directions and Rose to carry a map in her pocket. Her borrowed duplex stood on one corner and, on another several blocks away, stood Frances and her mother's narrow colonial with its picket gate and pepperberry wreath. The streets had a way of turning back on themselves, and, more than once in her wanderings, Rose arrived unexpectedly at Frances's gate or back at her own doorstep before she'd intended.

That evening, however, she'd found her way out of Tangletown to the wide avenue that ran past houses tall and grand to the great, gray mound of the Cathedral and then steeply downward to the riverbed, the wide Mississippi river basin where downtown St. Paul stood in its venerable grime. Though the sun had barely set, the city appeared so deserted it might have been midnight. An enormous black cupcake of a building, the Civic Center, entirely unpopulated, stood near to a blond temple faced in Greek columns, opposite a steep red brick, eight stories high and lined by a fire escape, the Catholic Youth Organization, no youths in evidence. Letting out her brakes, she blasted through a park, past a still fountain beside a stone castle with a clock tower, and then hurled herself through a red light.

In the gathering dark, in her dark green sweater, she couldn't be seen. Turning back uphill, she switched on her bike lamp. Its irritable stutter made more noise than light. She took to the sidewalk, head down, huffing, and so smashed into the only other living being on the hill, Alan Gilpin. Calling out hoarsely, he jammed her wheel to a stop with his foot and then grabbed her shoulders so she wouldn't fall.

"Are you okay?" he asked breathlessly.

Of course she was. Was he?

"Yup," he said and went on.

If chagrined, she was also thrilled. His rangy build was of the type that had always caught her eye, and he smelled frankly of sweat. But he was also gay. Rose thought of the commanding post the secretary's desk occupied in the front office of the music department and of poor Alan, conducting his business there while *The Beauty* tried to engage him over the xerox machine.

"Alan's gay, Frances."

"How can you say that? He brings women to concerts and things at the college."

"Well," said Rose. She thought he was. Some of the best ones were; Rose, in the course of her misadventures, had had to develop radar for that.

But it wasn't Alan who Frances yearned for. Gazing at the wall above the kitchen stove, where the absent Chairman Atkinson could be studied in triptych—first filling a folding cup from a spring, then handing it to his wife, and then, in priestly fashion, watching her drink—Frances choked out her confession in two words, the most important of her life: Harold Atkinson. The affair was long over—years over—but Frances would never be over *him*.

It occurred to Rose with a chill that Frances wasn't actually visiting her: she was visiting the home of her lost love. Frances declared she couldn't talk about it, then abruptly marched into the bedroom—the bedroom of her married lover, now Rose's bedroom—and, standing at the foot of the bed, declared her love for Harold Atkinson, and his for her—oh yes. They were sinners, she knew, and Rose might despise them for it, but Harold had been too lonely. So what if Doris couldn't have children? Doris had Harold! How could Doris cry herself sick every day when she had Harold?

What Rose could recall of Harold Atkinson was a pair of glasses with thick, dark frames and the boxy vest whose leather buttons she could not imagine wanting to unfasten. But there was a youthful version of Harold, many versions in the photos, large and small, that filled the mantel and lined the walls, photos of the Chairman and his wife in hiking clothes against the backdrop of various mountain ranges labeled *Urals, Alps, Andes,* his hair not yet gray, her freckled face lively, their hands joined, a radiant pair.

As the apartment would be occupied by Rose for nine months, why hadn't they put the photos away? Their closet was all empty hangers. The massive chest of drawers would remain mostly empty—Rose didn't begin to have the clothes to fill it. Getting into bed that first night, she'd rolled into a hollow, stretched her arm and encountered another, twin valleys in the double bed. She got up, tore off the sheets, and rotated the mattress, but it made no difference. The Atkinsons were long-married; the mattress had been much rotated.

But the male shape who filled the hollow was the Harold Atkinson upon whom Frances had fixed her heart, and, speaking of him, Frances gazed at the bed so yearningly that Rose feared she might lie down, and so led her back to the kitchen where the photos were, then to the living room, where the photos were, also, and finally out the back door, to sit on the bench on the back stair landing, where the view was of the treetops, and from which she could more simply ease Frances toward home.

"I've never loved anyone but him," moaned Frances, "and never will. Nobody knows. You won't tell, will you?" she begged.

"Why would I?" asked Rose.

Rose herself had been a late bloomer, a gangly girl who, at high school parties, had pounded on any piano in sight while her friends whisked in and out of dim closets and basements for groping and kissing. In the little New Hampshire town where she grew up, she'd been vice-president of student council and manager of glee club and had carried on vehemently platonic friendships with one boy or another. Love was way too much for her then. The very thought had made her silly and unable to think, had brought her, she'd felt, to the verge of disgrace not only before other people, but before herself, for she was a serious girl, and there was no dignity more monumental than that of a serious girl. She dwelt in a grand, if vague, future. While she lived under her parents' roof, she preserved her ignorance with a gravity past which no boy was bold enough to go.

So she didn't date. Her younger sister, Natalie, did, or ran wild, depending on who was talking. Their parents had been too engrossed to notice: her mother in oil painting; her father in religion. But if people said Natalie ran wild—and they did: there were rumors of an older man, a married man—Rose defended her hotly. Wasn't Natalie home every night, washing dishes while Rose dried? Not that anyone listened to Rose, who didn't even know what "wild" might be. Even Natalie mocked her. Rose, she said, would end up a nun.

Rose applied to a college far away where no one knew what to expect of her, and, making up for lost time, rid herself of her ignorance. By Thanksgiving she'd had several one-nighters—well, two—two young men whose names she could mention in coy phone conversations with Natalie, who was, after all, still in high school.

However, the thrill of proving herself at least capable of the motions of love left her shaken. If the earth moved, it moved too fast. Everyone seemed in a hurry those days, despite the languid clothes, the droopy mustaches, the flowing hair. She, herself, was in a hurry, terrified of missing something—the latest street theater, street dance, sit-in, and the pairing off in the dark.

But then darkness moved to morning and one woke up beside whomever and had to find something to say and a way to get out of there, to move swiftly, to *not care*. She hadn't been able to manage it. She cared about everything, the young man in bed beside her, whoever he was, no more than a boy, as she was no more than a girl; mean boys she couldn't like; sweet boys who made her nervous; other girls who might be her true friends or might not; the whole wide world. She'd wanted the world, and there she was, snarled up in it, with nowhere to rest except in music. She poured herself into music.

Her classmates began pairing off into established couples and she found herself wanting, for no good reason, to be phoned again by some boy, it didn't matter whom. She couldn't stand the randomness of it. At the start of sophomore year she got herself out of the dorm to a sunny rented room. Encouraging sly remarks about her off-campus freedom, she hid out there and devoted herself entirely to her studies and her music, while nursing a frail hope that she might one day meet someone she'd really want to know who would really want to know her.

Alone so much, she wrote clever, angry compositions which gained her attention, leery respect, and eventually prizes; one especially, which she titled *The Loser*, a chamber piece with a steady drone of cello, almost a march, over which poured, quite suddenly, skittering notes like a bag bursting and then a rustling and crackling like the contents of the bag being stuffed in again, quickly, quickly, while the march pressed on. Something about the piece made people laugh, and when she got up to introduce it, she learned to adopt a tongue-in-cheek tone, for the piece sounded not like losing, but finding and grabbing and winning. Taking top grad school honors, *The Loser* brought her to the attention of the college in St. Paul. That was her luck, as far as it went.

Ursula Kaiser, her best friend at school, had been far busier with men. One young man or another was constantly claiming Ursula as his own; and though she never seemed to take it seriously, and never let Rose feel a contrasting lack, she'd occasionally asked to borrow Rose's rented room for the afternoon so she could "you-know-what" with a boyfriend. She brought her own sheets from the dorm, and they'd always be gone by dinnertime.

On such afternoons, with a show of cheer, Rose took herself off to the library but, once there, found it hard to sit and instead wandered as though she had no place to be. It was fearsome, the "you-know-what" that so casually displaced her and left her exposed and perhaps pitied as she now pitied Frances.

She studied Frances, whose sobbing had subsided to a dry gasping. Rose knew that gasping, had sobbed and gasped that way herself over whozit and whatzizface. Oh, what was the matter? She and Frances were both young. What was this pathetic dredging up of the past? Life lay ahead. At least for the year ahead, they both knew how their bills would be paid—Frances for longer, the secretary job being open-ended.

"You simply don't know," said Frances, "what it is to be unlucky," and Rose laughed again, in spite of herself, in defeat, she would have said, though the laugh had an edge to it, an edge she could not deny. Frances wanted her pity? Very well, she'd have it. Rose would go on and prove Frances right. The past notwithstanding, she planned to be lucky. Every time she'd taken off her clothes for a new man, regardless of what followed, she'd felt a surge of triumph, of coming into her own, a kingdom forbidden to most others, to her own mother and father, for instance, whose misery and clenched rages seemed to have nothing to do with sex, not as Rose had sex. And would have it. She felt in her bones a renewed, humming promise.

Years later, looking back to this moment, it would strike her as fitting that Frances, in tears, should have brought her the news of love to come, and laughable, indeed, that she, Rose, had thought she could plan her luck. At that moment, she couldn't even hold to her scorn for Frances.

Seeing the sadness in Frances's face, all the bravado of *The Beauty* gone, Rose offered her hand, and Frances took it and stood up to walk home.

If Rose had been walking with Ursula instead, this might have been the start of a joke, one of their favorites. Back in grad school, Ursula had been in medicine, and the med school and dorm was far from the music building and Rose's rented room even farther off. However, they walked the distance one or two evenings a week, out amongst the sooty buildings of Philadelphia, Rose's dark hair bound up in a knot, Ursula's, red-brown, flying like a flag, and when eventually they reached Ursula's place or Rose's, they might turn around and walk back to the other's, because a woman wasn't supposed to be out alone after dark, although two together were okay; and so it should continue, they'd say, back and forth till daybreak. They never actually went till daybreak, walking from Rose's to Ursula's to Rose's again, but walking late as they often did, they pretended they could, no sweat, and the idea filled them with glee at how far they might accompany one another.

Rose's stride was too long for Frances. She shortened her steps. Did Frances like her? With all that complaining about Rose's luck, Frances might actively dislike her even. Did she like Frances? Stopping at the gate to her mother's house, where she still lived, Frances looked up and whatever she saw in Rose's face made her step backward. In response, Rose opened her arms to Frances, who clutched her convulsively. In spite of themselves, they were going to be friends.

Chapter TWO

L ove within a month, Frances had predicted. To amuse herself and kid Frances, Rose put up a calendar in the kitchen and marked a month ahead with an X. Unabashed by her storm of tears, Frances continued to visit every day, though now she was openly doleful, full of sighs and choked references to Harold.

"Hey, Frances, wanna shake the place up? Rearrange the furniture?"

"No," said Frances, but couldn't name a reason why. It *was* Rose's place for the year.

So she took down all the photos she could reach and put them in the empty chest of drawers and wrestled the chest and the mahogany table and chairs that filled the dining room and the great, wingback armchairs from the living room into the two matching studies, his and hers, Harold's and Doris's, that stood on either end of the apartment.

Rose would eat on the kitchen table. The bedroom was now clear of all but the bed and the window-lined front rooms of all but a couch, and while she worked Rose could pace back and forth through the rooms without having to watch where she was going.

Students were soon to arrive. She busied herself planning classes on three-by-five cards, absorbing Rules and Procedures, putting on the role of college teacher like a part in a play. It was a play for which she'd need costumes. Her lack of a wardrobe was not just the chic penury of grad school. Clothes had not concerned her parents, who didn't entertain and never went out, except for her father, to church. It was amazing for Rose to contemplate that she was about to earn a salary and would have money for clothes. Yet all she knew of how women dressed she'd gleaned from old movies on television.

On her bicycle, she ventured downtown to a department store—*the* department store, according to Frances, the *only* store for clothes—and, with a newly granted credit card, she selected her lady professor clothes: a shirtwaist dress with buttons from hem to collarbone, a sweater set in dove gray, a long skirt in tweed so craggy, twigs and pebbles seemed part of the weave. She roped all this to her bike basket and bore triumphantly back up the hill.

Reviewing the purchases, Frances made an odd little noise in her throat—Rose's taste was a bit governessy. There'd be cocktail parties, didn't she realize? There would be *evenings*.

Rose let herself be taken in hand. Half-naked before Frances in the department store fitting room, she tried on a half-dozen versions of the Little Black Dress that Frances was certain she needed. The fitting room was tiny, and though Frances averted her eyes, Rose couldn't hide the fact that she went braless. By contrast, Frances, beneath her sundress, possessed a crisp, molded quality that indicated foundation garments, even though she, like Rose, was far too slender to have anything to shore up or hold in. Frances, however, was not the one undressed, and Rose fought the feeling that she'd become a 4H Project, Frances's prize calf.

They'd been to the State Fair together, which in size and noise and embellishment made the county fairs of Rose's New Hampshire childhood seem paltry. The Minnesota State Fair had livestock barns as big as factories, separate barns for sheep, goats, pigs, roosters, and even rabbits, some of which seemed not rabbits at all but pastry concoctions in fur. There were tractors with ten-foot tires, wall-sized honeycombs crawling with bees, a lagoon with seven-foot sturgeon. Frances led the way amidst the steam of dry ice and the smell of crackling fat to buy them bits of meat and starch fried on wooden sticks, foot-long hot dogs and foot-high ice cream cones. On the Midway, which reached to skyscraper heights—and on that scale, even the Ferris wheel was frightening—Frances chose a hammer-shaped ride that arced up and down and swung full circle. High in the hammerhead, plastered to the safety bar, struggling not to barf her ice cream, Rose observed Frances as her eyes went huge and shot sparks and she laughed and shrieked. Rose instructed herself not to underestimate Frances. Inside that girdle was something wild.

"Hold," said Frances in the department store dressing room, placing Rose's hands in her hair and stepping back to look at the umpteenth Little Black Dress.

"Buy this one. It makes your rear look tiny."

"Oh?" Rose wasn't in the habit of considering herself from the rear.

"You'll want heels with it."

"Flats," said Rose.

"But not those," said Frances, who knew the shoe department as well as her own garden, which was small but burgeoning, double-planted and perfectly manicured, not a weed, not a shriveled leaf. She led Rose to pumps with leather soles and small, stacked heels, classics, she said, and then to the shoe repair window for Cat's Paws, little rubber heel reinforcements to be affixed before even a single wearing, adding years to the life of the shoes.

"Cat's Paws? Frances, you know everything."

She really seemed to. Just as she'd predicted, Alan Gilpin took a shine to Rose.

At the first department meeting, he approached her, faking a limp.

"The woman who ran over me with her bicycle," he announced, toasting her with his coffee cup.

"Shall I buy you a cane?" Rose retorted. He dropped the limp and sat down beside her.

She got through her first weeks of teaching with his "moral support." She was assigned a huge section of Intro to Music; beneath her lecture hall, Alan marched his Bagpipe Corps, bleating and wheezing. Routing his evening run past her duplex, he spattered acorns against her front windows. She retaliated with hot pepper cookies, alluringly set on a doily in his mailbox. He gnashed them down and then demanded to see just how such a treat was produced—a ruse—he knew the Chair's apartment and was avid to try out the antique Kitchen Chef range.

So began their joint cooking ventures. Showered after his evening run, he'd arrive at her door with groceries for a mouth-watering stroganoff or a magnificent paella. She sat him down to her millionaire chicken, amazed him with her blackberry crumble. They jabbered, shoulder to shoulder, at sink and stove in her kitchen or his, conversations that extended into late-night phone calls and picked up again in the office the next day.

Frances followed all this with a knowing eye and a brave little smile.

Alan called Frances flighty. "A flibbertigibbet," he said.

But Rose knew Frances had substance and, on an afternoon in mid-September, despite Alan's lack of enthusiasm, invited them both over for coffee.

Alan came early, arranged himself on the bench on the back stair landing, and stretched his legs in a lizardly fashion over the banister, his eyes half-lidded.

"*Well*," said Frances, bursting in, "aren't *you two* the item?"

"Item?" said Rose and beckoned Alan in from the porch.

"Running around campus together? Seen in the bookstore *holding hands*," she breathed.

"Holding hands? I don't think so," said Rose. She and Alan had visited the bookstore together and perhaps one had grabbed the other's hand in enthusiasm over some book or other, but nothing else.

"Oh, come now," Frances persisted. "You've been seen weekend mornings out to breakfast together with your hair all uncombed."

Alan gave a small, strangled cough. It had to be Rose who'd been seen with her hair uncombed. Alan always appeared well groomed, even in his sweaty running clothes. In this he more closely resembled Frances. But he did seem to like being seen with Rose, regardless of whether her hair was combed, and she felt the attachment to be genuine—he liked being alone with her as well. They were not an item, however. It was phony to let Frances think so, and there was something fraudulent also in the pose Alan struck and the tone with which he introduced Rose around campus. But maybe she, too, gained advantage by pretending to be half of a couple in public? It made her appear less lonely, anyway, than Frances.

"A busybody," pronounced Alan, once Frances had gone. "A Nosy Parker. She always has to have something to report." Rose rolled her eyes. "Really," he insisted. "She tattles to the Higher-Ups—not that I care what she says about us."

But there was no us—not really.

"The Higher-Ups," Rose said and sighed.

Alan had explained all about the Higher-Ups. His third-year review was upon him; he had two more years to go before he'd know for certain whether or not he'd be tenured. The only son of a single mother, a seamstress in Fargo, he knew exactly what he wanted: more of what he already had. His campaign was detailed and far-ranging. He saw to it that his students adored him; wrote and published, of course; and, in addition, volunteered for a bizarre variety of campus tasks, listable on his résumé but unrelated to music. He judged homecoming royalty, hosted alumni, lifeguarded faculty kids at the pool, and, in off hours, brooded on tenure. Rose let it be known she found this boring. In her opinion, he was in danger of reducing himself to his résumé.

"*Curriculum vitae*," he corrected. Résumé was the term for freelancers.

"Crummy little freelancers," she said. "Like me?"

"Oh, tenure's just a *thing*," he sighed. "You could get on the track if you wanted."

The college, like a number of schools in the region, styled itself as the Harvard of the Midwest, revealing a fear of inferiority. It nonetheless possessed an accomplished faculty, hailing from many lands, and the students were bright and lively. Rose could see the allure of tenure, but she wasn't getting on any track. Why was academic tenure the be-all and end-all? He could get work other than teaching. He could travel. Why, he could live in Paris!

On what money, he wanted to know?

He could teach English. She'd go with him. They would translate. They would cook.

"Cook in *Paris*?"

He could play music—pack along his instruments. She'd heard him jam with a rag-tag band of city musicians, all talented, but even so, he stood out. He cut a figure: his rangy height, his well-chosen clothes, his attitude, his car, a vintage gray-green Volvo with leather seats. He was making his way and Rose couldn't believe it really depended on a teaching job at a small college in Middle America. At any rate, tenure as a topic was becoming thoroughly tiresome.

Fortunately, he was open to distraction, dying to laugh, and game for any escapade. When distracted from the tenure thing, he seemed lighter than air.

Frances, by contrast, seemed heavier laden. Rose let her attention to Frances dwindle, returning her calls less promptly and then calling her almost not at all. She trained herself to walk swiftly through the front office, greeting Frances without really looking at her. Frances seemed to expect nothing better and Rose felt a pang. But the threesome hadn't worked and, except for the tenure thing, Alan was so much more fun.

"Rose Marie," he said one night. She'd let slip her middle name and he loved to tease. He was lounging in a bentwood rocker he'd rescued from a dumpster, repaired and painted a periwinkle blue with a cunning red stripe like a satin ribbon running over and around the runners. She lay on his long couch viewing a spray of reddening treetops through his windows.

"Rose Marie," he declared, "we have got to get out of here."

"Where to?" she said. "Downtown? To the old dead fountain and the clock tower?"

"You know nothing," he said. "Get up. We're going to Minneapolis."

Minneapolis: blues clubs, sidewalk cafés, the West Bank where a parade of mimes, druggies, and street musicians kept things stirring late into the autumn night. Here was the world: the thronged voices, bursts of song, the rustle of taffeta and click of dress shoes, on-and-off blare erupting through doors opening and closing. Alan kept them to the sidelines, to the edge of the street and the back of the hall, where he watched everything raptly, silently, observant of who was present, applauding discreetly, low profile, mindful of his reputation.

Oh god, the tenure thing.

They went to a weird staging of *Alice in Wonderland* in a cellar, where, to get to their seats, they had to crowd into an elevator with Alice herself. The elevator was lined with mottled brown paper, and as they descended, a hurtling sound suggested they were flying through a tunnel. Alice looked right at Rose and spoke: *Had she seen a rabbit, and was this the way to the tea party?*

Amused, Rose answered, "Yes, it is," but Alan took her hand and stepped backward. Rose couldn't stand it. "And here's your rabbit," Rose told Alice, presenting Alan.

Once in their seats, Alan slumped back and regarded her. She crossed her eyes at him. Abruptly, he leaned over and kissed her, a kiss that landed on her ear and slid down her neck.

"Hey now," she said, shivering.

"Oh? No touch?" He looked at her—a challenge.

"You're gay, aren't you?" she said quietly.

He looked away. "Who told you that?"

"No one told me. I just thought so."

"Oh," he said.

He didn't say she was wrong.

She'd noticed a tone when they were tired, a plaintive tone that went slightly mean. They were stuck somehow. She'd thought it was sex, or rather the lack of that possibility between them. She wished he'd just say so.

Instead, they raced onward breathlessly, to readings, dance-happenings, to an all-night jazz diner. They got almost no sleep.

"Gotta do it all now," said Alan. "Snow's coming." The weather, however, was merely cool, a mellow late September. Rose adopted an afternoon nap and paced herself to keep up with him.

They went to peculiar movies. Maybe in contrast to the wind instruments he taught—all that air—Alan had a hunger for movies with brutal plots and dim, earthbound characters, movies preferably with subtitles. Toward the end of September, they went to the fateful movie, the Hypnotism Movie, as Rose would refer to it ever after. As it happened, this was exactly a month after Frances had made her prediction. The X on Rose's calendar was by then buried under scribbled notes.

The movie's director was, in Alan's estimation, the high priest of German cinema, and rumor had it he might appear. They arrived an hour early and took seats twelfth row center, close enough to the front to really see but not so close as to crowd the podium.

Rose wore her Little Black Dress, deliberately overdressing to sass Alan, and a string of scarlet chili pepper beads, which clicked against each other as she moved. The beads were not a Frances selection, but papier-mâché from a junk shop. And, though she rarely wore makeup, that night she layered on scarlet lipstick.

Alan failed to notice any of this. He'd dressed impeccably—khakis and grass-green polo shirt—but his normally sleepy eyes were wide; his blond, almost white hair was up in a wild thatch that he kept smoothing down without success; and his beard, under the muted lights, seemed unusually black, a dark wedge into which his pale, thick mustache streaked like ash into charcoal. Nearly catatonic with excitement, he held his mouth in a grim, handsome line.

A tiny worm of something—jealousy? envy?—turned in Rose.

Whatever was exciting him had nothing to do with her. She remembered his lips on her neck that one time at *Alice* and stretched a leg over his ankle. He squeezed her knee without glancing at her, but she held her gaze on him, on the fine shape of his mouth, and went from there, stripping off his shirt in her mind, reaching for his fly. As though he sensed something, he shifted tensely. She gave it up.

A stranger sitting two rows down turned and, over the empty seats between them, caught her gaze and held it with an intent, slightly puzzled look, as though he were trying to place her. She had an impression of a face all angles and salt-and-pepper hair.

The room hushed and the filmmaker appeared—immensely tall, with deepset eyes, a lordly mane of hair, and a bearing so stiff, he might have been a medieval knight. Rose could almost hear the armor clank. Alan released a tiny sigh—apparently a dream come true. The director said hello with a barely detectable movement of his facial features. A voice called out to ask if it were true that the actors in the movie had performed under hypnosis. In clipped tones, he promised to return for discussion and signaled the lights down.

Actors in peasant clothing came stumbling into view in front of a nineteenth-century glassworks, fires in glass kilns burning within. As could be predicted, the hypnotized actors looked like fools: slack-jawed, slack-voiced, moving with nonsensical compulsion—a god's-eye view of human endeavor, if god had become bored and cynical.

Rose laughed unhappily. Alan shushed her.

Onscreen in a rustic tavern with plank tables and a dirt floor, someone began to play a hurdy-gurdy. The ungainly bloated lute, with a keyboard down the side and a crank at the end, creaked out a sound part harpsichord, part calliope: not an entirely unpleasant sound, and, by the music, Rose was led into the story. A pair of brothers—or were they friends?—

very close and very drunk, a flailing drunkenness under hypnotism—climbed up to a hayloft to sleep. In the night, one fell over the edge to his death. The next day, the other woke to find the body on the barn floor and began loudly to grieve. He seemed to know his mate was dead, but at nightfall he dragged the body to the tavern, where, demanding that the hurdy-gurdy be played, he embraced the stiffened shape and hauled it around the floor as though he could dance it back to life.

Rose was shocked to see herself in this: dead embraces, bodies she'd clutched willfully even after the life had gone out of it.

Someone two rows down glanced back in her direction, and silver threads lit up in his hair. She found herself lurched forward, gripping the metal back of the seat in front of her with both hands. She sat back and scanned the faces of the audience caught in the reflected light from the movie, and they were all—Alan, too—as slack-jawed and dead-eyed as the faces on screen. For the first time in years, she felt a horror of unfamiliarity and longed for family and scenes of childhood. Alan was the only one there who knew her at all. She reached for him. He caught her fingers, squeezed them absently, and let them go. She slid down in her seat, cringing.

Shutting her eyes, she thought of the little house in New Hampshire with its screen of quince bushes in front of the porch. Her mother still lived there, and her sister. They were fighting, Rose knew, though Natalie had graduated from college and should have been out on her own; there should have been nothing to argue about. Their wild-eyed father was off following his religious group across the Alleghenies. Ten years before, having converted from normal Christianity to something more electrifying, he sat their mother down and demanded that she submit to him, to his spiritual headship, whatever that meant. Maybe a form of hypnotism? Her mother had cackled, delighted, it seemed, to have a fresh outrage over which to fight. They gave Rose the willies. But even so, for a throbbing moment, trapped in front of hypnotized actors, she missed her mother and father and sister and wished for them all to come, to gather in St. Paul in her borrowed duplex, regardless of the fact that they'd spend the visit arguing, and Rose along with them, arguing, sulking, and stomping out for walks alone or in pairs, briefly allied: she with her father because they both believed in discipline; she with her mother because they were the artists; she with her sister because they were the children.

On screen, kilns exploded and the glassworks caught fire. Glass shattered, timbers pitched, and the actors shouted and ran. Her father would find this grimly right: an apocalyptic scene with a Christian lesson, one the filmmaker never intended, as her mother, were she present, would be sure to say. But what on earth did the filmmaker intend?

The house lights were up and Alan sat transfixed. With great effort, he turned to Rose to confirm that they'd witnessed something splendid. She glared at him, cleared her throat, and thrust her hand in the air. At the podium, the filmmaker lifted his chin in her direction.

"Is art a conscious act? Is an actor an artist, or a thing?" she asked.

He sighed and dropped his chin to his chest.

An edge in her voice, she pressed on. "And might I ask if you, yourself, directed this picture under hypnosis and who it was who hypnotized you?"

"These actors were not mere puppets," he said. "If I hypnotized you and gave you a knife and told you to stab your friend—" here he pointed to Alan, "—you would never do it."

She glanced at Alan, who stared at her in horror. She barked out a laugh. For a wild moment, she saw herself, knife in hand, going for Alan in his theater seat. He turned his head away. She was a philistine and a stranger. The filmmaker called for the next question. She crossed her arms over her chest and her beads clicked against each other.

"Nice chilies," said a voice below her. She looked two rows down into the angular face, the bright gray eyes lit up with amusement, the shock of salt and pepper hair. He sat tall in his seat and, despite the silver in his hair, his face was unlined and youthful. He drew a couple arcs on his chest and pointed, indicating her beads. She would remember that Guy Robbin, in his first gesture to her, had pointed to his own heart.

She was staring. She told herself to look away.

"You hated it?" He gestured toward the screen.

"Maybe," she said. "I don't know," and she felt herself relax.

"Right," he said. "It was too weird to hate."

When the movie let out, Rose watched as he unfolded himself to an immense height and turned in her direction. But Alan bolted from his seat and Rose, suddenly shy, hurried off after him. The evening had been exhausting and though she expected nothing more than an argument with Alan, she couldn't, at that moment, reach past the known for the unknown.

She and Alan were going to fight; she couldn't see how to avoid it. She wanted to ask to be dropped off at home, but he drove as though possessed to his place, gave her a glass of wine and, the very next moment, took the wine glass from her and pulled her to his bed.

He was rough and sudden, plunging into her. There was no laughter, no talk; all his lightness was gone and he lay upon her afterward, a slaughtered carcass, once she'd moved his hand away from the mechanical fumbling between her legs which he'd offered in afterthought. They were about to be very, very sorry.

"Well, this was stupid," she said, waiting for him to move his weight off her. "What are we—hypnotized?"

"Well," he said in a bleak voice, "isn't it always awkward the first time?"

"First and last as far as I'm concerned. I want what we had."

He rolled off and looked at her. She turned away from him, wrapping herself in the sheet.

"We still have it," he said.

"I doubt it."

"No, we do," he said, swaying to his feet. "Get up. I'm taking you to breakfast."

"At midnight?"

"Come on, Rose Marie." His voice was forced and trembling.

He handed her clothing to her: panties, nylons, Little Black Dress.

"Just pull it on any old way. We're going out to breakfast with our hair all uncombed."

Sitting across the booth from him in the all-night jazz diner, she cast her eye around for some sight or sound to provide distraction. None came. The place was unusually quiet and empty. She made herself look over at Alan and, for once, he held her gaze for more than two seconds. She did feel she knew him and that he had at least begun to know her. Could they love each other after this bad beginning?

She reached over and tousled his hair. Almost imperceptibly, he shrank from her.

Chapter THREE

They tried to act as if nothing had happened, loyally went on cooking together and phoned at night before sleep, though the conversations were strained and very much shorter.

She couldn't bring herself to blame him. She had asked for it. Sitting beside him at the movie, she'd summoned his attentions the way women did, with a look, a pressing of knee to knee. Why, then, had she been horrified to have his mouth on hers, to have the act of love under way? Was he gay, as she'd first thought, or was it just a lack of chemistry between them? He'd moved fast, torn through the streets, getting her to his apartment and to his bed. She'd been curious about what he intended, drawn by the glint in his eye and afraid that the flare of emotion was anger, that he suddenly couldn't stand her, and that the friendship, so newly begun, was about to be over. She had thought, as he pulled her to her feet, that he was about to say something terrible and then drive her home because she'd failed to love the Hypnotism Movie.

What was it about that movie that produced in him such a brash elation? People with their souls sucked out? The crashing wreck of everything? She'd been revolted. Hadn't she lined up her past mistakes to remind herself of such consequences, to fortify herself against unfocused eyes and colliding bodies? How could she, the very next hour, allow herself to be led where she'd just vowed she would no longer go?

Her body was desolate and confused. It was as though she'd been struck naked and couldn't get her clothes back on. Perhaps she wasn't made for love, and music alone was her calling. Perhaps she'd have to learn to ignore her body's foolish buzzing.

She'd have liked to phone Ursula—someone far away and not involved. However, back in Philadelphia, Ursula was having her own bleak time in the first grueling months of her medical residency: the twenty-four hour off/on schedule, the catnaps grabbed in hospital bunks, the food from vending machines. She was too poor to call Rose, too infrequently at home to have Rose call her, too busy to write more than cramped, unhappy postcards about her wretched boyfriend. She was fighting with her boyfriend, or her fiancé, depending. But fighting or not, Ursula at least knew what it was to live with a man. If Ursula answered the phone, what could Rose do but confess another misbegotten one-night stand?

Other people couldn't help, not Ursula, not her mother, who would blame her—Rose could blame herself without any help—and not her sister, Natalie, who would sympathize extravagantly, betraying pleasure in Rose's misfortune. And not Frances, who might find the story irresistible to repeat. There was no one to turn to—Alan, least of all.

To her astonishment, he tried again a week later. On his way out her door one night, he turned back, and as though executing a formal figure in a dance, placed his hands on her shoulders, pressed his mouth to hers and attempted to press his tongue between her lips. She clamped her teeth together and stood frozen. He turned and walked heavily down her stairs.

In the last days of September, crab apples dropped and mixed with leaves, smearing the paths on campus. From a stand outside the student union, she bought Concord grapes, a favorite fruit of her childhood, but found the popping skins and viscous flesh unexpectedly gross and tossed them. She went about her duties woodenly. The Midwestern accents, which she'd first found intriguing, now seemed exaggeratedly flat: words without nuance.

One day as she stood at the xerox machine, Frances laid a confiding hand on her arm. "You guys have a fight?" she said in that same flat accent.

But Rose had no intention of confiding. Frances had predicted the disaster—love within a month—and Rose didn't intend to give her the satisfaction of knowing that, a month to the day, something of that sort had happened, or a careless half-minute of it.

"You don't have to tell me," murmured Frances, blocking Rose's path to her office. "It's normal to fight." Frances opined that Alan needed understanding. "He's such a special man, don't you think? So *erudite*."

Rose regarded her.

"Erudite," said Frances. "And so very high-strung."

Rose walked into her office and closed the door. Erudite? He might be a Nobel laureate for all Rose cared. He didn't know the first thing about himself, kissing her as though he meant it. She knew when a kiss was meant. As to high-strung, she was high-strung herself. At the moment, she had trouble meeting her students' eyes, enduring their gaze on her, upon her body.

He hadn't wanted her. His touch had been experimental, self-absorbed, uninterested in her. She did blame him for that much. Oh, possibly he admired her physical form as an object in his collection, like his rocking chair with the ribbon stripe. But his touch between her legs after their rushed, nearly violent union had been hesitant, almost ignorant. He'd been what she might even call shy, turning his back to put on the condom.

Could it be, was it possible that, up to that night, he'd been a virgin? It seemed unlikely, but, if true, would explain a great deal.

If it was only that, well, she might even have been unkind in what she'd said and done or failed to say and do.

Leaving his kitchen one night, she turned back and asked if they could talk about it.

"If you mean our little sexual fiasco, what's there to say? You don't want to. I believe I've made clear what *I* want."

"Well, something's not right." She reached for his hand, drew a breath, and asked him.

His eyes widened. "A virgin? Oh, I don't think so." He withdrew his hand.

"Is that a no?"

He threw back his head and laughed harshly and for so long that she began to listen for him to draw a breath and gasped in, herself, to prompt him. He subsided into a chuckle of what seemed genuine merriment. He wasn't going to tell her.

She'd only been acquainted with him for six weeks. It was vanity to imagine she knew him. She could only learn what he chose to reveal.

"Look," he said. "Let's not and say we did."

"But I'm afraid we already *did*," she said.

"I love you, Rose." He kissed her, keeping his tongue to himself.

October arrived and snow had yet to fall. Afternoons were sometimes hot. Late one day, walking to the dry cleaners laden with her sweater set into which she'd sweated copiously and her splotched black dress—grease spots and the odor of sweat were not quite the professorial image; these professor clothes were expensive to maintain—she paused to check her wallet, when a voice called out to her, called *hi*, or *hey*, or something.

A man in a torn denim jacket and an old crushed fedora sat with a newspaper on the concrete wall. Not ten feet away, he regarded her in absolute stillness. Doubting herself, she'd half turned away when he called to her again.

"Seen any weird German movies lately?"

He folded his paper and stood to a sudden, staggering height. He took his hat off and she saw the flash of silver in his dark hair.

"I've sworn off the weird movies," she said.

She meant it. She'd take order and peace; calm, unexceptional days and nights; a load of work and a lonely bed. She was making more work of her teaching than it probably required: hunting down obscure recordings to supplement her syllabi, leading field trips to concerts, responding more intensely than was probably helpful to the tentative scratchings of her composition students.

His name was Guy Robbin. He wanted to take her for a cup of coffee. Or tea? Did she maybe drink tea?

As a matter of fact, she did prefer tea, but how would he know that? "I can't," she said and showed him her dirty clothes.

"But aren't you going to drop them off?" He flipped a long arm toward the dry cleaners. His eyes were gray with gold at the center, alive as an owl's. His long face creased into a grin. He seemed as sure of her agreeing as if they'd had a date.

"Oh, but I have a whole list here," she lied, and patted her purse. She wasn't going to just go off with him. The source of their acquaintance was omen enough, the Hypnotism Movie, which she was determined to wipe from her memory. She was a busy professor, not just a girl on display for anyone to say "hey" to and take for a "cup of tea."

On the following Saturday afternoon, however, across the river in Minneapolis, she caught sight of Guy Robbin again under the awning of a café where they'd arranged to meet. She had agreed to meet him, after all, as long as it was not on the spur of the moment. That way she'd had time to collect herself, to build caution, to think about what kind of life she intended and the conduct that would lead her there. That she felt something for him already, an unjustified something when she knew nothing about him, seemed a distinct warning sign.

She'd driven over in her "new" car, a rusty station wagon for which she'd paid a hundred dollars. Alan had helped her tape a scrap of carpet over a hole in the floor, not that he'd approved the ugly set of wheels. Let him sneer; it was transportation. She no longer needed a ride in Alan's Volvo to get to Minneapolis—now she could get there all on her own.

Though she was on time, perhaps even early, Guy was already waiting for her on the sidewalk. She was struck anew by his height. To greet her, he had to duck under the fringe of the awning. He waited for her to park. The station wagon was longer than any car she'd previously driven. As she struggled—she had no intention of parking crooked, nor two feet from the curb just because her heart was pounding—he turned his back to her and studied the display in the window and she caught her breath and wedged the car in.

He extended his hand and she shook it, a broad, callused hand. He looked her boldly in the eye, a look full of curiosity, yet not demanding anything of her, not yet. Over a cup of tea—they discovered they were both tea drinkers—over several cups, he told her he lived not in the city, but on a lake up north, lived alone there in a shack he'd thrown up next to the foundation he'd poured for the stone house he was building.

He was a strange creature, a boy from Mason City, Iowa who'd made it to Boston University on scholarship. But, not content to stick around campus when the wilds of Massachusetts beckoned, he had, in his freshman year, undertaken to read Thoreau's complete works on the banks of Walden Pond. And there he'd noticed new construction crowding the woods either side of Thoreau's neglected shack. He began a campaign of letters and speeches, but convinced neither the students nor the Board of Trustees to turn their energies to Walden's preservation. So he dropped out. What did knowledge matter if no one applied it where and when there was a crying need? He laughed as he told this—it was long ago. Back then he'd scrounged himself an actual soapbox and still had it, now turned right side up, holding stone-cutting tools.

As he spoke, he leaned to one side to look at her and then lifted his chin, laughing, his head held proud yet mobile on his neck. His face seemed all long angles, yet it was not a hard face. His cheek seemed a long expanse, a field, over the lower half of which spread the faint shadow of a whisker line like a patch of shade. And his voice: she wanted to close her eyes just to listen. His accent was Midwestern, but he played his voice like an instrument. A baritone, she thought: the occasional rumble, but bells in it, some sort of chiming.

As he described his stone house, it went up in her mind, thick bouldered walls. She saw grass growing on the roof, flowers, a goat tethered up there, grazing. She mentioned the goat and he chuckled—he'd only laid the first course of stone. But a sod roof was the right idea, and animals. A flock of geese, he thought. Goose eggs made tremendous omelets.

Like a house in a fairy tale, she said, and he rested his chin on his hand and gazed at her, unnerving her. His soft gray flannel plaid shirt had the slightest stripe of brightness running through it. His cuffs, rolled back, showed wrists surprisingly slender, though his fingers were wide and work-roughened. His gold-flecked eyes, which she'd first thought of as like an owl's, avid and unsettling, now seemed peaceful, almost lazy, like quiet water where a stream slowed and mica-spangled granite could be glimpsed below.

"And you live alone?" she asked, abruptly leaning back in her chair.

"Do I live alone because I want to, or because no one wants me?" He laughed and his gaze slid past her, took in the rest of the room, and returned to her.

He was spectacular, and she hadn't been the only one to notice. Other women in the room had looked up when they came in. The waitress had blushed taking his order, and she had felt proud for no good reason. She was nowhere near as striking as he; they weren't looking at her, except maybe to question why he chose her and not them, and he hadn't *chosen* her exactly; they were merely out for a cup of tea. All right, five cups. But it was an afternoon, just one, and who knew whether it would be repeated?

"I live alone because I want to live *there*," he said, and described the land an uncle had left him. Below the hill where he'd built his shack, a lake opened, a deep, glacial pool out of which northern pike like prehistoric monsters rose on his fishing line. He described the trees that stood on the lakeshore—a thick stand of birch, white as candles.

"Candles," he said, in that mobile, musical voice, not just telling her things but also, while speaking, in some way singing, making music: he was a musician, like she was.

"What?" he asked.

She'd laughed and had no idea why. He laughed with her, his eyes crinkling. Ah, he was kind. One of his eyebrows, she noticed, was set higher than the other. Above the higher eyebrow, a mole. Flaws. She liked that.

"Describe again—the trees," she said, and made herself listen to his actual words. They talked about what they did, where they'd traveled, what hurdles each had got over. They told about themselves and did not veer into detail about other people. His eyes did not shift from her as Alan's did; he held her gaze unswervingly and she did not look away. Yet they were careful; they did not note aloud how well they got on. They did not refer to love in the abstract nor in the concrete; signs and omens were not mentioned, nor fate.

Hours passed. She had to get up from the table to go to the bathroom. Her bladder ached even after she'd emptied it. Her throat was raspy from talking. Washing her hands rapidly, she went back to him, propelled like water moving downriver. It was that easy.

She found herself leaning across the table to tap out the rhythm and hum the last few measures of *The Loser*, the composition that had won her the prizes and got her the job at the college. She didn't mention the title of the piece, nor its meaning, but simply hummed.

He paused, calculating. She became aware that the room had filled and was noisy. Then he leaned forward and hummed into her ear, repeating back to her the final measure of her composition, note after precise note, as though they were alone in silence. He heard only her. And she heard only him.

She felt a burst of shock. It was as though everyone else in the world had died in the moment she relaxed and leaned across the table to hum to him, everyone erased except two.

Two, however, was a very small number. She wanted the world, the whole of it. She wanted to hurl herself into the thick of things. If she meant to write music, she had better get on it. What time was it? What was she doing sitting at a café table? What had he, really, to do with her? Why was he detaining her?

She got unsteadily to her feet, her hands shaking from what she told herself was an excess of caffeine. Out the window, streetlights were burning where only a moment ago it had been day. Earlier she'd felt a pre-monition of touch, which had slowly become a certainty, but now she didn't even offer her hand. The desire to touch him struck her as insane, akin to the impulse to jump off a bridge she'd set out merely to cross.

On her feet, she felt a surge of strength. Perhaps, at long last, she was learning caution.

Startled, he stood as well, towering over her. It took her breath away, his lanky height, the expanse of his chest, the grave, angular face, the keen eyes holding hers.

"I've got to go," she said awkwardly.

"You're married."

"Oh, no, not at all. Not in the slightest. It's just—my work. I've got to get to work." He nodded, puzzled.

But he had her phone number. She'd given it to him, and why not? It was just a number, just a series of digits, like a series of notes in a musical scale.

Chapter FOUR

His call came four days later, on an evening when she was up to her elbows in garlic. Her appetite had returned for Concord grapes, for long walks alone in the crisp air. The weather had grown chilly, but the world seemed hot with sound: dry leaves rasped underfoot; Canada geese cried out overhead, whooping and barking like dogs. Her senses lit up. She hungered for all kinds of cooking and eating, as long as it was in her kitchen, near her phone.

At the moment her phone rang, Alan was standing beside her, chopping scallions. He reached for the receiver, but she blocked his path, grabbed it with dripping hands and held it to her chest, catching her breath so she could answer calmly. He staggered back and stared as she plunged into her bedroom, stretched the spiral cord to a straight line, and closed the door.

Guy was up north, standing in a phone booth. He'd driven into town to get groceries and thought he'd call her if she had a minute, if she wasn't working, if she didn't mind.

"No, no," she said fervently, as though speaking a vow. But there was a dinner guest, a colleague. Could he call back in an hour or so? She was sorry—she knew he had no phone at his shack and would understand if he couldn't. She heard a muffled hooting—laughter?—and then his voice again, calm and formal. He wanted her to know there were bears in the oats.

"Bears?"

He would call back.

Alan sat with his arms crossed on his chest and his eyebrows raised in inquiry. She dumped lemon juice over the salmon and hustled it into the oven, cranking up the temperature. She had to feed him and get rid of him. Flinging roasted garlic onto the potatoes, she went at them two-fisted with the hand masher.

"Someone I met at the Hypnotism Movie," she began and stopped. She didn't really want to get into the movie with Alan again. "Someone I met," she amended, too late.

"The Hypnotism Movie? Is that what we call it?"

"The god*forsaken* Hypnotism Movie is what some of us call it."

"I thought you were with me. When did you meet anybody?"

"He was sitting in front of us." She plunked the food on the table and sat down. Her eyes strayed back to the phone. He darted his hand out and unplugged it. She whisked the plug back into place, leaving a blob of butter on the jack.

"Did you even see the movie, Rose? I don't think so. Not Rose Marie. She was too busy meeting someone. I take her to see the greatest living filmmaker. I dress her up, get her there—"

"Dress me up? I believe I dress myself."

"I guess you must. Take a look."

She went to the mirror that hung by the back door. Some of her hair had sprung free of its barrette and wisps were pasted to her face, along with a stripe of raspberry sauce eyebrow to chin. A crust of potato crumbled from her thumb as she gathered up her hair.

"So," said Alan. "I am watching the event of the season, the *Hypnotism Movie*—"

She'd somehow put on her sweatshirt inside out. She pulled it off quickly and reversed it, oblivious of baring her breasts in front of Alan.

In the front rooms, pages of penciled composition littered couch and floor. She was working again, quickly, rapturously as though racing some deadline. One new piece had Canada geese in it, baying and barking their way through a resistant, heavy hum, like an overcast sky. Another, a sketch for viola and cello, put forth a conversation in Midwestern accents—flat assertion that yielded up variations, bursts of melody, excitements. Alan's voice now, for instance, showed only by the slightest rise in tone that he was agitated.

"My *companion*, however—my fellow *movie buff*—has her attention elsewhere."

"Oh, no, no. I saw the movie," Rose put in.

"I don't *think* so. Too busy *meeting* people. And then she has the *temerity to face off* with the *filmmaker*."

"I saw every minute of that wretched movie," she told him. He'd started it. They'd have the big fight they should have had after the movie instead of that pitiful three-minute fuck.

She'd hated the movie, she told him, even if it was too weird to hate. It disheartened her and was everything she meant to weed out of her life, aimlessness and hopelessness, and if that reduced her standing in his eyes, if that made her a Pollyanna, then he could find someone else to gloom around with. She, on the other hand, would have hope. She would have love if she could get it. Oh, but she didn't mean, of course, that she loved *him*. He knew that, right?

She locked eyes with him in the mirror. He heaved himself up, stepped behind her, and wrapped his arms around her, resting his cheek against hers. "Rose, I'm gay, okay?" She nodded. "You won't tell anyone?" She shook her head.

They stood there, looking at themselves: her face hot, bright, and damp against his coolness, his eyes hard and a little frightened.

"You've found yourself someone?" he asked her. She shrugged. She would see. "I probably ought to do the same," he said.

She sat in the dark a few hours later, wrapped in a quilt on the kitchen linoleum, hugging herself and the phone receiver.

Late summer had been so dry, Guy was saying, that the wild berry crop was sparse, and four black bears, a mother and her grown cubs, had come in clear daylight to fatten for winter on a huge oat field nearby where the farmer was late in harvesting. They were out there all day, grazing and wallowing in the ripe oats, great hunks of oat straw hanging from their jaws.

"Roaring?" she asked. She wanted to hear that.

"Snuffling," he said. They were too content for roaring; they were sleeping out there now, their paws over their snouts. He thought he'd go and join them.

"Would that be safe?"

"It might be, if you came too."

"You're bold."

"So are you. You'd keep the bears in line."

"Do I want to keep anybody in line?"

"Right," he said. "Forget that. Off on the wrong paw. Why don't you come up here?"

"Like, on a weekend?"

"No, right now. Go get your car keys."

"Guy," she said, speaking his name for the first time.

"Rose. I'll meet you halfway."

But she had an eight o'clock class, she really did, and not one she could blow off.

He arrived at her door the next night, carrying a thick sheaf of oats tied with baling twine. She set it in a chair and he put his hat atop it as though it were a third person come to dinner. She'd cooked clam spaghetti, which, uneaten, grew cold. Standing naked in the kitchen later, they'd laugh at the big, congealed mass in the bowl and dig in, ravenous after exertion.

"How come you remembered me from the movie?" she'd ask him then. "How did you even find me again?"

"Luck," he said. "Destiny or doom."

In the Chairman's bed, he'd curled around her, gathered her against his long body and cradled her to him as though to protect her. It was a strange beginning. She wondered whether she appeared defenseless or forlorn to him. A moment earlier he'd been frantic to get their clothes off, but now he lay still.

"I've been waiting for you all my life," he said.

His smell flooded her with relief, an easy, human smell, with a touch of motor oil, a touch of wood smoke. She kissed him giddily, tasting his breath. Everything about him pleased her. He reached over the side of the bed for the pack of condoms in his jacket pocket and, giddy himself, pulled the wrapper open in mock terror as though it might explode. As she put in foam—she'd bought the contraceptive; she *knew* he'd call again; *knew* he'd come to her—he slipped his hands on her hands between her legs, interlacing his fingers with hers, and the spent plastic inserter went sliding across the sheet. He kicked it over the side of the bed and pulled her to him, cradling her. What was he waiting for?

Why the hesitation? It was clear they were going to be lovers. Why should there be anything dire in it, and why the first time, when there might be curiosity or impatience, but not dread, at least not before the fact? With Alan—though that hardly counted, so mistaken that it was nearly accidental—she hadn't felt the enormity of it until afterward. This, with Guy, was not mistaken. Yet it seemed there was something about to be lost.

She stretched her cramped legs and turned to him. When he entered her, he made a sighing sound and went on sighing as he moved. It wasn't thrusting, it was water on water, a strong current, the sound almost silent, a whooshing, water through water, then a sudden, steep falls and a widening into calm, into shallows. They rested and began again. Astride him, she gazed down into his face and thought of herself just days before, fleeing him. She knew him almost not at all. He was a stranger but he was hers. He told her he couldn't believe his luck. *His* luck? What world she'd feared giving up for him, she couldn't imagine. There was no loss here, only gain. Exultant, she cupped his neck in her hands.

Lying beside him, eyes closed yet unable to sleep, she imagined, with a creeping sense of mischief, the stoop-shouldered Chairman and his pale little wife making love in this bed. Now it was no longer theirs. Guy more than filled the other hollow in the mattress. She'd swept away their photos and furniture, and now she'd made the bed hers, repainted in water and fire.

Then, unbidden, the thought came of Frances in the bed and Harold Atkinson at the window, murmuring as he fastened his trousers, afternoon light seeping through the drawn blinds. The scene amused her, their furtive outlawry. But then it seemed Frances was weeping again, naked and bony and inconsolable. It shivered Rose, the thought of someone weeping where she herself lay. She felt her luck inside her, bright and heavy, something to which she had a duty. She pushed the thought of Frances out of the bed and opened her eyes on Guy.

It was a Tuesday, earliest morning, and she had class in a few hours but it worried her not at all. She might never sleep again, alert as she felt and in love. She was for the first time and knew it. Here was her luck, which hadn't seemed to come from outside her but rather had risen up from within, her very self made known to her, and great good fortune, part of who she was.

"Rose," he said, some hours later. "I think we could make—no, listen—" He took her hands between his and held them still. "I think we could make something perfect."

Make something perfect? What could be more perfect than what they already had?

She met her class only cursorily prepared, and then rushed back to bed. Wednesday night, then Thursday, he leaned to put his mouth to her breast and hours went by; she lay her cheek on his hipbone, took him into her mouth and the day was over and another began. They told each other everything, every story from birth to the present, with nothing held back. Describing herself, she became, more than ever before, someone in particular, Rose MacGregor, no other.

She acquainted him with her childhood, with her sister, Natalie: Snow White and Rose Red, as they were sometimes called, after the sisters in *Grimm's Fairy Tales;* the one dark, and the other fair—Natalie was very, very blonde. This was the less well-known story, the one without dwarves or royalty, in which the two sisters are peasant girls and Snow White plays the lesser role. The very capable Rose Red looks after Snow White's every need and preserves her from every harm, while earning the love of a man spellbound inside a bearskin.

"You," Rose told Guy. "You're the man in the bearskin."

Fanciful as the fairy tale was, it had made for Rose a sort of purpose for her life: the heroics of caring for a younger sister. She'd kissed boo-boos, chased bees away, and fetched many a cookie and glass of milk. This didn't produce the desired effect: peace, order, and gratitude. Instead, given so much, Natalie demanded more, rejecting the role of peasant girl, polite and tractable as Snow White ought to be. Fistfights had ensued. Once, Rose tripped Natalie and, when she fell, kicked her. How Natalie came to be lying unconscious with a bruise on her forehead had had to be explained. Relating all of this to Guy, she felt a tremor of the old remorse, but he laughed, and again she was set free. She could tell him anything.

In the tiny house in New Hampshire, Rose and Natalie had had the upstairs, a single room where her parents never came except to halt quarrels. Natalie was a slob. How was Rose to dress for school, do her homework, and get herself to bed with Natalie's dirty underpants, school books, and chewed pencils underfoot?

By the time Rose was in high school, their father had, to keep the peace, built a bed in the wall halfway down the stairs and Natalie slept there. Even so, Rose had to tramp through wads of papers and snarls of clothes to get past Natalie's bed and downstairs. Why anyone found

Natalie at all cute had been beyond Rose. However, as she confessed to Guy, Natalie had had boyfriends, while she had not.

"Why the hell not?" said Guy. "You're so pretty."

"I don't know. I was shy. I didn't have the blonde hair."

"Yah, yah," said Guy. He preferred dark hair.

"That's good," said Rose. Because there was a boy one grade behind her who, the summer after her high school graduation, came around to take Rose on walks. Almost a boyfriend, he sat with her on rock ledges long afternoons, where they exchanged poems and talked about nothing at all. But as soon as Rose was off to college and out of sight, Natalie, who scoffed at poems, led that same boy to a pile of feed sacks in a shed behind the Grange Hall and then told Rose all about it over the phone in a flood of guilty tears.

This occurred during Rose's first week in the college dorm, at the height of her homesickness. She hadn't known there was a pile of feed sacks in the shed behind the Grange Hall. She, who hadn't so much as allowed herself to picture the boy naked, now comprehended what Natalie must know and must have been doing with boys all along. Hanging up the phone, Rose went out that very night and grimly handed over her virginity to the first college boy who'd oblige her.

Guy probably didn't need to hear this.

"I don't care," he said. "However you got here, here you are."

She told him about Ursula and Alan and Frances, leaving out nothing and, as she talked, felt her burdens lighten and her luck grow. She stepped out of bed to play the cello for him, wearing not a stitch. Day and night mattered nothing—all the hours were theirs. And he wanted something still more perfect?

He wanted them to be together all the time.

"Looks like we are," she told him. He'd had a date with a well digger, set months in advance—he was weary of hauling water from the lake to mix mortar. But he'd called and postponed so he could stay with her a few days more.

"I mean, like stone. I want us to be like stonework," he told her. Stone would not burn, nor dissolve, nor, in the natural course of things, could stone fixed with mortar be knocked down.

But why should he be uncertain of her? In the week they had been lovers, she had given herself to him more completely than she'd thought possible. She had never had such days and nights and was not going to jump into the future when she liked the present so well. He could worry all he liked—why didn't he just do that, worry, while she took off his clothes?

It was Saturday afternoon, and fortunate that they were then at least partly dressed and sitting on the sofa, when the knock came at the door. Fortunate, also, that she'd tidied up, done a casual scrub of the bathroom and kitchen and neatened the manuscript piles. She had not been answering the phone, however, and it had rung a number of times that day and the day before. Alan, she'd thought, and hoped he'd wise up and let her be.

It wasn't Alan, but Frances at the door.

"I tried to warn you," Frances hissed. "I've been calling and calling." Stepping in, she stared at Guy sprawled on the sofa. "You're not Alan," she declared.

"'Fraid not," he said, suppressing a chuckle. He got up and extended his hand to Frances as Chairman Harold Atkinson and his wife, theoretically long gone to India, stepped in after her.

"Oh my god, Chairman Atkinson," Rose blurted. "What happened to India?"

"Nothing at all," he said. "We'll get there yet."

Doris Atkinson looked around her and let out a slow gasp. Though she was easily forty, given her slight stature, her milky, freckled face, and her crusty little eyebrows raised in outrage, she might have been a child as she looked up and down the apartment. Frances grabbed a chair from the kitchen and set it before her, but she stepped away and sank into the middle of the sofa.

"I know," gasped Frances. "It's not *my* doing."

"Oh god," said Rose. "Your furniture! It's fine. It's safe. It's piled in the studies." It *was not* fine. Why had she thought she could rearrange so much as a particle?

"We sojourned first in Vermont for the colors," said the Chair. "Then, on to New York City, where passport problems developed. It seems we left a visa behind."

"I'll make coffee," said Frances. Doris gave a sharp shake of the head, refusing, but Frances went anyway, detouring to close the bedroom door on the sight of tangled sheets.

"I'm sorry," Rose began and gestured about her.

"No, no, *not* to apologize," said the Chair. "Creative people, you know," he told his wife. "*We* are the intruders."

Guy cleared his throat and tried to catch Rose's eye. She wouldn't look at him.

He stood beside the sofa, which Doris had managed to occupy entirely by sitting in the middle. He stood across the room from Rose, yet a membrane of sex connected them; she could feel the idiot song of sex in her throat, still singing in her nostrils. An hour ago she'd walked the room naked, bursting with her luck. Now it seemed no luck at all, but a terrible lapse that had overtaken her. It was not her bed in the next room; she was only borrowing it. And here she stood, exposed, barefoot, her turtleneck hanging untucked out of her jeans.

Guy probably liked her that way—not a professor but just a girl, a teenager who had broken in to make a love nest with her boyfriend while the owners were out of town. She couldn't, wouldn't look at him. He'd fetched her a chair from the kitchen, but she couldn't bring herself to sit down, not while Chairman Atkinson still stood, his hand placed on the wall over a dark square on the wallpaper where a photograph had hung.

"Your photos! Of course, they're tucked away safe, I promise."

"Of course," he said. His soothing tone put her more on edge. Did she seem hysterical?

"And this is—?" He motioned to Guy, who had settled cross-legged onto the floor.

"Guy," she said quickly. "Guy Robbin." She sat.

"From Philadelphia, perhaps? Another composer?" She shook her head.

"Stonemason," Guy piped up.

"Ah," said the Chair.

Guy launched into a long-winded history of the building of their campus: where the stone and brick had been procured, who had done the work. The Chair pretended fascination. Doris examined her nails mutely. Did she ever speak? During the interview visit the previous spring, had Doris uttered a single a word in Rose's hearing?

Frances stepped in with coffee things on a tray and, pausing before the Chair to pour, bent and hitched her hip. Rose could not stop thinking of sex, of compulsive, hypnotic coupling.

Frances moved to Doris. "Milk. You always take milk."

"Milk," Doris whispered. "Just like a baby."

"Pardon me?" said Frances.

"Harold," said Doris. Her voice was gritty. "Harold," she said, while staring at Frances. "Is this what we call getting away from Frances? To sit as a guest in my own home? To be served coffee on my own china; to endure *milk* poured from the hands of Frances Dupre?"

Here was why Doris Atkinson had kept silent. But she was speaking now.

"You told her?" said Frances, the tray trembling in her hands.

"I am not entirely unobservant," said Doris. "Hasn't everyone told me, one way or another? Harold's colleagues, the students, the cleaning woman, so curious, so sorry for me."

There being no coffee table in sight, Frances set the tray on the floor. It seemed the affair was generally known, Frances the only one not to realize. She realized now. Rose got up quickly and Frances staggered to sit in the chair she had vacated. Frances, it seemed, was not just the source but also the object of gossip.

"I'll find the visa," Harold said, and Guy went with him to help move furniture so he could get to his files, leaving the three women alone.

"Now I'll lose my job," Frances gasped.

"Oh, I don't think so," said Doris. "No one could dismiss you for incompetence, and any other reason given to fire you would embarrass Harold. We won't embarrass Harold."

"No," Frances breathed.

Standing behind Frances's chair, Rose slowly, carefully tucked in her turtleneck. Her shifting of the Atkinsons' furniture was minor after all. But something equally unpleasant was dawning on her: the conviction that her appointment at the college had nothing, really, to do with her, not her talent as a composer, nor what she might have to offer students, but instead merely served the convenience of a professor getting out of a messy love affair.

Frances sat pale and absolutely still watching Doris Atkinson. Rose found herself doing the same. Doris, impassive, frozen except for the fiddling of her fingers, seemed almost to have the power to regulate their breathing. It was the power of the wounded wife. But an even greater power, a drag weight, could be felt from the far room where Harold and Guy rustled and heaved furniture aside. This didn't seem so much Harold's power over Doris—he seemed too mild to be oppressive—but rather the glueyness of marriage, the being together, no matter what, the "being together all the time," as Guy had put it.

Something in Doris's demeanor cracked and her face came alive with pain, an intelligent face, spirited, endearing, possibly even funny. "The blank walls remind me of when we first moved in—Harold and I," she said.

And like sunlight breaking through clouds, she smiled, her eyes fixed on Rose: a welcome unexpected and undeserved. And there seemed to be no warning in it, no warning intended. Still, all Rose had seen so far of Doris, her life, her troubles and how she coped, served as warning.

Frances spoke and Doris froze again. "Mrs. Atkinson," Frances said, in a small voice, heartbreakingly sincere, "you have no idea how much I admire and respect you."

Doris turned to her. "Frances," she said, "that's outlandish. Do you know how outlandish you are?"

Frances *was* outlandish. Her old fashioned views were outlandish, calling herself a *sinner*, labeling herself a *beauty*. Her straight-arrow femininity was outlandish. But her peculiarity was what made her Frances, and Rose wouldn't allow her to be condemned for it. She stepped out from behind Frances's chair, picked up the tray, and poured out a cup for Frances.

"Do you take milk?" she asked.

"Yes," said Frances, struggling not to cry.

Rose poured out a second cup and handed it, black, to Doris Atkinson.

Soon enough after that, the visitors were gone and Rose and Guy were alone again.

"Well, I guess you're all washed up. Promising young career in the ditch. Took the professor's pictures down off the wall? Moved his furniture? Fell in with a *stonemason*?"

She put the tea things in the sink and reached for him but he stepped out of her way.

"They're gonna take away your music license."

"C'mon," she said.

"I wouldn't dream of putting my grubby paws on you. I might smear up the résumé."

In his arms again and laughing, she gasped, "Please, *please* smear up the résumé." And they were, within a half hour, themselves again and the place and the world was theirs.

They had spent nine days in each other's company. If she felt a small ripple of a need to get away, it was only so she could step back and think about him. She was bursting with things to say, but *about* him, not *to* him. When, midday Sunday, he offered to go out for groceries, she let him go alone, and the moment he was out the door, grabbed the phone.

She dialed Ursula but set the receiver back down before it could ring. Ursula wasn't happy and it wouldn't be fair. Her fiancé had moved out on her and she was stuck alone with a lease in a rough Philadelphia neighborhood, working the terrible hours of her hospital residency. Her postcards had turned uncharacteristically cheerful. *Don't worry; I can see the humor in things when I manage to keep my eyes open.* This told Rose how bad it must be. *Amazing, the kindness of ordinary people,* wrote the formerly brash and sarcastic Ursula. *Sleep,* she wrote, *is better than food.* Calling at any hour, Rose stood the risk of waking her.

She called home instead.

Natalie answered distractedly. At the age of twenty-three, after college and a brief stint in a chiropractic school in Baltimore, she had inexplicably returned to stay with their mother, with whom she did not get along.

"*Marion,*" intoned Natalie, interrupting Rose each time their mother stepped within earshot, which would be almost anywhere in the tiny house. Rose heard their mother—Marion, as she was having them call her—in the background, exasperated, offering to go to the garden.

Then Marion was on the phone.

Rose didn't want to tell her about Guy. Marion had taken a mocking attitude on the subject of men ever since their father had, as she put it, *left her to her fate without him.*

"Rose, look, something's happening, okay?" her mother told her.

Rose asked what.

"Ask Natalie," her mother said and handed the phone back.

"You know how dramatic she gets," said Natalie. Rose heard the screen door slam. "So, tell me about what's-his-name."

"What is it, Natalie?" Rose insisted. In the brief silence, Rose pictured her sister as full and rounded as she was spare, white-gold hair like a waterfall, and blue, blue eyes, the same hue as Rose's eyes, MacGregor blue.

Marion, Natalie reported, had gone out through the garden. "So, hey," she said. "Speak up. You got yourself a *boyfriend?*"

Rose launched in, describing Guy, his looks, his voice, his land. She hadn't yet seen his land, but described it anyway, his oat field, his bears. Natalie would be none the wiser.

She described his body, giggling, and let her voice trail off suggestively.

Natalie egged her on. "He's got a freckle *where?*"

Rose excused herself and hung up.

What was she doing? Wasn't it private, what she had with Guy?

Well, but Natalie was far away. She was hardly going to travel halfway across the country just to judge for herself if Guy was all Rose said he was.

He came in just then, heavy laden with groceries, which he dropped so he could wrap his arms around her, clasping her to him as though he hadn't seen her in years.

Chapter FIVE

S he was startled by her body's vehemence, always wanting him. Everything had become easy. It seemed as if nothing could go wrong ever again. She set to her work with ease, relished her students, and when she and Guy went out together, caught and savored admiring glances.

He took her up north to his land. The thrumming of his truck motor detached itself from the urban roar as the city gave way to fields and woods. Within a half hour, they were in open country: acres of sunlight, barns like cathedrals, and thickets of pines like slabs of night.

A turn-off onto a narrow road took them through miles of pasture and oak scrub. Guy sat up straighter and started to whistle. Here was the oat field where the bears had loafed. A tractor driver lifted two fingers from the steering wheel. A woman digging potatoes raised her chin sharply in greeting. Rose was enchanted anew to discover this entirely separate life of his.

A dirt track lifted through a meadow. Below, the lake spread glistening through a vast stand of birches. The trees were like a fulfillment, each a candle, as he'd said, but taller and wider than she'd imagined and more plentiful; the trunks striped black over waxy white, and crowned with yellow leaves. As they got out, birds and wind resounded, shockingly clear.

Not to rush anything, he said, but couldn't she picture herself in a studio there? He took his boat out to fish, allowing her the pleasure of listening to the swoosh of the oars as he pulled, observing him at a distance from her seat at the foot of a birch tree. They cooked the fish over the open fire and, after lovemaking, dropped to sleep on the mattress on the floor of the shack where he'd managed clean sheets for her and dropped over them his zipped-open sleeping bag.

She took to driving up every weekend. The stonework grew: three courses high, then four; the walls immensely thick. He was building for The Ages. He'd begun an enormous central chimney that would open on two sides, the large hearth in the main room and a smaller hearth in the kitchen for a bread oven. The best bread, he claimed, was baked by wood fire. He switched on a cement mixer to stir mortar and fitted stones into the top of the wall while she sat nearby in a lawn chair, reading student papers and marking up pages of her music.

"Look at all this." He threw his arms wide, over the pounding mixer. "Look at us," he shouted, "you and me." She grinned and nodded, not looking up. He switched off the mixer and cracked in half a piece of granite. "It's like we created ourselves for each other, don't you think? Perfected ourselves, all these years—you for me and me for you?"

He had since childhood loved and believed only in nature. Rose didn't know whether she believed in god. Guy knew he did *not,* and when, in third grade, he'd made the mistake of sharing his views on the playground, he'd been showered with pebbles. Yet he had an obvious need of psalms and so invented them. "Look at us," he sang out. "I mean, whether or not we're married—isn't it just what we feel in our hearts?"

"Uh-huh," she said. "*What?*"

Was this a proposal? Did he picture his stone house complete with a wife in a big apron baking bread? She could snooze along on his theology, but marriage? She thought of Harold Atkinson's gluey possession of Doris and her own father bluntly commanding her mother's submission. Guy would never put it so baldly—he'd call it togetherness, call it *compromise*.

"What exactly are you saying?" she asked.

"You're perfect. You know that?" he cried, spreading his mortar-encrusted fingers, his long face flushed, his eyes on fire.

"Shut up," she said. It was true, he made her happy. She was absorbed in the music she was writing, mad, joyful music, and now there were lake sounds in it and the jittering of birch leaves. But she wouldn't be in his Hypnotism Movie. She had her own movie, thank you. She'd have things clear as this October day, with everyone scattered to their own pursuits.

He could catch a five-pound northern pike with the plastic spinner from a firecracker. He knew how to bake his own bread, and did, in a reflecting oven at the campfire—light soda bread, perfectly browned. Under the stars, he recited *Sam McGee* and sang old folk songs, vibrating his voice so it seemed he was making harmony all by himself.

She wrote about him, briefly, factually, to Ursula, curbing her excitement. She put a curb, also, on her phone calls to Natalie, who had taken to referring to Guy as the god, Rose's god.

"I hear you've found God," her mother had said, snatching the phone from Natalie.

"Oh, Marion. He's just—he's a very nice man."

"Do tell," her mother drawled.

Rose knew Marion thought there was no such thing.

Who could she talk to? She didn't dare tell Guy directly all she felt. He was much too prone to jump to conclusions.

"Frances," she began tentatively, one afternoon at the music department when nobody else was around. "Do you know you predicted it—me and Guy?"

"At a German movie," said Frances readily.

"Yes, and on the very day you prophesied. How do you know these things?" Frances smiled and admitted Alan had told her. Was it possible that she felt warmly toward Rose after so many weeks of neglect? Sharing a coffee break—why had they never done so before?—Rose waxed eloquent on the subject of Guy and found Frances receptive to every word, calm, self-contained, even pleased. After that awful scene with the Atkinsons, it seemed she had collected herself. A new nameplate—*Frances Dupre*, unadorned—had replaced *The Beauty*.

"Why don't you come over some evening?" Rose asked impulsively. Frances, she thought, did not get out much. She'd never met Guy properly. Saturday night, Frances ought to come over and join them for supper. Would she?

Yes, she would. And might she bring somebody?

"Of course," said Rose. "We'll make it a foursome, a dinner party."

Frances would bring Alan. Great—Alan. It had been weeks since Rose had exchanged more than two words with Alan. Now they'd all be friends: Rose and Frances, Guy and Alan.

But then the dinner party had to be postponed. On Saturday morning, Rose awakened with flu, wiped out, barely able to make it to the bathroom to vomit. Guy called Frances and Alan to cancel, and then stayed in the city to tend her.

It was blissful the first few days to find she could get sick, even very sick, without fear, now that she had people. Guy made soup and then broth, then weak tea and finally water, and fetched her campus mail every day. Alan taught her classes. Frances sent along get-well notes, knowledgeable of her symptoms. She realized they were getting acquainted without her and tried to get out of bed. Guy wanted her to go to the doctor but she knew what a waste of time that would be, bringing flu symptoms to a doctor.

A week passed and she was no better. Guy tended her very well; then it seemed he had taken her over. He knew before she did when she was going to vomit.

Late October had arrived and the nights were cold. A witch face went up in a window across the street, and a crayoned monster with tusks and smoking nostrils. A skeleton hung from a lamppost. The downstairs tenants ensnared the bush at the front door with fake cobwebs and plastic spiders. Halloweens back east were nothing to this. Pumpkins were amassed on porches for carving, doubling the population. Frances brought quantities of candy to lay in for trick-or-treaters. But when Rose propped herself up in a chair to carve her jack-o-lantern, the odor and the slime of the pumpkin pulp got to her, and she had to crawl back to bed.

Trooping through her bedroom on their way to the campus party came a cat with broom straw whiskers (Frances) and an enormous carp (Alan), his scales made of broken light gels scrounged from the theater department. Rose had hoped to go as guacamole, her chili pepper beads crowning her head. It killed her to have to stay home, but she made Guy go: he had an ax in his truck; he'd be Paul Bunyan. She waved them off from her post on the front stairs, beside a bucket of candy for trick-or-treaters, and then had to dump the candy, needing the bucket for another purpose. Back up in bed, she was forced to listen inertly as the doorbell rang and rang.

The first week of November brought a hard freeze. Up north, the well-digging could be postponed no longer, and Guy had to be there to oversee. Rose decided she was better. She could keep down rice and soft-boiled eggs. She told him to go, and he said he would if she'd go see a doctor. Why now, when she was up and stirring? Well, he insisted, just to be safe. Under his watchful eye, she made a morning appointment and then phoned Frances and Alan. She declared she was holding office hours, to be followed by the long-awaited dinner party—a pot roast with braised carrots and apples. She already had the roast defrosting, if Alan would bring wine.

Before he went, Guy pressed upon her cab fare to get to and from the doctor. He didn't want her behind the wheel. She told him she'd pay her own way or she'd walk; it was less than a mile. Then he'd just stay there, well-digger be hanged, and carry her down the sidewalk to the doctor in his very arms. She laughed and accepted his cab fare. He kissed her. He'd be back that evening in time for the dinner party.

But now he sat in his muddy boots by the door a scant five minutes early, stunned by what she was telling him. She knelt before him in her black dress, tugging at his bootlaces, her hair washed, combed, and pulled back in a knot, her face hidden, gray with fear and nausea. Their guests were coming—would he please hurry? On her own, she'd dragged the mahogany table and chairs back into the dining room. It had been more than she could manage. The roast was back in the freezer. On the table sat boxed pizzas and a bowl of salad.

"I didn't even know you were late," he said.

"I didn't either. My cycle's not regular." She should not have been pregnant. They'd never broken a condom, never ran out of foam, never "forgot." But here it was: statistical failure, the one percent. His features seemed to crumble. Without his sureness, she almost didn't know him. He gave his head a shake and then beckoned her to his lap. She backed away.

"Call your friends and tell them not to come," he said.

"It's too late. They're here."

She opened the door to Frances, who came twirling in on Alan's arm, breathlessly animated, stunning in a blue silk polka-dot dress that flickered and slid over her angles, doubling her every motion.

"Rose, how do you *feel*?" Her eyes were incandescent. It brought to mind the hammer ride at the State Fair, when Rose stood bracing herself and, as now, struggling not to puke.

Frances flashed to the dining room, dragging Alan with her, and peeked into the boxes.

"Pizza?" said Alan, setting his carefully chosen bottle of Cabernet on the kitchen counter.

She wouldn't meet his gaze, couldn't tell him what a fix she was in—not when she, herself, barely knew it. But, oh, she could feel it. Her gorge rose and she fought it back down.

Alan was wearing a necktie. He hated ties, and he seemed held in, bouncing on his heels in his dress shoes, very much on best behavior, in his "earning tenure" mode. Why? What he could accomplish there in her sublet toward earning tenure, Rose could not imagine. At least he was nicer to Frances. He was letting her boss him around, loading him with plates and silverware, instructing him as though he'd never before set a table.

Frances declared that she adored pizza, quizzed Guy about the well-digging, and, failing to note his muted response, turned her questions to Rose, who was thankful she didn't wait for answers. Guy hoisted himself up and clumped off after Frances, who bore the wine and glasses into the dining room. Was his footfall always so noisy? Maybe so. Hadn't he always been a bit of an oaf? Alan was creaking his chair, leaning back so the front legs lifted off. Alan was a nervous, pinched sort of person, wasn't he? And Frances—poor, lonely, pitiful Frances? She'd invited Frances as a kindness and here she was, Rose MacGregor, far worse off than Frances could ever be. What Rose wouldn't give to be Frances now, and out of it. What she wouldn't give to be completely alone—lonely, even. She'd be glad of loneliness. People could pity her, she wouldn't mind. She grasped the salad utensils and dizzily made her way to the table.

Frances had fished out of a drawer a framed photo of the Atkinsons, not on a mountainside but dressed up for some college event. Frances was in the picture. Cut off at the forehead, she stood directly behind Harold Atkinson, her arms crossed on her chest, elbows clutched tensely. She pointed herself out to Alan and laughed. The laugh was carefree. Rose found she was staring.

"It's okay, Rose," said Frances. "Ancient history. Alan knows and he doesn't mind."

Alan avoided Rose's eye. Something was going on here. She couldn't get quite what. Unable to bear the smell of vinegar, she passed the salad to Guy, who sat stupidly with the big wooden forks in his hands.

"Toss it, would you please," she said.

Alan took the utensils. Under the table, Guy reached and put his hand on Rose's knee. She felt his heat and sighed. Dizzy as she was, if he'd stood up, she would have gotten up to follow him. Nothing would have been easier than to follow him, whoever he was, however oafish, to some warm lair and curl up with him for good. Alan drummed a tight little rhythm on the side of the bowl. Rose groaned and got to her feet, letting Guy's hand drop.

"Rose, what is it?" asked Frances, with an excess of warmth.

Rose shook her head, sat down again, and suffered Guy to rest his hand a moment on her cheek. She lifted a slice of pizza. She watched the others chew and swallow.

"Isn't it amazing?" said Frances. "Love?" They were in the living room having coffee. Awkward for the first time that evening, Frances got up and slid into Alan's lap. As Alan gingerly closed his arms around Frances, Rose came alert and swung her gaze to meet his.

"Simply amazing," Rose said savagely and pitched herself to her feet.

"You guys have a fight?" she heard Frances ask Guy as she staggered to the kitchen. Gripping the counter, she pulled herself erect as Alan stepped in and closed the door behind him. They faced each other, glaring.

"What on earth are you doing with Frances? You haven't told her, I don't suppose."

"*Rose,*" he said. "How is it your business? What on earth is the matter with you?"

Guy and Frances came in. "I'm standing by you," Guy told Rose. "You know that."

"Rose is having a baby," Frances told Alan softly.

"So," Rose told Guy, through clenched teeth, "we're telling people? We're making *announcements?*"

"Not 'people.' Friends. Your friend Frances."

Rose turned to Frances, steeled for compassion, but Frances's face changed. Her mouth twisted unhappily and her eyes widened. Envy! So this, too, was lucky?

"Correction," said Rose. She might be in trouble—yes, pregnant, but who on earth said she was having a baby? Frances was in trouble herself, imagining Alan in love with her.

"Ah, Rose," said Alan, and put a hand on her shoulder. "Are you in trouble?"

She gasped and he enfolded her in his arms.

"Alan," said Frances. "What are you doing? You said it was over between you two."

Alan sighed. "Rose wants me to tell you I'm gay."

"Well, but we've been over that and you might not be."

"Oh, *really*," said Rose, tight in his arms, gulping for air.

Alan loosened his grip. Frances stood frozen, her face an empty mask. "Well, are you?"

She'd be crying in a minute, calling herself unlucky. She didn't recognize luck when she saw it: her life all to herself and unencumbered. If Rose could have gotten at even a shred of Frances's luck right then, she would have torn it from her. But luck couldn't be gotten from another, not begged, nor stolen, nor in any way exchanged.

"Don't try to help me." Rose shoved Alan away. What could they do to help her? Was any of them a doctor? Could any of them offer her so much as a knitting needle?

"That's enough," said Guy. "We've had enough now."

They went, leaving her alone with him.

No, of course she hadn't meant that about the knitting needle. Laws had changed. She could have it done safely.

"Uh-huh," he said. The dirty dishes stood on the table. He put his arm around her and maneuvered her to bed, undressed her, helped her under the covers, and gave her a brief kiss. He pulled a chair to the bedside and sat, gazing down on her. His face was absolutely calm.

When she awoke, it was morning, and he still sat in the chair beside the bed.

"What we'll do," he said, "is get married."

"I'm sorry?" She looked past him into an immaculate kitchen. She sat up and her nausea returned. "You mean," she sneered, "like, before god and man?"

"Not in a church. Of course not," he told her. But this was serious now. It was fate. Between the two of them, it wasn't just fooling around any more. It wasn't just fucking.

She got unsteadily out of bed and, keeping an eye on him, pulled on her clothes.

It had always been serious between them. It had never before been fooling around.

"Isn't love amazing," she observed bitterly.

"I've put it wrong. I want to marry you, Rose. Always have. You know that."

He seemed a simpleton, gazing at her, waiting for her to crush him. Well, it was crush or be crushed. She could see herself, five, ten years, down the dirt road beside the lake, fecund and brainless, her life gone, merged into mortar and mud. It even had a disgusting appeal. She'd be a slack-jawed thing in his movie, a wife and mother, would she? She'd just let them take her over, he and the cluster of cells inside her, which was, even now, doubling in size every few seconds.

"I've got to go out," she said and stepped past him.

He hurried after her to school and sat at the back while she taught. She stood in front of the classroom, a young girl, barely older than her students.

After class, he leaned into the office to speak to Frances, and Rose sped down the back stairs, drove to a motel nearby and got a room, got the name of a doctor, made the appointment, and called back to cancel classes. Frances asked where she was. There were students to see her. Guy—wait, she'd put him on. Rose hung up.

For twenty hours in the motel, she stared at ice-blue walls.

Then she lay on her back on a steel table with a nurse at her side who smelled of lilacs and held her hand primly. As she gulped and panted through the procedure, the nurse asked if she didn't think that perhaps next time she should use protection?

Poor thing, Rose thought—she hasn't heard that protection does not exist. And Rose would have enlightened her, too, had not the pain come on so strong.

Immediately after, she felt better, emptied out, unburdened. She brushed past the nurse, who reminded her she wasn't to drive. She walked to her car, the wadding between her legs hindering her gait. She pulled over every few blocks to lie down and rest on the seat, just on principle, she told herself, not because she was tired. By now she knew her way through the streets around the college, or at least had ways of getting lost and backtracking and finding her way again. She was maybe a little tired, but certainly her strength was returning.

She parked in front of the duplex and sat. It was done. The thing was taken care of. Ursula, she thought—she could tell her dreadful news to Ursula. Better yet, she'd tell her mother: in this she could count on her mother's interest and sympathy and on their shared relief at the outcome. She hauled herself up the back stairs.

On the top step sat Guy, red-eyed, unshaven, hugging himself.

"It was mine too," he declared.

"Well. Yes, it was," she said.

"It was my life too," he said, and stumbled off.

Good-bye, she thought. They'd known each other barely two months.

Chapter SIX

U rsula's hair was a shock: a reddish-purplish brush above her pale face, instead of the long, fluttering hair Rose was used to, hair in varying shades of brown, hair like a laugh or a shout. Ardent in conversation, the Ursula Rose had known in their grad-school years had tended to fling all that hair over a shoulder or to gather it into a hank doubled up in her fist. This new Ursula curved a palm over the top of her shorn skull, or placed both hands there, which, given her dangerous thinness, gave her the aspect of a prisoner of war in the act of surrender. Her hair was short, she told Rose curtly, so she didn't have to bother with it as she dashed to the bus to get to the hospital or woke in the awful bunks provided for the resident doctors-in-training.

Having no money to go anywhere, Ursula had done Thanksgiving alone. After her grimly cheerful Thanksgiving letter, Rose offered to fly back to Philadelphia at Christmas and Ursula said yes. She wheedled three days in a row off from the hospital rotation, a break she'd have to pay for by working straight through the eight days prior and the eight after. Rose, for her part, would take Ursula out for a big Christmas dinner at any restaurant she'd care to name.

"How about we cook instead?" said Ursula upon meeting Rose at the airport.

Better yet: Rose would cook while Ursula strode around the kitchen, talking, swearing, gesticulating, passing the odd dirty dish through the dishwater and putting it away with flecks of food still on it. They'd "cook together" and Ursula would be restored.

Stopping on the way in from the airport, they piled the grocery cart high. Rose picked the biggest turkey in the bin so there would be leftovers after she'd gone. Squash and broccoli went into the cart; potatoes, garlic, mayonnaise, yams, three kinds of olives, apples and a big bag of pecans, eggs and cornmeal for Indian pudding. Also boxes of noodles, cheese, flour, butter, vanilla, sugar, and chocolate chips. Did Ursula still have a yen for hearts of palm? Rose tossed in three expensive cans. The bill topped a hundred dollars, which Rose paid with a flourish.

Hauling their booty out to the cab, Ursula grinned, showing her teeth, a hint of the rascal Rose had known. She'd been dining from hospital vending machines, she admitted. Her eyes filled. "Just tired," she said, and began an emergency room story but fell asleep mid-sentence.

In the back of the cab, Rose eased bags of groceries to the floor, making room for her sleeping friend to lean against her, preferring Ursula's troubles to her own.

As the Minnesota autumn had progressed, as November turned bitter and December came on, she'd awakened in the mornings, warm in the bedclothes, but sensing cold outside like a great ice dome under which life twitched and scurried; and before coming fully alert, she'd hear herself ask aloud, *what's wrong?*—as if someone might answer. Then it would come to her. It was Guy not there. She remembered her cheek against his chest, his hand wandering over her breasts, and the pain of her longing crushed her. She hated him unreasonably for getting her pregnant, for trying to marry her, and at the same time for being someone she would miss so horribly.

Her skin broke out and her hair went dull and flyaway no matter how she tied or pinned it before marching off to her teaching. She missed his eyes, his jokes, his voice. She remembered how he'd hesitated that first night, remembered the dreadful pause. And here was the reason for dread: that, once parted, she would yearn for him, not as for lover of a few weeks, but as for part of herself now missing. Even now, as she was driven through the streets of Philadelphia with dear old Ursula snoring against her, she couldn't help sense Guy out there, living and breathing.

Ursula stretched, arched her back, and pushed her long legs against the cab floor so her head nearly touched the roof. The shorn head gave her the look of Joan of Arc, which suited her.

In her med school class of '75, Ursula had been the only woman, a fact brought to her daily attention in unpleasant ways despite her official warm welcome. Whether by necessity or by nature, she'd moved through her training like a guerrilla, swift, stealthy, and taking no prisoners. Her specialty was the lethal comeback. She was quoted by people who hadn't even met her.

"My legend," Ursula scoffed, but Rose believed the stories were true.

It was said that one day in Anatomy, Ursula had been requested by a sneering professor to come to the board and diagram "the male reproductive apparatus." She'd picked up the chalk and taken her time about it, going into detail. When she stepped away, the professor had drawled, "Miss Kaiser, though she may not realize it, has drawn the male member in the erect state."

"That's the only way I've ever seen it," said Ursula.

There followed a scene in Dissection when Ursula, assigned to work alone on a female cadaver while the rest of the class worked around her in pairs on dead males, one morning found a set of severed male genitals stuffed up between the legs of her cadaver.

"I guess she died of boredom," Ursula had observed in her small, clear voice, a voice that carried. Rose laughed aloud thinking of it. In the cab, in her sleep, Ursula turned toward her.

Rose had often wished for similar exploits. The grad program in music had been no more hospitable to females. Its famous program director, whom Rose also suffered as adviser, relished commenting on the rareness of talent and its unexpected indicators: a sense of humor, for instance. His brand of humor ran to sex, crude talk of banging the girlfriend while the wife came up the stairs. If, in telling one of his jokes, his eye fastened like a hook on Rose, she always managed to pass the test, not by laughing—she rarely laughed during those years, unless alone with Ursula—but by keeping herself from glowering. She presented a smooth countenance, absent-minded, as though unreachable, lost in thought, in music. There was no subject the program director couldn't turn to sex, and the other professors felt called upon to chime in; worse, the other students repeated the stories, chuckling experimentally, distracting themselves from the director's lack of interest in the music any of them were writing.

Rose's joy in music only just barely kept her going. One or two other female students would appear at the start of each semester and then fall away, but Rose marched straight through without leave or transfer; and she did it by keeping her head down, a strategy that never produced any zingers—none to compare with Ursula's.

Ursula found a fascination, regardless, in all Rose had to report. She claimed most doctors were frustrated artists and would, if not for lack of talent, compose or write or paint instead. Rose doubted it. Anyone who really wanted to could compose or write or paint. Compared to music, mending and saving lives seemed more unquestionably worthy. Life without music would hardly be worth saving, answered her friend who was already in name a doctor, Doctor Ursula Kaiser. This awed Rose and made her nervous.

When she was nine years old, Rose had had a boil lanced below her knee. The doctor had enlisted her mother to keep her from kicking, and he carved and carved as though he were boring a hole through her leg, while she, screaming, wet her pants and heard the pee spill to the floor. Ursula had been incensed at the story, furious that the doctor had failed to administer anesthetic. But Ursula herself now yielded the knife and something in her humor might be that way, too, something in Ursula's truth-telling. They'd chosen each other, however, because they were in some way alike, serious young women, comrades, equals. The hours they spent together were no mere pastime; and nothing had ever polluted things between them, as envy and pity had between Rose and Frances.

Toward Rose, since her disastrous dinner party, Frances had been distant but sympathetic, swapping envy of Rose for pity. With Ursula, there was instead a striving to be worthy of each other. Rose hoped to be worthy of her friend, both of them alone and both lately thwarted in love.

Regardless of her legend, Ursula did not hate men, nor was she indifferent to them, and men were crazy about her. She didn't fall in love often, but when she did, she fell hard, which was how she'd come to lease a huge apartment with barely a stick of furniture on a street so dangerous, she had to walk with a freon shriek horn.

The cabby pulled in at a smeary dumpster, and Rose paid him and woke her friend. They hauled the groceries, two trips up the graffiti-splashed, glass-riddled stairs.

The apartment filled the top floor of the narrow, crumbling house; six rooms within a mansard roof. Fifteen tall, arched windows spanned ceiling to floor and let in sun from every direction. East to west, the light flooded gorgeously across bare hardwood floors and lit up the handsome double bed with a carved headboard—Russian folk art.

Her last year of med school, Ursula had met Bogdan, who'd dropped out of medicine to pursue his interest in his native land and its literature, from which he quoted tonelessly. His main virtue, to Rose, was his devotion to Ursula. He monopolized her in every setting, hunched over her, running on about her charms. *Light of my life, fire of my loins,* he called her (Nabokov); *a beauty that could overthrow the world* (Dostoevsky). Unfathomably, Ursula declared him handsome and demanded agreement from Rose. He was tall but spindly, his hair sloped down his forehead in a brownish gray pelt, and when he smiled a set of crooked teeth seemed to pop forth. Having no sense of humor, he was immune to Ursula's powers of deflation and he never lowered his voice, but spoke his love talk to her always as though they were alone and not, for instance, in the middle of a crowded party.

Rose kept to herself her opinion of Bogdan, which was odd, given that she and Ursula prided themselves on telling each other everything. As Bogdan and Ursula had sometimes borrowed Rose's rented room, Rose felt implicated in their union. Bogdan was penniless and lived in his car. Without Rose's room to go to, they had only the smelly car or Ursula's narrow bed in the dorm and the impeding presence of a roommate. Ursula had brought her own sheets and aired out the room afterward and made up the bed nicely.

But then Rose gave up the room to move to Minnesota—and where were Ursula and Bogdan to go? He found the airy apartment under the mansard roof, a place worthy of their love, and, plunking down a deposit "borrowed" from Ursula, promoted himself to fiancé, and had them buy, on her credit, the double bed with the headboard carved in Russian wedding symbols: apples, a duck, a drake, and a branch of spilling grapes, all nicely rendered in birch. And then, five short months after he and Ursula had moved in together, Bogdan had vanished.

Ursula thought it must have been her fault. She'd been grouchy adjusting to her residency. Or maybe he'd run completely out of money and been too proud to say so. Whatever the reason, Ursula was now stuck paying the rent alone. She'd leave the minute the lease was up. She was nearly through her training and would find a practice to join somewhere else, *somewhere far, far away.*

"Minnesota?" said Rose.

"Why not?" said Ursula.

The future, however, could wait. They'd have Christmas, three whole days, three days together in the light-enchanted rooms behind the triple locks.

Though they hadn't really planned it that way, they never left the place at all. There at the top, it was actually hot once they—Rose—started cooking and baking. With the oven and the stove burners blasting, they traipsed around in their underwear.

Christmas Day, they sat on folding chairs with a card table between them, on which the roast turkey rested on a hospital tray and the rest of Christmas dinner was set forth in what, in Ursula's kitchen, passed for dishes—olives in a jar lid, mashed potatoes in a rinsed take-out box.

"He was a rat. Bogdan was," announced Ursula. It was the first time she had ever criticized Bogdan, at least in Rose's hearing. "He was a ratty rodent," said Ursula, rolling her r's. "And you knew it all along, Rose. You did!"

Rose shrugged. "Eat," she commanded her friend.

"Maybe he's gone to Russia," said Ursula.

"To Siberia, I hope," said Rose. "Take bites. Chew. Swallow."

Bogdan had disappeared without a call or a letter, without so much as a postcard. But Ursula guessed she was over it. Weeks and weeks had passed; she guessed she was over him.

"That's good, Urse. Maybe I am too. Over him," said Rose.

She found it difficult to speak Guy's name, and it wasn't till the day after Christmas, when the visit was nearly over, that Rose brought herself to tell everything.

She found it hard to begin. That afternoon, after Guy had walked away, she'd at first welcomed the loneliness. To be lonely felt good; to be silent felt right.

"I know," said Ursula. She was in the bathtub. Reaching back to scrub her neck, she slopped water over the side.

But, as Rose's memory faded of pain and the suctioning of the clotted blood running through a clear tube from her body to a drain, as days passed and she thought she was calm again, she found herself noticing babies.

Ursula interrupted with a story of her own about a messy triage and Rose realized she'd fallen asleep in the tub and awakened talking.

"Let's get you to bed," said Rose. She'd managed to get them to bed late each night of the visit, to bed if not to sleep.

"Count sheep," Rose had said the first night into the alert darkness. Urse didn't answer. Asleep, thought Rose. But later, she roused herself to hear her friend wandering.

Ursula declared herself unhappy to hear all Rose had undergone without telling her. They were side by side on the bed again, leaning against the headboard, nursing cups of tea. As Rose went on with her story, Ursula cupped first one hand and then the other over the top of her skull, as though holding her brain in place, and kept setting her cup down. And kept falling asleep.

"Your abortion. Oh, god. I'm losing it, Rose."

Rose began again, but Ursula broke in. "I don't fall asleep in emergencies, I don't think, but who would tell me if I did? *Shit*, I can't concentrate. I'm sorry—please go on."

Rose told her to snuggle down under the covers. She needed sleep. The story could wait.

"No. Tell me now." Ursula got up and walked to one of the long windows and stood looking out at the hard winter sky. It was one of her most endearing traits—she could look away and yet concentrate all the warmth of her listening, and thus allow Rose to unwrap slowly whatever it was that needed telling.

Leaning against the window, however, Ursula gave a sudden jerk and started in again, mid-sentence about the triage, how blood had sprayed the team and she hadn't minded, how she, as leader, had shouted orders and they'd gotten the job done. She'd been good at it—really good, abso-fucking-lutely a performer. She turned and regarded Rose with puzzlement. "I'm a monster," she said. "You had an abortion. Tell me."

"I am." Ursula dug her knuckles into her forehead.

When she found herself noticing babies, Rose was struck with the thought of herself as that, as the pulsing newborn she must have been, and it made her yearn for her mother. But she knew better than to ask

Marion's comfort. Marion would not have been sad for Rose, but would instead have praised her for "dealing with realities."

"Dealing with realities," Ursula intoned, Marion to a T: half smug I-told-you-so, half barely able to be bothered. They'd met one another's families, and Urse was a deadly mimic.

"So I didn't tell my mother. It's weird. Because she *would* have approved."

"You'd want her to disapprove?" Ursula leaned her forehead against the window.

"Yes," Rose continued, choking the words out—it was too pathetic, too obvious, too much what she felt—"because, you see, I was her baby once, and what if she had wanted to do that? You know—to flush away—to rid herself of *me*?"

Rose waited for what Ursula would say. She had finally gotten it out, and was grateful to have someone she could tell. She'd declare that, too, in a minute, her gratitude to Ursula, how much she needed Ursula.

"Well," said Ursula, turning a blind face, eyes closed, to Rose. "It was just a cluster of cells. You lost a cup of blood at most."

Rose regarded her. She could not have heard what Rose had said. She wondered how much of what she'd said had transmitted to Ursula, what parts, flashing on and off like a strobe. She wouldn't hold Ursula to blame, but she felt a lonely sinking into a deeper chamber of herself, her heart, her uterus. Someplace hidden and resoundingly hollow.

"I'm sorry," gasped Ursula, her eyes flying open. "What am I saying? It was a baby. Your child, who would have looked like you and talked like you—"

"Let's not get carried away," said Rose. Even more than grief, she had to admit that she had felt relief, immediate and persistent relief to have it gone—the fetus gone and her mother far away enough that if Rose never told her, she'd never know.

"I'm in trouble," said Ursula and came back to the bed and slumped down, resting against Rose. "I have to get out of this situation. It's making me unfit to be with people. I'm going to quit. Really. You can go in with me Monday and I'll do it—I'll tell them."

"Now, now, Doctor Kaiser," Rose said. They'd got themselves into a state, cooped up in the apartment. Rose would be flying out to Minnesota the next morning. They mustn't lose heart. They'd stay in better contact. For the moment, unless Ursula meant to go to bed and to sleep, they ought to bundle up and collect the freon horn and go out walking.

Chapter SEVEN

R ose lived a nun's life that winter: up early, compose an hour, tea and toast, classes, coaching sessions, a Coke at lunch to keep her alert through class prep and on into the evening when, after a quick supper and more tea, she turned herself over entirely to her music. And if, in the late hours, she went stale, she availed herself of the phone: Ursula, when she could get her, or Alan, though with Alan she had to steer clear of the subject of Frances.

Frances and Alan were still on, somehow. Rose had stumbled on the two of them kissing in Alan's office. However, when Rose called Alan late at night, Frances was never in evidence. At school, Frances was polite to her, correct and clear, and, as time passed, seemed no longer to notice her and radiated neither envy nor pity.

Rose had a student, Victor Zeiss, who seemed especially bright and funny but had trouble retaining concepts. He came by her office hours twice a week for tutoring and, during their talks, developed the puzzling habit of changing the subject to himself. One afternoon, she saw he was flirting with her. The realization overtook her physically: she caught herself blushing and had to think why. He gave a light, triumphant laugh. He was not much younger than she, five years younger at most. He had a marvelous, broad face and high coloring. She enjoyed his easy conversation. Had she somehow beckoned to him? He sat there, watching to see what she'd do.

She'd do nothing. Another student would be along soon. Her office hours were always full; in fact, other faculty teased about her popularity, which annoyed her. She was there because of music. She took a breath and brought Victor back to music.

Some of the music she was writing might be terrible, she suspected—unconsidered, unformed, and raw. But it was going—all flow and no ebb. She seemed made to work. The end of the school year and of her appointment was drawing nearer, but she'd saved fully half her salary. The money would last at least another nine months and wherever she went, she'd be writing music. She'd sent for a brochure from the Minnesota Composer's Guild. If she could win a concert grant, there'd be money to rent a hall, hire professional musicians and play to an audience far beyond students and professors at college recitals. She had purpose and focus. Her road lay straight ahead.

One night while she was washing dishes, Guy knocked at her door. She felt a startled ache at the sight of him, of his work-roughened hand on her doorframe.

He hadn't called first, he said, because he thought she might refuse to see him. She brought him in, made tea and let him talk.

He had lived in the neighborhood all winter and had sometimes seen her at a distance, he said, but had tried to keep out of her way.

Out of her way? Was she so harsh a person?

Come spring, he'd go north. As he described plans for the summer's stonework, she rediscovered her pleasure in the directness of his gaze and the melody of his voice. If this had been the olden days, they'd be, by now, a settled pair—married with a baby on the way—and working out how to stay close, now that the "being in love" was over. But it wasn't the olden days. She hadn't had to marry him. Had she loved him? Oh, she had. But it was over and she'd survived. She had, deep inside herself, changed the subject. Still, she felt how much she liked him. She almost wished he was speaking a language she didn't understand so she could simply enjoy the sound. His voice was a clarinet, and then it seemed he was cooing at her. He reached for her and she leaned back. He shuddered and clasped his hands. She thought she'd better wake up and hear what he was saying.

"I'm sorry," he said. "I'm sorry."

"What for?"

He shook his head. "Look. Can I call you?"

She'd be leaving her borrowed apartment soon, as the school year was winding down. Come summer, she'd be gone and he'd be up north. What harm would it do if he called her?

He dropped in again every few nights, calling ahead with shy formality. Once, for no reason she could think of, she put her arms around him as he stood at the sink and he turned and, with great relief, kissed her. But she wouldn't let him lead her to bed and he didn't press it. He imagined she was afraid. Of what? Of getting pregnant again? She was, and his tender concern touched her, but really her mind was elsewhere.

She asked him out to a college recital. They went and she enjoyed being seen with him. She took care that the students—that Victor Zeiss—should see them. Victor caught her glance and raised his eyebrows. All evening, to her surprise, she was more aware of Victor than of Guy. But Guy wasn't stupid. She couldn't parade him around and then send him home like a schoolboy.

On the first warm day in April, he went up north. It was understood that she wouldn't visit—there was only the shack with the one bed. Still, she caught herself longing for open sky and birdsong. And, as it happened, she knew someone else who lived in the country, to the south.

During her grad-school years, guest musicians frequently performed in

Philadelphia, among them an astounding cellist named Lila Goldensohn. Goldensohn gave a disheartening first impression: stiff and unsmiling, she took her place onstage, her heavy black hair massively subdued in a gold clip like something she'd killed for a trophy. Her brow weighed down over her eyes and her prominent jaw clenched as she lifted her bow. She was only a little older than Rose. Her concert career had begun in her teens; she'd been a prominent soloist for years. Rose had wondered that she couldn't afford to relax a little.

The moment she drew her bow across the strings, however, her stage presence no longer mattered. The sound eclipsed the sight of her, as though the ear could for once overthrow the almighty eye. In the fluid notes that crested and fell, the surging and slowing and rising again, Rose heard, that first time she'd witnessed Lila Goldensohn, what she had previously known only in her head and had never been able to produce in her own playing. The sound emerged as though from a single body, musician and instrument as one, and each note seemed sung.

Rose had ventured backstage after the concert and, trying to express her excitement, had burst into tears. She was mortified, but, to her surprise, the cellist was pleased. The forbidding features relaxed and her eyes, under her heavy brow, seemed actually to twinkle. When Rose tried to withdraw, leaving way for other fans, Lila stopped her and asked Rose her name and address to add Rose to her mailing list.

Rose ventured that she would write music for Lila.

"Really?" murmured Lila. "Well, maybe you will."

Every few months afterwards, Rose had received a notice detailing concert dates, though always with the same grim photo of Lila, glowering over her cello. When Rose came to St. Paul, she'd sent along her new address to Lila's management, but, for a time, heard nothing. The sound of Lila's cello was never far from her mind, and she frequently put on a Goldensohn recording when she went to bed, so that exalted sound was the last thing she heard before sleep. Then in late winter she received not a concert notice, but a letter with a Minnesota address.

I have retired from the concert hall—in fact, I no longer play. I'm out here on my farm with a bunch of women, not a hundred miles from you. Why don't you pay us a visit?

It was March then, however, and every weekend seemed to bring a fresh blizzard and travel warnings. Rose found it difficult to fathom that Lila would quit music. It seemed wrong, offensively wrong, when she played so sublimely. Rose's disappointment was, of course, for herself, though she had no reason to believe that Lila, with her Carnegie Hall dates, her raves in *The Times* and her following in Europe, would interest herself in the work of an unknown.

Rose wrote a brief letter expressing delight that Lila lived so near and defiantly enclosed a short piece for the cello, a piece of her own music.

At length, Lila replied with a letter very much like the first. *I'm afraid I haven't opened your score. Josie, the other musician here, has taken a peek at it and says it's good. Did I mention I own a farm here? We're the great farmers. Why don't you come out?*

On the Friday before Easter, Rose drove her beat-up station wagon out through the city's western reaches, past the Flying Cloud Airport to where the highway dropped south into the wilds of the Minnesota River Valley. In the fragile warmth of April, the willows and sumac, swamp alder and cattails were poised to unfurl in all shades of green. Her front seat rode high, the springs and upholstery bearing up stoutly over the rusted wheel wells. Despite a chilly breeze, she rolled her windows down to let in birdsong and the almost-audible rustle and buzz of growth.

On a rise above the Crow River, to the east of the tiny town of Cosmos, off a county road and down a dirt track that ran a mile to a grove of ancient elms and willows, the farmhouse stood, and the barn—not a fat, red, gambrel-roofed dairy barn, but a steep, weathered white, with a tin roof that swooped up to the ridgepole, making an incurved mountain shape behind the house, which was a story and a half and many-windowed. At first view, the house was all eyes.

Rose cut the motor and got out. Out of the stillness, sounds oozed and burst: the push of river water, grass rubbing on grass, and another sound, a chorus of nasal yawping and blatting. Then laughter burst, entirely human, and a white-blonde woman in a long chambray dress came zigzagging around the corner of the house, chasing a white-blond boy who was juggling an Easter egg. Her skirt gathered up in a fist, the woman halted and signaled to the boy, who rushed indoors as she strode forward in welcome.

"Here you are, Rose. I'm Wilma," she said, and wrapped her in a quick, cinnamon-scented embrace. "You can't go in yet."

Yawping again—voices, but not human. Bleating. A small sign over the front door read: *The Goat Pasture.* Wilma led her on a tour of riverbank and goat shed, where half a dozen black and white ewes, heavy-uddered and shaggy, rushed to them. Rose had never before seen goats up close. Leaning over the fence, she reached and buried her hand in warm, coarse hair.

Wilma shouted toward the house, "Ready or not!" and they went inside.

A bow dragged across cello strings. In the middle of the front room, dim at first, after the dazzle of outdoors, sat Lila in overalls, bent to her instrument, her untamed hair spread across her shoulders, playing with her unmistakable verve the short composition Rose had sent her, while a woman with a dark little rattail down her back played accompaniment on piano. Rose was struck dumb. The sound was all she'd hoped. Entering the fullness of the music felt strange, like setting foot on unknown land, though she herself had mapped it.

Then came a second shock: Lila looked up and Rose saw she had a beard. Dark, soft bristle covered her jaw line—a beard was what it was, and a mustache. For a split second, Rose felt tricked, as though this were some sort of masquerade. But it wasn't a costume Lila had on; it was something that grew from her body. Lila put down her bow and Rose approached and embraced her awkwardly, avoiding her face. A peculiar smell enveloped them, pungent and slightly chemical. Rose glanced at the cello and the open case, wondering at its source. Lila put her hand to her face. Rose let her breath out and brought her hands together, applauding.

"You *rascal*," she said. "I thought you'd given up music."

Lila grinned back at her, beard, mustache and all. "Maybe you'll talk me back into it."

"Oh, I will," said Rose.

She was soon introduced to Josie at the piano, to Wilma's little boy, Noah, and to the other "farm girls," as they called themselves—round-faced Dinah and skinny, nervous Peggy, who presided over the kitchen where a vegetarian supper was in progress.

The house was as plain as a convent or a Shaker house. Pictures on the walls were hardly needed: the many windows brought in the outdoors in great swaths of light, hot gold and fuzzy green. The front room—or common room, as they called it—held a scattering of ladderback chairs along with Lila's huge rocker, polished cherrywood, silent on its runners. A dining table at one end folded in or out to seat as few as two or as many as ten. On the river side, three bedrooms were tucked under a wide stair-case which led upward to a low-ceilinged master bedroom, reserved to Lila as owner of the farm, which had belonged to her grandparents. There was running water in the house, but no indoor bathroom. An outhouse stood in a screen of lilacs. It was a two-holer but could be locked from inside. Rose wondered if she would have to share it, if she would mind. A half-moon window was cut high in the door.

They gave her the little room upstairs across the stairwell from Lila, a room with a round window that looked out over the meadow. After rice, asparagus, goat's cheese, and apples, Rose lay down beneath the round window, but, jittery with delight, she barely slept. Light sleeping seemed a feature of the place, though it might have been the effect of spring. Downstairs in the common room, in the wee hours, she found Wilma and Josie playing Chinese checkers. Above them, she was almost certain she heard Lila wandering.

At first light, Rose stumbled outside over the soggy ground. Sunrise was huge in flat country. Swallows dipped, chattered, spiraled. Her eyes filled with sky and wind and grass; her ears, with a vague, oceanic roaring.

Why did they call the place the Goat Pasture, she wondered. Why not Chanting Wind or Star of the Prairie? *Goat Pasture* seemed so prosaic.

"You don't know goats," observed Peggy.

"Anyway, it's a prosaic sort of place," declared Lila. "No fancy philosophies, just the land, and each person doing as they please."

Rose extended her stay until the last possible moment, dawn of Easter Monday. The night before, they fired up the sauna, shed their clothes, and hung them on pegs on the side porch, the seven women and the boy. The cedar-lined hutch held a metal barrel of glowing rocks. They sat thigh to thigh on facing benches. At first it wasn't quite hot enough. Peggy stood and climbed lithely into Dinah's lap, snuggled against her breasts, and Dinah leaned down and kissed her.

"Look at the lovebirds," Lila growled.

Rose hadn't realized. She tried not to stare. She'd known lesbians, though never, she didn't think, at close range. She wondered whether the little boy ought to be seeing this. But it was only affection, after all. It wasn't as though they were *doing it* in front of him. "It"? What exactly did they do? Rose suppressed a giggle—it seemed somehow silly, the thought of what they did. Wilma dumped water on the rocks, Dinah and Peggy moved apart in a cloud of steam, and Rose was abruptly ashamed. How dumb not to have known. She'd been quick enough, meeting Alan, to think he was gay. But then he'd proved her wrong, hadn't he, carrying on with Frances? What did she know about all that? She imagined another woman's body would be familiar, and at least there'd be no fear of getting pregnant.

So it was that sort of a thing, a lesbian commune. Were all of them that? Late at night, she asked Wilma.

"Not exactly," Wilma told her. "I'm bi."

Rose regarded her.

"I go both ways—men and women."

"Oh," said Rose quickly.

"That's how I got my Noah." Wilma nuzzled the little boy, who'd fallen asleep against her. Wilma had known Lila since high school and, when

Lila inherited the farm, had come out there with her little boy, leaving her husband behind. He'd been a good husband but couldn't tolerate Wilma's need for an occasional girlfriend—had been heartbroken by the girlfriends. Josie came next. She'd been Lila's secretary during her concert years. They'd found Peggy at the food coop in nearby Litchfield, and Peggy had brought Dinah; like in "The Farmer in the Dell."

"So Peggy and Dinah are a couple. And Josie's with me sometimes, though not so much lately. And Lila is, well, Lila. Like Garbo, she walks alone," said Wilma. "And you?"

"I like men," Rose said quickly.

Wilma shrugged. Rose was welcome all the same.

Following the Easter visit, she drove out as many weekends as she could, sending music ahead. Lila always greeted her, ready and rehearsed to play. She commented sparingly, offering here a change of tempo, there an observation that she "wondered" about a certain passage. Rose didn't mind Lila's censure. Lila's ear seemed unerring, and Rose had three new ideas for every one Lila "wondered" about. More rarely, Lila called a passage "interesting"—her highest praise. Letting her gaze linger on the leonine mane and the jar-like, bearded jaw, Rose sometimes slid into thinking of Lila as a man. That was incorrect. Lila was just as much a woman as she, and when Lila played her music, Rose was led deeper into what she'd begun to explore, her soul's own country. Lila cut Rose's gratitude short. Apparently, the music meant something to her too. One evening in mid-May while they all sat at the table after dinner, the breeze blowing through the big room and spreading the fragrance of lilac, Josie leaned back in her chair.

"So, Rose, when are you moving in for good?"

"Oh, well," Rose spluttered. "Have I been invited?"

"*Lila*," said Wilma, rolling her eyes.

"She talks about it all the time," said Josie. "I thought you two had it worked out."

"I could rent a room in Cosmos so as not to overuse your guest room," Rose ventured.

"It's not the guest room," said Peggy. "We call it Rose's room, as if you didn't know."

"We'll be renovating the barn this summer," Dinah put in. "Guests can sleep there."

"I could do the barn," said Rose. She'd buy a hammer. They could teach her how.

"No," said Lila. "You'll be writing music." Josie got up, cleared the last of the dishes, and neatly telescoped the table, arranging Rose and Lila to sit face to face.

"Look, I've got to contribute," said Rose, "to the work and to expenses."

But the farm was paid for, Lila insisted. The taxes were nothing, and food and utilities cost at most fifty dollars apiece a month. "If you're going to be beady-eyed about it."

"I am," said Rose. On her savings, she could, at fifty dollars a month, live for a great long while at the Goat Pasture. She'd carpenter and garden. She'd write music day and night.

The school year ended in a happy rush. She couldn't wait to shed her teaching clothes and get out to the farm. They were going to show her how to grow things. The others were putting seeds in the ground as she taught her last classes and gave her exams. With hardly a backward look, she packed her clothes, her books, and her cello and returned the Chair's apartment to the state in which she had found it—every piece of furniture, every photo back in place, every floor and fixture scrubbed—and then turned the key over to Frances.

And so, for a time, Rose left the city, left Tangletown for the wide-open prairie, for clarity, and for what she expected to be a very much simpler life.

Chapter EIGHT

T hey crossed their own small, arching bridge over the river to the garden, a narrow strip that ran a quarter mile along the river. It amazed Rose to shout and see tiny, distant figures look up and wave. The farm girls taught her to weed without disturbing seedlings, to stake tomatoes and peas, to take the small, shaggy teat of a goat in the crook of her thumb and spiral her fingers closed in a rhythm that not only coaxed forth milk but also, they assured her, gave pleasure.

They lived outdoors, hauling food to the new gazebo in the meadow built by Dinah, who allowed Rose to help, ignoring her initial clumsiness, so that now, as they began work on the barn, she could whack in a nail with two blows. She wrote Ursula, rhapsodizing about the capabilities of women and, in detailed treatises with diagrams, urged Guy to take up gardening. They subsisted royally on so little, amazing meals from their own hands—mountains of greens, goat's-milk yogurt and cheese, rhubarb sweetened with honey. Out in the orchard where the bees were kept, Rose stood transfixed while Wilma lit smudge pots and Noah pulled honey-comb drawers from the hives, his slender arms in their thin sleeves dripping with smoke-drunk bees.

In the heat of the day, they shed their shirts and worked, naked to the waist under the sun—all except Lila, who kept her bra on, as her breasts were heavy. At dusk, they went down for a plunge into the river where it turned below a limestone bluff and deepened into pools hollowed in rock. Shaded by the bluff, the water ran swift and cold there; overhead, chittering swallows popped in and out of nests in the bluff's limestone face, where there were baby birds, unseen but much heard. The swim was like waking a second time. Rose found the differences among their naked bodies marvelous—not that she'd be caught staring, but such variety: breasts of all different shapes and sizes, some barely there, a smooth rise of muscle, a tiny peak of nipple, some high, some heavy. Lila's lolled on her chest, lifting a little in the river current, heavy breasts below that bearded chin of hers, just another form of womanhood.

Summer in full leaf and flower thickened sounds, complicated the wind, adding infinite sighings and slurrings. A beehive was like a tiny orchestra hall, the hidden musicians uniting in a humming, sizzling, end-lessly varying chord that transferred swiftly to the music Rose was writing. New sounds woke up old sounds, her earliest melodies and rhythms, which told of her own journey. She had somehow gone back to her childhood, to the initial thrill of sound.

The whole place worked a harmony, yet remained full of mysteries. From an oval frame at the top of the stairs, Lila's craggy-faced grandpa gazed down on them. Whatever he might think if he could actually see what his farm had become, he would have admired their industry. Every day of his working life, he'd strode out to make a success of the place, achieving, if not indoor plumbing, the purchase of a Studebaker sedan in a bright robin's-egg blue for Lila's grandma. Beneath coils of rope, amidst rusted junk, the old car still sat in the barn, the blue-green color showing in patches through dust and bird droppings. Nobody knew if it still ran.

Dinah's car was sufficient for errands, and now there was also Rose's station wagon.

Lila, herself a mystery, sometimes rambled off in the middle of a workday. She was entitled: it was her farm. They were all free, in fact, to do as they pleased. Rose, for example, was not required to share the outhouse, regardless that the seat had two holes. *Occupied,* she called, the door locked from within. *Come again another day,* she sang out against intruders. They went their separate ways as they liked, but usually preferred to be together, Lila and the farm girls and little Noah and now Rose, working and playing and merging, day by day, she felt, into a deeper and deeper harmony. Peggy was sometimes irritated by Rose's habits, that she failed to screw jar lids on tight or used the wrong soap, confusing Basic *H* (Household) with Basic *L* (Laundry). The tiny disagreements were a part of everything, though, spice in the food.

Rose saw that, up to then, she'd looked upon other women as rivals, crudely classified by their power to attract men. She recalled herself gloating over Frances's envy. So Frances was below her; Ursula on her level or a little above; and her sister, Natalie, far enough above to cause anger and fear? The Goat Pasture blasted all that away—any illusion of rank in luck or beauty or talent. If Rose wrote music for two hours every night, if she drafted a Composer's Guild Concert grant proposal and enclosed Lila's letter of reference, it was merely because it pleased her to do so, as, for instance, Peggy chose to devote hours and hours to the goats, currying and filing hooves and horns. Powers were many and varied; each person shone forth with an individual light.

Rose declared it paradise. Did they realize this was paradise? How long would it last? Why not forever, living together, into old age? She felt for the others a democratic fondness. Friendship seemed no longer suspect and love perhaps merely an extension of friendship, though she was not in love and did not miss it. The peace and freedom she now had seemed better than love, and she was almost never alone. It felt to her like the end of loneliness.

Needing little from town but hardware and what groceries they couldn't produce themselves, they rarely left the farm. Instead, the world came to them. Josie's college roommate came, a laughing red-haired girl who baked pans and pans of brownies. Peggy's twin brother was the first to try the new guest quarters. One night's sleep in a hammock in their barn, he said, was equal to sleeping a week anywhere else.

Rose wished for a visitor of her own, someone to show off to, and why not, when she had paradise to share? She wrote Alan and Frances as one, wishing she had done so before—been supportive of their love—and invited them "to Eden." She invited her mother and her sister. So what if her mother was bitter? Women could have sharp thoughts. And as for Natalie, Rose could easily forgive her little sister for the trifling hurts of the past. Why, even the MacGregors could live peaceably at such a place as the farm. Neither her mother nor her sister answered her letters, however. So one evening, before supper, she put aside self-consciousness and picked up the phone, the only telephone at the farm, which hung on the wall in the common room.

"Only women?" cried Natalie. "Don't you miss men?"

"Do I miss men?" Rose repeated for the general entertainment. "Hardly even think of 'em." She muffled the receiver against her chest and shushed the others. Lila's laugh was loud.

"Here's Mom," said Natalie. "Don't listen to her."

"Well," said Marion wearily, "you really should get a load of Natalie."

"You guys have a tire swing out there?" said Natalie, recapturing the phone.

"Natalie, put Mom back on. There's something you're not telling me."

"Look, will you, for once, let me handle things, myself—just *for once*, Rose?"

"Handle things? Is that what you call it?" said their mother in the background.

"You guys have a swimming hole?" Natalie persisted.

Of course they did. Rose had written to them all about the swimming hole.

"It's so hot here," said Natalie wistfully and hung up the phone.

They might come, Rose reported uncertainly. After all, who could resist paradise?

Rose was like a puppy, it was remarked. Still energetic after supper, she raced through the meadow with Noah in the fading light where fireflies flared in the grass like low-flying stars. All the while, Lila followed her with her eyes. Rose felt this and wanted to please, so grateful for the turn in her life, for the turn in her music.

Looking at Lila in open regard, Rose found nothing that should be altered. The beard and the smell were trivial. The smell Rose had noticed her first visit was not a chemical but a human smell, strong, rancid, almost burnt—Lila's smell. Afternoons, they played side by side in the gazebo and Rose told herself she was used to it. Then it occurred to her that this might be the smell of fear. Why should Lila be afraid?

Rose undertook to draw her out. She brought one of Lila's old concert announcements to the gazebo and set it on her music stand. "I wonder about this photo."

"What? No beard, you mean?"

"No," Rose scoffed. "You look like someone's forcing you to play. Why is that?"

"You know something?" Lila set her cello aside and turned her gaze full on Rose. "People don't like me."

"What do you mean? People love you. You get invitations all the time—I know, I've collected the mail. They keep writing even when you don't answer."

"I've conducted a career *in disguise*." She picked up the card. "I had to shave not just in the morning, but again, right before a concert, or it showed."

"What a hassle," Rose agreed.

"And I had to douse myself with perfume, as I'm sure you now realize."

"Jesus. But why? I mean, what *is* it, Lila?"

"Oh, let's not delve into endocrinology." Lila let the card drop and glared. "I mean, yes, the Mayo Clinic is just down the road. Any time I care to surrender, they're ready with heavy-duty electrolysis and pills for me to take the rest of my life just to keep from looking and smelling *like myself*."

"All right. But look, Lila, you've got your friends."

She thought a moment. "I have a farm. I've used it to buy friends."

Rose rocked back in her chair, stunned. This was in no way true. "Forget it," said Lila, getting up and stumbling back against her cello case. "I can't stand myself half the time anyway."

Rose stood and opened her arms and Lila clutched her hard, giving off such a smell it took her breath away. Rose made herself inhale and carefully laid her cheek against Lila's. The beard was surprisingly soft. After a startled moment, Lila thrust her away and rushed out.

She didn't show her face at supper and Rose feared she'd caused serious offense. When she climbed the stairs to her room, Lila's door was closed. But the next day, Lila seemed to follow her everywhere, sometimes watching her, sometimes turning awkwardly away. Rose started down a bean row, picking full-grown beans and leaving the little ones. Here came Lila, picking haphazardly, big beans and little, and flinging them wordlessly into Rose's basket. At supper, Lila slid into the chair beside her, speared a piece of eggplant off Rose's plate and, not looking at her, gobbled it down, grinning. Rose grinned back and her stomach turned over.

"Oh, that Lila," said Wilma, as Rose sat down beside her on the front steps, breathing in her cinnamon fragrance. It was like resting by a bakery.

"She says nobody likes her. I think someone must have broken her heart," said Rose.

"No, I wouldn't say so. Not yet, anyway. But I believe our Lila's finally in love." In the yard, Noah launched a cartwheel amongst the fireflies.

"Oh," said Rose quickly. God, she was slow. She turned the thought over in her mind. The sudden ache in her belly—was that excitement, or dismay? She lay sleepless that night, aware of the rustling in the room across the stairwell, of the corn shooting up outside, the cabbages swelling and involuting, the crickets and katydids aggressively, helplessly sawing away.

Quite unexpectedly the next morning, while she was sweeping the haymow, a familiar gray-green Volvo pulled in. Alan! Giving him a tour of house, garden, and barn, introducing him, Rose regained composure. She was overjoyed to see him. He'd stay the weekend, wouldn't he? They'd make stuffed chilies and raspberry pie.

He would. But all was not well with Alan. He was on the run from Frances. He'd broken it off with Frances. He was gay, as Rose well knew. He glanced at her nervously.

"Ah. So you've found somebody?" she asked.

"No. I thought I had. He was just a flash in the pan. But what a flash." Still, Alan was terrified Frances would make hell for him in the department, with his third-year review upon him.

"I don't think Frances would do that."

"You'd be surprised. She thought she'd changed me. I'm afraid I let her think so."

The morning was hot and they were sitting on the shaded bank of the swimming hole, dangling their feet in the water. He rotated a toe absently, his face pale and strained, staring into the water. "I want to apologize to you, too, Rose. I never should have touched you."

"*Alan*," she said, "I'm over it." She reached down and splashed him. He regarded her. "And tell Frances from me, *tough titties*. She was warned."

He snorted. "And you? What are you doing out in this nest of lesbians?"

She wanted to know how he first knew he might be gay.

"Lookit, Rose," he said. "You aren't."

"How would you know?"

"No kidding—are you really? Which one?"

Rose hesitated to lay claim to Lila and felt immediate shame. He'd absorbed Lila's beard and mustache without comment, but still, Alan was, well, so elegant.

"Nothing's happened yet," Rose admitted.

"Listen," he said. "Don't do it just to try it, no matter how logical it appears." He was ashen. "God—poor Frances. I could never, *you* know, without pretending. I wanted her to hold still so I could *fantasize*—shit!" He brushed at his eyes. "She was always kissing me. And wasn't *that* unreasonable. It would have been better if she'd been one of those big rubber dolls."

"Spare me," said Rose and took off her clothes and slid into the river.

Sweat and tears poured from his face. She reached up and pulled him in after her. He dived and swam upstream where, in his soggy clothes, he treaded water, looking up into the noisy swallows' nests. Then he swam back to her. They embraced briefly underwater and she felt a long-forgotten thrill as her breasts pressed against the flatness of his chest. She did miss men.

At dawn, he was up, playing his trumpet. He trooped to the garden with the rest of them, stripped off his shirt, and tied it around his head Gunga Din-style. At night, he regaled them with movie plots, whistled theme music, acted the parts and drafted the others into it—Lila as Ahab to his White Whale. When he had to drive back, they stood on the porch and waved him off.

"I like your friends," Lila told Rose shyly.

The liking would soon be tested. After supper the next night, while Noah cranked the honey extractor and Rose and Josie played four-handed ragtime and Lila glided soundlessly back and forth in her rocker, there came a rap at the door and Frances stepped in.

She had updated her image: a leotard with a wrap-around skirt in some subtle Indian print, a pair of slim sandals that clicked as she crossed the threshold. She looked fierce and proud and incapable of tears. She looked, Rose thought, actually beautiful. She turned her head rapidly, searching the dusk-lit room.

"Rose," she cried, "I know he's been here. I want to know what he told you."

"Why, Frances," said Rose, getting up to embrace her, but Frances would not allow it. She had spotted Lila and was staring pointedly, her chin jerked upward in Lila's direction.

"Perhaps I should introduce you," said Rose dryly, "or maybe we could start with a tour?"

"Who is that wolf-woman?" Frances demanded quite audibly from the front step, shaking Rose off. Rose hustled her out to the barn.

"If you're going to stay, watch your tongue. What's the matter with you, Frances?"

"What's the matter with *her*? What's the matter with the whole fucking world? And who said I was *staying*?" Rose had never before heard Frances swear. Rose sort of liked it.

"Suit yourself," she told Frances.

"I will," said Frances, climbing to the barn loft, getting ahead of Rose as though she, Frances, were giving the tour. "By the way, have you looked in the mirror lately? You're a mess. Who would ever believe you were once a professor?" Rose tried not to laugh. "You've got dirt in your nails and your hair is parted crazy." In spite of herself, Rose raised her hands to her hair.

Frances dropped into a hammock, swung her knees up under her, and tucked her skirt beneath them. It was dark in the barn, but Rose refrained from lighting a lantern. Fun was fun, but she'd didn't really feature a prolonged session out in the barn with Frances.

"It's you he loves, isn't it?" said Frances, low and tragic.

"No, Frances," Rose replied, aping her tone. "He's gay."

"How can I believe that," she whispered, "after the way he's loved me?"

Rose thought of Alan's lovemaking, the awkward drop of his weight on her. "It's probably not my place to say, but maybe you should expect more for yourself," she told Frances.

"Then you don't know what we had."

"Frances," said Rose, "if you persist in not understanding, you'll force him to be cruel."

"Who made *you* the authority on love?" Frances swung out of the hammock and marched to the stairs. Rose didn't see how she could move so fast without tripping and falling in the dark. "He doesn't love you," Frances flung back over her shoulder. "At least he's got that much sense. I'll leave you to your *wolf women*," she cried as she strode across the yard. "Go ahead, claw up the dirt. Howl at the moon! Grow hair all over your bodies, for all I care!" She hopped into her mother's Rambler and was gone.

Rose stood in the yard. Not a sound came from the house. Then a gurgle of laughter came through the screen, and as she stepped inside, it turned into a roar. Josie hugged her. Dinah pounded her on the back. They'd all been through it. Not everyone could "get *down* with the farm girls." And really, Frances was hilarious.

Almost before she could catch her breath, the next visitor arrived. At least a phone call came first—Guy asking when he might visit. Rose warmed to the sound of his voice but thought she had better broach it with the others. Was she having too many guests?

They didn't count Frances, they said, and Alan was practically one of them.

She described Guy, his land, his lake, his stonework, and surprised herself by blushing.

"An old flame," observed Wilma.

Dinah's interest perked at the mention of stonework. The barn foundation needed attention. Noah asked if Guy could bring his rowboat and take him fishing. They wouldn't kill any fish, he assured his mother—they could throw them all back.

Wilma laughed. "Sounds like he'd better come."

Lila sat, a thundercloud, in her rocker. The others drifted out, leaving her and Rose alone.

"If you're going to fuck him, you'll have to take it to the barn."

"Oh, Lila, look," said Rose. "And anyway, that's all past."

"What do I care? Do as you like." She gazed out into the dark. "You're neglecting your music." It was true. Since the afternoon she and Lila had embraced in the gazebo, Rose hadn't written a note. Alan's visit had distracted her, and then Frances. "It's got to be every day," said Lila. "There's the concerto to revise and the sonata to finish."

It was startling, how closely Lila tracked her work, more closely than Rose herself did.

"Righto," said Rose. "Start up again tomorrow?" She'd invite Guy, say, in a month?

Lila nodded. "Forget it. Forget what I said. You do whatever you please. It's just—I have to hear them at night—Peggy and Dinah, *you know*," she said in a defeated voice. Rose did know. Sounds from the downstairs bedrooms carried clearly up through the floor.

"Should I say something to them?" Rose asked.

"No. It's not like I'm against it or anything." Lila bit her lip and fled the room.

Again, they worked side by side every afternoon in the gazebo, speaking shorthand, cello to cello. And though their subject was music, Rose was newly aware of Lila as a creature and forced herself to consider that Lila might love her. If so, it was, at the very least, an honor.

On a bright noon at the end of August in the high tide of the vegetable harvest, Guy arrived, towing his boat. He took them all in at a glance, his eyes lighting up at the sight of Lila. She offered him a grand smile. Did Rose just imagine they were squaring off? Peggy and Wilma, haggard from a week of canning and freezing, groaned aloud at what filled Guy's boat: bushels of corn, tomatoes, zucchini, and melons. He winked at Rose, who went red, recalling the garden behind his shack. Why had he let her preach gardening to him on and on in her letters?

Anyway, he wasn't foisting vegetables on them. There was a farmer's market nearby, and he would take his vegetables to market, along with anything they might have to sell.

"Honey," said Noah. "Can I come too?"

"Of course you can," said Guy. "Do you call everybody honey?"

"I mean *sell* honey," Noah protested.

"All right, honey," Guy answered.

"Shut up, honey," Noah hooted and the yard resounded with laughter.

Guy was a hit and Rose was relieved. She watched him put himself at ease among them, washing vegetables for market, inspecting the hives with Wilma and Noah and then the barn foundation with Dinah. When the hour arrived for the afternoon swim, Guy shed his clothes without hesitation. Her heart began to pound and she had to look away from the whole naked lot of them. She wanted him to herself. After supper, she lit a lantern and they climbed to the barn loft alone together to settle him in for the night.

As they stepped into the big, airy haymow, he let out a rippling laugh. "Rose, Rose, who's the dog in the manger?"

"What?"

"Well, they don't think *I'm* a lesbian. You've got them all half in love with you."

"I doubt it. And anyway, I might be. I could be bisexual."

"Right," he whooped.

"Shut up," she said. But he was kissing her, and oh, she was kissing him back. He held her away from him.

"Are you sure I measure up?" he asked. "That swarthy one, what's her name—Lyle? She's got a better beard than I do." She struck at him and he caught her wrists.

The hammock wasn't much good for lovemaking. They loosed a straw bale and threw down a tarp and then sheets and a quilt. He'd brought condoms and her foam supply from his cabin. She wanted to know how he'd been so sure of her.

"Shine on, harvest moon," he sang.

They loved by lantern light without hesitation, with such familiarity, not caring that the straw beneath them was lumpy. It was like a long-pent exhalation, loving and subsiding and loving again. And if she should get pregnant, why, she'd raise the baby there, among goats and swallows. She could share the raising of it with him, but there'd be no marrying. She didn't even have to say it. Many months ago they'd collided and wrecked, but the broken bond between them seemed mended. Had anything broken, really? She couldn't help how much she wanted him. Peace and work went only so far. Stroking his belly, she thought of the others in the house, and felt a bubbling exultation that she had something no one else was having—a man.

And then she was flooded with shame. And blamed him for it. In what she thought of as her better self, she was stung, even as she thrilled to his lovemaking. He didn't know her quite so well as he assumed. She thought of Lila in the house and grieved, knowing that, though the lights were out, she would likely be awake and listening, aware that Rose had not come in again. An hour or so later, Rose heard, at a distance, a bow draw across a cello, bringing forth the sound that only Lila made. Lila, of all people, ought to have love.

For that reason, two nights after Guy had gone, very late, when she heard Lila pacing her room, Rose crept across the hall and, not letting herself know just what she was doing, let herself in.

Chapter NINE

S he thought she'd seen a light under the door, but the room was dark when she stepped inside. The bed was rumpled, but nobody was in it. A wing chair seemed to hold a thick shape, but, as her eyes adjusted to the dark, she saw it was only an upended bolster. A distant yard light shone down through a window over her bare feet and picked up the purplish crescent beneath a toenail where she'd dropped the posthole digger on herself the week before. She pressed the spot with her other foot. It didn't hurt any more. A dry breeze stirred a froth of willow branches. Through the open windows came the gurgle of the river. She was wearing only a T-shirt and underpants and now thought of her robe, though the night was hot. Her mouth was dry and her heart had begun to pound. Something moved in the far corner. She made out the mirror and the reflection of willow branches waving there. A pressure bloomed in her head. Her gorge rose and she swallowed. Homophobia, she thought to herself, a new word in her vocabulary, a word with a rolling sound that would be perfect sung in an operetta, if it weren't synonymous with hatred and fear. She really had to laugh, having thought herself so free of it. But she couldn't laugh. She could barely breathe. She'd just steal back to bed. Lila had gone off somewhere. Rose had proved she was no coward; maybe that was enough for one night. She'd go back to bed.

They'd been up before dawn to avoid the heat and lugged full bushels of tomatoes across the bridge to the pump for washing, and then into the house where Noah helped Peggy cut out the bad spots till he got bored and ornery, started pinching people and had to be sent outside. Rose scalded, Wilma pulled off skins, Dinah cored, and Josie packed jars, which Lila sealed and timed, ten minutes per batch in the pressure canner. They were going to fill every one of her grandma's two hundred canning jars. They chatted and then lapsed into a busy silence. Then someone started a song and the others joined in. Every hour they all switched jobs. They rarely worked in such close quarters all day long, and Lila, just another among them, chatted, laughed, and sang.

She'd even told a joke: "Why does Helen Keller masturbate with just one hand?"

"Lila," said Josie with mock severity, "not while we're handling food."

"What's 'masturbate'?" asked Noah through the screen door.

"When you make yourself feel good," answered Wilma.

"Okay, Lila, why?" asked Rose.

"So she has the other hand to moan with." There was a burst of surprised laughter. Rose laughed hardest. Had she ever heard Lila tell a joke before?

"I don't get it," whined Noah.

"Helen Keller was deaf, so she talked with her hands. I'll explain later," said Wilma.

Peggy wasn't laughing. "That's a cruelty joke."

"Oh, no—it's a pleasure joke," said Rose.

Peggy took a swig of water, eyed Rose, and shrugged. Lila was very pleased with herself. Arms covered to the elbows in black industrial rubber gloves, she stood fanning herself nonchalantly. Why, she's happy, Rose thought—my cellist is happy.

Lila threw a smile in Rose's direction, but her gaze was inward. It occurred to Rose that she'd been thinking of Lila mostly in terms of how Lila felt about her. That, by now, was impossible to miss. And Rose had profited from it. Without responding, she'd allowed herself to be enveloped by Lila's feeling for her, had wrapped herself in its magnetism. She'd become Rose the beloved. Because Lila was fascinated, Rose had found a new fascination with herself, and it had aroused energies and hopes. But what of Lila? She stood in the glow of her joke, flapping the huge rubber gloves, self-possessed in a way Rose had never seen. This was Lila the almost-beloved, not hidden behind a cello but standing in the open.

"Rose?" said Lila out of the darkness, and what Rose had thought was a robe on a hook turned in her direction.

"Yeah, it's me," Rose croaked and cleared her throat noisily. "Can't you sleep?"

Lila boosted herself up onto the end of the bed and sat with her legs dangling below the hem of a thin cotton nightgown. It was a high bed with spindle posts at each corner topped by oval, pointed finials. From one of the finials, the threaded end of a bolt protruded. Rose stepped forward and closed her hand around it.

"There used to be wood all around the top," remarked Lila. "Like a picture frame—*The Long Night of Lila. Lila in the Twisted Sheets.* I took it down, but I couldn't get that bolt out."

"I could help you," said Rose, jiggling the bolt back and forth.

"Mmm," said Lila. "Maybe not right now."

Rose let out a laugh, trying to ease the tightness in her chest. Besides being high, the bed was long, homebuilt by Lila's grandpa, who had stood six and a half feet tall. Letting go of the finial, Rose picked up a corner of sheet and rubbed it between her fingers. Small blue morning glories twined over the smooth cotton: expensive fabric, inviting sleep. Passing by Lila's open door, Rose had noticed the sheets, yet she'd never till now been over the threshold. No one came in here except Lila. Lila was not the chatty type. She'd never invited anyone in just to hang around.

"Why aren't you asleep?" Rose asked. "You're always up at night."

"Well, I'm sorry. What do you want me to do—tie myself to the bed? If I'm awake, I'm awake." Lila's sulky tone was somehow reassuring. Rose boosted herself up onto the bed.

They sat there side by side at the foot of the high bed.

"It's like a riverbank," Rose suggested. "We're trailing our feet in the water." Lila's smell wafted over her. She inhaled it, resisted, and then commanded herself to breathe deeper. A familiar smell, she told herself. She looked over at Lila through the moonlight and smiled.

Lila smiled back and then looked away. "You really want to do this?" she asked Rose.

"I don't know. To tell the truth, I feel strange."

"*You* feel strange?"

"Want me to go?"

"No!" Lila reached out, gripped Rose by the wrist, then opened Rose's hand and, trembling, stroked her fingers.

"It might be my ignorance," Rose ventured, "like the way I used to feel about boys when I was, oh, ten or eleven. My mother explained what she called 'intimate matters' early. She claimed she didn't want us to be shocked when we heard. I think she just wanted to be the one to do the shocking. Of course I was shocked. I was dumbfounded. *Fitting your private parts together?*" This was the wrong tack. Rose let out a jittery laugh. "But I guess you learn by doing. My, don't I have a lot to say?" she rambled on. "Maybe learning to love someone of your own sex is part of a maturing process most people never even approach. Do you think that might be?"

Lila was quiet, stroking Rose's hand. "Why do *you* feel strange?" Rose asked her.

"We could light a candle. People do that, don't they?"

"Good," said Rose and hopped down from the bed. There were candles in the kitchen. To get a candle was simple. She felt a springiness in her feet, a longing for the feel of the stairs, though coming back up might be a different matter. As if sensing this, Lila kept hold of her.

"I've got one here." She led Rose to her bedside table, which had a handsome oval top over a little drawer. Lila gestured and Rose opened the drawer to find a new candle wrapped in cellophane, a crystal holder in the shape of a star, and a small, full box of matches. So Lila had prepared for her? She felt a tightness in her head, and her heart pounded in her throat. At least she had something to do. She unwrapped the candle, twisted it into the holder, and lit it. Up on the bed, Lila slipped under the sheet.

The mattress was hard and yielded no hollows, no hint of the craggy old man, nor of Lila's grandma who had predeceased him, leaving him to sleep alone his final years in that bed. Here he was in Lila's face, in her heavy brow and square chin, as she lay curled facing Rose, following the contours of Rose's body with her hand, but not quite touching her. Outside, a breeze lifted the willow leaves and let them fall, like respiration. Lila closed her eyes.

"It's hot," Rose murmured, leaning back against Lila's bank of pillows. Rose ran her eye down the bearded face, the cheek bisected by its dark swath of hair, the shadowed eye socket, deep and creaturely, the shoulder, the breasts showing through the open neck of the nightgown, the higher breast resting on the lower, heavy and glamorous—breasts a man would like. Rose banished the thought, disgusted with herself. Why think of men? Why study Lila like a specimen? Apparently Rose could not be trusted. This lay heavily on her. Lila lay still. Rose couldn't justify staying there propped up on the pillows above her, and so she slid down. "Are you asleep?"

"No," whispered Lila, not opening her eyes.

Rose raised herself on her elbow. She ought to know what to do. She understood her own body and would understand Lila's. She should just lean over and kiss her. Lila moved her chin down a little and her mouth was obscured in shadow. Alone, Rose could reliably give herself pleasure and knew what it took to come—wetness and, with the fingers, this, and then this. But Lila lay there not moving, not speaking.

"Are you very tired?"

"No."

Rose felt a faint annoyance. Was this, she wondered, what a man felt when a woman lay passive? Had she ever been like this? She couldn't think. Yes, there had been times, but only when she hadn't really wanted to be there, the times when she'd stayed in bed with someone after she knew she should have been gone.

"It's okay," she told Lila. "We don't have to do this."

"But I want to." Lila opened her eyes.

Rose reached tentatively to stroke Lila's thigh through the thin cloth of the nightgown. Lila shifted and the cloth moved up and Rose put her hand on Lila's bare skin above her knee, where hair grew thick and soft. The smoothness of the hair on the warm thigh was pleasant. There was nothing wrong with Lila's body, she told herself sternly. Lila lay there watching her. Come on, Rose told herself, you do know what to do. Reach between her legs. *Reach,* she told her arm and wrist and hand. But she'd frozen.

A fury had come into her. Quite apparently, Lila expected her to lead. But why on earth? Why Rose, who knew nothing about loving women? Lila was the one who had fallen in love with her, not the other way around. *Not the other way around.* The truth hit her. She hadn't come out of desire, but out of gratitude and curiosity and restlessness and resentment against Guy for his self-assurance in bed. She'd come out of compassion—or was it pity? Lila seemed to want her so badly. She'd come because, finally, she couldn't see why not. Now she saw why not. She'd thought she might feel her way into love with Lila, might be educated into it. She'd been ready to respond, she told herself with failing conviction. She'd better get out of there.

"You see," said Lila, "I've never done this before."

"Oh," said Rose. She did see. She saw Lila bashfully turning her back while stripping off her clothes to swim, saw her shying off down the stream by herself, always keeping her breasts in harness in the bra, always keeping her bit of distance. In the laying bare of her body and in the uses of her body in love, Lila was a child. Rose's heart sank. She wanted to take her hand away from Lila's thigh, but it wouldn't move. Lila gave a luxuriant sigh.

If even then, Rose thought later, Lila had turned and embraced her, she might have been able to get past her dread and discover a new self, a self that loved women, that loved Lila like everything else on earth, a self that loved its own body enough to love another like it. But maybe love of self was nothing like love of another, two separate things, like breathing and eating. Breathing, one did without thinking. To eat, one needed the prompt of appetite.

She turned her head aside to avoid Lila's odor. It reminded her of insecticide, or burnt plastic, or the emission of a paper pulp factory. She thought of the people living in the neighborhood of such a factory, how they acclimated themselves till they no longer noticed the stench. Lila lay gently beside her. Rose's head hurt her horribly. She was going to cry.

"You know something," she said, "I'm awfully tired," and succeeded in moving her hand from Lila's thigh.

"Well," said Lila wistfully, "we did do tomatoes all day."

Rose pulled herself up to look at the clock on the bedside table. "Just past three."

"Yeah," Lila said, her voice flat.

She knows, Rose thought. Hugely relieved, she sagged against the bedpost and closed her eyes.

"Couldn't you just sleep here beside me?" Lila asked.

Rose opened her eyes and nodded. The least she could do was to stay the night. Lila stretched out beside her, holding herself still, as if to avoid disturbing Rose. Rose accommodated her by pretending to sleep till morning.

When Lila got up to go to the outhouse, Rose escaped to her room, grabbed her overalls, went out and flung herself down in the tall grass by the beehives at the far corner of the orchard. She woke to a dark shape looming between her and the sun—Wilma in a head net.

"Well, well," she said. "How's the baby lesbian?"

"What?" said Rose.

"Lila. It's unbelievable. She's on air. What's the matter?"

Noah came trailing along with his smoke equipment, and Rose staggered up and fled to the swimming hole, stripped and washed herself, put her clothes back on, smoothed her hair, and marched to the house. As she approached, she heard Lila's cello, playing Rose's music, strong, ardent, more than certain, a simple lyric line rising into an anthem.

Chapter TEN

Two days later, a Sunday, or First Day, as the Quakers called it, Rose sat in Quaker Meeting in Litchfield, thirty miles from the farm. She knew of the Quakers from her years in Philadelphia and wanted to sit in silence. She needed a plan, a fresh start, her own Quakerly First Day, although she knew the purpose of Quaker silence was not for making plans. You sat still, you cleared your mind, and you waited for your soul to speak. There was no leader. If someone preached, it wasn't from a prepared text, and, mercifully, no one was required to respond. Even so, she hoped to hear no preaching that morning. She wished merely to sit in silence among strangers, as one might sit at a train station where newspapers and coffee were not offered and where trains never came.

She made herself still and closed her eyes, but the room was busy with sound. It was a dusty old room in a disused union hall. From the twenty-odd souls in the circle of folding chairs came sighing, throat-clearing, coughing, and sneezing. Fabric rubbed on metal, shoe leather rubbed on wood, weight shifted noisily, and her thoughts sped back again and again to the scene of the accident or, rather, the crime.

She couldn't call it bad luck. She'd brought down the misery on herself and on Lila and on the whole household. And she'd been warned. Hadn't Alan told her plainly not to try it, and shown her what would happen, taking her to bed when he didn't want her? She recalled the aftermath, how abandoned in her skin she'd felt. And she hadn't even been in love with him. Lila, because she was in love, had it much worse, and with Lila Rose hadn't even followed through. At least Alan had committed his body to her, however briefly. But Rose hadn't even given Lila that much. She hadn't even given her some real act to regret.

When she'd marched back to Lila in the house, following the cello music to its source, she'd passed through the kitchen where, amidst the dregs of tomatoes, Dinah and Peggy had beamed approval, pleased with her, or so they thought. She'd nodded grimly and, glancing at the mirror over the sink, noted her red-rimmed eyes and her crazily parted hair. Frances, once again, had been right—Rose had let herself go. But she couldn't tidy up then. She marched on to Lila, who paused, mid-phrase, and looked up shyly.

"Rose."

"We've got a misunderstanding. It's not happening. It's not going to happen." It was labor for Rose to get the words out.

"It's not," said Lila.

"I can't do it with you."

"You can't," said Lila.

"No, I can't, and please don't repeat everything I say."

"But the thing is, you did, a little. Last night."

"No, I didn't. Not really. That was just—oh, Lila, I was being polite."

"But you came to me of your own accord."

"I made a terrible mistake."

"But you said you needed to learn."

"I was mistaken."

"Well. You could just sleep beside me. Just sleep."

"No, I can't even do that. I didn't sleep."

"Well, so? I didn't sleep either. Big deal."

Rose took a breath through her mouth. She couldn't stand Lila's smell. If this was the odor of fear, however, Lila now had new reason to be afraid, thanks to Rose. Lila now had reason to be afraid of the affections of her own heart.

In the circle of Quakers, Rose opened her eyes on an older woman across the room whose white hair fell straight to her shoulders and whose prominent brow and nose seemed sculpted—Justice with Her Scales. The woman sat at ease, forearms on thighs, hands deeply creased, dirt showing under the cuticles. This was how Rose's hands might look in forty years if she went on gardening. But she'd lost her garden. She'd been thrown— *she had thrown herself* out of Paradise.

At least she'd known better than to leave room for doubt—she'd done enough damage. "I'm not going to be your lover," she'd told Lila. "It's not in me."

Lila's eyes had widened. She'd put her hand over her mouth.

"It's not in me," Rose had concluded, "and I don't want to."

Somewhere in the past, she could hear a voice, a teacher or her mother, going up the scale in fury: *You don't want to? That's your reason? Because you don't want to?*

It didn't seem like much of a reason. Why couldn't she love Lila all the ways Lila loved her? Did she, deep down, think herself superior?—too good for Lila, better than Lila because she had neither mustache nor beard nor funny smell?

A whining buzz in her head focused into a fly that landed on her wrist. She opened her eyes again to the Quaker Meeting and shook the fly off. Sunlight poured through banks of dusty windows onto the plank floor in grainy streams. The Quakers around her sprawled or perched upright, some with eyes closed, some vaguely gazing. Two seats over, a little girl toyed with a shoestring beside her mother who sat with arms folded, chin sunk on chest. A dark man in a summer suit had fallen asleep, his arm thrown back and his mouth agape. A blond teenager in denim cutoffs, hair tied back with a leather thong, stretched his legs. The faces in repose seemed fatigued and sunken, the bodies burdens to be carried. Even the ponytailed young man, now leaning forward into a dusty sun ray, his eyelashes golden and his eyes perfect ovals, seemed to suffer his life restlessly. His gaze met hers and moved on. No one seemed to know anyone else, not even the mother and her little girl. In silence souls might speak, but they spoke only to themselves. Each sat alone, suffering the others, merely pretending any relation, a handful of people flung randomly together in a time and place. That's all we are, Rose thought; that's all we ever are. She could barely breathe.

And what was love? Lust-driven and hypnotic, a way to stay busy, nothing more, even if the lovers never let themselves realize, even if they contrived to extend their delusion over a lifetime. Her "luck" in love was nothing to be proud of but, rather, marked her as a troublemaker, someone who, drawing other people in, brought an increase of confusion and grief. And friendship was make-believe as well, though at least its claims were fewer.

She could hear her mother's voice: this was *dealing with realities*. Why should Marion need friends when she had painting? Why need daughters? Even motherly love was a burden, and to pretend otherwise would only prevent her daughters from learning to stand on their own. Two seats over, the little girl caught Rose's eye and splayed her fingers, laced with shoestring, and neatly inverted them: cat's cradle. Smiling shyly, tender with expectation, she waited for Rose's approval. Rose nearly groaned aloud.

"You don't want me," Lila had said, putting her cello aside, nearly dropping it.

"I should maybe pack up and go," Rose had replied.

"Don't insult me," cried Lila. "There's more to our life here than what I might desire."

"There's a great deal to our life here," Rose had quavered.

"Don't you leave me over this," said Lila.

Rose jumped. Had she gasped or cried out? The Quaker nearest her had touched her elbow, and the white haired woman across the circle had got up and was extending her hand. Rose looked into clear, gray eyes beneath the straight brow. Everyone was shaking hands. Rose blushed, returning the handshake, recognizing the traditional signal of the end of Quaker Meeting. The room filled with talk. The mother pulled her little girl to her and kissed her. The boy with the ponytail leaned over and put the sleeping man into a headlock. These people did know each other, of course. It was only Rose who was a stranger.

"Emma Williams," the white-haired woman said, still shaking Rose's hand.

Rose nodded, got up, and hurried out. She sat a moment behind her steering wheel and then pointed her station wagon back to the farm.

It didn't seem right to leave, not abruptly. It seemed wrong to stay, but just as wrong to go with the harvest at its height and more tasks than hands to do them. There was corn to slice from the cob and freeze, leaves to strip from the cornstalks for the goats, sunflower heads to hang to dry, carrots and rutabagas to dig up and bury in sand vats in the root cellar, sauerkraut to render from the overflow of cabbages. An excess of zucchini lay in a putrid dump by the compost pile, in need of layering with straw. Nobody spoke any more of each one doing as she wished. The seeds they'd sown in the spring now entrapped them. Rose had to stay till the harvest was done.

Alongside the others, she hauled, stacked, dug, raked, and attempted to keep up conversation as though all were well, as though this were still her home. The others were friendly enough, and Wilma still seemed to like her. If Rose had wanted to learn to love a woman, why hadn't she gone for Wilma, someone easygoing and pretty and sweet-smelling, someone resilient who would move right on if things went wrong? Or Ursula? What a match they'd make, they always said, if one of them had been a man. But they hadn't meant it. There'd been no catch in the breath saying so, no heat, no flash of the eye. Ursula liked men. As did Rose. Exclusively? Now she'd never know. One experiment of that sort was enough for a lifetime.

She could work all day and not think, but then evening would come on. She no longer slept in the house—not with Lila just across the hall. She bunked in the barn in a hammock lined with flannel sleeping bags, a visitor again. From deep in her swaddling, she gazed up at nails she herself had pounded in, framing the new windows. She inhaled the fragrance of straw bales she'd helped stack for winter mulch. She'd never see the straw released again. She slept there then, but by the time the straw was unloosed on the snowy garden, she'd be gone.

If Rose was miserable, however, Lila was like a wounded bear. She joined the others each day in field and kitchen, refusing the relief a walk alone might give her. Music was forgotten. Perhaps Lila had never cared for Rose's music but had only wanted her in her bed? At meals, Lila sat gruffly staring at her food, sighing repeatedly, each sigh a stifled moan.

"Lila?" Josie whispered one night after she had moaned for ten minutes straight over her soup bowl. She looked up, startled. She hadn't realized the others could hear her.

Next morning, she sent word through Josie that she wished Rose to resume their afternoon music sessions and, doggedly, they managed it, distant and formal and focused to task.

Rose was not reassured. The short walk out to the gazebo proved difficult enough, even with the distraction of music still ahead. But coming back in was excruciating. Rose wanted to fall behind but felt constrained to keep step with Lila. Should Rose arrive at the house first, she had to check the impulse to open the door for Lila, which Lila would not allow, insisting, instead, that Rose precede her. Then she'd have to pass as Lila stood facing her, gripping the door knob, the only moment Lila looked directly at her any more, the gaze heated and bereft.

Sundays, Rose returned to Quaker Meeting. Ursula would've had a good horselaugh if she could have seen Rose with hands folded and eyes downcast. They'd indulged in a certain amount of satire of Philadelphia Quakers, a certain amount of *theeing* and *thouing*. But now Rose sat, and in the silence her eyes frequently filled with tears. She had no idea where she was going. She longed for Ursula, who was her friend but unsentimental, who perhaps also recognized the lie of friendship, the fraudulence of *thee* and *thou*.

Even now, when she knew better, Rose noticed herself lurching toward warmth, every week seeking the empty chair beside the woman with straight white hair, Emma—Emma Williams, who, one Sunday when Rose was again in tears, reached and laid a hand briefly on her arm. Rose imagined herself in Emma's eyes, a lost soul. She was twenty-six years old—too old to be a lost soul.

An ivy vine climbing up the yard light turned crimson. Sumac flamed. The pippins and crabs ripened and then the Paula Reds and the Wealthies, bringing a round of paring and coring and canning. When the apples were done, Rose would leave the farm.

Then, on a night in late September, sometime past midnight, the phone rang in the house. Rose was awake in the barn and heard it. A moment later, Wilma summoned her in.

Natalie stood in a phone booth a block from their mother's house, crying so hard she could barely speak. "I'm pregnant again, if you want to know."

"Again?"

"Yes, again. I'm handling it myself. By *myself*."

"Okay. All right. Breathe," said Rose.

"Mom's trying to get me another abortion, but there's this official *waiting* period and they make you talk to the hospital *chaplain*—it's the law or something. He's a guy from school, Rose—the chaplain—Mr. Goshen, you know, our old *algebra* teacher."

"Oh. Uh-huh. Take a breath, Natalie."

"He *flunked* me, if you remember. I've got to get *out* of here. Say something."

"Poor Natalie."

"Right," she sobbed.

"You want to come here," Rose guessed.

"I understood I was invited." Natalie sobbed harder.

She was right. Rose had invited her any number of times in the letters she'd written.

"Natalie, now, let me just think a minute."

While Natalie plugged in quarters, Rose felt her spirits lift. Her little sister's predicament stirred in her a feeling of elation, so completely did it change the subject from how she'd spoiled things at the farm. She might be of use again. She might be of use to Natalie.

"Now, look, Natalie. I've got to think this through and call you back."

"Think *what* through?"

"There are other people to consider. I don't live alone here, you know."

"Can't you ask them now?"

"It's the middle of the night."

"I *know* that. It's the middle of *my* night too."

"Everybody's asleep," Rose said, but it wasn't so. The household was rousing. Wilma handed Rose a cup of tea. Dinah staggered out, followed by Peggy. Josie peeked in.

Rose pressed the receiver to her chest. "It's my sister. She's pregnant and needs an abortion. There's some sort of waiting period."

"Some state laws are medieval. New Hampshire's one of the bad ones," offered Josie.

"Natural cycles is all it is," said Wilma. "Conceive and carry or cast aside—the earth is always shedding things."

"Zucchini," said Peggy ruefully. Rose stuttered out a laugh. Peggy smiled at her.

"Barbaric, what they think they can do to a woman's body," said Dinah, warming to the subject, "constrain her and interrogate her."

"Natalie, sweetheart," said Rose, "I'm going now. Call me back tomorrow?"

"Don't hang up," said Josie. Lila loomed on the stairs.

Noah stumbled in. "What's going on?"

"Rose's sister is coming for a visit," said Dinah.

"She's pregnant," said Wilma, hoisting him to her hip.

"I want a brother," said Noah.

"Lila?" said Josie.

"Have her come," said Lila. "She'll be safe here. I know a doctor in Litchfield. I don't think she'll be made to wait."

Rose was stunned. When her own welcome at the farm seemed about used up, she could not fathom why they'd shelter Natalie as well. But Lila had spoken.

Two days later, Rose and Wilma drove over to the bus station in Litchfield. As Natalie stepped down from the bus, the shirt she was wearing billowed out. Spotting Rose, she dropped her duffel bag and opened her arms, revealing her enormous belly.

Whatever quarrel she'd had with their mother about the hospital chaplain had long since expired. It was months too late for an abortion.

She wanted to see the swimming hole first. She threw off her clothes and ran whooping into the river, then lay down on her skirt to sun herself, full breasts sagging either side of her domed belly. She was eight months gone. Rose sat a little way off, dangling her feet in the water.

An outline of truth did exist in what Natalie had told Rose over the phone. It was a second pregnancy; the first had been terminated at the hospital after a humiliating interview with the chaplain, who was, indeed, Mr. Goshen, their former algebra teacher. Natalie declared she'd never set foot in a hospital again.

"You cannot imagine it, lying on that table," she said. "You cannot possibly know what it's like." And Rose did not enlighten her.

After the abortion, Natalie had begun saving to go back to Boston—she hadn't, after all, quite finished her chiropractic studies. But while she lived at home and saved up, she couldn't *not* see the baby's father. She was so sad about the baby, and he was the only one who understood. She'd gotten pregnant again almost right away.

If a baby was to be born, who would raise it, Marion wanted to know? Who would take responsibility? Natalie would, of course, *by herself.* It was unbelievable that Marion was ever actually a *mother.* Natalie had managed, up till then, to conceal the identity of the father. But she would tell Rose: it was the pharmacist, if Rose remembered him. They both sang in the Unitarian Church choir, Natalie and the pharmacist, and things had "got going" in the choir loft after practice was over. It was cozy up there, if Rose remembered that thick carpet.

Rose remembered, all right—the pharmacist with his green eyes, so sincere behind his wire-rims, so interested in the high school girls at church. She recalled the rumors about him and Natalie, rumors against which Rose had defended Natalie, who'd repaid her by calling her a *nun.*

All that was long past, however. Natalie was in trouble now, real trouble.

The pharmacist had turned out to be as big a jerk as Mr. Goshen, said Natalie, treating pregnancy as a misfortune rather than an act of nature. He'd even tried to make Natalie take drugs to bring her period on. She certainly saw how Rose could live without men. What she needed was someplace safe to have her baby, someplace where life was met with love. Now that morning sickness was over, she absolutely loved being pregnant.

"It's a miracle," she said. "That's a cliché and I don't care." She yelped as a ripple crossed her belly and the tip of something protruded and vanished. She yanked Rose over and pressed her hand to her navel. "Feel it move and kick and run."

"Run?" said Rose.

Natalie was deliriously happy at the farm, uncomfortably reminding Rose of herself back at the start of the summer, tearing around, praising everything. The nearly-dead garden was bliss. The chilly barn was heaven. For all Natalie knew, it was: she was sleeping in Rose's old room. Natalie would cook or something—make herself useful. But her first experiment shattered a pitcher and her second set a toaster afire. She was expelled from the kitchen. Next, she took up decorating—the farmhouse seemed plain, had anyone noticed? She took Dinah's pruning shears and blunted the blades cutting bales of sumac in six-foot lengths and sticking them all over the house in gallon jars—jars Peggy needed for sauerkraut. The sumac immediately began to shed. Rose bundled it up and got out the broom while Natalie chuckled, claiming to like the look of leaves and berries on the floor.

"Leave it, why don't you?" she said. It became her phrase as she lost steam every day and, by afternoon, lowered herself into Lila's rocker, watching while the others trudged in from the garden and Peggy lit the stove.

"Leave it, Peggy. We can eat cold stuff for supper," Natalie would say, without seeming to notice that Peggy ignored her.

She claimed the rocker for her own. Rose advised her that the chair was Lila's.

"Oh, bosh," said Natalie, "two against one," meaning herself and her baby.

Chapter ELEVEN

Guy sent Rose a hand-drawn postcard of a bear holding a sprig of oats. It was October again; the seasons had revolved a year since they'd met.

Going to bed each night, she stepped out of her sweater and overalls in the frigid barn, boosted herself into the hammock in her underwear and socks, zipped up the sleeping bags, opened her legs, and brought herself to climax, the quickest way to get warm and drop off, and nothing to do with love. Oh, maybe she thought of Guy while she touched herself, but in the light of day she wasn't even answering his letters.

The harvest wore on, constant motion, no pause. Each day was shorter, each night longer, though sleep was brief in the chilly house and in the even chillier barn, which seemed to Rose with each passing night less of a shelter. Wilma lent her an old muskrat coat, which she laid over the top of her sleeping bags and arranged and rearranged throughout the night, covering her face with fur to warm it, uncovering it to breathe.

Even so, she awoke stiff-necked, her lips chapped and her nose nearly blue with cold.

She always woke first and so took the chore of ringing the farm bell before dawn to summon everyone for a wash and quick breakfast and then to the garden or orchard to make the most of daylight. Rain turned them indoors to shell soybeans, hone tools, and caulk windows. Breeding time for the goats arrived and, as they kept no bucks, they had to transport their goats to a breeder. One of the goats failed to get pregnant and kept going into heat, bleating, twitching, mounting the others, and had to be returned to the breeder again and again.

Rose learned to rest on her feet—sitting down, she risked nodding off. She had no time to write letters; her hands were full with the harvest and the two hours of music with Lila each day, bleak but constant, and her hands were full with Natalie.

Evenings, they sagged into the sauna exhausted, all except for Natalie who sat pert and lively, presiding over her belly. Natalie, of course, could not perform farm labor.

When the late apples were crated and stored, Rose turned her mind to leaving the farm. But she couldn't just walk away, not with Natalie happy there. Rose fretted for her sister. Her swollen shape proved that human love, however deluded, was itself designed for harvest. But, pregnant and unpartnered, Natalie was, Rose thought, the loneliest thing alive.

But she seemed not to know it. Despite her ungainly belly, Natalie moved with ease. Her hair was so long she could sit on it, and there was so much of it, it seemed to shed light around her. She would lug the rocker around the common room to follow a patch of sun and her laughter cascaded tunefully over all.

She had her own rhythm, a routine of sorts. She awoke mid-morning when Rose brought her a cup of tea. Still in bed, she did leg lifts and pelvic tilts while Rose held open a naturopathic text on pregnancy to which she matched her poses. Next, she brushed her hair, chatting amiably about how life had been and how it would certainly have to be in the future, while Rose struggled to keep her eyes open. Rose was, of course, used to her sister. She saw herself in the tilt of her sister's head and took comfort in her voice, a voice she'd heard, after all, every day of her life as a child. Sometimes Natalie reached for her hand and Rose came alert, reminded of the catastrophe of her own pregnancy, and had to take care not to grip back too tightly.

At eleven in the morning, Natalie snapped into focus when she walked down the lane to the mailbox, which, on two occasions, yielded small checks from the pharmacist which she used to buy skeins and skeins of yarn. It seemed Natalie had learned to knit. A fine thing, Rose told her, but even if she wasn't able to do farm labor, couldn't she pitch in to keep the rooms tidy and perhaps wash a dish or two? Their mother had never enforced routine; she'd left that to Rose. What else could Rose do now but play Rose Red again to Natalie's drifty Snow White and do things for her sister? Rose addressed herself to chores with energy enough for two, she hoped. Or for three—the baby was eating by proxy. She doubled her deposit to the farm account. But it was a little strange that Natalie should be so unaccommodating to the strangers who had taken her in and so very relaxed about plans for the future. Rose had expected worry and at least some physical discomfort. Instead, there was the laughter and all the blonde hair.

Rose noticed her own hair becoming a bother and asked Wilma to cut it all off one night—to hack it down to an inch. With winter coming on, she'd lose the warmth of it, but no matter how tightly she braided it or tied it up in her bandanna, she was finding the weight of it bouncing on her neck bothersome. Natalie stood and watched, appalled, as the hair came off, fifteen inches dumped unceremoniously into the trash. What Rose had left was not a crew cut, as Natalie termed it, but a nice, neat cap of dark hair, twin to Ursula's. Rose took pleasure in scandalizing her sister for a change.

Natalie had started teasing Rose about the farm. Oh, Natalie loved the river, the land, the buildings; but the people? No, it wasn't the lesbian sex. She was all for love—found it "cute" that Dinah and Peggy "got it on" and observed that Lila's beard "fit her personality." What she didn't get was why they were all working themselves to death. Oh, the tension, the furious effort, the striving. She raised herself up from her pelvic tilt on Rose's old bed and made marching motions; she brandished an imaginary hoe; she mopped the imaginary sweat of her brow. Rose tried to shush her, but she was funny and knew it.

Rose wrote a sonata to welcome the baby and made the mistake of mentioning it to Natalie, who started bringing her knitting—peculiar little sweaters and booties in rainbow colors and a big scarfy tube of a thing she called a baby sling—out to the gazebo when Rose and Lila were at their music. Rose was, at first, flattered, but then saw that Natalie was looking for entertainment. She began to make a game of Lila's demeanor. Behind Lila's back, she frowned and nodded and sawed one knitting needle against the other.

Rose ignored her. One afternoon, however, Lila wheeled on Natalie. "Yes?" she demanded icily.

Natalie folded her hands innocently over her knitting, but Rose sent her back to the house.

"I'm sorry," Rose told Lila, who shrugged and smiled halfheartedly, staring off at Natalie's retreating back. Rose realized with guilty relief that the burden of critical scrutiny had passed from her to Natalie. Still, she felt responsible for keeping Natalie out of trouble. And as the days passed, this proved more and more difficult.

Coming back from Quaker Meeting, the one time in the week she had to herself, she came to expect to find discord: Natalie and Peggy in a screaming fight over blonde hairs left in the kitchen sink, Peggy too furious to listen to Rose's peacemaking, Natalie placidly pointing out that the only mirror in the house was the one over the sink.

Wilma took Natalie aside to suggest ways she might make friends at the farm. Natalie reported this with a secretive half-smile, and Rose felt her hopes rise, imagining a change of heart in her sister and then, perhaps, in the others. But when Rose went to thank Wilma, she shook her head, calling Natalie "a hard nut to crack."

And so Rose was at first relieved when Guy drove down one evening and, on meeting Natalie, seemed to take a shine to her. Spotting the truck, Rose charged out to greet him. He pulled abruptly out of her embrace to examine her head.

"What have you done?"

Natalie sat on the steps, watching as he turned Rose's head from side to side and tugged at her short hair disconsolately.

"This is Guy," said Rose. "My sister, Natalie."

Guy looked over. "Hi," he said unsteadily.

"I feel as if I know you," said Natalie and smiled and cast her eyes down to her belly. What did she mean, know him? Rose hadn't mentioned Guy to Natalie since some crazy phone calls way back when Rose and Guy were first courting, more than a year before.

Dinah stuck her head out the door. "How many extra for dinner?"

"One, two," Natalie told Dinah, indicating herself and Guy.

"Just one. We feed you every night, I believe," said Dinah and banged the door shut. Natalie staggered up from the step and Guy hurried to her. She allowed herself to be supported into the house, where he held her chair for her and scooted her in and, in afterthought, gripped Rose's chair back and then, observing the roomful of women already seated, laughed helplessly and sat down. He turned back to Natalie.

"You're having a baby."

"Mmm-hmm," she said, beaming at his idiocy. "Due any day now."

Rose was startled. She'd imagined it was still a while off.

"I wouldn't trust due dates," said Wilma. "It may be some time yet."

"The hospital all ready for you?" asked Guy.

"Hospital!" said Natalie. "Better the woods or the open field."

"Oh, really?" said Rose.

"They all think once I'm in labor, I'll be helpless and they can cart me off to the hospital." This was surprising to hear, as no discussion had taken place. But that was, in fact, Rose's plan.

"Indigenous women did it themselves, you know," Natalie went on.

"Gave birth in the field, cut the cord with their teeth, tied it off, expelled the placenta, wrapped the baby in a sling, and went on back to work." She didn't mention to Guy that she actually never went to the field or did any work besides knitting.

"She's kidding," said Wilma and cast a worried eye in Rose's direction.

"You just watch me," said Natalie.

Guy toasted her with his apple cider. "You're out of your mind," he told her. "I'm going to build you a cradle."

"I wouldn't encourage her," Rose told him when they'd gone out to the barn for the night.

"I would never have guessed you two were sisters. She's a strange creature," he said. They fluffed up straw, laid down the tarp, and spread the sleeping bags over them.

"She's a lunatic. You said so yourself."

Guy kissed her but, despite the long string of lonely nights that had preceded his visit, she could not bring herself to make love. She felt she had to confess about Lila, her night with Lila. Not that she and Guy had any kind of agreement, but she thought he might sense something.

"So you lay in bed with her. You didn't do anything."

"Well, no. If you want to look at it that way."

"Learned your lesson, I guess," he said. She couldn't argue.

Lying wrapped up with him, she was for once warm enough in the barn, but too tired for anything but sleep.

He had to go the next morning—there were only a few warm days left to mix mortar. He was working atop a scaffold now; his walls were nearly ten feet tall.

"You ought to see it," he told Rose. "My stone house," he explained to Natalie, who'd come out while they were saying good-bye. As he drove out, Natalie followed his truck the length of the driveway, waving energetically, apparently no longer needing to be supported. Rose came with her and waved to Guy with even greater strenuousness, satirizing her sister.

He returned a few days later with a newly varnished pine cradle. Natalie was beside herself. At the sight of the cradle, she ran and kissed Rose and, tilting her head against Rose's, peeked shyly out through her hair. "What a boyfriend you've got," she said, loud enough for him to hear.

That night in the barn before sleep, Guy observed that the farm girls seemed to lack sympathy for Natalie. "You all could be nicer to her," he advised Rose.

"*Us all?*" She couldn't imagine what more they could be doing for Natalie. Weren't they feeding her and sheltering her? Didn't Rose, herself, wake her sister every day, bring her tea, and get her on her feet while listening to her prattle to the point of stupefaction, while everyone else was hard at chores?

"They could let her help out in the kitchen," Guy suggested.

"Ah, but she breaks things and sets things on fire. And she's not really a 'helping out' kind of person. She only ever goes her own way."

He frowned. "Well, anyway, I told her to stick up for herself."

"*Wonderful,*" Rose groaned. She'd noticed Natalie at supper, sitting quietly with her back straight and a glint in her eye.

Rose was, again, too tired to make love, and the next morning she woke, still fuming. Wasn't she paying Natalie's way, in money and in labor? Didn't she hustle to soothe ruffled feelings all around because, despite Natalie's stated wish to stay on the farm, she'd made trouble there, as she always did?

"Okay," said Guy. "What do I know? I'm just a lonely man on a rock pile." He pulled her to him, but she had to get up—she was late to ring the morning bell.

And then he had to go.

On a morning soon after, while Rose was rinsing breakfast dishes, Peggy paused in her recitation from the ledger, the spiral-bound farm log that was read from aloud each morning: chores, requests, and reminders to note, add to, or cross off. It hung on a nail on the side of a cupboard, available to all.

"Who wrote this?" said Peggy. "I can't read it."

Wilma tried. "Something 'the flubbing' . . . 'morning.' I don't know."

Rose dried her hands and went over to see. It was Natalie, sticking up for herself.

"What does it say?" insisted Lila.

Rose laughed uneasily and read aloud: "In case you haven't heard, morning does not begin until fucking nine o'clock, you maniacs. Keep the noise down."

Rose took a breath. The others were not to trouble themselves; she'd see to Natalie. They went on to the next item and soon enough scattered to the day's work, Rose to rake dead cucumber vines from the hill behind the tool shed.

Natalie had declared war, had she? Rose let ten o'clock pass, when Natalie would expect her tea. Rose heard the mailman come and go. A little before lunchtime, Natalie appeared behind the shed where Rose was raking, and, gathering up a heap of vines for a cushion, plopped down, calm, rotund, and self-satisfied.

"So, what did they say?"

"Sorry?"

"About what I wrote in the Big Book."

"No one could read your handwriting."

"I'll bet *you* could."

Rose turned her back and dug her rake into the hill.

"Okay. I'll write my message over again in block letters."

"Natalie," said Rose sternly, "do you really think your needs should rule the farm?"

"It's not just my needs, it's a *normal* need. Sleep is. People go a little crazy without it. Take a look around." Natalie cast a sly glance toward the garden where Lila was on her hands and knees, pulling mud-caked carrots, while Josie struggled up the row with a bushel of squash. Rose fought down the urge to shout at Natalie. Taking a breath, she listened to the distant crush-crush of a cabbage head on the kraut grater. It was a calming pulse.

"If you'll excuse me," she told Natalie, "we've got work to do and we don't have much time. There could be a hard freeze tonight."

"Come on, Rose. No one needs to slave like this. You know how much sauerkraut costs in the store? Ninety-eight cents a quart. And potatoes this time of year? Thirty cents a pound. Nobody has to bake bread any more. Nobody has to leap out of bed at five A.M. to dig potatoes. This is not pioneer America. We are not fucking Giants in the Earth!"

"Uh-huh," said Rose. "Did you know that I'm the first one up every morning? I'm the one who rings the bell?" Her hands on the rake handle trembled. She was going to lose her temper.

Natalie was genuinely startled. "Oh, really? Why?" she asked. "Can't you sleep? What's the matter with you?"

Rose's anger died. It was the first time since Natalie had come that she'd asked Rose about herself and, for a crazy moment, Rose was tempted to confide in her. But about what? About Lila? About how the farm had seemed in the spring and how it was now, how she had loved it and how she despaired of it now? She did despair of it. If she was the first up every morning, it was only because she was too cold to sleep. She'd imagined it a world apart and a new way of life, but underneath, it was as tangled as anywhere else, the people strange and the work arbitrary. They lived here, nonetheless, she and her sister; it was their home, their shelter of the moment. Rose felt the start of tears.

Natalie waited, her blue eyes sunstruck, her hair a gold corona. "Oh, I forgot," she said and reached into her pocket. "You got a letter."

Ursula, Rose thought. She had managed since her downfall with Lila to write one letter—a letter to Ursula, a dread confession, quoting the last written words of Admiral Scott before his death from cold and starvation: "the causes of the expedition's failure are these. . . ." She'd admitted to Ursula, at least, that the farm hadn't worked out and that she was stalled there until she could see Natalie though childbirth and figure out what to do with her and the baby. Once she'd sent Ursula the letter, she found she couldn't wait for a reply and so had driven to the phone booth in Cosmos a couple days later and had hazarded a call.

"I'm on my way out the door," Ursula had said. "Oh, shit, Rose. Call back?"

"Sure."

"But you won't."

"The phone's in the middle of the common room, remember? There's no privacy."

"Yeah, yeah. Listen up. Is she getting prenatal care? Is Natalie seeing a doctor?" Rose had hesitated. "Right. I have to say, I don't get you, Rose, inviting Natalie."

"I didn't really have a choice."

"Right. Only Natalie has choices. Fucking Natalie," she growled. Ursula did have some experience of Natalie, who'd visited Rose in grad school and run up the phone bill, alternately cooing to and arguing with some boyfriend back home—the pharmacist, Rose now realized. Once, to Natalie's wide-eyed astonishment, Ursula had untangled Natalie's hair from the phone cord and hung up for her, mid-call.

"You hold on," Ursula had commanded Rose as she stood in the phone booth. "I'm coming."

"You can't afford it," Rose protested. "Not the time off and not the money."

"You came to me in my time of trial," declared Ursula. "I'm coming to you in yours."

"Is this my time of trial?" Rose was beginning to suspect that all her times were of trial, and it touched her that Ursula might come. Maybe friendship wasn't such a shuck after all.

A letter from Ursula would at least offer further advice on how to manage Natalie.

Rose knew, however, as soon as she closed her hand on it, that the letter was not from Ursula. The paper was heavy and textured, and the envelope's return address was embossed.

The Minnesota Composer's Guild. Dear Rose MacGregor, We are pleased to inform you—and Rose read no further. She'd grasped what it meant and was shouting.

The grant she'd applied for—she'd gotten it. She'd won. There'd be money to hire musicians for a whole concert of her music in the Cities. She was going back to the city. She was going to be somebody after all. The charming little farm was about to be a memory. Natalie would give birth soon, but so? A wild young girl gets knocked up—ordinary life, unremarkable. Natalie would need to be settled someplace, but Rose was on her way now. She'd written the sonata for Natalie; she would put her sister's name in the concert program. Natalie was lucky, really, to have an about-to-be famous sister.

"What is it?" demanded Natalie.

But Rose wouldn't let Natalie be the first to hear. She ought to rush to Lila, but she didn't want that either. Anyone could see Lila had let her career go, retiring to a farm way off in the middle of nowhere. She'd be one of those musicians of brief fame. Lila had talent. It was sad. She was probably lucky to have met Rose; maybe she'd be a footnote.

Rose saw herself on Guy's arm at her concert. What did it matter if they were or were not lovers? He'd be her escort—he owed her that much. They'd be the handsome pair. He'd have to buy a suit. No, a tux. Gripping the letter, she backed away from Natalie, who looked at her strangely and let out a nervous laugh.

Rose didn't know where she was going, but she couldn't stand there a minute longer. She turned and ran to her car. The keys were in the ignition. She started up, backed around, and drove out, gazing into the rearview mirror where she saw, with a shivery stab of satisfaction, Natalie standing dumbstruck, exactly where she'd left her.

Chapter TWELVE

T he phone booth stood in the bright sun, trapping heat. Rose let her barn jacket slide to the floor and with bemusement studied the mud-encrusted overalls and the frayed sweatshirt underneath. Who had she been when she'd put on those clothes? It was as if someone else had dressed her. She lifted and let fall each foot, clunking the heavy-soled secondhand Red Wings, breathed in her own sweat smell, and ran a hand through her stubbly hair, picturing herself in a photo: The Composer in Her Brief Farm Phase.

She'd driven off without her wallet or address book, but knew the numbers by heart and would call collect. Bells would ring at her command in Alan's rooms in St. Paul and Ursula's in Philadelphia, and from those rooms life surely opened outward. Who could say but she'd have a concert in Philadelphia one day soon?

Soaking in the heat inside the booth, she gazed out at the squat brick and shingle storefronts of the one-block main street of Cosmos, and the towering conveyors of the grain elevator, and the prairie beyond, vast and lost. She could love the prairie and not have to live in it. To the rhythm of a distantly ringing phone, music tumbled inside her. Ursula would shout and Alan would ask a jillion questions. But neither was home.

She thought of Emma Williams. She and Emma had taken to sitting side by side at Quaker Meeting, and one Sunday, invited on the spur of the moment, she'd followed Emma out on the highway from Litchfield halfway to Hutchinson. They'd turned onto a gravel road at a sign in the shape of a winged corncob—she thought she could find it again—and turned again at a round barn and the next place was Emma's.

Emma's farmhouse sprawled in a grove of oaks above a pond. The house only seemed in poor repair: she primed and painted one side of it a summer, so it stood in various shades of blue-gray, various stages of fading and cracking. The inside walls had turned brown under years of wood smoke and the furniture was a worn hodgepodge, but the place was full of books and pictures and there was a lamp to turn on at every spot a lamp could be wanted.

On a rise above the pond, two upholstered armchairs, which had been surrendered to the sun and rain, creaked and sent up puffs of dust when the two of them sat down there. Mother of several grown children, grandmother of many more, Emma was now on her own—no one but herself and the weather—and loved it. A husband had drunk himself out of the picture long ago, she told Rose with a dismissive wave of her hand, and she'd gone to work for the county—no choice, mouths to feed—while studying law at night.

"Law," said Rose. "Wow."

Had Emma always looked the part, Justice with Her Scales, or had she grown into it, Rose wondered? Was there something in Rose that would develop so that, years in the future, younger people might say to themselves that hers was the face of music?

Emma had passed the bar and become a public defender, *but no bleeding heart.*

"A public defender," said Rose. "Wow."

"Wow," Emma had echoed and had tilted her head back and raised her eyebrows and grinned, no longer ancient but a kid again. In that look, Rose had recognized the offer of friendship but had been too snarled up inside just then to do more than sit silent, and so had gone away without telling Emma a thing about herself.

My friend, Rose allowed herself to say as she turned at the flying corncob.

A dizzy little rhythm in her head changed into something that loped along. She'd never mentioned Emma at the Goat Pasture. This was misguided loyalty, she realized, fear that the others would think she was making friends elsewhere, moving on. How had she gotten herself into such a state, inhibited, mistrustful of herself and other people, unable to take the open hand of friendship? Oh, she *was* moving on.

Emma's truck was missing, but affixed to the door was a dog-eared note, much punctured by tack pricks: *Back soon—Come in.*

Rose sat on the steps and took her letter out. She read it closely and then stood up, her heart pounding, and went in and spread the three pages of it on Emma's table. Here in fine print was her project description in her own words: a concert of her music *featuring the cello soloist Lila Goldensohn.* She hadn't remembered proposing that.

"Why, Rose," Emma called through the screen door and burst in, dumping a chain saw. Embracing Rose swiftly, she spotted the letter. "Why, you clever thing," she said, scanning it. "You're a composer! Is this the biggest thrill in maybe a hundred years? And you never breathed a word."

Rose laughed and blushed. She'd been right to come to Emma.

"I'm going to buy fifteen tickets," declared Emma. "You sit down here and tell me all about yourself, starting at the beginning."

Self-consciously, Rose sketched in the peculiar parents and the wild sister and then added a piano, warming to her story of Musician as Lonely Young Girl. But as she approached the present, dread crept in. She was going to have to bring Lila into it.

"My god, Lila Goldensohn! Rumor has it she lives around here, though nobody's ever seen her. Do you mean to say you know her?"

She admitted she lived on Lila's farm, at least at present.

Emma was astonished. "No, really? What's she like?"

Rose didn't want to say.

"Ah. Shy? I've read she's a hermit nowadays."

It was a startling thought. Did Lila ever leave the farm? Rose couldn't think of a time when she had. Except for the defunct Studebaker, dusty and cobwebbed in the barn, Lila had no car. Could she drive, even? Did it matter? Lila kept to her land and the rest of them, Rose included, mostly did the same. Perhaps Lila had sworn off the world for good and would refuse to play Rose's concert, and that would be that. And that would be best. Could she still cut Lila from her grant proposal? Alan would know.

She said goodbye to Emma, drove back to the farm, told her news, and suffered everyone's congratulations. They seemed genuinely happy for her—jubilant, even—all but Natalie, who kept to the background with a fixed smile. Even Peggy threw her arms around Rose; Dinah pounded her on the back; and Lila, electrified, tripped over Josie as she thumped upstairs to get her cello.

Rose wanted to call to her to wait, to have caution. Rose was the one who'd started it with Lila, rushing backstage, bursting into tears, begging to write music for her. But she'd tried on Lila's life and it hadn't fit. It was an episode and it was over.

Throughout that evening and into the night, well past bedtime, Lila could be heard at her cello up in her room, playing Rose's music. At a late hour, the music halted and angry voices erupted. Out in the barn, Rose got up and looked down on the house to see Natalie's light on. The voices died out, the light switched off and, as Rose bundled herself back into her hammock, the cello resumed. Lila did, indeed, expect to play Rose's concert and so was about to have her feelings hurt. Again. As soon as Rose could manage to pack herself and Natalie up, she was out of there.

Or so she thought.

The first obstacle was Natalie, who refused to leave the farm. She was settled there, she told Rose. She would not go to the city. It would be bad for the baby.

Rose couldn't fathom this. Didn't Natalie complain about the farm all the time? Didn't she hate everybody? And, Rose ruthlessly pointed out, didn't everybody hate *her*?

Oh, *well*, Rose could say whatever mean things came into her head; she could strut around in her *concert grant* britches—Natalie wasn't budging. Rose could leave her there; Natalie wouldn't stop her. Why didn't Rose just do that?

Well, Rose couldn't. Other people were involved.

Her second obstacle was the grant proposal, what she'd laid out in her own words. She wasn't sure how to get out of it.

As she backed out of the driveway on her way to Alan in the city, Rose saw Lila striding to the barn, rocking chair hoisted overhead, with Natalie in shouting pursuit. Under Natalie's weight, one of the runners had come loose. Rose couldn't just leave Natalie at the farm.

Now she sat at Alan's table, eating the enormous chicken sandwich he'd made for her and moaning as he told her, gently but firmly, that Lila could not be cut from her program. He'd worked his Composer's Guild sources, and word was that Rose's great coup had been to engage Lila to perform again, that Lila's letter of recommendation had virtually assured the grant.

"Well, then, I'll just hand the money over to Lila," said Rose, sinking into gloom.

"It's no reflection on you. This is politics. It's marketing. It's publicity." His phone was ringing, but he ignored it. "Be strategic, Rose. Use your luck."

"You don't know the half of it," she told him. "Lila and me."

His face darkened.

"I know you warned me."

"Yeah, well, I'm guilty of my own experiments, as we know." He knelt beside her chair and put his arms around her, his eyes so unbearably sad that she had to look away across his shoulder. Friendship, mutual solace, whatever it was, she needed him. She needed him to know every agonized detail of what had and had not occurred between her and Lila. That monstrous night, half enacted, half smothered, still clung. She couldn't see how she'd ever arrive at comfort with Lila the way she and Alan had, able now to put consoling arms around each other. She couldn't imagine Lila looking at her any way other than with that dead look, the look of someone who's hopeless but keeps going through the motions, a look she could expect to see the night of her Composer's Guild concert, the concert that Lila was apparently destined to play.

Alan's phone rang again. "Some student. Some godforsaken committee member. At ten rings, they'll quit." At twenty rings, he picked up and handed the receiver to Rose.

"Well, here I am," said Ursula.

"Ursula! Oh, god, Ursula, I need you," said Rose, not hiding her tears.

"I'm at the frigging Goat Patch, if you want to know."

"*Where?*"

"Where are *you*? I've only got till tomorrow."

"On my way."

It dawned on Rose as she drove back out of the city that the hard freeze had come overnight and ended the growing season. The grass had gone papery. Leaves fell in clumps, and whatever remained in vegetable and flower beds was wilted or blackened as though a malevolent hand had passed over.

It was night by the time she reached the Goat Pasture. There were people in the gazebo—Lila, layered in sweaters, playing while Josie held a lantern and turned pages—and Guy's truck was parked at the barn, beside Ursula's glossy rental car.

On the front step, Rose glanced in through the window and stopped at the sight of Guy, bent over the wood stove, apparently alone. As he fed a log in, the fire lit his hands and his shirt front and his open collar where his chest disappeared into mossy shadow. In the fire's glow, his lidded eyes were lively above the stillness of his bones. How long had it been since she'd really looked at him? She wanted to take his face in her hands. However painfully, she was coming alive again. Old hungers were surfacing: hunger for a place in the world, for friendship and for every other possibility. Why not love? Maybe her long penance was over for her sin against Lila, for the earlier trouble she'd gotten into with Alan, and for the misfortune of her pregnancy and how it had undone them, herself and Guy, so near to the beginning of their love.

She stepped inside.

Strangely, a bed sheet was tacked up over the kitchen doorway and, behind it, a light cast huge shadows. A humped form lay on the table and someone stood alongside, poking at it and murmuring. Guy straightened up and put his finger to his lips.

"Ursula?" she called.

"In a minute," said Ursula from the behind the sheet. Guy led her outside.

"What is it? Is the baby coming?"

"No. It's an examination. Prenatal care."

They stood awkwardly in the evening chill. She reached for him but he held her back. "Your grant. Why didn't you tell me?"

"How could I? You don't have a phone."

Across the meadow, Lila's cello ceased, and in the house, Natalie started to cry. Rose felt her heart contract at the sound, though it was nothing more than what she'd imagined hidden beneath Natalie's laughter all along—the sound of lonely misery.

"I was about to write you," she told Guy, tensely. "Please, I just heard about the grant myself, only the day before yesterday."

Lila and Josie approached across the meadow as Ursula stepped outside. Natalie, swiping at tears, peeped out through the open door.

"You're letting heat out," called Lila.

"I am not delivering your baby," Ursula told Natalie. "I've got to go back first thing tomorrow. Which is when you go out and get yourself a doctor. Agreed?"

Natalie looked from Ursula to Rose to Guy. "All I want," she sniffled, "is to sit in a stupid rocking chair."

"It's being reglued," Lila said and pushed past them into the house. "In or out?"

Natalie took a step backward and Lila closed the door.

"The baby seems fine," Ursula said. "God looks after fools. She's fortunate."

Natalie opened the door again and peeped out. Her belly swelled toward them. "I can't come out in the cold," she said bleakly. "That would be bad for the baby."

There was the immediate question of where people would sleep that night.

"Emma," Rose told Ursula. "A woman I know nearby, a friend. You and I will go to Emma's."

"You're just going to leave me here?" quavered Natalie.

"I thought here was where you wished to be," said Rose.

Natalie sighed and closed the door, and Guy turned to Ursula. "I don't see how you can call her fortunate."

"That's because you're a sucker," Ursula retorted.

"And you're fucking rude." He turned on his heel and walked away, and Rose noticed anew the length of his stride and his grace. She was indeed coming alive again.

"He's going to sleep in the barn," she told Ursula.

"Well, you better get Natalie out of here before someone wrings her neck for her. *That* would be bad for the baby." Ursula barked out a laugh. "So this is paradise."

"Yah, well," said Rose, "post-snake."

"Paradise, either way." Ursula took a step out into the yard and spun under the prickling stars. "I ought to move out here."

"To the Goat Pasture?"

"God, no. But to someplace quiet. To wherever you are, Rose."

"You have to go tomorrow *morning*? This isn't a visit, Ursula. It's a hit-and-run."

Ursula sighed. In the nearly twelve months since their previous visit, her hair had grown out. Rose was the one with the haircut now. Ursula's good, thick, healthy hair fell, chestnut-brown, again to her shoulders, but her face still seemed tired. They wrapped their arms around each other and Rose dodged the thought that her only true friends were people she almost never saw.

There was Emma, however. She was making friends with Emma.

They climbed into the rental car, she and Ursula, and rolled down the windows and screamed into the chill all the way to Emma's. Ursula hollered to the fence posts and the withered fields and the sky that Rose had won a concert grant and was on her way to greatness. Beside Ursula, her worry over Lila dwindled and her anguish over Natalie drained away. Rose didn't need to confide in Ursula so much as to roar alongside her.

They began to spin the tale of the Pregnant Maiden of the Goat Pasture. Arriving at Emma's, they repeated it all for her—Rose mimicked the mischief and Ursula the pathos. Though amused by their monkeyshines, Emma grasped the difficulties and proposed to take Rose and Natalie in for a time. Natalie would not have to face the city. Rose could drive over to rehearse with Lila—Emma sensed discomfort there—and then drive home to Emma's.

"Do it," said Ursula.

Rose was staggered by the offer. "But you live alone," she said. "What about your privacy?"

Emma's answer came bold and merry. "I'm no bleeding heart—don't worry. It's a big house and from time to time I enjoy taking in strays."

"But you haven't met Natalie."

"The Pregnant Maiden? Can't wait." Emma shot Rose her wide-eyed grin.

The next morning, Ursula went and in the evening, they packed up to move—Rose and Natalie with Guy, who stayed over to help, though there wasn't much to carry: a box of clothes and books, a file cabinet of manuscript pages, Natalie's knitting bag, the pine cradle, and Rose's cello.

Good-byes at the Goat Pasture were muted. Rose would be back within the week to plan her concert with Lila. Only Wilma and Noah bundled up to wave them off, just as they'd come out in greeting upon Rose's first arrival. She recalled her first view of the house, with its many windows that had seemed to examine her from every angle. Now, in the dark, the shades were drawn, the eyes closed. Then the short caravan, Rose's station wagon and Guy's truck, rounded a bend and the house disappeared from sight.

Emma shook hands gravely all around and sat Natalie down to discuss the birth. A doctor was mentioned, and a hospital nearby.

"*Emma* understands," Natalie whispered to Rose with reproachful good cheer, though Rose wasn't fooled. Whatever Natalie might say, she'd been taken in hand.

Emma settled Natalie in a little room at the top of the stairs, right next to a bathroom so she wouldn't have far to go. Guy was given sheets and blankets for the front-room sofa, and Rose was directed to the bedroom beside the kitchen, below the stairs.

Warmed by the proximity of the kitchen's wood stove, her memories of the hammock in the frigid barn hurtled into the past. Wide awake, clean from a bath, at ease, almost happy, she sat up in bed. Guy was no more than a few feet away. She wanted to go to him. And why not? A burning log collapsed in the stove. Under the sound, Rose crept to the door. The knob, turning back, gave only a slight crackle, but as she slid over the threshold, the floorboards groaned. He was only past the staircase and around the corner, but it wouldn't do to wake Emma. She paused and sat down where the moon cast shadows of oak branches on the bottom stair.

Creaking footsteps, not her own, approached. She heard a whispered exclamation and slow, muffled progress. It had to be Guy. He'd had the same thought and was coming to her. Giddy, she stifled a laugh and moved up the stairs out of the moonlight where she couldn't be seen. His shape loomed below her. She watched for him to reach for her doorknob and to find the door open. But, instead, he turned and started up the stairs and, before she knew it, was tripping over her, gasping and grabbing the railing.

"Guy," she whispered, shocked, shoving down what was welling up inside her, unready to know what she now knew. "Guy, where are you going?"

Chapter THIRTEEN

He wanted to take them both, Rose and Natalie, to live with him up north. And the baby. The stonework was finished and he'd frame up the house by spring; there'd be plenty of room.

"I see," said Rose, "a harem."

He hustled her up the stairs. The little room under the eaves held a wicker armchair stacked with towels and a narrow bedstead where Natalie lay waiting, the covers pulled back in welcome, her breasts loose inside the open neck of her nightgown and her hair tumbling free. Guy shut the door behind them. The air smelled of freshly bathed skin, Natalie's, and of sweat, Guy's, an odor that tugged familiarly, nauseatingly at Rose.

She'd thought she could reach out and draw him back to her, had she? Too much had happened. Things beyond her imagination had happened. The music that had been a constant inside her since the news of the grant, the surging and trilling, went silent.

"No, of course not a harem," Guy was saying. He'd never meant to touch Natalie. That was wrong. But she needed holding. Anyone could see she needed to be held. Rose should be the one to hold her. They'd all be together and things would straighten out.

"Ah," said Rose. "I'm the chaperon."

"*What?*" gasped Natalie. "What are you *saying? She's* not a part of it."

"Oh, I'm not—no fear." Rose's throat tightened and her stomach heaved.

"Rose, I'm sorry," Guy said, and murmured to Natalie to lie down.

"Don't tell me what to do," said Natalie.

"You need your sleep. We can figure this out later." He put a tentative hand on her head. "We'll go now. You sleep."

"Never tell me what to do," declared Natalie.

She swung herself up out of bed and into the wicker armchair, displacing the stack of towels, which cascaded to the floor. She arched and gasped. Guy reached a hand behind her and began rubbing circles on the small of her back. It seemed to Rose a practiced gesture.

How exactly had they managed to get this going right under her nose? They'd gone for a walk once or twice to build up Natalie's strength, Guy had said. *Strength,* was it? But hadn't he slept with Rose in the barn every night he'd stayed over? And Rose was never away from the farm, except the previous two nights. She'd slept one night at Alan's and then the previous night she'd spent with Ursula at Emma's. That was when.

Natalie caught Guy's free hand and held it. "It's not wrong—what we are to each other. Don't we have a right to be happy?" She stared up at Rose. "Don't I?"

Guy stood caught in the headlights. Well, Rose would not spare him. Had he actually, the past two nights, crawled in with Natalie across the hall from Lila? Natalie would not have consented to sleep in the barn, so he must have. The disgrace of it, the creepiness—the pair of them trooping down in the morning, shamefaced or defiant in front of Lila and the rest.

"I see," said Rose. "I get it, Guy." She waited till his eyes met hers. "Natalie's almost me—right? You can pretend it's your baby."

"I'm not you," said Natalie.

"You shut up," said Rose, quaking with rage, her self-possession deserting her as Guy massaged and massaged her sister's back.

Natalie was undaunted. "You did have his baby, but you killed it."

Guy shot a hand up to Rose in appeal.

"What else did you tell her?" asked Rose. "What I'm like in bed? The sounds I make?"

"What do you care?" Natalie broke in. "You barely pay attention to him. You hardly know he's alive."

Then Rose was on her, roaring. The heel of her hand struck Natalie's chin and knocked her jaw upward, crashing her teeth together. Rose clamped down on her sister's shoulders, but Guy stepped between them, freeing Natalie, and put a hand over Rose's mouth and held her back as she roared, wordless, into Natalie's face, roared out all her freezing nights in the barn and all her lonely girlhood, the butt of Natalie's jokes, that outrage not dead and buried, but mounting up in a long, unbroken blast. How could someone as sloppy, as trivial as Natalie get her hands on Guy? How could Guy allow it? Roaring at him now, roaring out their lost days and nights, their chance meeting, their wondrous hours—her Guy, her bear in the oats wrested from her, her hope and pleasure swallowed up in the bloated figure of Natalie.

Rose ripped Guy's hand away from her mouth and quieted her voice. "Okay," she said. "We're not waking Emma, but you're not staying, either. You'll have to go. Both of you."

"Right now?" said Guy, ready to obey her.

Natalie drew a sharp breath. There came a whooshing and her night-gown was drenched, thigh to foot. She stood. "Oh, god," she said and rushed out.

Guy let Rose loose. She swiped at her hands and arms, ridding herself of his touch. A puddle ran from the wicker chair to the floor. Rose bent and stacked up the towels and took one to wipe up the wet. She wouldn't look at him.

Emma called from the bottom of the stairs, "Hello, up there. Everything all right?"

Natalie opened the bathroom door. "Active bladder," she called.

"Ah, yes," Emma said and padded off to her bedroom at the back of the house.

Natalie reappeared and lowered herself, groaning, toward the bed, and Rose and Guy cracked heads, bending to try to help her down.

"Leave me alone, both of you," she said. "I've got to change my nightgown."

As if she had anything to hide, Rose thought. But they went.

"Rose," Guy said, behind her on the stair. "I've only held her and kissed her a little. It's never gone beyond kissing."

She laughed mildly. She'd seen Natalie waiting to take him into her bed. He had crossed over a very wide river and sunk the boat on the other side.

"First thing tomorrow, you go," she told him and quickened her step through the dark, and then he wasn't behind her any more.

Emma, in plaid flannel pajamas, stood brewing tea in the kitchen.

"The noise woke you up. I'm sorry," Rose muttered.

Emma handed her a cup of tea. "My hearing's not the greatest any more. No, you didn't wake me. I was on a prowl and saw the light upstairs." But even halfway deaf, Emma could not have failed to hear Rose roaring that way. She still felt the vibration in her chest. Her teacup shook in her hand.

Emma reached and put a finger on her wrist. "What is it?"

Rose flinched. Again, she saw herself step into Natalie's room, Guy ahead of her, Natalie's face showing fierce exultation till she saw Rose. Again, she heard the placid little voice: *You barely pay attention to him. You hardly know he's alive.* There was truth to that. She'd neglected Guy, pushing him away when it suited her, leaving him to tag along till she was ready for him again.

"You've got nothing to be ashamed of," said Emma. "You didn't get her into this. That young man of hers—he's the one responsible. He's here tonight; all well and good. But has he put a ring on her finger? Has he put a roof over her head? Does he have any plan at all?"

Rose barked out a laugh. Apparently, it had not occurred to Emma that Guy might be—might have been—Rose's boyfriend.

Guy and Natalie. It even made some sort of sense. Maybe they belonged together. Preoccupied as Rose had been with her troubles at the farm, with her grant and its promise of a new start in the world, she had failed to follow where love was going. Love was, as always, on the move, pushing things out of its path, strengthening or breaking things. The *strength* Guy had built up in Natalie, or Natalie in Guy—it hardly mattered who started it—the building into a *we* had cast Rose out, a lonely *I*, and just when she'd started to desire again. What her grant could do for her seemed nothing, seemed ashes, compared to what love could do, not to strengthen, but to disgrace her. She was going to have to live this down. She could start by telling Emma. She made herself meet Emma's eyes.

"Well," Emma was saying. "You're just the sister."

Right. This might not be about her at all, but the story of Guy and Natalie. And Rose was "just the sister," the one who'd unwittingly brought them together.

"It's easy to get wrapped up in other people," said Emma, "to lose sleep they ought to be losing." She frowned. "Have I said too much?"

"No, Emma, you're dead on. I'll let them lose the sleep." Rose pulled herself to her feet. She'd explain it all to Emma another day. She glanced through the doorway toward the darkened staircase. "Do you have a dog?"

Emma shook her head. Rose shrugged—she'd thought she heard a panting sound somewhere in the house just then.

She went back to her bed and dumped herself down. *Let them lose the sleep.* She forced her eyes closed and saw Guy standing at Natalie's bed. His clothes dropped away and his cock sprang upright. She told herself to quit—not to do this to herself. He'd said there had only been holding and kissing. But, really, why should they stop there? Nothing was stopping them. Certainly not Rose, not the sister who'd brought them together. Natalie on the bed would be harder, but Rose could do it—spread her sister's legs apart beneath her huge belly or hump Natalie up on all fours so he could enter from behind.

Natalie cried out. An actual cry, distant in the house. And then another—an alert, gasping cry. Rose and Emma converged on the stairs.

On the bed stripped of all but a bottom sheet and towels underneath her and a belt looped either side of the footboard, leather belts of Guy's, homemade stirrups, Natalie lay, pressing out her feet, her arms stretched overhead, her hands clamped to the bars of the headboard.

"I'll call the ambulance," said Emma.

"No," gasped Natalie. "Not the hospital. Not lights and steel tables and strangers."

"You can't do it this way. It's too risky."

"Guy, don't let her," panted Natalie.

Emma turned to him. He stared, unseeing. Natalie drew a breath and brayed.

"Call the ambulance, for Chrissake," said Rose.

Emma dropped to her knees and tugged the towel smooth under Natalie, and reached for the stack of towels on the floor—Emma's towels. "You had this all planned, I see."

"I'm sorry," said Rose. "I didn't know."

"Well," said Emma, "why should we argue? I, myself, came into the world this way, right in this house, as a matter of fact, possibly in this room. We'll need a sheet of plastic to protect the mattress and boiled water, lots of it. And basins. Have you sterilized the towels?" she asked Natalie, who sat up, shaking her head and shivering.

"Lean back," said Emma. "No rush. How long have you been in labor?"

"Since supper."

"And your waters broke—"

"An hour ago." Now Rose understood the source of the flood that had drenched Natalie's nightgown and puddled the chair. Natalie regarded her. Between them was the unspoken accusation: Rose had shouted at Natalie, had struck her *while she was in labor.*

Rose returned the stony look. She had not known Natalie was in labor; Natalie hadn't seen fit to tell her. Emma sent Rose to the kitchen to fill and heat the teapot, the double boiler, and the soup kettle and to turn on the oven for sterilizing towels. Rose turned from Natalie. She'd be the sister; she'd heat water and carry basins. But she hated Natalie all the same.

In the hour it took to boil water and cool it and fill pitchers and gallon jars and set them in a row outside the birthing room, Rose turned herself into a bystander, coming and going, passing Guy on the stairs. He reached to touch her shoulder once and she quickly moved out from under his hand.

Natalie lay on sheets and towels over crackling plastic. Emma unfastened and cast aside the leather belts from the footboard.

"A trip to the olden days," she said, and beckoned to Rose to make a sling with her, the two of them kneeling either side of the headboard. Natalie was told to sit forward, and Rose and Emma joined arms, hand to elbow, and braced her from behind and then she lay back and Emma and Rose extended, each of them, an elbow around front, over which Natalie was to hook her knees. And when she had each knee in place and, between her legs, gripped their free hands, the human sling went taut, and Natalie was entirely contained in their arms and, at the same time, able to open her thighs. Her nightgown was bunched to her waist. Her underpants were soaking.

"You can take those off," said Emma and released Rose and set a lamp low at the foot of the bed for later, when it would be needed. She switched the lamp off. It might be a while yet, she told them. Natalie should rest and Rose might read a book, and Guy—well, Guy would do whatever he pleased.

Emma installed herself with a book in a narrow rocker outside the open door, where she read and hummed. Obediently, Rose went downstairs to the bookshelf and found a Western with a sunset on the cover and settled herself back upstairs in the dampness of the wicker chair. She read and reread page one, in which a cowboy put a halter on a horse. Emma noticed she was not turning pages and suggested she go downstairs to nap. Rose gave a fake yawn and stretched but settled back to her page one, seeing not a cowboy, but Doris Atkinson the previous autumn, that terrible afternoon when she had observed Doris enduring Frances and Harold in the same room. She felt a sudden affinity for the pale, shattered woman. But here, in the room under the eaves, the room with the strange odors, something was about to transpire and Rose found herself interested. Something, someone was coming.

Natalie slept and then she was astir. She tried to get up. She lay back down.

"Are you hot?" Emma asked. "Shall we take this off?" She gave the nightgown a tug.

Natalie cast a wild look in Guy's direction.

"Oh, I wouldn't spare his feelings," said Emma.

They lifted off the nightgown and Natalie leaned back, her breasts and nipples bloated above the mound of her belly and her vulva, enormous, exposed between her open knees.

Emma cast an eye on Guy, and, obediently, he looked.

"You're okay. You're good," he told Natalie, his voice unsteady.

Was he turned on by the sight, Rose wondered? Did this fulfill his notion of womanhood? She felt a prickling of remorse. No matter what Natalie had done, she was in childbirth now. This was, undeniably, womanhood, a grand, momentous thing.

Natalie smiled wanly up at him. "We could name him Guy, Junior."

"Oh?" he croaked. He leaned back and his shadow seemed to fall over backwards.

She yelped and bore down.

"I'm not sure you should be pushing yet," said Emma.

Natalie lifted her chin sharply toward the spot between her legs. They saw a slight bulge.

Emma and Rose knelt and made their sling, and Natalie gripped and the bulge vanished.

"Not so hard yet," said Emma. "Try to hold back."

Natalie was thirsty. Emma went to crack ice. The grandeur of birth, was it? The roiling mass of legs and belly seemed to yield up nothing but chaos and stink.

Natalie again lay against Rose and Emma, her hair matted, her skin very pale. A freckle by her ear seemed as dark as ink. She tensed and Emma and Rose tensed with her, cradling her. And they stood and stretched and then she tensed again and then again so soon after the previous time that they had to stay kneeling in place.

The clock read 3:30. The bulge between Natalie's legs was enlarging by degrees.

"His head," said Natalie.

Between her legs, between the lips, a dark something showed, partly hairy, partly smooth, perhaps a head. A little dent and a slit in it—perhaps a wrinkled eye.

"Push now," said Emma, and swung Natalie's knee to Guy and moved to crouch between Natalie's legs, reaching in with her hands. "And now." Natalie bellowed.

"God," said Guy.

The head came and then the shoulders and the rest, sluicing fishlike into Emma's hands, and she scooped it up and laid it on Natalie's heaving chest. A baby. A baby who breathed in a tiny heaving counterpoint.

"It's a girl," said Guy.

"Very good," said Emma, laughing.

"Oh," said Natalie and closed her eyes.

With sterilized sewing scissors, Emma cut and tied the cord.

"Now, hold her," she urged Natalie, who, her eyes still closed, allowed Emma to move her arm to curl limply around the baby. "What are you going to call her?"

"She's a girl, so I don't know," said Natalie remotely.

Rose sneaked a hand up and grasped the baby's foot. Satiny, sticky little foot. Natalie's arm loosened around the baby and her hand wandered down to the pulsing cord.

"Yes," said Emma. "Take your daughter, Guy. We've got to push that placenta out."

Guy sat gingerly and held out his hands, eager, uncertain. "She isn't mine," he admitted.

"Yes, we all feel that at first," said Emma and no one enlightened her.

Natalie swayed to her feet and squatted and the placenta spilled out, purple and white, ridged and ruffled and slick with blood. They couldn't help staring, all but Emma, who was gathering towels and pouring water.

Rose filled a basin and took the baby from Guy, who didn't protest, and went to the wicker chair, where she sat with her knees together, nestling the baby between her thighs and, no one stopping her, bathed the little thing and, with a clean washcloth and pins, fashioned a diaper.

Swaddled in a towel, the tiny girl frowned and twisted her mouth. A cheek caved in and then rounded out again.

The silence inside Rose had broken out in chanting, a many-voiced tumult. She closed her fingers around the tiny hand. *Who are you?* This was Natalie's—*Natalie's* baby, she told herself sternly, but it seemed irrelevant.

"What's your name?" she whispered. Beyond her in the room, Emma helped Natalie into a fresh nightgown and Guy gathered up the soiled bedding.

"What's your name?" Rose said aloud. "She's going to tell me," she informed them.

"Really?" said Natalie dully and lay down again.

Rose knew it was not her right to do this, but no one seemed to be stopping her. In her lap, the tiny, wobbly being opened one dazzling eye and then the other and looked at her.

A name floated up.

"Marguerite," breathed Rose. "Marguerite MacGregor," she said aloud.

"After who?" said Natalie.

"After no one but herself."

Guy stopped. Emma cast a startled glance at Rose and the baby.

"All right," said Natalie. "We'll call her Marguerite."

Chapter FOURTEEN

T he Composer's Guild was housed in an old brick warehouse in downtown St. Paul, in a room whose stark length was interrupted by great pillars, each hewn from a single log and bolted into an iron framework overhead, evidence of the lumber barons and ore magnates who had built the city. The vaulting space dwarfed the Guild filing cabinets, table with phone, and scattering of chairs. A poster-sized portrait of Beethoven floated on a wall, insignificant as a postage stamp.

At a table beneath a huge, arched window, six people were gathered ahead of Rose, who'd had unexpected trouble finding parking. She was never late—she hated to be late—but here she was at grant orientation, slipping into the last chair. Her hands were freezing from her struggle with the pay envelope at the unattended lot next to the freeway, and now she was sweating in her woolens. She'd worn (what else?) the twin set and tweed skirt Frances had correctly termed *governessy*, and here came the Director in her silks, her auburn hair with its chic white streak.

Rose gripped the small hand and felt the bones crunch. "Sorry," she said and sat.

The Director turned up the wattage behind her smile. "Rose Mac-Gregor," she announced to the room. "Rose has just come in from the farm. Lila's farm."

"Not quite," said Rose. She'd come from Emma's.

"Lila Goldensohn, you know," the Director purred.

They were already acquainted, Rose and the Director. When Rose had come to town the previous fall to begin her appointment at the college, the Director had hosted a reception for her at the Guild, ostensibly to meet other composers, though wealthy patrons were rather more in evidence. The Director had ferried her from group to group of tanned, expensive people, introducing her and dropping names.

Rose had studied in Philadelphia—she must know George Crumb? Or Rochberg, surely? Richard Wernick?

"Not personally," Rose had answered, which wasn't quite true. The famous names had trooped through her grad program; some had even been her teachers and she had known them as students always know their teachers. She knew them, but they didn't know her. She couldn't say the same of Lila. She was going to have to admit that she knew Lila. Personally.

The Director handed her a blank name tag and without forethought Rose wrote, "I know Lila Goldensohn," and slapped it on her chest. Baring her teeth, she surveyed the circle.

"Har, har," said a white-haired, white-bearded man who shook her hand damply. Beside him sat a kid in big glasses whose grin seemed to split his face, then a bald guy who raised his jaw in her direction as he rocked a motorcycle helmet on the tabletop, and, beside him, in a cape, a gloomy young man with one continuous eyebrow crossing his forehead and a boot placed aggressively on the window sill. Rose took a second name tag, scribbled her name, slapped it up over the first, and turned to the remaining grantee, a thin-lipped, restless person with a ruffle at her throat whose name was actually—she held still a moment and Rose confirmed it on the name tag—*Melody*. Rose swallowed and extended her hand. Melody shook her fingertips. *My people,* Rose told herself grimly. They were not a community but hungry competitors, ranked, no doubt, from first place to sixth in a file somewhere in the room.

The Director, a composer herself who rarely had time for her own work, though that was another subject altogether and none of *their* concern, declared her pleasure in awarding the grants, speaking of the rareness of talent, a rareness akin to that of unicorns. Rose nearly choked. *Unicorns.*

The Director got up to take a call. "New York," she said, winking and beaming.

Rose caught herself sitting up straighter and deliberately slumped back. She would, of course, love to have her music played in New York City, but it was highly doubtful that the Director could, by picking up the phone, hand out fame and fortune. Still, who could say? Melody, with a wriggle of the shoulders, scanned the ceiling, eyes alight. She imagines she's being discovered, thought Rose—she thinks she's a unicorn. Maybe the others *were* unicorns, brilliant and justifiably self-regarding, in contrast to the marginally talented Rose, who had hitch-hiked in on the coattails of a famous musician.

"What's the matter?" the fellow in the cape asked her. "Or do you always scowl?" He radiated a savage, almost feral smile. "You're not paying them; *they're paying you,*" he told her.

"Right," she said and rubbed her eyes. She had no excuse for behaving badly. A folder inscribed with her name in gold calligraphy was set at her place at the table. She opened it.

The grant was not large—twenty-five hundred, from which to pay musicians, hall rental, and copyists, and if there was any money left, to pay for her time. If she was extremely frugal—she'd copy her own music and make do with Lila and one or two other musicians; she needn't hire a whole orchestra—the grant, added to her savings, would cover living expenses through winter and spring. She wouldn't need much, living at Emma's. In fact, her life had emptied out so completely, she felt nearly disembodied. There was music and there was Emma.

Guy had packed them up, Natalie and himself and the baby, and gone.

It had been a shock to see them get into the truck. Rose had diapered and bathed Marguerite every day—Natalie was exhausted and having trouble nursing—and had rocked and sung and played music to her. But of course Rose couldn't nurse her. And had no say over her. The truck's passenger door, which had once belonged to Rose, gave out its peculiar sound, opening and closing, a screech and then a groan, now merely a noise a truck door made, and the driver was merely someone she'd once known, loading up his woman and his baby.

"It'll be all right," said Emma, as the truck pulled out. "You can visit them."

But would she? She couldn't imagine missing Guy and Natalie, and she could do without the crying in the night; but, quite unexpectedly, she felt unsure she could do without the baby: the dense, wobbly weight of her, her heat, her firm, tiny grip, the silken nape of her neck, her unfocused, rapt regard of everything around her. Even at a week old, Rose imagined she saw personality. Marguerite seemed eager but deliberate, ready for joy but cautious—sensible, even. Could a baby take after its aunt?

They were gone. Her life was her own again, and she stood there weeping.

"Oh, now," said Emma.

"No, really," said Rose. It was time to make a clean breast of things to Emma, however awkward. She admitted that Guy had quite recently been her boyfriend and choked out what had happened with Lila too.

Emma offered a handkerchief, but no reply. They got up and went their separate ways: Rose to her music, and Emma to clean up her gardens for winter. When they met in the kitchen to prepare supper, Emma had not yet spoken.

"What you must think of me!" Rose blurted. "Would you like me go?"

"Why, Rose, I'd be bereft."

"So I can stay?"

There was pain in Emma's answering smile. "You don't trust anybody, do you? Not even yourself. Though why should you," Emma added, gently, "after all the shenanigans?"

"I do trust you, and I want to stay," said Rose. She'd pay rent; she'd buy the groceries.

Emma laughed. "Not the groceries." But she'd take rent. She suggested a figure ridiculously low. Rose doubled it.

"If you must," Emma said, "but what I'd really like is to go with you once in a while when you and Lila play."

Rose wished she'd thought of it herself. She and Lila, with Josie on piano, practiced every evening in the common room at the Goat Pasture, and, once she began bringing Emma, it went easier. Because Emma was a guest, Peggy brought refreshments, Josie told jokes, and Lila's silence seemed mere shyness. And if her circumstances there seemed in some way a drab afterlife, Rose was at least able to pursue her music now without distraction. In the steady hours, she finished two long pieces, three short, and a brand new, tiny, jazzy piece dedicated to Marguerite: a concert of ninety minutes, she figured, adding in intermission.

She'd figured wrong, however. She was not to have her own concert. When the Guild Director returned from talking on the phone to New York, she clarified this "minor matter." The Guild only had the budget to publicize three concerts. The winning composers would be paired. That way they'd split hall rental. They'd each have more money that way, didn't they see?

Rose realized she was gaping. "More money, but less music," she said.

The Director turned a corner of her mouth up in Rose's direction and a dimple sank. Best to be realistic, she said. Pairing up, they'd increase their draw. This was Minnesota, didn't they know, with its liberal tradition, its populism? The Board liked to spread the money around.

"Two composers for the price of one," observed Rose.

"New music by unknowns," the Director said and sighed. Their concerts *were* central to the Guild's mission, but not even the Board could be counted on to attend.

"Not even to hear music by unicorns?" said Rose and told herself to shut up. Careers theoretically were launched from this room, reputations made. The Director let out a silvery giggle. They'd have to drag in family and friends and any other unicorns they happened to know and beg their musicians to do the same. The Guild would pay for jug wine, crackers, cheese; and the Board's bright idea of the season was to mount the concerts during Winter Carnival to piggyback onto Carnival publicity, though who that might draw, one couldn't say—ice sculptors or the guys who tromped around in helmets—Vikings? Vulcans. But, oh well, the main thing was to hear one's music oneself, wasn't it? And, of course, it would all look dandy on the résumé.

So this was it, Rose thought, her Concert Grant? Her turning point, her luck? But didn't luck always go this way—a brief sense of arrival, quickly overthrown by strangeness? The Chairman of the Board, the Director was saying, liked to participate hands-on. He'd paired the composers for their concerts, drawing names out of a hat. The white-haired man was paired with the grinning kid. Santa and The Elf, thought Rose. The motorcycle man and the young vampire were paired—a Vulcans' Concert.

Rose realized who was left. Melody adjusted her shoulders.

"And the distaff end," the Director said sweetly.

"From a random drawing out of a hat?" said Rose. "I want to see that hat."

The Director threw back her head and laughed. "Aren't you a breath of fresh air? Now, *here's* a thought: Lila Goldensohn will bring in a crowd if we bill your concert as her comeback."

"Why, *yes*," said Melody and tugged at her ruffle.

The Director winked. "Just something to ponder."

Rose was crushingly tired and baffled by her own unruliness. She wrote down her phone number and passed it to Melody; it seemed they'd be working together. The huge project she had been counting on to fill the winter days had collapsed to nothing. She'd have a mere half-hour to program. She could be ready the next day.

When the meeting ended, she fled to a nearby gas station and, in the restroom, changed out of her sweaty woolens and into the jeans and flannel shirt she had bundled in the car, intending to head back to Emma's and go straight to bed. In the rearview mirror, she noticed a patch of dried baby spittle on the collar of her flannel shirt and scratched it until it powdered off. She took a detour up the hill to Tangletown. She might sack out on Alan's couch, her head felt so heavy.

But she didn't go to Alan's. The address she sought was across a thoroughfare that separated the college from a scruffy commercial block—used bookstore, greasy spoon—behind which stood several apartment buildings divided into efficiencies, catering to students.

Guy answered the door with the baby asleep on his shoulder. For a stunned moment, he regarded her. A month before, she'd hated him, but now she smiled and said hello.

He hooked an elbow around her swiftly and she let herself be hugged.

"I should have called first," she whispered.

"Not at all. You're family." He swung aside to let her in. "This is only temporary, now."

The windows in the tiny place looked out on a brick courtyard devoid of sun. The floor was black beneath ancient varnish, wood or linoleum—who could say? The plaster walls were pocked and scarred, and the air was thick with smell: sour milk and pee beneath Pine-Sol. But a bunch of daisies packed a jelly jar on a huge pine table, Guy's handiwork, pegged and joined like the cradle and the double bed in the corner of the room.

Natalie sat on the bench at the table with her shirt open.

"Honeypie, it's your sister," Guy said softly. "Get up and give her a hug." Natalie complied, draping her arms briefly around Rose's neck.

"Should I make tea?" she asked wanly.

"I'll do it. You sit back down and do your nipples." Guy unfolded a lawn chair for Rose. Natalie toyed with a tin of ointment, pulling the lid off, pressing it on again.

Marguerite slept meltingly on Guy's shoulder as he puttered at the stove. She'd grown in the month since Rose had seen her, though it was hard to see her with her little face squashed up against Guy's neck, her mouth pulled downward and her eye aslant. Rose could not imagine ever having been so tiny—small enough to be lifted to Guy's shoulder and to rest upon him completely. The thought made her throat constrict. She wanted Marguerite to wake up so she could hold her.

Guy put a hand on Natalie's back. "Come on, honeypie," he said. He'd never called Rose honeypie, but the patience in his tone made her glad of it.

"We're treating her for mastitis," he said. "It's common in new mothers."

"You got her to go to a *doctor*?" Rose exclaimed.

"I'm here," said Natalie in a tiny voice.

"And Marguerite to a pediatrician."

"Don't talk about me like I'm not here."

"Sorry," said Guy. "I'll shut up and let you talk to your sister, but you've got to—" He motioned in the air in front of his chest.

Natalie sighed, reached a finger in the tin and, lifting from a great harness of a bra the cap of cloth over a breast, stroked gingerly around the edge of a swollen and cracked nipple.

"What happened to you?" Rose whispered.

"A baby," she said grimly.

Guy caught Rose's eye. "They're doing fine. It's a period of adjustment," he said, and, as if on cue, Marguerite popped her head up, looked around, and let out a wail.

Natalie stiffened and Rose jumped up. "Let me take her."

"Okay," said Guy doubtfully.

Rose cradled the satisfying weight. For a startled moment, Marguerite gazed up.

"Remember me?" Rose breathed. If so, it was beside the point. The baby leaped at Rose's chest, mouthed her shirt front, and then drew in a breath and screamed, her face convulsing, her tiny fists flailing, and her feet pressing Rose's side, trying to launch herself away.

Guy put an egg timer on the table and set it. "Just five minutes," he said, and took the shrieking baby, placed her in Natalie's lap, and crooked her arm up.

Natalie tipped her head back and, without looking, guided the baby to the nipple. And as Marguerite quieted and suckled, Natalie began gasping with pain—terrible, asthmatic gasping.

Guy picked up a brush and stroked her hair. "Good job. It's okay if it hurts. We're getting there," he told her as he lifted and let fall the yellow hair.

An alarm clock rang. "You've got to go," murmured Natalie. "He's working three jobs. He's insane. He. Never. Even. Sleeps."

He was driving a school bus, selling Christmas trees, hauling firewood—jobs that allowed him to pop in every few hours. The teakettle whistled, and he leaped up. The timer dinged, and he gestured from one side of his chest to the other, until Natalie, without glancing at him, put Marguerite to the other nipple. Haggard but bright-eyed, he stood in place and did a little dance. And the point of all his effort? That Natalie should nurse her baby? Something she should do on her own?

He's buried now, Rose thought. Yet she couldn't mistake his joy. He loves them, she told herself severely, and the thought brought no jealous pain. A happy, busy man, he had hugged her hello and now pressed her hand good-bye.

Rather him than me, Rose thought. If Guy hadn't taken Natalie on, it might well have been Rose in that little apartment, cajoling and comforting, working odd jobs, doing diapers and ointment.

Reassured, she sped off to her music.

Chapter FIFTEEN

In her room at Emma's, Rose paced the plank floor, then knelt or stretched out on her belly, scribbling. The days passed and the pages piled up. Thanksgiving filled the house with Emma's kids and grandkids, though the day after the feast, Rose could barely remember a name. At Christmas she dumped presents on Marguerite—a plush elephant, a red rubber ball, and a muffler with small round brass bells sewed to the edge—and at Alan's Christmas table she ate roast goose basted with gin, the startling bite of the juniper berry sharp and singular.

Hadn't she always meant to learn to be alone and like it? She watched as Emma washed dishes or stood at the window or read in her easy chair: a human race of one, lively or lazy, responsive or shuttered up in herself, a world complete. Solitude asked nothing and entangled no one. The dramas of desire and of rivalry now seemed peculiar. Between her and Emma, shared meals and conversation occurred only by happenstance, pleasurably unplanned.

Though Rose was alone, music accompanied her and drew people toward her. The Winter Carnival approached like a throng heard from a distance. And though her concert—hers and Melody's—was scheduled last in the series, she could already sense an audience assembling, people stepping toward the concert hall from near and far. Ursula was coming and bringing a mystery guest. Rose's mother was coming and, more astonishingly, her father, who had mailed back her concert announcement with a message scrawled on it: *I'll be there.*

The third week of January, the Carnival began, and she was up in the city nearly every day, summoned by the Guild to go out and make publicity. Gamely, she trooped through the ice palace with the other composers, judged the Klondike Kate singing contest, and cheered the Frigid Thirteen Half-Marathon. Summoned to the Carnival Ball, for which a floor-length gown was required, she went out and rented a bluish thing patterned with icicles. The hem at her toe amused her. When since the dress-up games of childhood had she donned a garment that trailed to the floor? And an actual ball! At the prompting of the Guild photographer, she danced with the Snow King, who managed a jitterbug, red-faced and dripping in his fake ermine.

To cool off, all one had to do was step outside. With a troop of Girl Scouts, she dug through a snowbank on a fruitless search for the Carnival Medallion, which was snatched up by a hockey player who hadn't even followed the clues in the paper. The Carnival wasn't fair; it was wild, brisk, Schnapps-flavored, meant to bestir and keep people warm; it was reckless and inane.

She suffered the Carnival's worst—the assault of a Vulcan. Otherwise ordinary men, Chamber of Commerce types, the Vulcans got themselves up once a year in black face, black gloves, snowmobile suits, and crested helmets, and, beyond their dubious ceremonial purposes, were permitted during the weeks of the Carnival to grab and kiss any woman they encountered on a street corner, in a post office line, in a grocery aisle, wherever opportunity arose. Naturally, women scattered at the sighting of a Vulcan.

Rose was on an elevator digging through her knapsack, riding up to use the Guild copier, when a Vulcan stepped on and smeared her with his sooty face and smacked his lips wetly on hers. She shrieked, shoved him, and jumped out.

He stood at the open elevator door, cackling. "It's for fun!"

"For fun?" she gasped, her back shoved to the wall, her heart pounding.

"For luck," he declared, mildly outraged, as though she had scorned a gift. It was more a mugging than a kiss, but the heat of his mouth had brought a pang of loneliness.

Still, if he said it was luck, she'd take it as that. Her faith in luck was back, full force.

The Guild grant was turning out to be lucky. Things were coming together out of what she hadn't planned and couldn't predict.

The concert hall, for instance. A musty box with creaking seats, its quaint proscenium stood four feet above the floor and its upstage wall revealed a mural by a lost artist of the WPA: an outsized rendering of Thomas Hart Benton's *Persephone*, with alterations. Dressed as an American farm woman, the nubile goddess rested on her mossy bough, as in the painting, but the red dress shed at her feet had been picked up and put back on her in the mural, and the color of the dress was revised to a "Minnesota nice" salmon pink. And the peeping farmer was altogether gone, replaced by waving grain.

The suggestion that *Persephone* be painted over, made by the assembled composers to the building manager, had been met with a numbing silence.

"Very well. She does not exist," the Guild Director had crisply concluded.

Rose and Melody had then sneaked in and spent a pointless afternoon—Melody directing, Rose pulling and shoving—trying to coax the rickety frames of the Guild's sound baffles to meet and cover the mural. But the mural was too large. No matter what they did, the colossal head mooned above and the sleepy eye stared down into every seat of the first ten rows.

The mural was not badly executed, though. The grain, ten times life-sized, was ripe and plump. Oats, the building manager confided. *Oats.* The tree cradling the goddess was thick and black, possibly bearlike. Rose shut her eyes and the shapes of bears emerged, growling like distant thunder. She opened her eyes on the goddess and pondered how she might be put to use.

Luck seemed to arise from whatever lay at hand and whoever stood nearby. Josie allowed Rose to discover that, besides piano, she played violin, and with nimbleness and spirit. So Rose arranged her half-hour of music for Lila on cello accompanied by Josie on piano and violin. It simplified everything to work with just the two of them. Progress was so rapid, Rose suspected them of rehearsing extra hours. She was utterly, goofily grateful to them, and when they refused extra pay, she began sneaking the money into the farm's bank account.

Daily, she brought them fresh pages. A piece took shape from a sketch she'd begun long ago at Guy's shack and another from a dance she'd started before things had gotten heavy at the farm. Then the two pieces gelled into one and she heard human voices, as well as cello. She had just enough money and just enough time to hire singers—a choir of six voices, five women and a man, whom Josie would conduct.

Her sense of good fortune wavered only at the mention of Lila's comeback, the campaign to make something splashy of it, which the Guild Director waged with sly asides and "just a thought" notes that Rose ignored. Finally the Director, with Melody at her side, sat Rose down and threatened to go directly to Lila, and Rose decided she'd better get there first.

On a snowy night at the end of rehearsal at the Goat Pasture, when Josie had gone to brew tea, Rose spoke up. "They want to call this your comeback."

"Yeah," said Lila. "They would."

Outside, half a foot of new snow blew around in a stiff wind. The windows in the common room were frosted over and icy grains flung themselves up against the glass.

"They can forget it," said Rose. "I have no intention of exploiting you."

"Exploiting me?"

"My music ought to stand on its own."

"Well," said Lila, "I suppose I could play with a bag over my head."

"What?"

"Rose, I want you to use me. I'm using your music to play. And cash from a mysterious source keeps finding its way into the farm account." She cocked her head and smiled at Rose, a smile that seemed to lack sadness.

"Well, are you? Making a comeback?"

"Who the hell knows? Let the music be heard."

Josie set out the cups and poured. Rose's car, she reported, was buried to the bumper and the driveway could barely be seen. So that night Rose stayed over in her old room across the hall from Lila. They nodded good night, closed their doors, and she fell to sleep instantly and slept hard. Sometime in the night she halfway heard a noise, somebody coming up the stairs, but she didn't awaken till morning, when the world outside blazed with a post-storm glare.

The concert would be billed as a coming-out-of-retirement for the famous cellist. Lila would shave her mustache and beard and come into town to give interviews.

Melody appeared to gloat at the news. Not to be outmaneuvered, Rose seized on the question of the order of the program, and when Melody claimed not to care—"I'll go first or last, whatever"—Rose put her own music both first and last. *Marguerite* would begin the concert: a rousing minute and a half of cello, a tease for the Goldensohn fans. Melody's part would follow, with her harp bits, her flute bits, and her unusual use of the xylophone. Once they hit intermission, however, the rest of the concert would belong to Rose. *Marguerite* would be preview enough to bring the audience back to their seats, and then it would be Rose's concert to the end.

She was finally ready. She had to be. Josie came with Lila to the city and met with Rose's choir for rehearsal, after which there could be no more changes. Her work was done. Aware of the temptation to review and reconsider and make herself a nuisance, Rose grabbed her coat and hat at the end of rehearsal and made for the door. Lila caught her eye and winked. She and Josie were heading back to the farm. From then on, they'd rehearse without her.

"You try to call; we won't come to the phone."

"Righto," said Rose. She stood outside the rehearsal hall, flexing her fingers inside her mittens. She was staying at Alan's till the concert and could head over there. Or she might go walking, get herself a bowl of soup, jaw with some stranger about the blizzard in the forecast. She might wander over to see her mother, who'd flown in the night before and was staying at Guy and Natalie's, sleeping on the floor on a futon, which she described over the phone in her bright, angry way as "great fun, happy torture."

Rose had offered to pay for a hotel room. Her mother did *not* have to sleep on a futon.

"Oh, but I do," her mother had said. "For family togetherness. Just ask your sister."

The particular edge to her mother's voice let Rose know a major battle was brewing, and she thought she might as well go over. She was glad of any excuse to visit Marguerite, though it was maybe too obvious that she went over there mainly to catch the baby up for delicious minutes of wide-eyed nonsense, of babbling, peeping and gurgling.

"She's not just a plaything," Natalie would grumble.

"Oh, but she *is*," Rose maintained and Marguerite would, often as not, giggle obligingly.

Rose found Natalie in a chair at the window with Marguerite tipped to her breast as though nursing had never given her a moment's trouble. She smiled one of her new-mother smiles, half self-satisfied, half aggrieved. Their mother sat on the rolled-up futon, drinking whiskey from a mug. Natalie let it be known that she was offended. She was offended that their mother had come for the concert and not for the birth.

"As if I should have known when you went into labor by *pan-maternal telepathy*," said Marion. Had Natalie even called once the baby was born?

"She doesn't love Marguerite," declared Natalie.

"Oh, sure she does," said Rose. Marion said nothing.

Guy stood at the sink, his back to them. "It can't be forced, Natalie," he said, his voice so low Rose could barely hear him.

"Oh, *right*," said Natalie. "It's just a matter of *preference*. Like, does she like the color *blue*; does she like scrambled *eggs*; does she like Marguerite?"

"If you force it, it can't come." He shot Rose a haggard look.

"*Thank* you, Guy," cooed Marion.

"I can't really say you're welcome," he muttered.

"Don't pretend you're not on her side," Natalie spat at Guy.

"Oh, dear," said Rose.

He cleared his throat and reached for his jacket.

"Milk," said Natalie, "and orange juice." He put his head down and went out.

"She wants to make me into a grandmaw. Do I look like a grandmaw?" drawled Marion.

She looked ageless and fierce, her eyes bright, her lips pursed and moist.

"I believe you redefine the term," said Rose.

"She won't even hold her granddaughter," said Natalie.

"*Honestly*," their mother said and extended her hand as though she could hold the baby on her open palm.

"Give her to me," begged Rose.

Natalie shook her head.

"Look, I spread myself at your feet." Marion swooped her arms open. "I sleep on a rock for you." She slapped the futon, which gave a resounding thud.

Natalie turned away and fixed Rose with a stare. "So Dad's coming?"

"Where's he staying?" asked Marion. "In some church basement?"

"No idea," said Rose. Since his scrawled *I'll be there,* she'd heard nothing at all.

Marguerite's nursing pulsed noisily over the traffic sounds from the street outside. They sat without speaking. Guy came back in and set a quart of orange juice and a gallon of milk in front of Natalie. She read the labels and nodded. He opened the fridge to put them away.

"I don't know why Dad's making such a big deal, coming out here," said Natalie. "It's not like he can afford it. And it's not like you're getting *married* or something."

Rose saw Guy tense as Natalie looked his way. Would he marry Natalie? Already they squabbled like married people. Rose considered. It didn't seem to bother her.

"So, Rose," said their mother. "Let's hear about the concert."

"She has her fucking concert. I have my baby." Natalie stood abruptly. "You know what she said?" She cocked her head toward Marion. "*Babies? You've seen one, you've seen 'em all.*"

The baby released the nipple and lolled, drowsy and goggle-eyed.

"That's what she said about you, Marguerite." Natalie handed the baby to Rose.

"Hi, sweetie," Rose murmured, entirely useless as referee. None of what they said seemed to touch her. Her mother and sister and Guy, too, seemed eccentric and cranky but harmless, really, comical and vaguely dear. Her mind was already in the concert hall.

Natalie was right—she had her fucking concert.

She was going to move the sound baffles apart to reveal *Persephone* completely. Her choir on risers right below the goddess would wear salmon pink—even the solitary man in the choir had bought a tie to match the dress in the mural—and when the choir sang and growled, whooped and snuffled as the score demanded, Rose hoped everyone would feel free to laugh. Her big piece was called *Bears in the Oats,* and it ran twenty minutes. In her mind, both Lila and Guy were in it, rolling in the oats, she hoped, eating their fill; and everyone else she knew was in it, forgiving, forgetting and satisfied.

From a passage from Flaubert, she'd fashioned a text for the choir to sing:

> *Human speech is a cracked drum*
> *upon which we beat a rhythm for bears*
> *though what we meant, and all we meant,*
> *was to make a music to melt the stars. . . .*

And the cello would lead them all on, a throng of bears, to fresh, untrammeled fields.

Chapter SIXTEEN

The lobby of the concert hall was packed. There was hardly room to open a handbag or reach into a pocket for a ticket. The Guild phone had rung off the wall that week, but still there'd been no inkling of a crowd quite so large—true to prediction, the other concerts had played to tiny houses. Inside the hall, the house manager scrambled to open a second section of seats and then a third and was calling for a vacuum to run over upholstery dusty from disuse.

Rose slouched in a seat down front, pretending to have a purpose there. On stage, a tuner hunched over the piano, working his way down the keyboard. His dark, close-cropped hair and his baggy suit made him seem not of the present time, but someone beamed in from the harpsichord era. He glanced at her over the tops of his wire-rims.

"It's okay?" she asked. "The piano?"

"Yup. Perfect." His flat, Midwestern accent dispelled the harpsichord era. "And, of course, snow improves acoustics."

"Huh?"

"Quiets the street. Wraps the music in a blanket."

He grinned. He was teasing her, the nervous composer. Everyone seemed to know who she was. The house manager shooed her out to the lobby to meet her public.

The Director, her lock of white hair in a cunning little plait, pounced on Rose. "It's a triumph," she said, "a triumph."

"Let's hear the music first," muttered Rose.

"And in this weather," the Director trilled, dashing across the lobby to pull people inside and close the doors that were letting in the wet and the cold.

Snow had fallen heavily since morning, a storm that had created a moving cloak around Rose as she'd wandered the shops near the college to buy flowers and presents for her musicians and singers. By noon, streets and sidewalks were clogged and still it had gone on snowing. Travel advisories had been posted, but Lila and Josie were safely in town already, in a room in a grand old hotel nearby to the hall. Rose had wanted them each to have a room of her own or a suite with two bedrooms—she was paying; they should have the best for luck. But they'd refused, agreeing only to let her take them out for a meal after the concert.

She'd burst in on them that morning, though there was nothing left to say. Josie was fussing over collars and hems and Lila stood at the mirror, applying foundation thickly over the rash on her freshly shaved jaw.

Rose had wanted to reach out and stroke that lonely jaw. Their music would bring people out that night. They'd be desired, she and Lila, that night, and for something higher than physical love, something for which solitude had prepared them. Loneliness would not touch them that night, could not hurt them, should be celebrated, even, seeing what they were able to do, each in her solo orbit.

More people were crowding into the concert hall, wedging the doors open. Sand and salt crunched on the terrazzo floor. In a dim corner of the lobby, the other composers huddled with Melody, who was clad in lace and attended by a pair of small, frightened daughters in identical velveteen. Perched on a stairway overlooking the lobby, Rose gazed down on the park where the Carnival ice sculptures stood, pitted and half-melted beneath the new snow.

"A night composers dream of," said the Director, gliding up the stairs to link arms with Rose. "Look there. It's the critic from the *Star*. I hope you're happy."

Rose felt lightheaded and blank, but happy? No—she was itchy with dread.

"And the guy from the *Dispatch*. Dear lord, the critics are here, and they *never* come," breathed the Director.

Rose's work was done, and she understood her ceremonial function. She'd chosen her clothes with almost superstitious care: short, black leather skirt; black stockings; cobalt-blue heels; and retro black cardigan, embroidered and beaded, which she'd buttoned up backward so her front was draped with a net of jet beads. Who *was* that in the mirror with the shaved legs, the sparkling chest, the hair brushed to a luster, the fiery lipstick?

Alan approved entirely—high time she let the world see she was beautiful.

Could wear beautiful *clothes*, she'd retorted. She felt not so much beautiful as armored.

If luck could be bought, she should be very lucky. Concert costs, clothes, restaurant meals, and presents had spent down the grant money entirely and bit into her savings. However, she had a new job with Artists in the Schools and she'd found a sublet in the city. And it had been easy to tell Emma, who had seemed to expect that Rose would be going.

Guy appeared across the lobby with Marguerite on his shoulder, muffled to the chin in the jingle-bell scarf Rose had given her at Christmas. Natalie, in a hooded shawl as large as a blanket, leaned cozily against him. Their mother shook snow off a wide velvet hat, showering her neighbors. She snapped her eyes around the room, found Rose, and waved. Then her hand stopped mid-air. At the end of the lobby stood Rose's father.

No one had seen him in the five years since he'd quit the family home for a cell of a room and a chair at a communal table, somewhere in Kentucky. Rose could hardly sneer—except for particulars of belief, his commune was probably something like the Goat Pasture. He wore a gold cross, visible from a distance. Tall and rangy, his hair grayer and longer than she had ever seen it, he had on his ancient black suit, which she and Natalie had always called his fancy suit, but which was really his only suit. He straightened, sucked in his gut, and stepped toward their mother.

Marion raised a hand again in frantic summons to Rose, who fled into the coatroom and peeked out from among the coats to follow the progress of her parents' reunion. They faced off a few feet apart. Then the crowd pressed in on them and her mother unexpectedly moved up close and placed a hand on her father's chest. And he reached up and covered her hand with his. What on earth? After all the rage and accusations? The sight of those two hands, one covering the other, burned Rose's eyes. Their need of each other seemed somehow pathetic, something they ought to have forfeited by now. But, of course, Rose was stronger than any of them.

Oh, why had she invited them, her wretched, complicated family: father, mother, sister, baby niece, and Guy, whatever he was—her sort of brother-in-law? Her concert would soon begin in front of them, becoming theirs as much as hers, theirs to consume and dismiss and turn quickly into the past—Rose's little evening, remember that?

The house doors opened and the lobby began to empty into the auditorium. Someone spoke her name at the coatroom door. She pulled the coats close and peered out. It was dear Alan, who'd blasted her with bagpipes that morning as she lay asleep on his couch. All day he'd been dragging in boxes of food, flowers, and drink for the after-concert party he was giving her. He turned and shouted a hello, and Wilma hove into view wearing a cotton rainbow of a dress, too flimsy for winter, beneath the ratty old muskrat coat that Rose had used as bed covering her final nights at the farm. Noah, in a little suit, clung to Wilma's hand. Peggy and

Dinah came after, dressed in skirts and hose and looking about them faintheartedly.

Rose huddled more deeply in among the coats and stroked a Persian lamb, softly whorled and glistening with drops of melted snow. It gave off the warm scent of cedar. She took it from its hanger and slipped into the flow of its satin lining. It fit her, the sleeves so long she could scrunch her hands up into the cuffs. In the pocket she felt a lump, two lumps—foil-wrapped chocolates. Nice ones, embossed with fleurs-de-lis. The coat fit her like an embrace. It was her night, wasn't it? She wanted the coat. She'd steal it, walk out of there and keep on going.

The coatroom attendant cast a kindly, myopic eye on her.

"Jitters," she said aloud, and slid out of the coat and hung it up, but took the chocolates. She'd do them an honor, the woman who owned the coat and the man who'd undoubtedly bought it for her. Rose had no one to buy her a coat, and it *was* her night. They'd be feeding the composer. Chocolates. She noticed that she seemed to have lost her mind.

There was a commotion in the lobby and a sharp voice called, "Rose? Rose MacGregor?"

She handed a chocolate to the coatroom attendant and made her way out.

Frances stood at the ticket table without a reservation. "I'm on your list, aren't I?"

They hadn't spoken since the night that summer when Frances had rushed away from the Goat Pasture, bidding Rose to howl at the moon.

"Friend of the composer," Rose blurted, and Frances snatched up a ticket.

Rose spotted Emma, motioning frantically for her to go into the auditorium. The doors were closing. Alan was saving seats, and Emma would wait for Ursula, who was coming from the airport.

Rose made her way in, unsteady in her heels, feeling herself watched. A seat was taped off for her at the end of a row near the middle of the house. She sat down heavily and looked to see who might be sitting next to her. No one she knew, she was relieved to find.

She was wrong. Victor Zeiss, her former student, his hair now grown to his shoulders, turned to her with a slow smile, and beyond him sat a whole row of her former students. She could have screamed. Had everyone she'd ever met in her life found their way to the concert hall? Of course they had. She'd invited them. Across the aisle sat Professor Harold Atkinson in velvet jacket and ascot, and Doris Atkinson in silky blue.

"Nervous? No, not *much*," observed Victor.

She'd liked him, she remembered. Or he'd liked her. Something. She tugged her skirt down.

"Cute," he said. "Very cute, professor. Or may I call you Rose?"

"You always called me Rose." She handed him the other chocolate. He grinned, unwrapped it, and popped it in his mouth. The house lights dimmed.

Lila and Josie took their places in the dark and, as the audience quieted, began to play. To start before the lights came up had been Lila's scheme for averting any applause that might greet her reappearance on stage. It didn't work. As soon as she was halfway visible, a cheer broke forth from the packed hall and a dozen people jumped to their feet.

Lila raised her bow, the crowd quieted, and she and Josie began again. *Marguerite*: little peeping noises flew up the scale. The violin lifted the heavier voice of the cello, the way Marguerite could raise Rose's spirits and make her forget her burdens.

It was over almost before it began—a minute and a half, and it was done.

Was it any good? A silence fell in the concert hall, a puzzled silence, she feared.

Victor turned to her and mouthed, "Wow," as applause broke, loud and zestful, with a stomping of feet. Several rows ahead, Guy raised Marguerite aloft, once, twice, three times.

Lila and Josie bowed and went off, clearing the stage for Melody's musicians, and Rose sagged in her seat, relieved, even if the applause was more for Lila than anything else.

To the sound of a harp, Rose became dimly aware that Emma had come in with Ursula, who was wearing a wild, feathered thing around her shoulders and leading some tall person.

It seemed barely a moment later that intermission arrived. Guy, on his way to the lobby, paused at the far aisle, his face flushed. He jiggled Marguerite's arm, making it wave to her. "*Bears in the Oats?*" he called, pointing to the program. "My bears? *Our* bears?"

"The very same." She hadn't thought to warn him.

He gave her a long look. She struggled to her feet and went to hide in the dressing room.

It was very quiet there with Lila and Josie. Ten minutes and it would be their concert, Rose's music all the way to the end.

She was in her seat again and Lila's bow was in motion and Josie's fingers moved across the piano keys. Rose tried to listen. The notes clipped dryly by. The young man beside her, Victor, reached over and shook her elbow and she realized she'd been humming along.

"Sorry," she gulped.

He rested his hand on the back of her neck. It felt warm and strangely welcome. She had the shocking impulse to rub her neck against his hand. She shrugged and the hand dropped away. She fingered the beaded sweater on her chest and then realized she appeared to be caressing herself. Applause erupted. She brought her hands together.

The lights went down and as the sound baffles were moved apart, a spotlight widened on the pink-clad Persephone mural, and the choir in pink took its place on the risers in front of the recumbent goddess. Laughter. The concert hall bubbled and filled. Wave followed wave of laughter; people laughed and then laughed at themselves laughing. Josie lifted her baton once, twice, three times.

And at last, Rose dropped into her music as the choir sang, growled, and breathed, and in the pauses the audience answered with laughter, and then with what seemed to be a sighing in unison. The cello stood alone and then picked the choir up on its broad back, a bear in the sun. The choir sang a roaring chord and the cello ruminated, chewing on an oat stem.

Guy was seated just three rows in front of her. He held his head absolutely still as Lila launched into the final movement. Marguerite was pressed up against his shoulder and, as Rose watched, she reached and buried her hand in Guy's hair and twirled her fingers. Rose couldn't take her eyes away from that little hand, twirling a lock of hair, those tiny fingers trailing over the tender skin beneath. The touch was merely that of a baby at play, yet it seemed to generate heat, a heat akin to her mother's hand pressing her father's chest, a heat both fascinating and dreadful—what touch promised, what it could not provide.

The final movement was a solo called *Never*. Rose couldn't quite explain the title, but it seemed Lila could, asserting what might be and never was, leading them through desire and onward, not bravely so much as steadily, for bravery existed in the company of others, but became mere steadiness in solitude, though no less difficult for that, and then became ease—*not* resignation, never resignation, but peace. Natural as breathing. The music breathed.

Rose wondered how she ever could have wished to be rid of Lila. Lila was her greatest luck, her example. If Lila could stand it, she could. She could go it alone.

And now there was nothing left to hope for or to dread. Her concert was over. She made her way up the aisle, heading backstage, as people, strangers, grabbed and hugged her.

"Thank you. Thank you for coming," she said. She recognized a critic and veered away, but he stopped her and offered his hand.

Then the Director slid into place beside her. "My god, he shook your hand."

Wilma, Dinah, and Peggy surrounded her. Little Noah bowed at the waist. Then Alan clasped her to him, followed by Frances, who enclosed Rose's hand in both of hers.

Alan would expect Rose back at his place for the party by ten o'clock, no later. He and Frances withdrew and stood conversing, apparently at peace. Frances reached and put her hand on Alan's arm, and Alan stood unflinching. All was well, if only Rose could feel it. She tried to summon a feeling of well-being which surely should be hers now. Harold and Doris Atkinson ferried up and Doris said a friendly hello to Frances. Peace. All manner of things were well. Then her father's arms were around her. "Praise the Lord," he said, beaming, and then the crowd intervened and he edged off toward the table where Emma was pouring wine.

Rose's mother gripped her elbow. "I don't know about the pink," she said. But before Rose could ask her to clarify, Ursula's arms were around her neck and a feather boa was choking her and Ursula's mystery guest, a gangly man with a sloping forehead, stood by.

"Remember this old thing?"

Rose brushed feathers out of her face. A name floated up. Bogdan. Bogdan, the Russian scholar, who'd left Ursula stuck with the apartment lease.

"Nice music," said Bogdan.

"Nice?" cried Ursula. "No, it was brilliant. *Brilliant!*" Her tone bespoke passion and privacy rather than argument. Ursula and Bogdan were together again? How on earth, and *why?*

"All that pink? I don't know if I'd say brilliant," said Rose's mother. "There was a certain kitsch factor, wouldn't you say, Ursula? Wouldn't you have to say?"

"Hel-*lo*, Marion," Ursula sang out. "And aren't we in form tonight?"

But Marion didn't hear. She'd gone off to Rose's father and the glass of wine he held out for her. Emma, at the refreshment table, gave Rose a bright salute, but the sense of well-being Rose had summoned would not come. As she watched, Emma hoisted a wine jug, and her hands shook so badly she had to put it down again. She turned away and hugged herself a minute, and Rose realized she'd seen this once or twice before, a new aspect of Emma, aging and uncertain.

Lila. Rose needed Lila. The sight of Lila would restore the evening to her.

"Excuse me," Rose said to the latest well-wishers. "I've got to thank my musicians." She made it to the apron of the stage, where a hand caught hers and pulled her down. Guy sat there, his eyes streaming. He swiped at his face and bounced Marguerite, who craned around to look at him and fussed uncertainly.

"Thanks for coming," Rose said lamely. "I should have warned you about *Bears.*"

He shook his head. "I made my commitment," he managed to say.

"Oh? You guys are getting married?" She found she could ask quite casually.

He looked at her hard and shrugged.

"It's okay," she said. "You love her."

"Do I?" he said, his voice breaking.

She pulled back. What was he doing? She'd made her peace with her solitude.

Natalie flung herself down beside them. "Oh, here you are. Guess what? Dad's taking Mom out for supper. They're *talking.*"

"Great. Wonderful. Excuse me." Rose got up and nearly ran.

The backstage corridor was packed. People were asking for Lila, but the dressing room door seemed to be locked, so Rose went in another way.

Lila sat in a chair with Josie in her lap. They were locked in a kiss, so absorbed in one another they did not see Rose at first. Then Josie jumped up and they moved apart.

"Oh, my," said Rose, unsteadily. Of course she should have knocked. But all day she'd been coming and going from their dressing room.

"Well," said Lila gently, "yeah."

Rose took a breath. "Okay," she said. "Okay. I mean, congratulations."

"We did good?" Josie asked her. Lila laughed awkwardly.

"Wonderfully well," Rose said. "You played utterly, fantastically well."

"See?" said Josie. Lila wrapped her arms around Josie again and grinned foolishly.

"I think," said Rose, "I'll just step out and clear my head. Oh, but you must be starved."

"We'll go and claim a table," said Josie.

Rose slipped out the stage door and into the park, no coat, no hat, stepping gingerly in her heels. The snow had stopped and the paths had been plowed. Under a clear sky, the temperature was dropping, turning the wet sidewalk to ice. She teetered along a row of lights, pretending to tour the half-melted sculptures—an eagle, a lightning bolt, and a lion.

Tomorrow the reviews would be out and they'd be good, possibly raves. That was something to hang on to: columns of black and white where her name would appear, her place in the world. Perhaps she would recognize herself in print.

She examined the eagle with its beak and wing tips melted, the lightning bolt softened to a standing noodle, the lion with its face melted smooth of features.

No matter how people had flocked to her concert, she'd go to bed by herself that night, while Lila curled up with Josie, Ursula with Bogdan, Natalie with Guy, Doris Atkinson with her Harold, possibly even her mother with her father. Emma was alone, but she'd had her husband and her children. Rose had made such a big deal, such a cause of being alone. But that hadn't been hard to accomplish, had it? What was solitude but an absence, a lack? Really, it was nothing at all.

PART TWO

"Now you are tangled up in others and have
forgotten what you once knew. . . ."
                            —Kabir, "The Radiance,"
                            version by Robert Bly

Chapter SEVENTEEN

On a bright Sunday afternoon in late March, the week before Easter, Rose lay in her kimono, lolling in bed on her sun porch, when a knock came at the door. It was not a knock she knew, not Alan's boom-boom, nor Frances's rhythmic rat-a-tat, nor little Max's soft thud when Frances held him up to do the honors. The Gilpins—Alan, Frances, and their son, Max—lived upstairs, and their descending footfall usually warned her before any knock came.

"Just a sec," Rose called and tightened her sash.

Downstairs, the front door lock had been changed the week before by Alan. He was president of the condo association and security-minded: outside locks should be changed every two years. It was, however, a *lit*tle schizophrenic, to use his phrase, that he hadn't yet managed to deliver new keys, so the front door stood unbolted all day. Anyone could be knocking. Though the tangled streets of the neighborhood around the college tended to discourage outsiders—so easy to get lost there—it was still a city neighborhood, and the only thing between Rose and the street was her door with its peephole. She peeped out and didn't see anyone. The knock came again, down low.

She opened the door to a strange little creature, a girl of five or six. There was something of the wild animal about her, like a squirrel or raccoon. Her snarled brown hair was held back by a worn velvet headband, and she twisted her hands—paws, really: her fingernails seemed both sharp and bitten—and gazed at Rose through widely spaced eyes of a peculiarly intense shade of blue. In her patched-together jacket, which seemed to be missing buttons entirely, Rose recognized something, and looked into the blue eyes as into a mirror, feeling absurdly that she was looking at herself. Yet a real little girl stood before her.

"Aunt Rose?" the girl said, in a tiny, tremulous voice.

"Marguerite?" breathed Rose, and knelt. "You're Marguerite, aren't you?"

The girl nodded curtly.

"Well, *come in,*" said Rose. She hadn't seen her niece since Natalie and Guy had struck off for Mexico a month after her Composer's Guild concert, on a winter vacation that had stretched into years, six years. For all Rose knew, they'd settled there.

The little girl took a step inside and looked around, and then peered up at Rose through her lashes. It was pure Natalie, that look, exact to the tilt of the chin—dauntingly innocent and at the same time obscurely scheming.

"Where's Natalie?" asked Rose, craning into the hall. The little girl stood at the threshold of the sun porch, leaning on her toes toward the unmade bed.

"Where's your mama?" Rose asked again.

The girl wriggled out of the knapsack on her shoulders and let it drop to the floor.

"Guy's sposed to get me," she said.

However, out the windows, all the parked cars were familiar. Guy's truck, if he still had the truck, was nowhere in evidence.

"Uh-huh," said Rose. "Your dad's coming to get you?"

"He's not my dad." She tiptoed back to the kitchen. "Guy?" she called.

"Guy's with your mom, do you think? Maybe they dropped you off here for a visit?"

Marguerite shook her head.

"Well. Are you hungry? Can I take your jacket? I'm very glad to see you."

The girl pulled the patchwork closer, dragged out a chair from the table, and sat. Once a plate of scrambled eggs was placed before her, she warily picked up her fork. Her chin floated only inches above the tabletop. Rose reached for the phone books little Max sat on, but Marguerite refused them.

"I'm not a baby."

"No, you're not," Rose carefully agreed.

"I'm in first grade. At Lincoln School."

"I see. Where's Lincoln School? Someplace close, or far away?" Every town and city in the country probably had a Lincoln School.

Marguerite shrugged and swallowed her mouthful of eggs. "I'm on Easter vacation."

Rose buttered and offered a caramel roll. And could not resist resting a hand briefly on the shoulder of her small guest, this little girl with blue-blue eyes whom she herself had named. Sunlight rolled from the porch through the living room, pouring over the piano and into the kitchen alcove where they sat. The apartment was like one great room: dark woodwork, glossy white paint, and long oak floor. Rose used the sun porch for a bedroom and the little space behind the kitchen as her study. She had no need for doors to shut—she had no one to get away from.

Munching the caramel roll, the little girl slid from her seat and stepped toward the piano, pausing at the telephone by Rose's big chair.

"Do you want to make a call?"

Marguerite considered, shook her head, and went on to the piano, reaching out to stroke its cherrywood side. A baby grand with exceptional tone, though requiring frequent tuning, the piano was a thirtieth-birthday present Rose had bought herself three years before, when the Chamber

Orchestra had commissioned a song cycle. She sometimes felt that the piano was an island on which she stood with her cat. Or maybe it was her good ship—evidence of having traveled far.

The girl regarded the open keyboard and wiped her hands on her jacket.

"Go ahead, Marguerite."

"Meggy."

"You go by Meggy?"

"Yah." She pressed a key, and then dropped both fists onto the keyboard. Rose came over to demonstrate, but the girl was back at the table, examining the last of the rolls.

"Listen, Meggy, do you think you could explain how you got here and what we're doing?" Meggy reached a bitten hand to her face and rubbed an eye. "You don't have to worry. You can stay here as long as you like." Rose handed her the roll, and she slipped it into some inner pocket behind the fraying flaps of her jacket. "I've got plenty of food, you know," said Rose, "and you can sleep on my couch or in my big bed with me if you want."

"Your big bed!"

Meggy rushed to the porch, dived into the covers, and fingered the scalloped satin edge of the comforter. Then she pulled the comforter over her, leaving no part exposed except for feet in muddy little shoes. Rose reached and slipped the shoes off. Her tortoiseshell cat emerged from under the bed and fixed them with an outraged stare.

"Jewels, this is Meggy," Rose told the cat severely.

From deep in the bedding came a whimper of joy. Meggy peeked out, eyes aglow.

Footsteps came up the hall, followed by a tapping at the door. Natalie, Rose guessed.

It was, instead, the piano tuner, the baggy-suited one from that long-ago night of her Guild concert. She'd gotten herself on his waiting list soon after she bought her piano, and after a wait—he was a sort of star among piano tuners—he had come and acquainted himself with her piano, which he'd approached like a trainer approaching a horse. Writing out his checks, she'd sometimes struggled to keep a straight face, having overheard him in his baggy suit and his suspenders, earnestly talking to her piano.

She'd left him a message, the day before, that one of her keys was sticking, but she hadn't expected him to come around so soon, and certainly not on a Sunday.

"I'm in the neighborhood," he said, looking past her to the piano. He gave his case an easy swing, though Rose, having hefted it, knew it weighed a ton. He was slight in build but obviously stronger than he looked. She stepped aside, adjusting her kimono.

Meggy came and peeked from under her aunt's elbow as the tuner reached into the piano. He had short, dense, dark hair and a mobile face that would have been clownish if not for an impression of stillness and shyness. His hands were big and knobby at the knuckles and moved with their own separate life, as when, while in conversation with Rose, his fingers went on with testing and tuning and sometimes played a progression of notes and chords.

"Your daughter?" he asked. Meggy went starry-eyed and picked up the end of Rose's kimono sash to rub between her fingers.

"My niece," she said proudly. "Meggy, this is Graham Lowe."

He ran his fingers down the keyboard. Nothing stuck—it was as though healed. But he wasn't satisfied. "I'll have to come back," he said and went.

Meggy piled back into the thick of the covers and lay humming through goose down.

"Meggy, can you hear me? Guy's going to pick you up? Do you know when?"

"*Now*," came the little voice, sleepy and a touch cranky.

"You go on and sleep," Rose said and ran upstairs to consult Frances and Alan.

When she'd first bought her condo, the Gilpins had so admired it that she'd felt obliged to call them when the one above went on the market. The turn-of-the-century brick building was sullen and sooty on the outside but had treasures within: parquetry tiles at the entryway, leaded glass that shot rainbows, wainscoting never touched by paint. The oak floors resounded satisfyingly when Rose played, and the high ceilings made the smallness of the rooms seem snug rather than closed-in. She knew the people above and below, and no one objected when she pounded away on the piano or droned on the cello. The Gilpins never did, even when Max was tiny. And as Max was of the shouting, galloping sort, things were in balance between the two households, at least with respect to noise.

The Gilpins' condo ran the length of the building, affording them a nursery for Max and an ample master bedroom at the back. For obvious reasons, Rose was glad that Alan and Frances didn't sleep on the sun porch directly above her bed. Their living room overlay hers, but Rose's view was into a thicket of mulberries, which gave forth a thrumming, chiming, rasping, ever-changing bird concert when she threw the windows open in summer. The Gilpins' view soared out over the rooftops to the bell tower of Old Main on the campus where Rose once again taught, and where Alan had, five years earlier, succeeded in winning tenure.

Rose was now up for tenure herself and recalled how nervous Alan had been those years before, and the grief she'd given him. Now she understood what had made him so nuts: the awareness of judgment from every quarter, of the criticism possible from any faculty member or staffer, any student, or secretary, even, that might tip the scales, though by appearances they were all such pals, such a community. She had no real reason to worry. Her music was getting wide play and, as she was the only composer on campus, she was considered a shoo-in for tenure and had been told so, the murmured assurance passed on to her in the tone of the ultimate compliment. It had actually begun to annoy her. She wanted the job, but she could do without the secret handshake.

She hoped tenure was worth it to Alan. He'd paid an enormous price for it. It wasn't her business, but she couldn't help think of the household above her as brought into being by accident—or rather by misadventure.

On an afternoon five years earlier, Rose, just rehired at the college, and Alan, his tenure decision imminent, had stood side by side, sorting through their mail slots. There was nothing unusual in Frances chatting away in the Chairman's office, but Rose and Alan, by mischance, were hidden from sight behind the Chair's open door. If they'd been standing even a few feet over, Frances would have seen them and shut up. As it was, her clear, low voice emerged as though on a ribbon of foul-smelling smoke. She was telling the Chair that, since he had asked, she found Alan a bit peculiar, though terribly nice, of course. Hearing this, Alan had turned to stone, while Frances went on to say, in a quiet little voice, that Alan was maybe a trifle needy toward students, seeing as he lacked a family life, and that it possibly made for a not quite healthy, not entirely wholesome atmosphere.

Rose had been unable to drag Alan away and, afterward, failed to dispel his fright. She told him Frances's opinion meant nothing. It was known that Alan and Frances had had a failed affair, that Frances would have an ax to grind. *Since you asked,* Frances had said, but that was no proof that the Chair *had* asked her. Chairs had to nod and let people run on about things. Rose had assured Alan that what Frances had said was more a reflection on her than on Alan—*she* was the lonely, needy one. Why, she'd gotten involved with Atkinson himself, once upon a time—didn't Alan remember?

Of course he remembered, but it made no difference. The fact that he'd met every tenure requirement and that everyone knew that his relations with students were above reproach seemed to mean nothing to him. Rose commanded him to stand back and let the wheels turn. Instead, in a fit of proving himself to be unpeculiar and thoroughly wholesome, he took Frances to bed again and then, seeming to turn his whole life over to the proof, asked her to move in with him. To Rose's mind, it was a slow-motion wreck, the accidental overhearing, then the extreme and lengthy response. By the end of the school year, he and Frances were engaged.

Maybe they did cherish each other, the Gilpins. They seemed to. Having had Max, they were in deep, and Rose with them—she was god-mother. She saw them daily, ate with them—if she wasn't at supper, they'd want to know why—and counted herself lucky, never as lonely as she would have been without them. But she was also, secretly, their anthro-pologist—and a skeptical one. How could she not study them? She wanted to know if long-term love—if marriage—was ever any good, and the Gilpins were her only example close at hand.

Six months after Max was born, they'd moved in above her and begun the habit of leaving their door open to her, literally ajar every night and all day on the weekends. Their door opened into a book-lined foyer, and no one walking by could see very far in. And no one but Rose and her cat would venture beyond Max's scissor fence, which expanded to the width of the doorway. Her firmament, she called them, her domestic heaven, which was where she went once she was certain Meggy had fallen asleep.

"What's happening in heaven?" she called out, and followed Jewels in, stepping carefully over the turrets and buttresses of Max's multicolor block castle.

All was going smoothly in heaven. Alan crouched on his hand-knotted Oriental rug, blowing razzberries on Max's belly, both in a roaring frenzy. At three, Max had a voice bigger than his size, a shock of hair black as his father's beard, and his mother's sharp nose and chin.

On Alan's wonderful old couch where Rose had slept so many nights, now freshly upholstered in many-leafed tapestry, Frances reclined, pre-viewing the *Sunday Times* Arts Section for her husband. The picture of chic wife-and-motherhood, she wore a nubby tunic and wide trousers, knockoffs from the pages of *Vogue,* chosen by Alan and tailored by a pal in the college theater's costume shop. Her closet was full of handmade one-of-a-kinds, and her hair was shorn to a close helmet, boyish except for the way it came to smooth points either side of her chin. Alan had chosen her scent, a man's cologne, actually, but who was to know? She moved with a newly won grace, courtesy of modern dance class, and now knew when to throw a pose, exposing her remarkable profile. Alan adored showing her off, and Max, whenever he could. They made a winsome picture: elfin child, gamin wife, handsome, athletic father and citizen of growing substance: condo president, head of faculty oversight, chair of the Minneapolis Jazz Festival.

The Gilpins' burgeoning style spilled over onto Rose. Alan had forced her to retire her old station wagon, replacing it with his leather-seated Volvo when they upgraded to an Audi. Rose had mounted a protest—*what am I, your daughter?*—but he'd threatened to sink the Volvo in the river *after* he'd sunk her station wagon. So Rose accepted the car and, likewise, Frances's expertise concerning dress for her premieres. She allowed herself to be dragged out to try on and actually buy wonderful clothes. However, she never managed to inhabit what she wore quite as Frances did, and her life was never as full as theirs.

She had her premieres. And, as Frances' prediction continued in force, there was always some new man ready to grab Rose up and ask her out. But what did it matter, if whoever it was grabbed but couldn't take hold? An affair would flare up and then fall to ashes, ashes piled on ashes, a deepening bed of ashes. Each man was in some way wrong and seemed to know it—the men disqualified themselves almost as quickly as she did. She'd lost confidence in trial and error and had come to doubt her own judgment so far as to feel almost virginal again, not older, but startlingly young, and uncertain what her life should be. She confided it all in Frances and Alan, who seemed rather to enjoy guiding her. She was not their daughter; she was their friend, and had given up scrutinizing friendship. If she had people close enough to share meals and confidences, she thought it ought to be enough, even if it didn't always feel so. She did have a life. She had the Gilpins. She had students and colleagues. A strange, small part of her exulted that she was still alone, that she'd managed to come this far unencumbered, that no one and nothing could impede her work. And, really, how could she tend a love affair when she was always leaving town, often for weeks on end?

She'd secured a commission from an orchestra out West, and she was writing a symphony.

When she was feeling optimistic after an award or a new commission, the lucky-in-love hope sometimes returned, and she imagined she'd finally meet some conductor or star musician who would match her in the limelight and make her long wait for the right man seem prudent. The conductors and star musicians she knew, however, were married, gay, or preoccupied. And she had to admit that she was finding it increasingly difficult to meet men anywhere at all. Maybe she'd gotten too picky. Maybe it was her age. She had the beginnings of crow's feet.

She went out at night with Alan and Frances as a threesome. They did not allow her to baby-sit Max (there were students for that), but dragged her along to movies and concerts. Third wheel, she called herself. But they seemed to require her presence. This was the shaky side of things, their need of Rose as a buffer. Alan had had a series of boyfriends Frances knew nothing about. As secretary, Frances worked regular hours, whereas he came and went and could claim night rehearsals and coaching sessions where none existed. Rose was sometimes aware of an unfamiliar footfall overhead in the day and of other sounds. And, of course, he told her things. Frances was in the dark, he liked to say, and Frances enjoyed being in the dark. He claimed to have a divided heart, which wasn't so bad—sort of like being ambidextrous.

"And she *does* know," he was wont to say. "On some level, she knows."

"But not on any useful one," Rose would reply. She worried that Frances might be suffering, as though from an undiagnosed illness. Alan's voice at times became satirical in his wife's presence. Sometimes he took a tone so fey that Rose had to look hard at Frances to believe she didn't know. Rose was forever on the verge of raising a question about it to Frances. But something in Frances, a fierce, deflecting self-possession, always stopped Rose from saying anything. Maybe Frances did like being in the dark.

Though muted around Alan, Frances still had her wild side and an unexpected sense of humor. It was a mistake to laugh *at* Frances, but Frances, telling stories on other people, could render Rose helpless with laughter. Frances claimed that Alan talked in his sleep and would answer questions and even sing if she started him on a simple tune—"Three Blind Mice," for example. She offered a wicked imitation of his sleep-stupored singing voice, the tune precise but the words all vowels as though he were toothless or drugged or hypnotized.

However chatty she might be about other people, Frances revealed none of her troubles to Rose. Alan maintained that they hadn't made love in the three-plus years since Frances had become pregnant with Max. But could Rose believe him? They were so demonstrative, Alan and Frances. They claimed each other in dozens of ways: Frances leaned against Alan; he rested his hands on her shoulders; and they kissed casually, publicly, sometimes with a quick mingling of tongues.

How could Rose say what made a marriage? They drove her a little crazy with what she might be missing. Not that they were stingy or exclusive with affection. Doubt and envy lay uneasily buried beneath Rose's gratitude for the tenderness they offered her. They hugged and kissed her every day, Frances on both cheeks, French-style, and warmly, as though for her own comfort as much as for Rose.

Rose sometimes deliberately put them at a distance, demanding to stay at home with Max, sending Frances and Alan out without her.

Frances, too, on occasion put a distance between herself and Rose by being disagreeable. Why Rose would keep a studio at the Goat Pasture, Frances couldn't fathom—that godforsaken farm with those peculiar women? Then Frances would remember genius, Lila's genius: Rose went out there to be near Lila's genius. Frances believed Alan also to be a genius. Her views on "peculiar" people were in this way consistent.

Frances admired Rose, too, tremendously; but luck was the theme, rather than genius.

Rose decried her luck in love, but Frances sweetly contradicted her.

"Look what a life you have. Look at your concerts, your awards, your travel."

It was true. Rose had all those things and was likely to go on having them. Tenure would soon be made official, probably in the upcoming autumn. The Chair liked to say how glad he was that the college could boast a really good woman composer.

"As opposed to one of the many lousy women composers?" Rose wanted to ask, but she knew the Chair could do without her being difficult.

Doris Atkinson had succumbed to what, after testing, had proved to be early Alzheimer's and was no longer seen in public. Her appearance was said to be unchanged, smooth and freckle-faced, youthful as ever, but she was unaware of who or where she was, and messy as a toddler.

Frances reported all this. She went several times a week to help with Doris. Rose didn't quite get this. Had Frances not seemed happy with Alan, Rose might have surmised that Frances, in making herself such a constant presence at the Atkinsons', was gloating over a fallen rival.

The Chair, at any rate, meant to compliment Rose, his "really *good* woman composer," and did much to help her. He saw to it that others in the department covered her classes when she needed to travel, and Frances and Alan brought in her mail, took phone messages, and fed Jewels. And when Rose was home, they were there to turn to in times of sorrow, irritation, or anger. Or of puzzlement, such as now, with the startling arrival of Meggy.

"Here you are," said Frances, casting aside her *Times* and bounding up to kiss Rose.

"You'll never guess who I have downstairs. All by herself."

Frances loved to guess. "Lila? No, Lila's still in London. Emma?"

Alan, his back on the rug, elevated on the soles of his upturned feet the delirious Max, who shot out his arms and roared airplane noises.

"Give a clue. Young or old?"

"Very, very young." Max dived from his perch and thrust himself into Rose's lap. She closed her arms around him and dipped her nose into his hair, which smelled vaguely soapy and vaguely doggy. "Marguerite. My niece, Marguerite. Six years old and all by herself, out of the blue. I don't know where she's come from or where she's supposed to be."

"She play wif me!" boomed Max.

Soon they were gathered in council—Frances, Alan, Max, Rose, and Meggy—at the Gilpins' table, eating Alan's delectable lasagna. His cooking had always been good, and now that he had a chef for a boyfriend, it was out of this world. Meggy asked for seconds and stared at her plate as if she couldn't fathom the flavors.

"So, Meggy," said Rose. "You came today just like magic. How'd you get here?"

Meggy said nothing, her eyes on her plate.

"You say Guy's coming to get you?"

"Sposed to." She swung her gaze solemnly around the circle. "It's visitation."

"Visitation?" said Frances. "That's divorce talk."

But to Rose's knowledge, Guy and Natalie had never married.

Meggy looked at Rose. "I can stay here if he doesn't come?"

"Absolutely."

The girl nodded as though sealing a contract, then opened the patchwork jacket and, from the pocket of her frayed overalls, brought out a scrap of paper with a penciled number on it. Rose dialed the number, but there was no answer. On a hunch, she tried directory assistance and found a new listing in St. Paul for Guy Robbin, the number matching the one on Meggy's paper.

Later that night, after talking Meggy out of her jacket, out of the crushed bit of roll in her pocket—there'd be fresh rolls in the morning—out of her overalls and her grayed underwear, and into bath and bed, Rose again dialed Guy's number, but without success.

Chapter EIGHTEEN

They were having a wonderful time, a time out of time, she and Meggy, her sprite, her mystery girl. Rose had to continue meeting classes, and so persuaded Max's daycare to take Meggy on a temporary basis. Rose was delighted to pay for that and for other things. She took pleasure in fulfilling Meggy's obvious need for a change or two of clothes and a nightgown.

And there was also the jacket. When she'd gone to get Meggy's clothes from the dryer that first night, she'd had a bad moment. Looking at the jacket closely, she saw just what was familiar about it: the patches were squares of fabric from her own clothes, good blouses and dresses she'd mailed to Natalie, care of Guy Robbin, General Delivery, at the Texas town on the Mexican border from which Guy's postcards had come. Apparently, the clothes had got through to Natalie, but why she'd cut them up and patched the pieces together so shoddily, Rose couldn't imagine. When she lifted the thing—jacket or wrap or whatever it was—

from the dryer, the zigzag stitches came apart and the batting shredded. In a single washing, it was ruined.

Not ruined, Alan told her—never say ruined. His pal in the theater costume shop mended the patchwork, then added ripstop nylon beneath and gussets to expand the size, a fleece collar, a hood, big pockets, and a zipper whose bright brass tongue zipped to Meggy's chin. Walking along the street with her niece, Rose saw her own history skipping ahead: plaid gabardine, freshman year of college; scarlet corduroy, antiwar marches; black crepe, that first little black dress Frances had chosen for her. The sight made Rose absurdly happy, as if bits of the past had come to life again and started off on their own toward new conclusions.

Rose had taken up running the previous spring, three miles each morning, an exhilarating if lonely endeavor. The route she took was down the big avenue to the cathedral and back, and, as she ran, she studied mansions and gardens. She'd come far in her career—how far might she go? Ridiculous thought. What would she want with a house with fifteen rooms?

She sometimes wished Alan was running with her, but he'd given it up in favor of weight training at the YMCA, which was one of the settings for his other life, so she didn't attempt to follow him there. When the weather turned chill, she kept on running. A cold January morning might sting; but after ten minutes at an even pace, she would warm up, and the repeat motion gave rise to a steady thrill, a sense of herself as unstoppable.

Sometimes she'd wake in the middle of the night to her own heartbeat, which seemed overly loud in the dark. Running after such a night made her feel that she was catching up with herself, calming her heart with a burst of legs and arms, like persuading a car engine to a lower idle by pumping the accelerator. She'd never been so healthy. Periodically, she took herself to her doctor to hear once again that she was fine. He made her listen to a recording of the heartbeat of a healthy, adult woman and then, through his stethoscope, to her own heart. Then he'd ask if she was having enough fun.

She thought so. She was thriving—a steady income, commissions, future seasons taking shape. She'd struck a vein, and grant was followed by fellowship as the powers that were—foundations, orchestras, arts boards, endowments—hurried to endorse one another's judgment. Not that merit had no bearing. She was good, but she was also in fashion, a woman composer. And while she was hot, she was making the most of it. She was now recognized on the street in St. Paul, if that was a sign of thriving, and invited inside the mansions to sit on the down-filled furniture and partake of food prepared by private chefs under multi-prismed light, herself an ornament, *our composer.* Neighbors, former students, and even vague acquaintances looked for an excuse to chat with her, asking in hushed tones about the latest concert, the upcoming premiere. She'd been interviewed and photographed often enough that complete strangers sometimes greeted her by name, and if that unnerved her, she recognized it as success. She'd wanted the world, and she guessed she had it.

Lila had recorded three of her pieces and, in lieu of a royalty, had built Rose a studio, a quiet place of her own at the Goat Pasture. A white hut with a steeply pitched roof on a knoll overlooking the river, it had a futon that rolled up into a cabinet, and its own tiny kitchen with a wood stove. Rose had country and city and music and people, even children—Max and now Meggy, who was hers so all-of-a-sudden, not just for an afternoon, but hour after hour.

Putting Meggy to bed beside her, Rose found her own heartbeat hardly worth notice. She'd smooth a lock of the little girl's hair or adjust the comforter to cover a small foot. From time to time she tried to get Guy by phone, but was pleased enough to find him never at home.

The front door was once again secure. She'd leaned on Alan to distribute new keys and gotten him to make an extra set for Meggy, a key for the front and a key for her apartment, so Meggy would always have them, strung on a ribbon with a cardboard tag labeled "Aunt Rose."

Meggy didn't care much about keys, but she reveled in her new clothes. She arranged and rearranged the dresser drawer that Rose cleared for her. In her new nightgown, blue with white stars, she danced dizzying spins.

She was not a sprite from fairyland, however, but a little girl who'd been dropped among people she didn't know, a child unused to such attentions. Sometimes she became overexcited. Sometimes she seemed to hold it against Max that he had a rocking horse, an electric train, and a set of a hundred building blocks, all colors, with a canvas tote to carry them wherever he might wish to build. Left alone with Max, Meggy clocked him on the head with the largest block in the set and then pronounced him spoiled when he let out a roar and Rose and Frances came running.

It was agreed that all Meggy needed was a little more spoiling herself. But then, several days into the visit, Meggy woke, sat straight up, and asked Rose to buy her a mini-bike. For a blind half-second, Rose could see it: Meggy on a miniature Harley—did they make such things?—with a helmet, of course, and a flying scarf. Still, actually buy a motorbike? They couldn't do something so dangerous without asking Natalie.

"What if we can't find her?" said Meggy.

Rose wasn't ready to consider that. "Oh, she'll find us. We'll just wait until she does."

"My mama would say yes," suggested Meggy with Natalie's sidelong grin.

With reluctance, Rose brought herself to say no, that six was too little for a motorbike. Meggy's face fell. She pulled the covers over her head and would not come to breakfast.

Rose was struck with wonder at the depth of Meggy's wanting, the powerful certainty that a motorbike was the essential thing, the only thing that would satisfy her. She recalled herself at Meggy's age and her everchanging visions of things to have. She remembered, too, how she'd strived to be good. It was a revelation that Meggy could tell fibs, could be greedy or messy or too rough, and none of it seemed very wrong. Why being good had been so important, Rose couldn't say. And it pained her not to get Meggy what she wanted, whatever it was, just because she wanted it.

Still, Rose was finding it somewhat tiring to attend day after day to the wants of another creature, however small and darling. Her life was, to an extent, on hold. A fatigue was building in her that early morning runs did not dispel. It occurred to her that she might not merely be running, but running *from* something. She always came back, though, to Meggy safe in bed behind locked doors, ready with her shy good-morning.

As the visit lengthened to five, then six days, Rose noticed, in addition to fatigue, trouble coping with Meggy in the afternoons and evenings, once she'd picked Max and Meggy up from daycare. She wanted to do better than dumping the two little combatants in front of the TV. A Parcheesi tournament led to flung dice and upturned boards. They went to the zoo, which, in March, was smelly, stuffy, and mud-tracked.

There was always shopping. Meggy was avid for shopping, and Rose kept meaning to curtail it, but a pink corduroy Easter dress with a ruffle at the neck and bird-shaped buttons seemed, once glimpsed, a necessity. Easter loomed at the end of the week. Meggy should have a basket and candy eggs and a chocolate rabbit. Rose was thrilled and exhausted and growing seriously uneasy about this extended game of theirs, hers and Meggy's. Was she the loving aunt, or some outlaw harboring a tiny fugitive? Had the little girl run away? Should Rose be calling the police?

Saturday, the day before Easter, seven days into the visit, Rose drooped in her big chair while Meggy and Max sat hypnotized in front of cartoons. Out in the street, a motor sputtered and died. A crow cawed in the mulberries, and then a commotion began out on the stairs, and there came a pounding on her door. The children continued to sit perfectly still and looked up only with reluctance when Rose opened the door to Guy, in a fury, who ran to Meggy and clutched her to his chest. Directly after him came Natalie, who rushed to Meggy and grabbed her hand.

"Give her to me," said Natalie. "Give me my baby."

"Until five, she's mine," he growled.

"That's only twenty more minutes," said Natalie.

"Would somebody like to explain this, Rose?" Guy said between clenched teeth.

Alan and Frances craned in from the hall. Frances beckoned to Max to run to her. "I hope it's okay that we let them in," said Alan.

Guy turned to Rose. "Am I welcome here?"

"Of course," she said, and waved Alan and Frances off.

She told Guy to sit down and pulled out a chair for Natalie. Meggy sat in Guy's lap, winding her arms through his. Natalie looked older: her face was puffy and lines had appeared, etched deep into layers of Mexican tan. Guy looked simply like himself.

During the week Meggy had spent with Rose, he'd been the one who'd called the police to report his former girlfriend and her daughter missing, the daughter with whom he had visitation rights that week.

"He took me to court," said Natalie. "Can you imagine?"

"*After* you threw me out and told me I'd never see Meggy again." He turned to Rose. "What—haven't you heard?"

"Not a thing. Nobody's told me anything."

"I thought you were on her side," he said. "She told me you were on her side."

"I haven't spoken to Natalie in, let's see, six years. Nobody's called me," said Rose. "I thought you all were in Mexico."

Not at all. Once Meggy was old enough for school, Guy had insisted they move back up to the States, to Minnesota; but there, things had fallen apart. He and Natalie had never married, though he'd certainly call this a divorce. He had an apartment and Natalie a room in a boarding house. Keeping the lights off, she'd faked a disappearance for most of the week; but when, that day, she'd gone out for groceries, he'd stepped out of his truck to meet her.

"You want to know where I was?" said Natalie. "With a friend you know nothing about."

"Oh, I doubt it. You were hunkered down in that room all week with the lights out."

"He is disrespectful," said Natalie, ticking off her complaints on her fingers, "he is controlling, he is disloyal." She looked, Rose thought, extremely frightened.

"Yeah, and four more pages of that on her legal pad. I also have rights."

The judge had not cared to read Natalie's legal pad. A court-ordered psychologist had offered the opinion that Meggy had bonded to Guy as her father, and, as certain hair-raising items had come to light about Natalie's mothering, the result had been visitation rights for Guy.

"Not that rights mean anything," he said.

"That's the system for you," said Natalie. "Men handing out rights to each other."

"We were together *six years*."

"Five and three quarters."

"As man and wife."

"*Man* and wife. That's the system for you."

"Sharing the same *bed*."

"Guy," said Rose and cocked her head toward Meggy.

"It's okay," said Natalie, stretching an arm across the table toward her daughter. "We don't keep secrets, do we, Marguerite?"

"Meggy," said the girl and stared blankly, her eyes like bright, receding stars. She began chewing her fingertips, like working her way along an ear of corn.

"She knows all about it. She knows how he is. Don't you, baby girl?"

"Jesus," said Guy.

"Watch your language," said Natalie.

Meggy plugged her mouth with her thumb.

"My *language*?" said Guy.

The friend Natalie had been "visiting" that week, the one about whom Guy knew nothing, was Jesus Christ. Natalie caressed the syllables—*Jesus Christ*.

"What happened to Quetzalcoatl, God of all the Aztecs?" Guy demanded.

Natalie had never before been religious, and it struck Rose that her sister's tone smacked of their father, who would certainly accept collect calls if the subject was Jesus.

"We've eaten the Aztec diet," said Guy. "And we've gone through a round of peeing and crapping from a squat on the toilet seat, in imitation of the ancient peoples."

Rose laughed in spite of herself and then swallowed, catching Meggy's gaze. Meggy regarded her as across a great distance and sighed.

"Five minutes more," said Natalie.

Guy staggered up, and Meggy slid off his lap. Quickly, he gathered the girl back to him, sat again, and tugged her thumb from her mouth, which released with a wet, popping sound.

"I've been in church," said Natalie and folded her hands. "I've been in the church, day and night, praying I would see my daughter again."

"What are you *talking* about?" said Guy. "You never left your apartment till now."

"The church of my own heart."

"That's strange," said Rose, who was in sudden danger of slapping Natalie. It had dawned on her what had transpired the past week and why. "Isn't that strange," said Rose, thinly, "when you knew where your daughter was all the time; when you could have come to see her at any moment?" Then she could have kicked herself, glancing at Meggy, who gazed at the ceiling, rapidly sucking her thumb again.

Rose calmed herself and lowered her voice. "Meggy, why don't you run upstairs to Frances and Maxie?"

The girl shook her head.

"All right," said Rose. What could she do but forge on? "Let me see if I've got this. You brought her here, didn't you, Natalie? Dropped her off without a word. A very nice surprise for me, Meggy," she told the little girl, "though I had to wonder: what was the plan? 'Guy's sposed to get me' is all you can tell me, Meggy. But," Rose gently concluded, "it turns out Guy can't come and get you, Meggy, because he has no idea where you are."

"Know what, Guy?" Natalie got lightly to her feet. "Meggy had your phone number. She could have called you if she wanted. Think about that. And now, time's up."

Natalie beckoned to Meggy.

"*Wait* a minute," said Rose and reached for the girl as Meggy headed toward her mother. For a fraction of a second, Meggy hesitated.

"We'll follow the law," barked Natalie, "since he brought the law into it." She hoisted her daughter and plunged out, Guy following, into the raw spring night.

Rapidly, Rose emptied the dresser drawer into Meggy's knapsack and stuffed in the patchwork jacket and the Easter dress, tucked around the Easter basket which held the candy and Meggy's set of keys. On the street, she shoved the things at Natalie, gave Meggy a hard hug, and then made herself go back inside. From her porch, she looked down to where Natalie and Guy stood shouting and Meggy hung against her mother, her thumb still planted in her mouth. She gazed at the little girl and closed her eyes, memorizing her. There was no predicting when she would see her again. Rose kept her eyes shut until the shouting faded and motors started up. Then they were gone and quiet enveloped her. She felt her heart start to clang.

A half hour later, Guy was back at her door. Uncertainly she let him in. He set down a six-pack of Dos Equis. "This is not my proudest hour." He pulled his hat off and swiped at his eyes. "Fuck. Why didn't I think to call you?"

"It's okay," she said, but it wasn't. She was so tired she could barely move, and part of her was jerking down a street somewhere, flung into a rattletrap car with Natalie driving. He took off his coat, and she let him rummage around and cook them something, half-listening to his rueful tales of their life in Mexico, the crazy jobs he'd taken: oil rigger, shrimper, pottery salesman. Rose was not much of a drinker, but before she knew it, she'd killed two beers.

They'd lived on the edge of the jungle in a thatched house. Natalie had tried to turn them into, first, Aztecs and then, when she found out about the blood sacrifices, Mayans. She'd had them sleeping in hammocks, grinding corn, chewing chicle sap. The locals found it comical, and Guy had seen their point. That's how he'd been *disloyal.*

Rose started to laugh, not because this was funny or funnier than any other remark of the evening, but because a wave of involuntary laughter was overtaking her, rising from her noisy heart. Guy stopped trying to talk to her and, as he cooked, sang a Mexican song, all vibrato, as she laughed herself silly.

"This is good," she said, taking a bite of his huevos rancheros and laughing. "So, Guy, whatever happened to the ol' stone house?"

"It's still sitting there, half-built, in the wind and rain."

"In the wind and rain," she cackled.

"Well, but that can't hurt it. The stones won't crumble, at least not in our lifetime."

"No," she said, and smacked her bottle down on the tabletop.

It was her third—she'd be sorry in the morning. That, too, was funny.

"So. I'll be starting on building it again."

"Okay. Do that. You do that. Put in windows and give it the roof with the grass growing in it and everything. I mean it. I'm not laughing at you."

She switched on the lamp above the table and his hair shone, now more silver than dark, his only sign of aging. He stretched a long leg and rested it on the table. She recognized the jut of his hipbone beneath the thin, threadbare denim. So he and Natalie were done. Rose had stopped laughing, but that didn't mean she had to behave. Coolly, she considered him. Her nights alone stretched back for months uninterrupted—except for the nights with Meggy.

"Rose." His eyes were deep and lively and then sad. "Really, I've been sorry about what happened for a long, long time."

"Want to hear something insane?" she broke in. "I wish Meggy was mine. I really do." How contented she'd been, sleeping beside Meggy, and how soundly she'd slept.

Unexpectedly, her eyes filled. He reached to touch her cheek, which came alive in the warmth of his hand. He knelt and wrapped his arms around her as she'd imagined he would and had probably invited him to do in a dozen wordless gestures.

But were those the same gestures Natalie used? It wasn't so easy to dismiss Natalie. Six years he'd had with her, hundreds and hundreds of nights *sharing the same bed*. He must know Natalie by now far better than he ever knew Rose. He'd gone from Rose to Natalie maybe at first out of some resemblance, some novelty in such a different version of the same flesh and blood. But now it was Rose who might be the substitute. For a moment Rose was more Natalie than herself and hated him with her sister's smug fury for thinking he could without difficulty move from one to the other. So, when he put his mouth on hers tenderly, knowingly, and the tip of his tongue slipped between her lips and nudged her teeth, she jerked her head back and leaned out of reach.

Chapter NINETEEN

S pring was on the way, then summer, the season of weddings. Rose could expect a fistful of invitations and would not be able to turn them all down. Colleagues were getting married, musicians and composers, and old friends from grad school and college, and her own students, even. The whole of her world appeared to be staggering toward the altar.

Her dreadful era of weddings had begun four years before, with Frances and Alan's. Theirs had been simple: she wore plain white; he wore plain black to the chapel on campus; and they recited vows from *The Book of Common Prayer*. Both mothers had cried, and so had Rose, relieved that she could. Even the petals scattered down the chapel sidewalk had seemed spit from a cloud of doom. It was partly what she knew about Alan and Frances, but Rose had witnessed so many dazed brides and baffled grooms, so many seething mothers and harassed fathers of both, that all weddings had come to seem in some way mistaken or goofy.

She'd stood by as one bridegroom ended his vows by proclaiming his bride to be the best woman he'd ever met, the best God ever made. This unexpected twist in the liturgy brought laughter from the congregation. The other women present, those less perfect creatures, took care not to meet one another's eyes, particularly the single women stranded in the pews, untouched by foolishness, no one's best anything.

Not that Rose yearned to be married. How could she, without a bridegroom in sight, without a candidate, even? She'd read in the paper that single people slept more soundly than marrieds. If her own fitful sleep was the standard, marriage was truly to be feared. She'd read that unmarried women reported the highest levels of happiness. Could they be entirely candid, these reports of happiness and sound sleep? No one else was there to witness whether the solitary sleeper slept. There was no test, like a throat swab, for happiness. Was she happy? A lame question. Who in their right mind could give a simple answer?

She was busy. Her symphony would premiere the following March—Women's History Month, naturally. Orchestra conductors and music directors—men, almost all of them—imagined they showed themselves to be enlightened by commissioning female composers to celebrate women. A new piece for Amelia Earhart's birthday or Louisa May Alcott's or Eleanor Roosevelt's or to celebrate the women who fought for the vote? Of course! Rose was thereby presented as a woman among women, but not a composer among composers. Was it any wonder that the music produced this way, lacking true artistic endorsement, often carried an underlying sadness?

Rose, however, was determined to rejoice in her commission. The suffragists again? So be it. Her symphony was commissioned to celebrate the birthday of Susan B. Anthony, and though she was tempted to call it *Susie's Birthday*, she'd turned in *Symphony #1* as her title, endorsing herself with the implied promise of symphonies to come.

Once the initial thrill of receiving the commission passed, however, anxiety set in. The size of the project required her to refuse other commissions, and in the works-in-progress section of her tenure portfolio, smaller works with a number of orchestras would fill more space than the single symphony. Still—a symphony. What could be grander? It would be the one egg in her basket: *Symphony #1 by Rose MacGregor, slated for world premiere by the Seattle Sinfonietta.*

On a blustery Saturday in April, when the memory of Meggy had faded and life had got back to normal, a piece of the symphony came to her whole. While her laundry tossed in the basement dryer, she stood barefoot in a T-shirt and stained sweatpants at her windows, gazing out on budding mulberries. It was spring by the calendar, but the floor was freezing. She raised a foot to rub on the back of her leg, and began to hear clearly the concluding movement of her symphony, as if it already existed and was simply being played to her.

The phone rang—a bossy buzz. She let it go unanswered, though she was loath to miss a call. She didn't get them that often. The phone stopped ringing and the music went on and on, filling her with a jolting sense of luck.

She would have gone straight to the piano—except, at the moment, it was being tuned. Graham Lowe had been right; the troublesome key still stuck. He'd been working all morning, hitting the one note and muttering in that way of his, and now he was adjusting the pitch of the keyboard— he was nothing if not thorough—and his hands running up and down the keys were swamping the music in her head. And the phone was ringing again.

Answering it, Rose couldn't help but crowd him. Her phone table stood beside her big chair, not three feet from the piano. His ancient suit coat lay across the back of the chair, and he got up and whisked it out of the way as she sat and lifted the receiver.

"Guess what?" It was Ursula, tremulous with excitement. "Rose, Rose, Rose, Rose—"

Rose took a breath. "You're getting married."

"No, no—let *me* say." There was a clunk—Ursula had dropped the phone, and then she was back, fresh from being kissed. "Oops—kissing. *Married! Me!* We wanted you to be the first to know."

"Wow," said Rose.

"Wow?" said Ursula. "Is that all you can say?"

In an orderly row on the piano bench sat Graham's hammer, mutes, and tuning fork. Atop a dishtowel spread over his tool case, he now began unpacking his lunch. He adjusted his suspenders and set out a pair of sandwiches in wax paper. He unwrapped a sandwich, shrimp salad, held it midair, and met Rose's eye.

"Look, can I call you back?" she asked Ursula.

"Rose, *don't* you hang up."

"Have you called your mother? Call your mother, Ursula. I'll call back."

She put down the phone and regarded the tuner. She didn't need a witness to this news, this latest nail in the coffin of her youth. And the music she'd caught hold of for her symphony was slipping away.

"D'you want some privacy?" he asked. "I can eat outside."

"It's too cold," she observed grumpily. "And you need something to drink with that."

He brought out an orange and a pocketknife, cut it in half, and sucked it. Then he tipped the other half toward her, exposing a shock of crimson.

"Blood orange," he said. "Try it." A bloody color ran through the strands of orange pulp as though the fruit had hemorrhaged. He handed her the second sandwich. "You sometimes forget to eat when you're working?" he asked in the mild tone he used with the piano.

He stood and began packing his case. "You want to call your friend back. I'll finish another time."

She sat holding the sandwich, which smelled enticingly of shrimp and celery, and the gory half-orange, which gave off an innocent citrus fragrance.

"No," she said, "I don't want to call my friend back." It seemed she might burst into tears. "Hey, I'd take any excuse *not* to call my friend back right now."

"Ah," he said as though he understood. He gazed at her, his alert, brown eyes flecked with gold. But it was agony for her to be seen just then. She swallowed hard and set the sandwich and the half-orange back down on the towel on his case.

"You go ahead and eat," she managed to say. She wrote his check, put it on the piano, went to her porch, pulled the French doors closed behind her, and flopped down on her bed.

Ursula was getting married. It would have to be faced. She now lived in Madison, Wisconsin, where she'd taken a job at a hospital. Rose, at first, had been overjoyed. They'd traded weekends, Madison or St. Paul, going out to bars, dancing as often with each other as with the men who asked them. But then Ursula became hard to reach by phone and coy, and then, on a weekend when Rose had driven down, understanding she was expected, she'd found Ursula still at breakfast, scrambled eggs and mimosas, at two in the afternoon with somebody named Bruce.

"Why, Rose, here you are," Ursula had cried with a woozy, unfocused joy. There was no third place set at the table.

Bruce: large, dark-haired, and heavy-browed, with a cleft chin and a forehead lined with kindly wrinkles, a reliable man, an anesthetist. His would not be the worst face to view just before going under. But why did Ursula have to *marry* him? He'd be perfect for a marriage joke, one of Rose and Ursula's anti-marriage jokes: *Please, Doctor, don't put me under!*

Rose and Ursula had been weathering the wave of weddings together and privately howling over mincing brides and stumbling grooms. And they'd promised each other they would never, never surrender. But now, several months into knowing Bruce, Ursula had taken Rose by the shoulders and asked whether she didn't, herself, need someone to come home to and, yes, perhaps even children? As if all of that could be had for the wishing. For Ursula, apparently it could. She'd changed her mind and here he was: solid block of manhood, source of children.

Rose was thankful that Bruce, at least, seemed incurious about her love life. As he got to know her, he kept track of all she told him in a gentlemanly fashion and refrained from joining Ursula in hand-wringing about finding someone for Rose, now that Ursula was so happy.

Maybe happy now, but Rose still imagined she'd hear any day that Bruce had done something dreadful and been sent packing, just as Bogdan the Russian scholar had, without warning. Ursula hadn't forgotten Bogdan's eight-month disappearance and the matter of the apartment lease after all. On a day soon after their reunion, he came "home" to find the locks changed and the phone unlisted. Bully for Ursula, Rose had declared. And now she caught herself hoping the same thing would happen to Bruce. Was she against her friend's happiness?

If she was unhappy that Ursula was so happy, maybe Rose deserved to be lying stricken on her bed on a bright Saturday afternoon. She hauled herself upright, meaning to go and call Ursula back, when her symphony flooded her anew. It was happy music, confident—defiant, even. So Ursula was getting married? That was not original. A crutch was what it was, a retreat from the world, an end to adventuring, possibly a defeat. The phone rang again and she unplugged it. She meant to get that music down on paper.

When she plugged it in three hours later, it was already ringing.

"Poor Rose!" said Ursula. "I'll bet you've been calling and calling. My mother's telling everyone, and my phone's just been ringing off the wall."

The wedding date was set for July, three months away. Ursula now announced the first item on what would prove to be the endless wedding list: a dress for Rose as maid of honor. Ursula had already found her gown and Rose's dress in a bridal shop in Madison.

Two weeks later, Rose dragged herself down there to try on the dress. As she stepped out of the fitting room, she had to wrap her arms around herself to keep from spilling out of it. Ursula had chosen white cambric for herself, soft white on white, flowing to her toes in an ivy pattern with the simplest lines at waist and neck. But, bafflingly, Rose was to be a milkmaid in shiny roses, or were they peonies? Call them blossoms, great blossoms as big as cabbages, and call Rose Bo Peep, Bo Peep as a hooker, bare-shouldered, the bodice of the dress so tiny it almost wasn't there. Unfortunately, the dress fit, what there was of it. And the spilling-out was to be prevented by a corset. Ursula didn't notice Rose's dismay. A remote look had come into her eye: part dream, part steel. Rose, speechless in the face of it, allowed herself to be fitted with the corset, for which she was required to pay sixty dollars plus five hundred—*five hundred dollars*—for the dress. She took both home in a box and stowed them on a high shelf out of sight.

Ursula wanted a wedding in the country.

In early May, they sat at Rose's table after a long lunch. All meals with Ursula were now long and lingering, full of gazings into the middle distance. The weather was mild. The fragrance of narcissi floated up from beds below the windows. Rose was half sorry she'd planted them—a bulb bed wasn't a farm garden, and she was wearying of the insistent waves of citified blooming: crocuses, then daffodils and narcissi, then tulips, and then spirea, which she refused to call by its common name—*bridal wreath.*

"Someplace in the country," repeated Ursula, chewing her lip.

"The Goat Pasture? You've gotta be kidding."

"It's awfully pretty out there by the river. We could use your studio to dress in."

But Rose didn't want her studio to be a dressing room for a wedding and she wouldn't inflict heterosexual rites on Lila. The farm girls barely knew Ursula. Rose didn't want this argument. She chewed her lip and tried to gaze into the middle distance herself.

"How about Emma's?" Rose said finally, sick of the standoff.

"Bingo," said Ursula.

"Why didn't you say so, if that's what you wanted?"

"Because you'll have to ask her. I couldn't possibly. I'm the bride."

Not even Emma's would do, however. That big, round barn neighboring Emma's—the farmhouse behind it was standing empty, wasn't it? Could they, for one day, pretend it was their own? The barn could be cleared out for a wedding, couldn't it?

Rose wrote Emma, though it wouldn't be quite the breeze for Emma that Ursula seemed to imply. Emma had suffered a stroke the previous winter, and her face was now lopsided and her speech slurred, though her mind was as sharp as ever, and she could by means of pen and paper make herself understood. Emma wrote the neighbor. Yes, they could use the house to dress in—Emma had the key—but they weren't to touch the stuff in the barn. At the center of the pasture next to the barn was a great old oak tree. The wedding would be staged in the pasture beside the round barn out beneath the oak.

A week later, Rose and Ursula went out to broadcast the pasture with flower seed from a colorful can, *The Flowered Meadow*. Cows would likely eat or trample the poppies, cornflowers, and daisies long before July, but Rose didn't mention that to Ursula and instead ran whooping through the mud while Ursula stood beneath the oak. Eventually, Rose dragged herself over.

"I never thought getting married could be so much fun," said Ursula, unsmiling.

Behind her friend's back, Rose made devil's horns. Ursula groped a hand behind her, pulled Rose close, and interlocked their arms. However bossy she was, she also clung to Rose just then, and Rose tried to forgive her. Rose tried to forgive Ursula's abrupt turn from the understanding they'd shared that, regardless of any boyfriend or husband, they each, at heart, stood alone. Alone and free, Rose told herself—she was, anyway. Rose was.

In Ursula's presence, she could now let her mind wander freely. She even worked on her symphony, jotting on a notepad she kept in her pocket. Ursula never seemed to notice, and it was easy to keep her talking. What she felt, what people said and what she said back, what she'd eaten the night before and what she'd fed Bruce, was what she and Rose talked about. However boring it was, Rose let her run on. It seemed the kindest thing, and also the easiest. Brides were fundamentally nervous. And brides were also *not* to be opposed.

They were wandering through a department store—the one Rose had first been led to by Frances, the Minneapolis store, which was bigger and grander than anything in Madison. People were to phone the store and choose from Ursula's registry list, and Rose was to fetch the stuff back to St. Paul in her car and stow it in her condo.

"Terrific," said Frances. "So simple for everyone." Frances had come along to help pick out things for the bridal registry. Something was wrong, Rose was aware, overtly wrong, upstairs between the Gilpins, but Frances betrayed nothing but excitement. She knew the store; she knew the ropes about weddings. She was flushed and jittery, more excited even than Ursula.

Ursula and Bruce would need things, Rose allowed. Besides their enormous student loans, they possessed between them Ursula's bed, her card table and folding chairs, a frying pan, a soup kettle, and odds and ends. Both sets of sheets Ursula owned were blotched and discolored: Bruce was prone to nosebleeds.

Ursula beamed approval on the bridal registry salesman who broadcast enchantment with all things wedding and was dressed in a dark vest and a starched white shirt that had obviously never been touched by a nosebleed. He led the delighted Ursula not to sheets and towels, but to the crystal department, where she now posed with a gold-rimmed compote before a mirrored wall.

Trailing along with a felt-tipped pen and the registry packet, Rose read aloud the price tag on the bowl. "Three hundred fifty dollars."

Ursula raised her eyebrows and smiled.

"Superb taste," chirped Frances.

"*Frances,*" said Rose under her breath. Ursula's widowed mother lived on a shoestring. Bruce's people ran a bowling alley in Pocatello, Idaho—how much money could they have?

"Think of a table with that compote at its center or a buffet with masses of candles, each floating in a smaller matching bowl. Imagine cocktails at twilight," intoned the salesman, "each sipped from a crystal cocktail glass, perhaps tinted garnet, perhaps tinted green."

Rose muttered to Ursula about the families, the money.

"Sshh," said Frances. "It's her wedding."

"Think of color and shine working together," the salesman crooned, "if you have the wit to approach it that way. Picture your home as a composition."

Ursula turned brightly to Rose. "Like music."

"Why, yes," said Frances. "Each place setting like a movement in a symphony."

"Oh, let's leave music out of it," said Rose, her voice sharper than she intended. Frances and Ursula stood blinking at her. Rose turned to the salesman. "I can't help picturing your commission. There are quite a few things she actually needs. I think we'd do best on our own."

"Rose, Ursula is getting *married*," said Frances quietly. "It'll never be like this again. Let her choose her crystal, for Chrissake."

The salesman looked at Rose sideways through his eyelashes, gently took the registry packet, and located *Name of Bride*. "Ursula?"

"Excuse me, Frances, *cocktails at twilight*?" Rose turned to Ursula. "You know what Frances does with her wedding crystal? Takes it all out and dusts it once a year. Could we just have a moment of common sense here?"

Ursula flashed Rose a look. "Actually," she told the salesman, "I'd appreciate your guidance." She and the salesman linked arms and strolled onward.

"Maybe I *should* throw cocktail parties," Frances told Rose, as they followed behind. "Maybe that would be the solution. What do you hear from down below us?" she asked Rose suddenly. "Footsteps? Or actual conversations?" Frances flushed, and, not waiting for an answer, turned away, and cranked the handle of a crystal pepper grinder.

The previous night and the night before, Alan and Frances, who never argued, had, in the wee hours, raised their voices and raged. And Rose had heard it all. However solidly built their building was, in the still of the night, voices carried, especially those directly above. Rose had been up working when they started, and had crept, shamefaced but unable to stop

herself, to the back of her apartment, nearer their bedroom, and had sat
up with a cup of tea and listened.

Frances had wanted Alan to make love to her.

He'd told her to drop it.

But she wanted another baby.

What about what *he* wanted? Alan had said, not shouting, but using his
voice to imply that Frances was raving, his voice crisp as a singer in recita-
tive, his tone cold and magisterial. Rose had been momentarily ashamed
to be a musician, that musical technique could be put to such a use. Frances
had first argued and then begged: it was all she asked, all she would ask of
him ever again. Max woke up and started fussing. And Rose had listened
to it all, ignominiously, telling herself that, as godmother, she had to
keep track of things for Max's sake, while in truth knowing she had no
right to their troubles just because she was awake and alone.

"Footsteps, mostly, is all I hear," Rose told Frances and pressed her
hand. "And I don't mean to spoil Ursula's fun, but she's choosing stuff
people can't afford and won't buy."

"You'd be surprised," said Frances, "what people spend when it comes
to a wedding."

They found Ursula with a champagne flute, a plume of smoke
somehow captured in its stem. She bent her head over the glass, as though
drinking from it. She lifted a lock of hair behind her ear. She looked not
a day over fifteen. How had she grown so young? Her self-absorption
seemed the natural state of a newborn creature who has no idea what to
want, and Rose suddenly loved her again and feared for her.

The crystal with the smoke in it was absolutely gorgeous. Ursula read
the serial numbers and Rose recorded her wish for eight water goblets,
one hundred twenty dollars apiece; eight wine glasses at the same price;
eight champagne flutes, a hundred thirty apiece. Before they left the
store, Rose contrived to put on her charge card the eight champagne
flutes Ursula had specified. Adding this to the cost of the dress and corset,
Ursula's wedding would use up half of Rose's savings.

Home alone again, the warmth of her gesture went cold. She could no longer afford travel that summer—something that Ursula was never to know. Did Rose imagine she could buy Ursula's love, buy back their friendship? She could barely remember why they were friends. She tried to feel what it must be like to be Ursula. From the outside, it looked like Queen for a Day.

From the apartment overhead came murmuring and creaking. Frances and Alan were home and cooking supper, and Rose would be expected upstairs.

Alan, too, was playing some game, leaving Rose giddy little notes as he always did when newly in love, notes under her door and in her jammed mail slot at school. She could barely keep up with her teaching, given the wedding hoopla. She didn't want Alan's little notes and didn't want to catch signals he passed to her in Frances's presence. Final exams were upon them and student recitals and a first deadline for Rose's symphony, a firm outline and thirty pages of score—reason enough to excuse herself from supper with the Gilpins.

Sitting down to her piano, she dislodged a stack of unopened mail. There she found a letter officially requesting her participation in a custody matter between Guy Robbin and Natalie MacGregor, concerning Marguerite MacGregor. She was at first unnerved and then annoyed. No crime had been committed; it was family court. Natalie was also playing a game—outlaw, hermit, or heroine. And who could guess what game Guy might be playing? Rose was, fittingly enough, to report to a referee, a court referee.

She let the letter fall with the rest to the floor as the streetlight outside blinked on, and she turned to see it, first glowing pink at the filament, then wrapping itself in a white, steady light. That moment every evening when the streetlights came on, if she remembered to observe it, was one of her small joys, though probably too minor to be called happiness.

The fresh light coming through the window picked up a glint under the lid of the piano—a tuning fork, lying on the harp by the pins. She took it out and set it on the windowsill. The tuner must have forgotten it. With his orderly ways, his sandwiches wrapped in waxed paper, square and tidy as birthday presents, it wasn't like him, she didn't think. But she didn't really know him. She didn't really know anyone.

Chapter TWENTY

T he custody hearing was set for mid-June, and Rose would, of course, attend, though she'd told them she wouldn't take sides. Natalie was phoning all the time anyway, trying to explain her fitness as a mother, and Guy was phoning too. He'd asked Rose to give an affidavit about what had happened just before Easter—the facts, he said, for Meggy's sake. He pressed Natalie's address upon Rose: a rooming house in a rundown St. Paul neighborhood called Frogtown. He hoped she'd go over and see for herself before she gave her affidavit.

She drove by a few times and, once, parked across the street for a while. This was, she supposed, spying, but Natalie had resisted every hint that Rose might want to visit. Rose wasn't sure how Frogtown would help Guy's affidavit. She found a certain allure in the neighborhood, which was built over a swamp (hence the frogs) into which railway cinders had been poured. In the sinking porches and peeling paint, Rose felt a relaxation into circumstances. No one was on show here; the captains of their own fates and masters of their souls lived elsewhere. Rose supposed she was that, or trying to be. Here the strain was gone, all that effort, as Natalie had put it, all that striving.

The two-story rooming house where Natalie and Meggy lived lacked a coat of paint entirely and appeared to be capsizing, weighed down at the front by all the mailboxes around the doorframe. In the side yard, a catalpa tree, split almost to the root, unfurled a green canopy.

Rose would attend the custody hearing, and that was the best she could do. She wasn't sure where Meggy belonged, and her phone had become a hazard. If, when she sat down to work, she forgot to unplug it, the thing was sure to ring when she was in deep. And, often as not, when she plugged it back in, it was already ringing—Natalie or Guy about custody, or Ursula about her wedding, or Frances about Ursula's wedding, or Alan about his new love, who was called James, Alan complaining to Rose that she had not yet met James, that she had not sat down to hear about James.

The conductor in Seattle was also calling about what he and Rose both assured each other was a minor difference over the direction Rose was taking with her symphony. His name was Stephen Orrick, and his interest in her work had been a boost, her best luck yet.

She'd met him at Wolf Trap, the national park for the performing arts—or, rather, he'd made a point of meeting her, though she'd recognized him at once. As reputed, he looked like Tchaikovsky—high forehead, stiff brush of hair, bristling whiskers. He had raised from oblivion the Seattle Sinfonietta, had expanded it to a full-sized orchestra, had brought new audiences to new music, had gone national via radio, and now took frequent invitations to conduct everywhere else, adding radiance to his reputation and to that of his orchestra. At forty-seven, he was too old to be a Young Turk and too young to be an Old Master. This made him somehow easier to talk to. He was astoundingly friendly, almost deferential to Rose, as if she were the star and he the unknown. At that first meeting, he'd asked her to mail him everything she'd written. And she had, reams, with Lila's help to decide what was finished.

The previous two seasons, he'd featured several short pieces of Rose's work and each time brought her out to rehearse and took care to introduce her to audiences. Then he'd commissioned the symphony—in the name of Susan B. Anthony, true—but still, he seemed to have a real feeling for Rose's music.

And he treated her as a friend. He sent her intriguing things from the Northwest: green almonds encased in hairy hulls, smoked salmon. He had an actual life outside music, revealed when she stayed as his houseguest. He cooked, gardened, and conducted a baby orchestra at his daughters' preschool. Alexis and Starr, four and five, were a thorough part of everything he did. He took his afternoon "nap" sitting in a big chair with pillows behind him, propping up his ego, as he put it, while the little girls colored at his feet. He didn't actually sleep then, but instead made conversation with his wife, Leslie, or with Rose, or he chatted on the phone.

Leslie, a violinist in the orchestra, made Rose especially welcome—flowers in the guest room and orchestra gossip, though, naturally, she omitted the gossip about her husband. Conductors were notorious for carrying on with women, and Rose had heard this about Stephen Orrick. Now that she knew him, she wouldn't believe it. The cause of the rumors had to be jealousy. She'd spent hours alone with him, and he seemed to prize nothing above conversation. He liked to listen and he liked to talk. He was noisily political. Leslie rolled her eyes at his proclamation that he was more feminist even than she. But he walked his talk: made beds, mopped floors, cooked, and did the dishes. There was just no way to fault him. He had the energy of three men—or a woman and a half, as he put it.

The third week in May, Rose's outline and thirty pages of score came due. Almost before her package could have arrived, Stephen Orrick called to say that he found the music a little somber, a bit on the edgy side for a birthday celebration. Rose was known for vivacity, for effervescence, for great self-assurance—she'd written *Heart's Apple*, had she not? *Spirit Mechanics* and *Bears in the Oats*? Her work at its best, he thought, had a triumphal quality.

But effervescence was only one mode, Rose retorted, that of the twelve-year-old girl forever skipping through the daisy field. And she thought she might be coming to the end of bravado. There had to be something beyond it. Susan B. Anthony had lived a life of struggle. Surely the great woman knew moments of less than perfect self-assurance?

Unfortunately, there was little historical evidence of the doubts of Susan B. Anthony.

"Especially not on her birthday," said Stephen Orrick.

Susan B. was, indeed, renowned for giving herself enormous birthday parties, at which she made speeches.

"Failure is impossible," he said, quoting Anthony on her seventy-fifth birthday.

"I never said failure," Rose told him. "This piece is not about failure."

"Well, of course not," he said. "Forgive me. Should I leave you alone?"

"Oh, no," she assured him. She needed time to work, but she didn't want to be left alone, least of all by him, by them, the Orricks. Her trips out to Seattle restored her to herself. She was their favorite guest, they said, not just Stephen and Leslie but the little girls too. She adored the girls, their mischief and their chumminess. They reminded her painfully of Meggy, and when she bought them presents, she always bought Meggy a third and set it aside for the future.

At the moment, Natalie was not allowing presents. Presents were termed materialism. That Natalie was against materialism certainly matched her circumstances. It wasn't clear how she was getting by. A Frogtown chiropractor had employed her briefly, but she'd barely settled in at the reception desk when he decided he didn't need her after all. And just when they'd gotten a good thing going: he adjusted the body and Natalie, quietly and unobtrusively, she said, adjusted the soul. When he let her go, the reason he gave was that he could not afford her. But he was paying her almost nothing, and Rose should see his swanky office. And Natalie had been doing extra for him, putting patients at ease in the waiting room, engaging them in healing conversations. Jesus Christ figured in, of course, but also astrology. For instance, Rose and Jesus were both Capricorns—did Rose know that?—and that's why they both were so good at grasping the big picture. They didn't fasten on to details. They were also good at forgiveness—like the way Rose had forgiven Natalie over Guy. Where was Guy, by the way? Had he and Rose perhaps gotten back together? No? Well, that was good; it must not be in the stars. Really not? Fine, good. Back to the subject of materialism. The chiropractor couldn't afford Natalie. Money, materialism, had intervened. Did Rose understand how materialism had ruined the whole of society? Had she reflected on whether Meggy had really needed the expensive clothes and the Easter basket? What was the underlying message? What did Rose wish Meggy to learn?

Rose hadn't been trying to teach Meggy anything. There wasn't a message.

But Rose had promised her a mini-bike?

"Never," said Rose. "And as for the dress, I just wanted Meggy to have something nice."

But what Rose termed nice, Natalie suggested, was merely new. Wear something once, and it's no longer new. Had Jesus Christ insisted on new garments? Why did Rose think He'd been born in a manger and not in the palace of a king? How could a little girl learn to cherish all of heaven and earth once she got the habit of craning into every store window?

Rose couldn't think how to answer. Was it possible that a little pink dress could in some way harm Meggy? Could there really be something wrong with an Easter basket? A small but sparkling pile of things atop Rose's piano awaited Meggy, for such time as Natalie once again allowed a material life. There was a canary feather in a block of Lucite; a leather coin purse from Afghanistan, soft and pleasantly stinky; and a jade ring in a felt box. To this, Stephen Orrick, when he learned of Meggy, added a blue china egg from Tiffany's.

During his "naps" and late at night, after a rehearsal or performance, he liked to hear Rose talk. At first she'd been shy and, in the face of his well-ordered and very full life, afraid to reveal her own. But what she thought of as her chaos, he found intriguing. He couldn't seem to get enough of Ursula's wedding or of Alan and Frances's peculiar arrangement, and tales of Natalie made him roar and gasp.

When he presented the blue china egg for Meggy in its blue box, Rose was pierced with gratitude but felt secretly, aggrievedly, nonsensically that it wasn't nearly enough. She wanted Meggy to be Alexis or Starr—to have such a father and a life of plenty in a lovely old house. She, herself, envied Alexis and Starr—ridiculous, when Stephen was only a decade older than she and could never have been her father. Yet she found surprising comfort in talking to him and felt very much better about her life in the terms she offered him: the heroine, calm amidst storms. So it was perhaps her own fault that he saw her as above her troubles, always rising triumphal.

"Come out and see us," he urged her. "We'll cheer you up."

But she was cheerful enough and reasonably certain of the music, which was not so much gloomy as lucid; not somber, but free: Susan B. taking up and bearing her freedom. Rose would stay away from Seattle till she knew how to defend her ideas and had more of the score to show.

"Certainly," he told her. "Take your time. We can always postpone."

"Oh, no. No postponement," she told him. Any working composer knew that postponement could mean cancellation. Postponement was the anteroom a conductor let you sit in awhile, before sending you out into the cold. Not that she thought Stephen capable of that. "I'll be out in late June as planned," she told him. That would give her time to finish classes, hand in grades, and write perhaps thirty more pages of her symphony.

Then, on a day at the end of May, on her way out the door to her last week of classes, she received a call from Guy—another alarm about Natalie. Guy claimed that Natalie had taken Meggy out of school, that she was being held truant, kept out of sight in the rooming house.

Rose went on to meet her class. The thought of Meggy cooped up in the rooming house troubled her. Still, given the season, it was hard to get upset about a little girl sprung from school. Rose's students were loud and hilarious, and pranks were the order of the day. As she settled her books and papers at the front of the room, the sound system crackled to life and began to broadcast the bleating of a lamb. Another prank. This one got on her nerves. It was not a happy, frolicsome sound, but the cry of a young animal in distress, helpless and, worst of all, hopeful. Her students went into hysterics and Rose laughed, too, in spite of herself, as the little voice went on and on. Nobody knew how to shut the thing off. Rose dismissed her class and drove to Frogtown.

She stopped first at Lincoln Elementary School, which stood just down the block from the rooming house where Natalie lived. Meggy was at least registered at Lincoln School. On the playground, frantic simultaneous games of tetherball and soccer were underway, cut across by a game of tag between the boys and girls, in which the girls pretended indifference, prolonging the glamour of being tagged by a show of disgust and unwillingness to pursue, and then pursued. Meggy ought to be out there, tagging and being tagged, but Meggy was not in school that day, nor had she been seen at school the past two weeks, nor had the mother responded to calls.

Lukewarm sunlight fell harshly on the front of the rooming house. The broken sidewalk and ragged lawn seemed not so much self-accepting that day as defiant or possibly defeated. No one answered any of the buzzers. Rose tried the front door and found it unlocked.

The entryway swallowed her in a clammy chill. Behind closed doors, televisions tuned to different stations made war. Carpet remnants lined the hall, and, along its dark length, some child had dragged a fistful of crayons. An old woman, one eye crusted shut, directed Rose to the rear.

Natalie opened her door a crack and peered out from behind a chain. At the sight of Rose, her face showed surprise and then cunning. She whipped the chain aside, pulled Rose into the room, refastened the chain, and threw her arms around her sister.

Meggy lay asleep in the single bed, face down, wearing the Easter dress, which was now pinkish gray and flapped open at the back where the buttons had been. She rolled onto her side and revealed her thumb thrust deep into her mouth. Though asleep, she sucked hard, as though drawing nourishment from her own hand. Rose hadn't seen her for weeks, and the strength of her feeling for the little girl took her by surprise. She wanted to seize her niece and run. Instead, they eased down, aunt and mother, either side of her on the bed.

It was afternoon, yet Natalie still wore her nightgown. "Are you sick?" asked Rose.

"Oh, no. Just short of laundry. You caught us unawares."

From beneath the corner sink, a snarl of dirty clothes spilled out, tangled with the telephone cord. Natalie shoved at the pile with her foot. Under layers of dripping paint, the walls appeared to be sweating. Trudging steps approached in the hall. A toilet flushed so loudly it seemed in the same room with them. The school playground broadcast a distant din.

"Why isn't she in school?" asked Rose.

"She can have a day off, don't you think?"

Rose was not prepared for Natalie to lie to her. An instant shouting match was more what she'd expected. She let herself be led for a while. Natalie, at least, wanted Meggy with her. At least in this way, it had to be said, Natalie was a good mother.

"And how are you?" Natalie asked, snuggling up close. "You look a little lost."

Rose laughed quietly. "Might you be adjusting my soul now?"

"Well," said Natalie. "But I know how it is. To feel lost. To be lonely."

"And next we're going to hear about Jesus?"

Natalie chuckled. Rose chuckled with her. Childhood might have been easier for them if their father had succeeded in converting their mother to his sweet Jesus. It would have been more cozy for them if their mother had turned at least part of her energy to being kind. Rose could hear their mother's harsh laugh and see the deprecating shake of the head like a tossing of branches above them in the bitter tree of life. For their mother, kindness was the province of the weak-minded. Rose was unprepared for her sister's kindness. Natalie, sitting warm and close, so close that they breathed together, brought Rose a moment of unreasoning respite.

But then trudging steps came again and the toilet flushed deafeningly.

Meggy rolled over and gave a little snore. Rose cleared her throat. "Meggy's been truant for two weeks. Why have you taken her out of school?"

A metal wardrobe with its doors hanging open displayed a dishpan, hot plate, kettle, and bag of oatmeal. Natalie hauled out the hot plate and plugged it in. "We'll have a cup of tea."

"None for me," said Rose. "You need what you've got."

Natalie rolled her eyes and filled the kettle. "Consider the lilies," she said. The food shelf at church, if Rose had to know, had tea and oatmeal and macaroni for free.

"Macaroni?" Meggy croaked and sat up. "Are we getting macaroni?"

"Well, we'd have to get there early, remember?" Natalie replied. "Macaroni runs out by afternoon. Maybe Aunt Rose could drive over some morning and score us some?"

Meggy smiled and put her head down in Rose's lap and fell heavily asleep again. Rose stroked her hair tentatively. Natalie seemed not to mind.

Anyway, their father was sending Natalie a few dollars, and a man in his Christian commune, a Mr. Greer, who'd seen a picture of Natalie holding Meggy, had felt moved to pay the rent. Like a guardian angel. Wasn't that amazing? Mr. Greer had, in turn, sent a photo, which Natalie produced: a chinless face with a stripe of hair over a white forehead.

"What does he want, this Mr. Greer?" Rose wondered aloud.

"He wants to do good," said Natalie.

Rose felt a spasm of guilty relief that she wouldn't be taking on Natalie's bills again, at least not for the moment. And why should she pay Natalie's way any more than Natalie should pay hers? They'd had exactly the same start in life, Rose a mere ten months ahead of her. Did it follow that everything Rose had gotten for herself must also belong to Natalie? Rose sat benumbed, sunk in the pulpy mattress. Something shiny scuttled over her foot. She moved Meggy aside and went to the window, where heart-shaped catalpa leaves and spikes of flower buds pressed against the glass.

Then Meggy was up and at her side. "What about a mini-bike, Aunt Rose?"

"Meggy," warned Natalie.

"This is where we pray," said Meggy, raising her voice a little. Below the sill were squares of carpet padding. Meggy tugged Rose to kneel down beside her. "Like this. All night."

"All night?" Rose turned to Natalie. "You've got her up praying all night?"

"We sleep in the day," said Meggy. "But if you get tired praying, you can lean a little." She slumped against Rose, grinning. "What about a mini-bike?" she murmured.

"You know," said Natalie, "we can't just wander out in the daylight. He wants her. He could snatch her at any time and I'd never see her again."

"I don't think so," said Rose. "Guy's not like that. And I'd get her back in school or the judge is going to think you're crazy."

"Aunt Rose needs to go to the bathroom," said Meggy and tugged Rose upright.

"No, Meggy," said Natalie. "It's not a nice bathroom."

"Aunt Rose might need to go." Meggy unchained the door.

"Hmm," said Rose. "Maybe I do."

"Believe me, you don't," Natalie told Rose. "Honey, she's used to something nicer."

"I can probably stand it," said Rose.

"Suit yourself." Natalie grimly motioned Rose and Meggy out the door.

Meggy placed her hand on the crayon stripes that ran down the hallway. "I did that," she said and studied Rose for a reaction.

The bathroom gave out a sharp stink. Somebody's comb, trailing hair, lay on the ledge beneath a cracked mirror, and the bathtub showed an oily ring. Cups and toothbrushes were jumbled over the sink and toilet ledge. Meggy pulled down her underpants, hopped on, and peed. Rose looked for soap to wash Meggy's hands, but when she saw the cracked, muddy square on the soap dish, she let the girl finish rinsing with water.

"It's like the jungle. See, lion paws," said Meggy and crouched down and pressed her cheek against the filthy floor and pointed to the tub's clawed feet.

Rose pulled the little girl up. "How 'bout I carry you like a sack of flour?"

Meggy flopped her arms over Rose's shoulder and rested, an obedient sack. Rose started down the hallway toward the front door, but Natalie called out. Natalie was watching from her doorway, and so Rose turned and went back down the hall toward her sister. Two sacks of flour, their father used to carry them, belly-down over each shoulder, Rose and Natalie. Rose recalled the thrill of being lifted up and then the bony jostling of her father's shoulder digging into her, and the final and best part—the relief of being set down again.

"Aunt Rose says I can have a mini-bike," Meggy announced, climbing off Rose's shoulder.

"Meggy," said Rose. "We never discussed it."

"We did once," said Meggy.

"No," said Natalie. "The answer is no. And that's the end of it. Let's all remember I'm the mother here."

"Well," said Meggy in a feathery voice, "maybe you wouldn't have to be."

"Pardon me?" said Natalie.

Meggy cupped a hand at the back of Rose's knee. It was the lightest touch. "She could be the mother. You could be the aunt."

Natalie gasped and pulled the little girl into the room. Rose felt herself flush. Not daring to look at Meggy, she made herself look at Natalie.

"That didn't come from me," Rose said and felt instant remorse as Meggy began to apologize. Hadn't the little girl merely voiced Rose's wish?

"I didn't mean it, Mommy," said Meggy calmly, almost sternly. "I was just fooling."

"You hurt me," Natalie muttered to her daughter. "You hurt my heart."

"Listen," said Rose. "Kids say things."

Without thinking, Rose reached for Meggy, but Natalie tugged her daughter close and in a flash had them both on their knees on the carpet padding, hands clapped together, eyes shut, leaving Rose in the doorway. Without opening her eyes, Natalie gestured Rose to kneel down.

"Dear Jesus, protect us and lead us," Natalie intoned. Meggy opened a wary eye and quickly closed it. Natalie turned her sightless face to Rose. "Get out. I never asked you here."

"I know you didn't," said Rose. "But it looks like I had to come anyway. If you were handling things yourself, I'd never bother you."

Then Natalie was on her feet and shouting. "Get out and stay out. Nobody wants you here." She crowded Rose into the hall. Overhead, somebody began to pound.

Meggy craned around her mother. "Don't worry, Aunt Rose. She never stays mad."

Natalie, however, was in full cry. "Do you think for a minute I'd be standing here," she bellowed, "in this wretched house, in this godforsaken city, within your reach, Aunt Rose, if I had the means to get away from you?"

A door fell open down the hall and a big man with a yellow face and dark circles under his eyes, a great jack-o-lantern of a man, loomed out. Rose stepped back as he continued past them into the bathroom.

Natalie slammed the door on Rose, and the chain rattled into place.

Rose stood alone in the hall. The flush of the toilet rocked the floor. The big sick-looking man stepped out again in a cloud of stench and walked by. Rose collected herself and sped home.

Safe in her apartment again, she unplugged the phone, got out a bucket and sponge, and cleaned her own bathroom till it was spotless, even behind the toilet and the sink, places no one could see. Jewels got tangled underfoot. She stopped to pet her but petted too hard, and Jewels jumped away. There was dust, hair, and papers behind the bed—it was disgusting, how she'd let things go. Dusting the windowsill, she bumped the tuning fork, which clattered to the floor.

She plugged the phone back in, picked up the receiver, and found the piano tuner at home.

He sounded a little startled but, yes, he'd come over to get it, right then, if she wanted.

She did. She wasn't going to stop till everything was cleaned and put where it belonged.

The phone rang and she snatched up the receiver.

It was Natalie, remorseful now and in tears. "You won't hurt us, will you? You have to help mother and child stay together. Here—Meggy will tell you."

Rose hung up and unplugged the phone before Natalie could make Meggy say whatever she'd been rehearsed to say. Meggy had to be gotten out of there. Rose would give Guy his affidavit. Meggy would be better off almost anywhere else than with Natalie. She thought briefly of marching back to Frogtown and taking Meggy forcibly. But that would only bring a wrestling match, one she wasn't sure she could win.

She went forward with a dust rag over woodwork, high and low: baseboards, moldings, doorframes. She put oil soap and water in a bucket and, on her hands and knees, went over the floorboards, and as she scrubbed, the visit to Frogtown came back in hideous detail. A story for Stephen. It would be a doozy. She'd go to Seattle, to Stephen, right away—she wouldn't wait till she'd written more music. In Seattle, she'd find order and sanity. Stephen would help her with her music and her life; he'd help her figure out everything.

The doorbell rang and she buzzed the tuner in, unlocked the door to the hallway, tiptoed quickly across her wet floor to snatch up the tuning fork to hand to him so she could prevent him from tracking in, and slipped and fell, sprawling. In a blur she saw the tuner in the doorway. He grabbed for her and fell himself, and then they were on the floor together, his elbow on her knee, her ankle somehow over his thigh. She had the impression he'd fallen on purpose, he'd been so quick, and she might have been annoyed with him, besides being embarrassed and sore. Instead, she was overtaken by the odd sensation that she was looking at him for the first time, and a small voice inside her said, There you are.

There he was? Absurd. Even so, she saw, as though for the first time, the dark, close-cropped head, the clean-shaven face, the narrow nose, the gold-flecked eyes.

If he'd fallen on purpose, he was quickly on his feet again, disentangling them and holding a hand out to her. He didn't laugh, didn't even smile, but simply held her gaze and then glanced away and reached a hand to her piano.

"Have you eaten?" he said. "Could I take you out for supper?"

"Me or my piano?" Rose stuttered out and laughed, and then he did, too.

"You, of course," he said and, noticing her phone cord lying loose, reached and plugged it back in. And, of course, it rang.

Chapter TWENTY-ONE

F orty-eight hours later, Rose was in Seattle, up talking into the night. They sat, she and Stephen, in his study on twin leather recliners, perfect chairs, neither soft nor hard, as easy to rise from as to sit down on and angled toward a great wall of windows overlooking Puget Sound. In the day, the view was of the water and, at night, of the lights near and far. In lieu of a fireplace, Leslie had improvised on a low table half a dozen beeswax pillars which, when lit, produced enough light by which to read Rose's new pages of score. It was a perfect room.

Since the visit to Frogtown, Rose had barely slept. She'd been up at the piano through a day and a night and then had stumbled onto the train. She might have caught a plane, but given the wedding-bankrupt state of her savings, last-minute airfare was out of the question, and on the train she could spread out her manuscript pages and go on working.

What Stephen thought of her new pages, she wouldn't know until the next day, however. Leslie lit the candles between them, kissed Stephen, and went off to bed, wishing them well with their work. She didn't seem to know that her husband never worked at night.

"So," he said when Leslie had gone, "what's up?"

"Fresh horrors. Wait till you hear," said Rose. "I hope you're not sleepy."

"Never sleepy, never tired." He brought out the bottle of brandy and the glasses.

"Aren't you hot, wrapped up in that?" she asked him. He had the present she'd brought him from the train-station gift shop around his shoulders, an eye-popping red shawl like the one Susan B. Anthony wore. He'd crowed with delight, wrapped himself in the shawl, and worn it all day and to evening rehearsal, where he'd made a show of it to the orchestra, bringing Rose up to the front to narrate while he modeled it, and had put it on again to go home.

He shook his head, but loosened the folds of the shawl. The night was fine. The warm breath of early summer murmured through the screens. She slipped off her sandals and rubbed a foot against the leather footrest.

"So," she said and laid Frogtown before him, the dark hallway of the rooming house, Meggy's scribbles along the wall, that final sight of Meggy kneeling beside Natalie, their eyes squeezed tight. She choked out a laugh, but Stephen regarded her without gasping or laughing. Was it too extreme to be funny? And she hadn't even told it all. She'd left out the nasty bathroom. What was she doing, over a thousand miles away, serving Natalie and Meggy up for the amusement of a colleague? And failing— the story wasn't amusing.

"Well," said Stephen. "What else? Something's got you buzzing— something happy."

"No, really," she told him. "I need your advice." The family court date was approaching.

"You'll know what to do," he said. "C'mon, you've already decided."

It was true—she had. But she could feel her sister's fear. She told Stephen how Natalie had pleaded with her not to take Meggy away, how she'd put Meggy on the phone to beg.

"Duet!" cried Stephen. "Show-stopper of a tune—*Don't take away my baay-by—Don't take away-ay my mom!*"

"*Stephen.* "

"You're just a witness, Rose. And you'd be surprised what kids can survive."

"Oh, really?" How did he know? Had he been taken from his mother? What if he was down on his luck or crazy and a judge decided to take his daughters, she thought, but didn't ask.

That afternoon, while he'd studied her score, Rose had played with his daughters for hours, observing how safely they rested within their parents' custody. They had their own wing of the house, tucked up into the hillside, a bathroom and two bedrooms full of lovely clothes and toys. Built into the wall separating their bedrooms was a doll house with open windows and grand little doorways through which hands could reach. Like giants eyeing each other from either side, Alexis and Starr reached in to move dolls and furniture, while narrating their dramas. Rose had been assigned to be the weather. She was to shout for thunder and to use the flashlight for lightning. Water was, unfortunately, banned. Firecrackers too—she knew how their *dad* was.

"He says it's *dangerous,*" they sighed. Their life was *so* restrictive.

Rose related all this to Stephen. He didn't laugh even then.

"Two darling girls," he said, arching back in his leather chair, "with a happy life. But not a perfect life. For instance, how can they ever explain why their parents don't sleep together?"

"Uh-huh," said Rose, her voice carefully neutral.

Stephen did have a fault. He snored but refused to believe it. Rose had heard him from her bed in the guest room, barely muffled through walls and closed doors, the sound like a piece of paper caught in a vacuum cleaner. The earplugs had not been invented that could obstruct his snoring, Leslie had confided to Rose, laughing. But he was irrationally sensitive about it and had been horrified, insulted, *betrayed* to find Leslie gone if he awoke in the night. So Stephen had given up the marriage bed to Leslie—no, no, he'd sleep elsewhere; he would not ruin her sleep. He had a bed built into his study wall, recessed and hidden by a curtain.

"He only pretends to suffer about where we sleep at night," Leslie had told Rose. Behind the curtain on a rainy afternoon, Alexis had been conceived. And on a snowy one, Starr.

Rose settled deeper into her leather chair. Stephen's bed was hidden behind its curtain across the room, but she'd once glimpsed a snowy coverlet over a mounded mattress. A featherbed. Stephen seemed as easy as a god in his comforts. The lights on the Sound blinked and burned and bounced off the water, which, in the dark, seemed fathomlessly deep.

"You're not telling," he said. "What else?"

What was there to tell him? There was nothing but dark water. Ursula bobbed up. She would tell about Ursula.

She'd nearly been fired from Ursula's wedding. When the piano tuner plugged in the phone, it hadn't been Natalie again, but Ursula calling about whether to have mints or nuts for her wedding reception. "Oh, hello, sweetheart," Rose had said to soothe her friend. *Sweetheart,* she'd said, not *Ursula,* so, of course, the tuner had inferred that she had a boyfriend. She saw the effect of her words and was thoroughly annoyed with herself. He'd dropped his shoulders, pocketed his tuning fork, nodded to her, all formal again, and had gone out her door.

"The wedding," Stephen prompted. "You were fired from the wedding."

"Very nearly." As Rose began to tell it, she kept the tuner to herself. About him, there was nothing yet to say.

Over the phone, Ursula had demanded to know if Rose was paying attention.

"Why not mints *and* nuts?" said Rose.

"Because we're running out of money," said Ursula.

"Then neither."

"But we can't do neither, we can't do nothing, we can't just set empty tables. We'll be earning a ton in the future. We don't want to look back ashamed of a crummy reception. It's our wedding—it's supposed to be great. Bruce is out walking," she'd added.

"Ah!" said Stephen. "*Out walking.*"

"Right," said Rose. "The bride has been fighting with the bridegroom."

"Never mind Bruce," Ursula had declared. "Things have to be decided." Should it be initials or a quote on the personalized paper reception napkins; mints or nuts or mints and nuts in tiny china cups or in fluted paper matching the color of the napkins?

"Ursula," Rose had ventured, "I have absolutely no opinion."

"*Oh-oh,*" said Stephen.

"Well, I didn't say it *that* coldly. I just told her to do whatever she wanted."

"Wrong move," said Stephen.

"*Really,*" Rose concurred.

Ursula had burst into tears. "I want you to *help* me. To be *with* me through this—this nightmare."

"You're having a fight with Bruce. It'll be okay. He loves you."

"No, I am not having a fight with Bruce—I'm having a fight with *you.* If you don't have time for me, just say so. You don't even have to stand up with me if you don't want to."

"And you'd better want to," Stephen put in.

"Don't do anything you don't want to do," Ursula had concluded in ringing tones. "*You don't have to be at the wedding at all.*"

"Ho-*kay,*" said Stephen. "Bye-bye, Ursula. We don't need the stress."

"Oh, I can't drop out," said Rose, though, at the time, she'd pictured the swift donation of a bridesmaid dress and corset to the college theater shop.

"Why not?" said Stephen. "Shit. Don't tell me you're one of those *good* girls."

"You don't walk out on your friend right before her wedding."

"Sounds like the Good Girl Code to me."

"Is Leslie a good girl?" she asked him. He sighed. "And Alexis and Starr? Or are you raising them to be bad girls?"

"Don't change the subject."

Rose *was* a good girl. She had made profuse apology to Ursula and gradually the crisis was averted, very gradually—a half-hour later, she was still apologizing.

"You could reassure me," Ursula had suggested. "You could say you're looking forward to it, that it's an honor to stand up with me. Unless you don't think so. I mean, sometimes it's like I'm getting married *all by myself.* Even Bruce looks at me funny. You think he loves me?"

"*Oh,* yeah," said Rose.

"He calls me his tiger kitten," Ursula remarked and giggled.

"Ah," said Stephen. "The secret of Ursula—between the sheets, a *tiger kitten.* That explains the man's patience."

"Spare me," said Rose.

She'd had to stay on the phone with Ursula, working from tiger kitten back to mints and nuts, and when they hung up, it was past eleven, too late to call the piano tuner. But, while soothing Ursula, she'd studied his address. He lived just a few blocks away. For a shivery instant, while Ursula yammered on, Rose had imagined Graham Lowe calling her "tiger kitten."

She told none of this to Stephen. She wouldn't have him know she was aflutter over a piano tuner. She pushed back into the padded leather and gazed up into the starlight. The thought of Graham pleased her absurdly. A chuckle escaped her.

"*And?*" said Stephen. "If you don't tell me, I'll be forced to guess."

"The night wasn't over," she said.

Rose had gone to bed and to sleep. Otherwise, what occurred next would have been unremarkable. Instead it began with a scare—what she'd thought at first was a break-in.

"Have you ever," she asked Stephen, "been allowed to witness someone falling in love? Someone you thought never would fall seriously in love?"

"With you?"

"No—with someone else."

"I would think," he said, "one would rather participate than witness."

She regarded him. He seemed bored with what she had to say. For the first time in conversation with him, her life seemed to lose luster in the telling. He seemed to want her to say something in particular rather than anything at all. It had been a great freedom she'd enjoyed, the freedom to tell him anything at all. But perhaps she was the one who was spoiling things, dropping her candor and putting falseness between them, imagining he would judge her. It wasn't his fault he had money and prestige. Maybe he'd come from no money at all—he'd never breathed a word about his childhood. He might well have earned everything, as she had. Maybe the nasty bathroom in the rooming house in Frogtown wouldn't faze him at all. Maybe, too, he'd be charmed by her little crush on her piano tuner. She ought to stop where she was in her story, circle back and put in what she'd left out.

"Later that night," he said. "Go on."

She did not circle back; she went on. Later that night, after she'd gone to bed, she became drowsily aware that she was no longer alone in her apartment. For several minutes in that netherworld between sleeping and waking, she'd been unable to move, as though she were mud with roots growing through her. Really, she'd had the sensation of roots growing down, right through her shoulder and through her face, as though pinning her to the mattress.

"Uh-huh," said Stephen. "*And?*"

Why was he rushing her? She was performing, wasn't she? Maybe she'd shut up and *he* could tell a story for a change.

"*And,*" she continued. Paralyzed there in her bed, she saw a man's shape. And then she was up, screaming, making for the open window where she burst a hole in the screen, a nylon screen with a tear already in it, which, thank god, ripped open quickly. And she was out on the ledge in nothing but a T-shirt and underpants. Only then did she hear Alan shouting her name.

"The gay guy upstairs with the wife and kid?"

"My friend," she told Stephen.

"It's Alan. I'm an idiot," he'd called as she dragged herself back in through the window, the ripped screen burning her bare arms and thighs.

"God in heaven," she cried. She'd have him impeached of his condo presidency and relieved of his master keys; she was serious as a heart attack. She yanked on her kimono. Someone stirred in the apartment overhead—Frances, awakened by the ruckus.

"I know, I know," said Alan. "But I've brought James." He reached into the hall and dragged someone slender and dark-skinned into the apartment.

"Let's leave her be, man," the stranger said softly. "Let's get out of here."

"This is James," said Alan.

"He's a tiny bit drunk," James told her, "and we'll be going now."

"Rose," Alan breathed. "This is *James*."

"The chef?" she asked.

"No, no, man—the musician, the drummer. From Ethiopia," lilted James, toeing a beat on the floor. He had wonderful slanting eyes and a heart-stopping smile.

Reaching to touch James, Alan's hand had trembled. "I have to tell you, Rose, I love this man. I would give this man anything. I'm, like, new born. I know what love is now."

"Such poetry," said Stephen, dryly.

"From Alan, it is, believe me," said Rose.

"And this is Rose," Alan had concluded, "my best friend in all the world."

Was she? She hadn't seen anything of Alan in months. He was so busy with his several lives, he hardly had time for friendship. Stephen had time. Stephen was her friend. He was, yes, her very best friend now. She told him so.

"Thank you, I think," said Stephen, his tone every bit as dry as before.

"You're welcome," she said. Didn't he know that, given her life, friendship was nearly everything?

James had opened his arms and clasped Rose to him. He smelled lemony and she'd felt some high vibration as though his chest were full of birds, and her own chest seemed to take up the thrumming. A wild, willful look in Alan's eye recalled the night, years ago, that he'd taken her to bed. But he was no longer that angry boy and his look was warm, ardent and certain. She'd never before seen him so entirely happy. Swiftly, he'd moved to reclaim James from her. And then, footsteps were heard descending the stairs and Frances' soft knock came at the door.

Rose stepped out into the hall and, for the first time, told Frances a direct lie about Alan.

"White lie," Stephen put in.

"Frances," she'd said, "I'm so sorry," and quickly invented the unexpected visit of an old boyfriend. "I'd let you in, but he's not dressed."

"I heard you scream. You sounded frightened," said Frances. "I thought I heard Alan." Frances rubbed her eyes. "It's okay. You're not the only one to make a ruckus late at night," she said and went back upstairs.

"I don't feel so good about that," Rose told Alan when she'd closed her door behind her.

"It's been tremendous to meet you," James told her and gave Alan a tug.

But Alan pulled a chair out from Rose's table and sat heavily down. "I love this man." He flicked a hand toward James. "I would lay down my life for this man."

James chuckled.

"We know this, now," Rose told Alan. "We know this."

"Okay," he said, getting to his feet. "So let's tell Frances. C'mon, let's go tell Frances."

"Could be the rum's talking," observed James.

"Love. Is talking," said Alan.

"Really?" said Rose. "But what about Max?"

Custody was on Rose's mind—what should be done to get Meggy away, how to argue it and arrange it. She hadn't thought of it the other way, what a parent could lose in an instant.

"You could lose Max," she'd blurted out to Alan.

"Undeniably," said Stephen. "But it sounds to me like you care more than he does."

"Then I've told it wrong," said Rose.

At the mention of his son, Alan had uttered Max's name, and Max seemed to stand in the room with them, unable to see them, yet stopped, his wild animation stilled, while his father seemed to cave in on himself, to become, in an instant, elderly. He knew Max's need of him better than anyone, and his own need to be his son's father. Max would, of course, be fed and sheltered, but where? And from whose hands fed?

That humans should need each other struck Rose at that moment as a grievous condition, a ruinous necessity. Ursula needed Bruce so much that she'd become *not*-Ursula; Natalie, while unable to care for her daughter, nonetheless grasped Meggy to her; Frances wretchedly reached for Alan even as he turned her away; and Rose, too, clung at the edges, warming herself at the fires of other people's lives.

Alan had leaned himself against James and, forgetting Rose was there, begun stroking his lover's chest, sadly but ardently. They would not go up to tell Frances that night. But they had each other, and even to Rose it was so obviously the right thing for Alan that the consequences could not hold sway. She told Stephen so and then stopped speaking, her story over.

When Alan and James had left her, she'd been mad with arousal and lay down briefly to satisfy herself. Then she'd gone to her piano, and the pages flew, the music buoyant, tormented, but gaining power, as though she had drawn from the lives around her not a secondhand passion, but her own self in anguish and joy. Getting up from the piano to pack for the train, she'd realized she was rank with sweat. Under the shower, she'd sung her symphony aloud while the water poured over her. The singing continued now inside her head. Stephen was right—something was up with her, something more than worry and grief, something joyous.

He rocked forward and blew out a candle. "Ever done this?" He licked his fingertips and pinched another burning wick, then another, until only one was left burning.

Rose pinched the candle out. Then they were in the dark.

"Gimme the matches," she said.

"Well, and what about you, Rose? If you're not in love, why not?"

"Oh, I have my adventures."

"You're not one of those ironclad celibates, then?"

She laughed. "Like Susan B.?"

"I've got my theories about Susan B., behind closed doors with all those women."

"Hey, really," said Rose. Even with the candles out, the room had plenty of light. Or perhaps her eyes had adjusted.

"So. You're a lesbian, are you?"

"Oh, lord. Don't tell me—*just* because I have short hair?"

"You're heterosexual like me?" he said. "Well, how boring."

She laughed uneasily.

"I think you're in love," he said.

"Well, maybe with the idea of love." The brandy slid along her tongue. She rubbed the soft leather of the chair and turned away from him toward the lights on the water.

"Or maybe with your new best friend?"

She startled. That was what he'd been waiting to hear, that she was in love with him. The possibility hadn't occurred to her. Instantly, she knew to pretend otherwise. He'd got up to stand behind her chair. His fingers were moving through her hair. He was her conductor; they had work ahead; they couldn't afford to fool around. He was too old for her, nearly fifty. He was *married*.

"What are you *doing*?" she whispered.

"You don't have to whisper. No one can hear us," he said. This was true. Leslie slept in the master bedroom in another wing. "I'm touching your marvelous hair," he went on. "How does it feel?" Her skin buzzed. It felt lovely; how could it not? He knelt beside her. "Give me your hand.

C'mon—you've shaken my hand a dozen times. You've kissed me before, please remember."

"Yes, *publicly.*"

He took her hand, pulled her to him and kissed her, and she returned the kiss, self-consciously matching his pressure. How stupid of her not to see this coming. Rumors had warned her, but she had disbelieved. She'd wished for a conductor. She'd rejoiced when there was more to it—friendship, she'd insisted, pure friendship. The worst she'd been willing to think of him was that he was a little arrogant, controlling and shaping his world. She saw she was the same, insisting that things be the way she wished or foolishly pretending they were. Unlike Stephen, she lacked the force to make things be as she wished. She was a fool. She'd fooled herself. She'd pretended her way into this, this situation.

"So what you feel for me is only friendship?" he said with a wicked calm in his voice.

She regretted that it took no effort to get up from the chair. To exit the bed behind the curtains wouldn't be as easy. He led her there. The curtains parted silkily. She didn't want this. It wasn't love. She wanted to finish her symphony and see him conduct it. She felt not so much led as hoisted up, a sack of flour. He went on kissing her, and she went on returning his kisses promptly, like a student answering questions. The enthralling softness of his touch turned sharp, like a father's shoulder digging up into her belly. He unloosed her fingers from the bedframe and pushed her in. The featherbed puffed up around her. He was pulling his shirt over his head.

She was going to allow this, was she?

Chapter TWENTY-TWO

She was tense and wincingly dry, but he didn't know it. He was busy trying to get hard, holding himself over her as if he were in the up motion of a pushup, brushing his hips back and forth between her spread legs which she'd opened for him correctly, widely, a very good girl. If he was embarrassed by his lack of a hard-on, he didn't say. He wasn't saying anything, but working away, flopping against her. Leaning on one hand, he reached for her face, her jaw, and pulled himself up the bed and loomed over her, nudging at her mouth with his cock. She tried to suck, but he wouldn't hold still. He flopped against her lips and chin. It was the joke punishment: fifty lashes with a wet noodle, but she'd better not laugh. She'd better make a good job of it—fuck him and get out of there. She'd better mind his feelings. On paper, her career was in Seattle now. Her tenure application was laced with his name.

Better a participant than a witness, he'd warned her, but she'd stayed on alone with him in that room, the room where he slept, exposing herself.

The buzz inside her brought on by her thrill over Alan and James and stoked by her furious writing had halted. Her voice was stopped up in her throat. She was going to have to speak, at least to tell him to put on a condom. If they got that far. His cock flopped loosely against her face. She gasped, drawing breath when she could, as the doughy expanse of his belly pressed up and down on her, forehead to collarbone. He was older; of course he'd have a paunch. She saw the purpose of the cunning pleats in his Italian trousers. She saw how he worked it from the podium: the trousers outlining the slender legs, the blackness of the tailcoat drawing the eye up to the wide shoulders, the tails drawing the eye down and away from the vacant white shirtfront over the frog belly. To make room to breathe, she reached to raise his belly, but he batted her hands away. He lifted her chin, adjusting her to him. The lights on the Sound jerked in her sight as he bounced. One eye was blocked by his belly. With her other eye, she peered into the room and, between bounces, noted where her blouse lay on the floor by her sandals and her skirt, flung over the chair where a half hour ago she'd sat, yakking away.

She couldn't think of that now; she might, like a little girl, give way to tears—like Meggy, she thought, and then realized she'd never seen Meggy cry. Her heart contracted. Why did Meggy never cry? One of her eyes had started to leak, but Rose wasn't crying, *oh* no, she was not a little girl but a grown woman in bed with a man.

Why wasn't he getting hard? Maybe it was the brandy. He'd refilled his glass more than once that evening. Or maybe he didn't really want her either and would see that and quit. Maybe she'd be excused; maybe she could still face his wife in the morning.

He moved down again and spread her knees wide, grinding heavily on her. She rocked her hips a little, in time with his thrashing. If he didn't get hard, he might blame her. If he didn't get hard, they'd never get this over with, whatever it was going to be.

People would say she'd gotten to where she was—Composer in Residence, Seattle Sinfonietta—on her back. There was talk already, she realized. She heard again the wry remarks, saw the raised eyebrows, the winks in her direction. She saw now that people assumed she'd been sleeping with Stephen Orrick all along. Which might as well be true, if she were willing to pay this price to see her commission through to performance.

His words and his tone had seemed practiced, getting her undressed and under him. It was apparently what he did: took women to bed. She grasped that now. Of course, he was far from the only conductor to make his way across women's bodies, though he would gain nothing professionally by sleeping with Rose. It was likely just a reflex.

Wealthy volunteers, almost all of them female, who raised and maintained concert halls, who kept the books, paid salaries, funded commissions, and who saw to it that the seats were filled, did not do all that for nothing. The savvy conductor "played" the volunteers as a sort of second orchestra, and what better way to string them along, the bevy of them, than to offer at least the possibility of going to bed with him? Stephen had no paid staff, other than a stage manager and a secretary. Even the bookkeeper was a volunteer. Such women did not turn over their time—what might otherwise be full-time paid work—for the purely altruistic love of music. They did it at least partly for the life around the music: the gossip, the flirtations with artists, the intrigues.

Stephen gave a sigh and rolled off of her. "Well."

"It's okay," she said, her voice swift and quiet and not her own. "Really."

"I'll be better at it in the morning."

In the morning? "Sure," she said.

"Or shall we see what we can do for you now?" For the first time, he reached his fingers between her legs. She caught his hand quickly and raised it to her lips—she wouldn't have him find her dry, frightened cunt. Rarely had she thought of herself as that—hole to be plugged, cunt. And she wasn't even that; she had no desire. She turned on her side away from him. He ran his hands over her, touching her breasts and stroking her ass. Fear held her there beside him, fear of the harm he could do her.

"Ah, Rose. I knew you were hot. I knew you were a hot one," he said.

Why? Cold to her bones, she nearly asked him why. She couldn't see a clock. It was probably too late to catch the redeye flight from Seattle to St. Paul, and the train would not depart until the evening, but she could go and camp out at the station. She'd pack and head out. If she could only move.

"Well," she said, "I'm off to bed now," and with great effort sat up.

He wrapped his arms around her and pulled her back to him. "Nuh-uh. You're sleepin' wif me." Baby talk? He thought he'd hold her with *baby talk*?

"Look," she told him, "I can't be here when the house wakes up."

"Leslie's driving the girls over to church. They've got a thingie at Sunday school. We won't see 'em till lunchtime." He snuggled closer.

"Leslie," she echoed and waited for shame. Instead, what came was hatred. She hated all husbands and wives. Alan, she thought, would admire the arrangement—the guestroom so convenient to Stephen, the wife asleep out of earshot, off in another wing. Of course, Alan and Frances were a different matter: the tricks, schemes, and maneuvers seemed mutual. Stephen's Leslie had done nothing to coerce Stephen to marry her, as far as Rose knew. Theirs was a storybook courtship as they both told it.

"Do you like doing it in the morning?" he asked, his voice husky and sly.

Or maybe Leslie did know. She had, after all, lit candles for Rose and Stephen, turned off the lights, and absented herself. Maybe she knew all about his affairs; maybe she even arranged them, luring in female house guests to distract him so she wouldn't have to suffer his wretched love-making. How could Leslie stay married to such a man? Rose realized with dread that he was the sort she herself had sometimes imagined marrying, a prominent, accomplished man. This one had nothing to offer her, not even marriage, but even so, he had seized her and flung her down; he had taken her. Apparently she was easy to take.

His arms were tight around her. His palm, as he brushed over her breasts, caused her nipples witlessly to tighten.

This is sex, she told herself bitterly, what you long for, what you've been missing.

A whistling blew through her hair. He was snoring: an accordion with a toneless, gasping inhale and then a labored, whistling exhale. She let it fill her ears. She was going to travel on that whistle; she was going to get up and out of there. He shuddered, and his breathing seemed to stop. She waited as if at a deathbed. At length he sucked in again.

"I'm going to the bathroom," she muttered, wresting herself free and swinging her legs out of the bed. He half-roused, reached for her, and grabbed air.

She quickly gathered skirt, blouse, sandals, and wristwatch. She couldn't find her underpants, but he'd be handy, no doubt, at disposal of underpants.

In the guest room, she dressed, pulled on her jacket, thrust her feet into her running shoes, and threw her bag over her shoulder. She could already feel on her skin the damp pre-dawn air of Seattle. She hardly cared if she got lost; she had hours to find the train station—if only she weren't exhausted and dizzy. She told herself she would sleep soon. She'd nap next to some nice woman at the station, someone she could ask to guard her while she slept. She lurched back across the hall for her toothbrush, then sat on the bed to gather herself, and shouldn't have. It was irresistible not to tip over, to lie on her side a moment and close her eyes. Then he was standing in the doorway.

"So you're just going to cut and run?"

"Stephen," she said thickly. "Listen." She sat up and shook her head to clear it. She'd fallen asleep. "Look, Stephen, you're my conductor. The most talented conductor I know, certainly the most important—"

"What is this—an awards ceremony?"

"—the most important conductor I've ever been privileged to know."

"Past tense?"

"I really hope not. Please, I'm asking you to realize my position."

"Oh, I want to. All your positions. I'm better at it in the morning, I told you."

"That's really, I mean *really*, beside the point."

"Well, what is the point, Rose?"

In the doorway, he straightened and widened his shoulders. The room was filling with a dim, achy light that for a moment cast in grandeur the wedge of his torso. His eyes seemed carved, yet alive, blinking at her.

"You need love," he continued. "Are you too worried about your friends and your family, are you too worried about your *career* to let yourself fall in love?"

In love? She gave a startled laugh.

"Or are you just afraid?"

She stood up. In his mouth, the doleful litany of her worries seemed a lie, so clearly was he self-serving. Really, he did her a favor. Parroting her fears and her sorrows back to her for his own transparent purpose, he showed himself to be her enemy, and a stupid one. He stood blocking the door. If she was afraid, she was not going to show it.

"Are we in love?" she said. "I don't think so."

"But we are. Or could be in a second. Have you any idea how lonely you are?"

"You're a married man," she said. "And your wife, Leslie, is my friend."

"Leslie is not your *friend*. You are acquainted with her through me. To stay in this house, you would have to know Leslie."

What an asshole he was. Why had she never seen it? She'd exposed her sorrows to him, but he apparently had none, nothing but the snoring, nothing but the limp dick, whatever that meant—hell if she knew. She didn't know him or Leslie either. But she wouldn't let him go unopposed.

"I'll be the one to say who is and is not my friend," she told him.

"I thought *I* was the friend. The best friend?"

"It seems I was mistaken."

"Really?" he said, frigid and remote. "Then I'll get out of your way."

Yet he stood there. She waited.

"An ironclad celibate after all," he said, stepping backward into the hall.

"You wouldn't know," she allowed herself to say.

"Oh, you can't hide it. It shows. It shows in the music."

Her ears rang as though she'd been struck.

"I'm going." She'd get on an early train and get a connection back to St. Paul. She'd go to Omaha first if she had to. She'd go to Winnipeg.

"Christ. Aren't you tired?" His voice sounded normal again, almost warm. "Go to bed, Rose. I'll take you to the station in the morning."

But it was morning. A distant rustling came from the kitchen.

"God, she's up early," he said. *She*, the woman of the house, his woman, his house, his everything. His eyes passed over Rose and did not linger.

Leslie approached up the hall with steaming mugs on a tray. Rose couldn't look at her, but Leslie didn't seem to notice.

"Everybody's up early," she said pertly. "The girls are already dressed." She set the tray down on the guestroom bed.

Could she tell that it had not been slept in? Was there anything to remark in Rose being dressed while Stephen stood there in his bathrobe?

The breakfast room was spangled with sunlight. The little girls pranced in, all frilly dresses and shiny shoes. Rose looked past Leslie to Stephen and noted again the high Tchaikovsky forehead and prickly beard as though viewing a portrait. She couldn't fathom that she'd kissed him, yet a patch below her lip burned from his mustache. The girls chatted over their fresh-squeezed orange juice and croissants. She thought of Meggy and how she'd envied Starr and Alexis for Meggy's sake, how she'd imagined Meggy in this house, safe, prosperous, and lucky. She didn't know if she should fear for Alexis and Starr, but she no longer envied them. At least Natalie's troubles were out in the open.

She took the earliest excuse to leave the table. Stephen got his coat and met her in the foyer, handing her her underpants, tidily folded, if dirty, and her manuscript, stacked neatly in a new file folder labeled

R. MacGregor. She'd meant to leave it with him; she had her own copy. But she packed it without a word.

On the way to the station, he began speaking, mildly, a trifle absently.

"Many a symphony has been played too soon, of course. You need time. Lots of time. Brahms, as we know, took twenty years writing his first. Worth the wait, of course. So, let's postpone, shall we? A year at least." For the Susan B. Anthony Birthday event, he could substitute the Virgil Thomson/Gertrude Stein. Rose's commission would, of course, be paid in full.

As quickly as he dropped her at the station, he'd dropped her from his season.

She hadn't thought this could happen, and she had no alternative plan. She'd finish the symphony, of course, but who could say when she'd next find an orchestra to perform it? Her tenure portfolio was due at the end of summer, barely two months away. Once she deleted Seattle from her list of upcoming premieres, what would be left? Commissions and residencies couldn't be invented; new opportunities couldn't be hurried.

Gripping the arms of her seat aboard the train, she held herself up as firmly as she could. Even so, she felt herself falling as the train sped homeward. She rested her head on her bag between her knees, her purse buried inside it and, for good measure, her wallet tucked in her armpit, up inside her sleeve. Any money she had seemed about to run out. She rested her eyes and for brief minutes slept. The return trip took her through a day and a night and into another day.

And then she was home again in her condo, in her own big chair. And still falling. Her life *had* to be more than her career and surely could not be ruined by a single blunder. She needed food and a bath and sleep, but she couldn't move. The evening breeze rustled at her window, springtime pushing onward, ardent and naïve.

As though from another world, the sound came of Frances pounding on the door and calling out to her. "Rose, are you there? Are you all right?"

What day was it? Had Rose missed something crucial? "It's open," she called.

Frances came in with Jewels in her arms. Placed momentarily in Rose's lap, the cat jumped down, refusing to know her.

"What day is it?" she asked Frances and staggered over to her calendar.

"Tuesday, last day of May. Graduation was this morning," said Frances.

Rose had missed graduation—a mistake while under scrutiny for tenure, though she hadn't had any special duties, no speeches or presentations. Maybe nobody had noticed her absence. She double-checked Meggy's court date. It was not for another ten days.

"Dear, oh, dear," said Frances. "What are you doing to yourself? Old boyfriends in the middle of the night? Unplanned jaunts to Seattle?"

Boyfriends in the night?

"Oh," Rose groaned and looked away, remembering the lie she'd told Frances to cover for Alan and James. Frances was bright-eyed and lively, her coloring up, her very short hair not desperate, but endearing. Rose could tell Frances about Stephen. She'd been through a wringer or two of her own; Frances would understand humiliation.

"Well?" prompted Frances. "The boyfriend in the night and then Seattle? There's a connection?"

Rose decided there had better be. She put Stephen in her apartment in place of Alan and James. Then she put herself running after him to Seattle.

"Of *course*. Your conductor."

"You're not going to like this, Frances. He's married."

"Oh. No, I don't like it."

"But you know how it could happen," said Rose. Frances had, after all, carried on histrionically over the married department Chair.

"All right," said Frances. "It does happen. Is he nice to you?"

"Not particularly."

"Then dump him," said Frances.

"Okay," said Rose. That was easy.

Frances, full of kindly concern, studied her. "You want to find somebody all of your own," she said earnestly. "Someone in the free-and-clear.

Really," she said, "you would not believe the contentment." She seemed to glow. "Things get humdrum, of course. It can seem like a whole lot of nothing for a great long while, and then. . . ." She paused in mock suspense.

"And then?" Rose asked dutifully.

"And then your husband is making love to you again. Sometimes, once you're married, you hardly make love at all. Did you know that?"

"No, I didn't," said Rose, dully piling on another lie. Why Alan was making love to Frances, she couldn't imagine.

Chapter TWENTY-THREE

T he corridor on the seventeenth floor of the Ramsey County
Courthouse, City of St. Paul, was lined down one side with a
long bench where men and women divorcing or wrangling over
custody or suing for protection sat and waited to be called. A woman with
her jaw wired shut and a fading bruise all down her neck studied her
folded hands. Which of the men—if he was present—was the violent
boyfriend or husband or father could not be determined; no one sat
together here. Lawyers, social workers, deputies, and clerks cut through,
while, along the bench, calm prevailed, the horrid enforced idleness of
waiting.

The three MacGregors—Rose, Natalie, and Meggy—had arrived
early, Rose just a step behind Natalie, who'd turned and clasped her sister
hard to her. Meggy accepted Rose's hug with a polite, uninhabited smile
and they sat down. Guy wasn't there yet.

How Rose's days had passed since her return from Seattle, she couldn't have said. In the mulberries outside her windows, birds sang and sang, but she was sick of music, sick of everything. She'd slept; she'd taken bath after bath, but she still felt Stephen on her skin and his words of judgment were snarled up inside her.

"Mommy?" Meggy shyly uncurled her finger toward the far end of the corridor where, below a small window, an armed deputy sat. "What does he need a gun for?"

"Aw, don't worry, sweetheart." The deputy spoke up from ten feet away. "Sometimes the grown-ups in here get upset and I have to calm 'em down." A nervous shifting along the bench followed, as of birds rising and settling.

Maybe, as Stephen had suggested, lovelessness did show in Rose's music. How could she tell? She was cold and celibate, as doomed as any miserable soul here on the bench, where shoulders angled stiffly and averted faces spoke of a distance worse than that of strangers: the wish to become unacquainted, to have never met.

Rose bent toward Meggy. "I've got something for you."

In a cloth sack in her briefcase was hidden the small pack of treasures she'd long accumulated for Meggy: the canary feather in a Lucite block, the Afghan coin purse filled with dimes, a jade ring, a tiny black winged horse—Pegasus carved from a piano key—and even the Tiffany egg from Stephen—Rose could see no reason Meggy should forgo the egg just because of its source. Meggy's eyes glimmered at her, but the whiz of the briefcase zipper drew Natalie's glance and Rose stopped her hand.

What Rose most wanted to do was to slip down to the floor with Meggy and hand her presents, one by one. But even if Natalie would allow presents, Rose couldn't get down on the floor in what she was wearing. As if for a wedding or a funeral, she'd dressed in her linen suit: straight skirt and shoulder pads, the single professional woman, chic version of the maiden aunt. Why had she come so armored? Because she was ashamed of the situation? Because she wished to show the judge or anyone else who was watching that not all MacGregors lived like Natalie? A lot of good that would do Meggy.

"Later," she whispered to Meggy, who nodded agreeably, her eyes flat again, her shoulders held very straight under Natalie's hands. Her hair, though raggedly cut, was combed and clipped back with a plastic bumblebee barrette. Her T-shirt and shorts were a matching blue. She looked nice; Natalie deserved that much credit. The little girl's knees were scabby, though, and her rubber flip-flops seemed grievously wrong for court. But Meggy was not on trial—why should she have to impress anyone?

Natalie was the one under scrutiny, but seemed not to know it. Her hair hung lank and unwashed, and she wore an old plaid jumper of Rose's, which she'd transformed into overalls, the skirt slashed and re-stitched into trouser legs that bunched clownishly at the crotch. What was she thinking? Was she crazy? Well, yes, she was. She seemed to be.

At the appointed hour of their hearing, the escort deputy stepped out and called names, but no Natalie MacGregor and no Guy Robbin. Rose went to confirm that their judge was in court and that they were on the roster. They were—court was running a little behind. Here came Guy, late, and dressed little better than Natalie. He wore a derelict sport coat, jeans, and cracked work boots embedded with cement. He'd grown a beard but left it untrimmed, a bird's nest, and he'd water-combed his hair straight back. He had a sheaf of papers in his pocket that he couldn't seem to keep from rattling.

"Guess what?" Meggy whispered to him. "Our bathroom doesn't work, so we took a bath in the dishpan, like in Mexico."

"Really?" said Guy pointedly. Rose tried not to look at Natalie's hair.

"And we peed outside and pooped at the gas station," said Meggy, forgetting to whisper.

"Shh, Meggy," hissed Natalie.

Guy added a note to his sheaf of papers and Rose found herself annoyed. So they'd peed outside? Up north, Guy used an outhouse, same as at the Goat Pasture. So Natalie and Meggy were a little dirty? Hadn't Rose herself, just days before, stumbled off the train, grubby and sour-smelling? They were all travelers of a sort. They'd get through this and move on. There'd be a decision, peace, and eventually better or at least different days, a change of luck, maybe, though Rose was not keen just then on the subject of luck.

But she could be an instrument of peace. She'd made lunch reservations at the museum a block away. She spoke up to tell them so. Her treat. The museum restaurant had a nice buffet. There'd be chicken and shrimp salad, hot rolls and local strawberries, the fresh, soft kind that won't travel. After court, they'd break bread together; they'd talk things over and make arrangements. Alan, Frances, and Max were going to join them for dessert, for a sense of a wider community—Frances's idea. The museum restaurant overlooked the river. Meggy and Max could watch the barges and boats.

Guy stared at Rose without expression. She realized she was gibbering.

"The matter of Robbin versus MacGregor," announced the escort deputy.

They were led into a tiny courtroom with a platform at the end, just room enough to seat a judge and a court recorder, and, below the judge, a table and chairs. The judge sat close, almost on top of them. His platform placed him just a few inches above them and he may as well have been somebody's uncle in a choir robe—Guy's uncle, in fact. Though clean-shaven, his resemblance to Guy was uncanny: long nose, sharp jaw, bold gaze. Rose felt a surge of sympathy for her sister now taking her place before Guy and the judge, men who were about to confer over her, *men handing out rights to each other.* The judge's hair was combed straight back. Had Guy done the same deliberately?

He motioned Rose to his side of the table. Natalie hustled Meggy to the seats opposite him. Rose hesitated.

"I see that Mr. Robbin has brought counsel," said the judge, and the court recorder, a woman with brown hair hooked over her ears and a pair of hands joined to a machine, clicked into action, a sort of staccato accompanist.

The judge's voice, at least, was nothing like Guy's, but a big, deep voice, pitched softly to whisk over the surface things, a voice which, if singing, would boom and roar.

"I'll be speaking for myself. I'm prepared," said Guy.

"So am I," put in Natalie. "Don't think I'm not." Her tone was high and mean. Rose was surprised. She'd expected a show of meekness.

"So this is your counsel?" the judge asked Natalie, pointing to Rose, who still stood. Counsel? He'd mistaken her for a lawyer.

"The aunt," said Guy.

"My sister," said Natalie.

"Rose MacGregor." She went and shook the judge's hand. His palm was dry and neutral. Why was she shaking his hand? Because he'd mistaken her for a fellow professional, instead of recognizing that she might be related to Natalie—Natalie's sister and Meggy's aunt? Ashamed, Rose sat down beside Meggy.

"Ms. MacGregor," said the judge, addressing Natalie pleasantly, "as I said last time, it is improper for a child to be present at these proceedings."

"Where else should she be?" Natalie retorted.

"With a baby-sitter," he answered. "Perhaps the aunt?" He turned to Rose. "Would you take the little girl back to the waiting area?"

Rose stood quickly. There was suddenly nothing she'd rather do.

Natalie clamped a hand on Meggy. "My daughter doesn't leave my sight."

Did Natalie mean to misbehave? Did she not see that she was under judgment? Did she not understand the weight of everything she said or did there?

"Anyway," said Guy, "I need the aunt. I need her for corroboration."

The aunt. Rose was the aunt. Yes, Meggy's aunt, and glad of it.

"Don't we have an affidavit from you?" the judge asked Rose.

"Jesus," Rose blurted. "I forgot."

"Language," muttered Natalie.

Rose had meant to give Guy his affidavit. Where on earth had she been? All wrapped up in her work. And then, in Seattle. In Seattle, getting fucked, literally.

"But you're prepared to speak here?" the judge asked her.

"I need corroboration," Guy said, spreading his papers on the table. Did he have to be so formal? It seemed suddenly strange that he should get custody. Would he know how to talk to a little girl? What kind of father would he be? Grim and remote as now?

Rose nodded to the judge. She'd speak. But what would she say?

The judge cast his glance around the table and frowned. "As I've stated, I question the appropriateness of deliberating with the child present."

"Then call the thing off. *Postpone*," said Natalie in a tone so unruly, Rose turned and stared. Natalie sat heavily in her chair, large-eyed and pale, deathly afraid.

"Your Honor," said Guy. "Please. Since we've gotten this far." It was Guy who was meek now. Rose couldn't understand it. The facts were on his side, it seemed to her.

The judge cleared his throat. "These are adult matters."

"Meggy knows he's not her father," sneered Natalie.

"Ms. MacGregor," said the judge.

"She knows everything," Guy shot back, "the way you raised her."

"She'd better know. I want her to see what you people are trying to do to her."

"Ms. MacGregor," enunciated the judge. "Mr. Robbin." His voice, though no louder than before, exerted its force, and they all went still. "This is a formal proceeding. There will be no quarreling." The court recorder paused in her clicking. The judge looked up out the window, a tiny lapse in demeanor, and Rose thought she saw grief. Then he snapped his jaw tight. She could almost hear his teeth crash together.

"All right," he said. "You're raising a fine young girl here." Easy and warm as a friendly coach—a referee, as his title plate read—he turned to Meggy.

He was good, Rose realized; they were lucky. They might be lucky in him.

He explained custody, that the people present all cared about Meggy and what was best for her, and that more than one person wanted her to live with them. As he spoke, Meggy carefully laid on the table a small, grubby, nail-bitten hand.

"Do you have any questions about this?" he asked her, and Meggy drew a breath. "Any thoughts at all about where you would live? We're not asking you to decide."

Natalie leaned back from her daughter and closed her eyes.

"With my mama?" asked Meggy and Natalie exhaled noisily. But the girl's words had been a question, not a statement.

Invited by the judge, Guy then began reading from his papers. As quietly as she could, Rose unzipped her briefcase and fished out and placed the little yellow feather in its clear plastic block onto the table where Meggy had laid her hand. The girl glanced at her mother and gingerly closed her fingers around it. Natalie looked over and rolled her eyes.

He'd known Meggy from birth, Guy was saying. Meggy had known him all her life. He'd changed her diapers; he'd been up with her when she was sick in the night. She'd known no other father, and, until forbidden to do so, she had, of her own accord, called him Daddy. He'd been the one she came to first when she hurt herself and cried.

"I don't *think* so," Natalie growled. The judge fixed her with a swift glance.

"*Dia*pers," Meggy muttered.

"That was a long time ago, when you were in diapers," said the judge. "We know you're a big girl now." They exchanged a nod, grave, collegial— two judges who might, between them, straighten things out. Rose choked on the thought. How could they? How could any of this ever be set straight?

Guy started in again, started over, it seemed. Now he was saying all the same things but in legal language. He spoke of the need for stability and continuity of relationship, he spoke of the need for a father figure. The language was bland, almost hateful. Rose took out the jade ring in its felt box and offered it to Meggy. Uncertainly, the girl handed back the feather floating in its block.

"All yours," Rose whispered, "all these things are yours."

Her eyes on Rose, Meggy tucked the block into her pocket and put the ring on. Guy was speaking of Easter and of Natalie's defiance of the visitation order. Without even knowing if the aunt was home, the mother had abandoned the child on the aunt's doorstep, on a city street.

Asked for corroboration, Rose nodded. That was what had happened, and, of course, it was wrong, but she recalled the wonder of finding Meggy there at her door, the girl grown up from the baby she had cherished—her niece who could now sit to eat at her table and cuddle up with her at night.

"When," said Natalie hoarsely, abruptly, "are we going to talk about the law?"

"Ms. MacGregor, you will get your turn."

Guy set forth his worthiness as a father. Meggy meant the world to him. And he possessed the means. Unlike the child's mother, he earned a living—various odd jobs, but steady—and he owned property.

"A shack," said Natalie.

"Forty acres of woods on a lake. Compared to a room in a flophouse."

The judge rapped his gavel. Meggy jumped. "There will be no interrupting," the judge told Natalie, his voice barely more than a whisper.

"I've built a stone house," Guy continued fiercely. "The roof's raised—a grass roof, sealed inside. Sod is laid and the grass is growing. The windows are in. She has her own bedroom and her own bed." He'd show the girl the woods. She'd hunt and fish with him. They'd grow a garden. The court recorder sped along, her hands lively. Rose now understood Guy's neglected appearance. He'd been working day and night to make ready. She could see Meggy safe asleep within the stone walls or out on the grass roof, learning the stars, or running loose in the day among the striped birches, jerking her first fish from the water, growing strong and free and confident. Surely the judge could see it too. Guy had built his house; he should have his child. He'd be a fine father. Meggy should be allowed to receive what Guy was so eager and able to give.

The girl had been kept truant, Guy was saying. Despite his best efforts and those of her teachers, the mother had kept her out the last month of school. The judge had affidavits from the social worker and the principal. Guy paused as though out of breath.

"Send her to school? How am I to let her out of my sight when he could kidnap her at any time?" Natalie cried, her voice as ragged as if she'd been talking all the while.

Fine—let the judge see how crazy she was, thought Rose, and reached into her briefcase and brought out the Afghani coin purse for Meggy.

"*Kid*nap her?" said Guy. "I would never kidnap anyone."

"You heard me," said Natalie.

The judge rapped his gavel and lifted his voice and then dropped it. He was not, he said, the sort of referee who chased players up and down the field. This was not a squabble fest. What example, really, did they wish to set for a youngster? If they couldn't comport themselves, he would decide the case with no further testimony from anyone. Really, how could Ms. MacGregor answer Mr. Robbin if she didn't first hear what he had to say? Whatever her reason, if she spoke again before being called on, he'd have her escorted from the room.

Rose reached and tugged at the top of the coin purse, which emitted a sour whiff. Meggy sniffed and, fingering the dimes inside, gave the tiniest hint of a smile.

Guy's hands had begun to shake. The child had been kept truant. Instead of going to school, she was kept up all night praying. Was she properly fed? He didn't know—the mother lacked an income. She refused his money, though who knows how she might spend it? On religious tracts? On contributions to a lunatic church? And meanwhile, the living conditions! That very day, he'd learned that they lacked even a working toilet, he said, and he let his papers fall and turned to Rose.

"Right," she told the judge. "What he says is true."

Natalie jerked Meggy's chair closer. "Do us a favor," she muttered to Rose. "Go over and sit on his side."

Ignoring her, Rose rummaged in her briefcase and slipped Meggy the tiny black horse. Only Stephen's blue china egg remained to be handed over to Meggy.

"Aunt Rose," said Meggy softly, "we weren't supposed to tell about the toilet."

Rose nodded but kept her chair. Natalie had it coming. Natalie wasn't a bad person, just a bad mother, a frightful mother, fit for nothing but to follow her own crazy whims. She could follow her whims without Meggy. She'd be fine. She'd have visitation—Guy said so. He was saying that, if granted custody, he'd abide by visitation.

Under the tabletop, Rose handed Meggy the china egg. But before Meggy could close her fingers around it, it fell and shattered. Guy flinched in his chair. Rose asked the judge's pardon and bent to the floor to pick up the shards, but she was glad of the explosion.

It was the noise of breaking—Stephen's egg breaking. It was the end of bad things.

But now Natalie had her turn. Let her speak, thought Rose. Things ended so things could start over. Guy would get Meggy, and Rose would visit. She'd visit all the time.

"Mr. Robbin says he abides by law." Natalie, too, was prepared. She spoke word after careful word. Guy had never married her through six-plus years of cohabitation. He had never adopted Meggy. "If I understand the law, he has no parental rights," she said.

The judge cleared his throat. "Is that all you have to say?"

"It is," said Natalie. "I believe it's all I need to say."

It seemed to Rose a weak defense. She grinned at Meggy goofily, gawkily.

"School attendance is also a matter of law," observed the judge.

"I'll be getting her back in school," said Natalie.

"Oh?" said the judge. "Have you got her registered? Have you determined whether she can be tutored this summer or whether she must repeat the first grade?"

"I said I will get her back in school. She will be in school in September."

Weak, thought Rose.

"Very well," said the judge. "May I ask how you are living? Paying the rent?"

"We are not to be tempted by money," said Natalie and took the coin purse from Meggy's hands and pushed it over to Rose. "We will not worship mammon."

Another Christian paid their rent, she said, a friend of her father, a disinterested person, and Rose recalled the chinless man in the photo.

"May I ask," said the judge, "how you and the girl are eating?"

"Food shelf," declared Natalie, "if it's anyone's business. And clothes from Goodwill. Blessed are the poor," she said and joined her palms together.

Good, thought Rose. Let the judge see this too.

"Dear Jesus, enlighten our minds," intoned Natalie.

"All right," said the judge. "I believe I've got the picture." He continued to speak as Natalie continued to pray. "What we've got here is an eccentric situation," he said.

No kidding, thought Rose, on the edge of jubilation. Natalie lapsed into silence.

"We've got a mother who thinks prayer comes before earning a living or providing a nice place to live," said the judge. "We've got a father who has a more usual view, except he isn't actually the father. And we have a little girl who is at least adequately fed and clothed."

Rose felt her heart drop. Something was going wrong.

"Some of us may not like this," he went on. "Some of us may really disapprove of the up-all-night praying."

Rose bobbed her head like an idiot.

"I am constrained, however, to rule according to law," he said and flashed Guy a look of what had to be sympathy. But then the look was gone and the judge was stone. "For a legal stranger to get custody, conditions must exist which don't exist here."

Rose choked. Guy was on his feet. *"A stranger?"*

"Mr. Robbin, weeks ago, when you set this matter in motion, my clerk advised you of the difficulties," said the judge. The court recorder rattled on. Guy staggered down into his seat again. "You were told you could petition for custody. Anyone can do that. You were also advised that the rights of the natural parent were likely to prevail. Unless related by blood, by marriage, or by adoption, you have only as much legal right to the girl as a stranger walking by on the street."

"A blood relative," said Rose. "What about me?"

The judge frowned.

"Anyone can petition for custody," she persisted. "Could I?" She suddenly saw how it should be. She felt what she had to give. If the judge sighed, she didn't hear it. If he shook his head, she didn't see. Nor did she see Meggy looking up at her, dismayed. Instead, she remembered what the little girl had said at the rooming house in Frogtown. Rose again felt the little hand on the back of her knee and heard the suggestion that she, Rose, be the mother and Natalie be the aunt. Meggy *had* spoken, hadn't she?

"I'll take her. Let me take Meggy. I petition for custody."

Natalie stared. "You bitch," she said. "Have your own damned baby."

But the words were mere noise to Rose, a sneeze, a scratching on the table. Rose saw Meggy with her, breakfasts and suppers, the little girl's quiet breathing beside her in the night, the clothes she'd get her, after-school conversations, piano lessons, college. Rose's career might be wrecked. She might fail to win tenure. All of that could be faced, however. She'd have Meggy and she would cope. She'd wait tables, if need be. Nothing would prevent her from seeing that Meggy got everything—not a feather here and a ring there—but peace and plenty every single day and safety every single night.

Chapter TWENTY-FOUR

After her outburst in the tiny courtroom, Rose stopped and looked around her. Meggy was up in Natalie's lap, gripped tight, and both Natalie and Guy were staring at her as though she'd gone crazy.

The judge cleared his throat and studied Rose. An aunt did have a slightly better chance of gaining custody than someone unrelated, he said, but he was not allowed to rule according to his personal view of a case nor even according to common sense. Family law might be out of date; but without proof of behavior endangering the child's survival, the law required him to protect the rights of the natural parent. Natalie's rights.

So Rose had no claim either.

Beyond the laws governing music, she had never pondered law. She'd believed not in law, but in luck, something she thought one could make for oneself. She'd believed that something could be done about nearly anything. But nothing, it seemed, could be done here.

The judge concluded the hearing with what seemed to Rose to be a scolding directed at Natalie, not that a scolding could make any difference.

Keeping Meggy truant was illegal, he said, and he'd be checking that Meggy was back in school in September. Then he took up the visitation order. "I see that you are a strong-minded woman and determined to do things your way," he told Natalie. "You're the natural mother. We grant you that. You call the shots. You're the only one who can say whether this girl will be allowed to know the man she considers her father."

"She'll forget him," said Natalie. "I have."

"I doubt that very much," said the judge.

"How would you know? You aren't god," muttered Natalie.

"I'm not god, no—but I've seen quite a few families," he replied.

Rose saw he couldn't help. He couldn't even enforce courtesy. If god was the sort who refused to help, who let things go on without lifting a hand, then the judge might as well have been god, holding lives to the tracks they had already taken, making sure that none derailed, condemning each to carry on exactly as they were: Meggy condemned to Natalie, Rose to solitude, and Guy to his hand-built house with its empty bed for a girl who never came.

Guy spoke, his voice trembling. "Natalie," he said, "remember the day we met? All you wanted, you said, was to make a family. All you wanted was to share the upbringing with someone. And didn't I jump in? Didn't I jump in up to my neck?"

Natalie shrugged and looked away. It was over. She didn't have to bother with him any more. She moved Meggy off her lap.

"Well," she said. "I'll leave you to your regrets and I to mine."

"Listen, Ms. MacGregor," said the judge. He moved his gaze to Natalie, to Meggy, to Guy, and then to Rose, and he was no longer exerting power over them, but merely looking at them. "I've seen quite a number of fathers and daughters in all stages of life. They don't tend to forget each other. I've seen quite a number of aunts and nieces, and they don't forget each other either." Rose sat up straighter. "If you keep this girl from knowing other people, you'll keep her from what she needs. She needs a larger world. That world is right in this room, if you can handle your differences."

This was neither law nor luck; this was the common sense that could not defeat law, but Rose leapt at it. "We can do that," she choked out. "We can make peace."

"You're unbelievable," said Natalie.

Rose turned to her sister. She would apologize. Natalie had a terrible authority and Rose had been ignorant of that. To have misjudged Natalie's power had put Rose in the wrong. She had done harm and would have to pay—Meggy wouldn't look at her now.

"I'm sorry, Natalie," she made herself say. "I'm truly, deeply sorry."

"For what?"

Rose took a breath. "For trying to take your child from you."

"Okay," said Natalie in a strange little voice. It seemed to dawn on her that the ordeal was over. She gave a shuddering sigh and reached up with both hands and lifted her hair out of her face and smiled to herself, for an instant restored to the golden state she'd inhabited when she was pregnant and self-assured, overflowing Lila's chair.

The judge and the recorder got up and went.

And then they were descending, Rose, Natalie, Meggy, and Guy, hurtling downward in the courthouse elevator. Guy stood heavy in his work boots. Natalie's face was strangely mobile, now frowning, now grinning, as though her features were at war. Rose returned to Meggy the best of the treasures, the coin purse and the tiny ebony Pegasus, which had probably been ill chosen. In the pert spread of its dark wings was the fool's dream of escape, of flying away. Looking neither at the horse and the purse nor at Rose, Meggy added them to her bulging pockets.

In the elevator, that tiny, falling room, Guy asked Natalie if he could talk to Meggy for a moment. Natalie nodded and looked away and he knelt, seeming to collapse his big frame around the girl. Rose thought he'd hug Meggy to him. Instead, whispering to her, he cupped her shoulders, his long fingers nearly meeting in the middle of her back. Rose tried to stop up her ears. She couldn't bear to hear him say good-bye, to see him in defeat, this man she'd once so loved, this tall man with prematurely gray hair who had set out to build in stone.

Stepping off the elevator, she burst out ahead of them and turned and spread her arms to stop them. They would still eat together, wouldn't they? Their table was waiting in the art museum, the table overlooking the river. Her treat?

They stared at her. People were trying to get onto the elevator; they were gumming up traffic. Hadn't she made herself understood? She was taking them to lunch. She pointed. It was just a block away. She'd run ahead and claim the table. She dashed out into the blindingly bright day and grabbed a table, a big table, and sat.

If Guy had won custody, as she'd so foolishly expected, Natalie would have come to the table, clinging to Meggy as long as she could. Guy would have been diplomatic, saving his exultation for later, and then the Gilpins would have burst in and eased things.

The museum restaurant's windows were cranked open all along a curved wall that faced the river, and barge horns blew, low and sick-sounding, below the noise of street traffic. After twenty minutes, the wait staff began to fuss and glare. Lunch rush was passing and the largest table stood empty except for the one woman, waiting.

Rose laid money on the table, the sixty dollars plus tip she'd expected to pay for the lunch, not to please the wait staff but to stave off the loss she could feel coming, as though by paying she could forfeit money instead of Meggy. Meggy wasn't coming. No one was coming except the Gilpins, Frances and Alan and Max, and she couldn't bear to see them just then.

It was hideous to be a MacGregor. Other families worked things out—betrayals, disappointments, anger—got over things and went on together. But not MacGregors. MacGregors got mad, stayed mad, struck to kill but ineffectually, tangled themselves up and pitched over cliffs, clawing and scratching, drawing blood as they fell, forever falling but never hitting bottom, never coming to the end of anything. This seemed to be their law. Her mother and father's brief reunion, for instance, begun at her Composer's Guild concert those years ago, had, within the night, ended in quarrel. It seemed her father seriously thought that if her mother was pleased to see him, she would follow him to his Christian commune. Rose wouldn't be phoning either of them at their separate addresses about what had happened in court. They'd only be hot with opinion. It would not occur to them to offer comfort; they wouldn't know how. The MacGregors had neither good times nor bad times; they just had times, relentless times.

For instance, Natalie was not quite finished with Rose that day. Once she'd gotten herself back to Tangletown, Rose would find her door standing open, wet towels on the floor, her shampoo bottle emptied out, and, on the table, a note in Meggy's careful printing, obviously dictated by Natalie: "*Aunt Rose, you meant well, but I cannot be bought,*" and beside it, in a neat row, the feather, ring, coin purse, and tiny horse, plus Meggy's spare set of keys—the keys they'd used to get in—surrendered with its tag labeled "Aunt Rose." The coin purse, however, would be empty of dimes. A frail consolation: it had to be Meggy who'd taken the dimes and hidden them, maybe in her pocket, maybe in her shoes.

Later that night, Rose would drive over to Frogtown to find the room in the boarding house stripped and deserted.

Perhaps Rose sat so long at the table in the museum restaurant because she could feel all this coming. At length, she got to her feet. She couldn't bear to have Alan and Frances and Max walk in to find her alone and helpless. She bolted, and just in time. Emerging on the street, she saw, at a distance, the Gilpins approaching, little Max in the middle, the three of them swinging along, hand in hand. But as she turned to go the other way, the dark-headed figure she had thought was Frances resolved itself into someone else, someone taller, dark-haired, dark-skinned, and male: James. It was undeniably James.

Did Frances know, then? Was it all out in the open now? It had been

Frances's idea that they should come to the museum restaurant to help
bear up the sorry MacGregors. Were they, the Gilpins, so big-hearted and
tolerant, so peaceable that they could go forward like this: Max swinging
blithely between Alan and his lover, Frances alongside? But Frances didn't
appear. Where was she? What had they done with Frances?

Back at the condo in Tangletown, Frances was in her bed and threw
her arms open wide when Rose, after picking up the wet towels, after putting away the ring, feather, horse, and coin purse where she wouldn't have
to see them, made her way upstairs.

While court was in session, Frances had gotten a last-minute appointment with her doctor to confirm amazing news. She was pregnant—there
would be a *new baby* in the house. She was out of her mind with joy. And
apparently none the wiser about James. But she'd made her bargain, hadn't
she, pleading to Alan late at night that if he'd get her pregnant, she'd never
ask anything of him again? Given that, how could Rose fail to rejoice with
her? This was marriage, Gilpin-style, and who was Rose to judge, with her
own life emptying out like a sack with a hole in the bottom?

Seattle and Stephen had dropped away; Natalie and Meggy were gone;
and Guy? If Rose had let Guy come back to her, as he'd made clear he
would that night they'd downed all the Mexican beer, might they possibly,
together, have claimed Meggy? At least they'd be mourning together now,
mourning losing her as they never had that little wisp of a child of theirs,
the one who never was. For a week after the court date, she would try to
reach him at his number in town, until she got a recorded message that
the line was disconnected. And the letter she'd send up north, full of
sorrow, would go unanswered.

Just why losing Meggy was like death, Rose could not explain. That
she should lose people seemed to be her lot. Perhaps it was because of
some inherent lack in her. What could she do but cling tighter to
whomever was left: Max, Alan, and the pregnant Frances? To have
people, any people, warm and breathing and nearby enough to speak to,
might be all that Rose could hope.

Life with the Gilpins wasn't nothing. Frances had a rare capacity to make Rose laugh. In the throes of early pregnancy, nibbling her way through packets, boxes, whole cases of saltines, Frances was prone to utter pronouncements so inane that Rose's sorrow would, if only temporarily, crumble.

Frances now had everything she'd ever wanted of life, she said. She looked out on the world with a tenderness that encompassed Max, Alan, Rose, and probably the postman and the paper carrier. But no matter how silly she was, Frances knew how to comfort people. Frances made Rose laugh and let her cry. Her arms encircling Rose, Frances declared it all bad luck—the disaster with Meggy, the miserable business with the married conductor, the symphony "postponed" as tenure review loomed. Dreadful luck—no wonder Rose felt rotten. But Rose was to remember that luck could change.

Rose was tempted to retreat to this view, their long-held devotion to luck, good and bad. Perhaps her bad luck had nothing to do with who she was, or with what she did or failed to do, or with what she understood or failed to understand. Perhaps luck was impersonal.

"Exactly," said Frances. Rose was not to worry about *tenure*, however. She, Frances, would be sitting at the nerve center, fielding departmental correspondence and phone calls and squelching or amplifying rumors. Frances ought to be able to rustle up some tenure.

"Like scrambled eggs?"

"Something like that," agreed Frances.

Maybe this was true. It was dawning on Rose that she might have to fight for tenure and, if so, she was about to need Frances in a whole new way.

Frances cooed and clucked over her and, for an hour every afternoon, brought Max and his satchel of blocks down to Rose and went back upstairs to sit in the lotus position with a speaker set in front of her belly, playing the sound of the ocean to the unborn baby.

Max, likewise, was given to repetition. For his hour with Rose, he did one thing over and over. He built a high towered fortress of colored blocks, then knocked it down, roared and flung tears, and then picked up a block and set it atop another, cheerfully starting over. Rose wished she could spend her tears as quickly. She hated Max to see her sad.

She was his godmother, after all. Holding Max in her arms, swaddled in lace, five years earlier, she'd stepped forward with Alan and Frances and had promised in Max's stead to renounce the wicked powers of the world and to trust entirely in grace and love. That wicked powers existed in the world was easy to see and acknowledge. She'd believed in making the most of what she had—her talent, her friendships, whatever love she found. Wickedness, it seemed to her, was taking any of it for granted. But relying entirely on grace and love was something she'd never seriously tried, then or now, and it was difficult to see how that could possibly work for her.

Even more than Max, Meggy had been entrusted to her, that first bath after the birth a sort of baptism. Hadn't Rose been the one to take Meggy and wash her when she was fresh to the world and sticky, when Guy was too freaked out and Natalie was too dazed and exhausted? Hadn't Rose been the one to meet Meggy's gaze when the infant girl first opened her eyes? But where was Meggy now? Nowhere Rose could find her.

"There, there," crooned Frances. The wonder was that Rose got herself up and dressed every day and off to teach summer school. After all she'd been through, nothing should be required of Rose except to sit in a high chair and be fed mashed bananas, according to Frances.

Rose laughed helplessly at this. She hoped she was still capable, at least, of chewing her own bananas. And although Frances was great at making her laugh, she couldn't help notice that Frances never laughed with her but, rather, regarded her beatifically, with an odd sense of owning her that Rose found off-putting.

Wasn't there, when things got bad, someone who used to laugh with Rose, someone with whom she could laugh herself silly? There was. There was Ursula. Rose was on the phone with Ursula every day about the wedding, but seemed to have forgotten how to talk to her about anything else.

"So much has been happening," she told Ursula when she'd summoned her courage to confide, "but I haven't wanted to burden you."

"Whatever it is, please burden me," said Ursula. She'd hoped they might be particularly close at the time of her wedding and had wondered why Rose was so remote.

There was no point in being proud. Rose launched in, starting with the wretched night in Seattle and moving on to the disaster at the courthouse, but Ursula was absolutely quiet at the other end.

"Is this too depressing?" Rose asked. "Maybe not the stuff to be telling a bride?"

"Oh, no," said Ursula. "I'm fine. Really. Things are just about taken care of. And, Rose—this is so exciting. My dress arrived!"

The ivy-patterned cambric dress had come in an ivy-patterned box tied with wide white ribbons. Ursula had taken to untying the ribbons, opening the box, trying the dress on, and wearing it awhile every morning after her bath. "I like to walk around in it—I mean, just inside on the living-room carpet. You would not believe what it's like to be a bride. You've got to do this, Rose—I mean, you've just *got* to do it."

Rose agreed and let it go, whatever else she might have said, let it all be covered over by snowy white ivy-patterned cambric.

"You tell Frances she's coming to the wedding," said Ursula, "even if she's pregnant. And we've got to get a date for you, Rose—you can't just come all alone."

Rose thought of her piano tuner. He'd been standing in the back of her mind ever since the night she had summoned him to collect his tuning fork. But then the thing in Seattle had happened—she'd let it happen—and it seemed wrong to phone him, at least while she still felt sullied, while a creeping pressure still rose from her belly to her throat whenever she thought of Stephen. And then there was her weepiness, her unpredictable self-command. Would she ask her piano tuner out, only to cry on his shoulder? Was his a shoulder to cry on? By her lights, she was not allowed to call him, not then and maybe not at all. But she did. She called him.

She got his answering machine and hung up. Off on a short trip, his message said. He took trips, then? He traveled? She would see him in the normal course of things the next time her piano was scheduled for tuning, but she wanted to put them in a different setting—out somewhere, just as he'd suggested. But not at a big, public affair where people would look them over and ask questions. Not a wedding.

So she dialed him again and left a chaotic little message: she wasn't calling because her piano needed tuning—she didn't know if it did; she hadn't been playing—but would he, when he got back, go out to lunch? She hung up and then dialed a third time because she hadn't been sure she had left her last name and who knew what other Rose he might tune for.

"MacGregor," she enunciated into the phone. "Rose MacGregor." It hurt her to say her name—Natalie's name, Meggy's name. It was the only thing they still shared. And then, not even that.

A photo arrived in the mail, ten days after she and Natalie and Meggy and Guy had stepped out of the courthouse elevator together. Rose had to study the image to decide just what it was. Natalie was in the photo, and Meggy, and something that might be a wedding bouquet was clenched in Natalie's hand. She wore a plain whitish shift but did not have the look of a bride. Her eyes were slightly bulging and her lips were pursed as though she had a mouthful of something bitter she was waiting to spit out. Their father, the other prominent presence in the photo, stood in the back, beaming triumphantly, wearing his one and only suit. His arms spread wide, he held Natalie on one side and, on the other, a shadow of a man standing far enough from Natalie that their father's suit buttons could be counted, one-two-three, in the space between. The man was neither young nor old, and there seemed to be no division between his chin and his neck. Rose vaguely recognized him as Natalie's rent payer, the Christian man of the no-strings-attached, Mr. Green. Greer, rather.

Rose turned the photo over to read, in the block letters of their father's hand:

> *Mr. and Mrs. Greer on their wedding day, with their*
> *daughter, Meggy Greer, and the proud father of the bride.*

Meggy stood in front of them, leaning away, listing, lost.

Chapter TWENTY-FIVE

T he round barn matched the great old oak in the pasture in size and shape. Three hundred years old, according to Emma, the tree stood in full summer array, a mountain of leaves stirred by the breeze; and the barn, though only relatively ancient, displayed glories of its own: silvery boards pierced by sunrise streaming through cracks and knotholes. The site had its charms, Rose would admit. Barn and tree, bride and groom—things would come that day in pairs.

The day had dawned clear but chilly. Minnesota summers could cough up an April morning in July, and this was one. Shivering in jeans, a sweat-shirt, and running shoes sopping with dew, Rose paced the processional path she and Ursula would take from the farmhouse near the barn to the tree, maid of honor to be followed by bride, another essential pair. Enough of tears; Rose was getting her grip again. In the grass, from the Flowered Meadow seeds they had broadcast back in May, a daisy showed here, a poppy there, a burst of blue flax. All around her were examples of people arranging their lives, putting things in order with an eye to stability—Alan and Frances and Ursula—compromising and arriving; particularly Ursula, her best friend Ursula, in the soon-to-unfold glory of her wedding day.

Not that Rose could bring herself to love a wedding. Ceremonial custom, as explained by Ursula, required the maid of honor to attend the bride from the moment she put her dainty toe to earth at the wedding site. Rose had greeted this piece of information with a horselaugh, but Ursula meant it: seven in the morning onward, regardless of the fact that the guests would not arrive till two. Knowing better than to argue, Rose had gotten herself out to the site very early to get her bearings before anyone else arrived.

In the empty farmhouse, she discovered a small room at the top of the stairs with a window overlooking the barn. No bigger than a cell, the room held nothing but a doubled-up canvas sack of straw, striped canvas, rotting to pieces: a straw mattress was what it was, bedding of the pioneers. She unfolded it, dusted it off, lay down on it, and got right up again. It was all lumps, no softness. Downstairs in the kitchen, which was to be bridal headquarters, she improvised a broom from a bald mop handle and a box of rags. She'd be a pioneer that day, a maid of honor, a maid venturing through the wilderness of wedding. After the vows, once the bride and groom had made their grand exit, the maid of honor was to stay on at the wedding feast as bride's representative until the last guest departed. How late? Who knew? Sometime after midnight or later, guessed Ursula. This added up to twenty-plus hours of wedding—a day and night that Ursula would remember in detail for the rest of her life. It would be Rose's honor, she told herself sternly, to stay on till the last dance was danced, the last crust chewed, and the last drop swallowed down.

To her credit, she showed no outward sign of wedding stress except shadows under her eyes from the late nights on the phone with Ursula and the thousand trips to pick people up at the airport or once more to Minneapolis to haul back department-store loot: boxes and boxes wrapped white-on-white. Guests were, as Frances had predicted, dumping bundles on Ursula's registry choices, and Rose was the one who had gotten that started, priming the pump with her hundreds of dollars of champagne flutes, just as she should have, she told herself. It was money spent in the cause of her friend's happiness.

Lacking a dustpan, she knelt on the farmhouse kitchen floor next to the pile of dirt she'd swept up and, holding the door open with her shoulder, flung it in handfuls over the threshold out into the yard. Then she set her mop inside the door and got back into her car. The night before in St. Paul, she'd gotten the box of her wedding garb down from quarantine on its high shelf and had hooked, tied, and cinched, and had practiced, in front of the mirror, smiling in it. The more she smiled, the less sincere she looked, at least to her own eye, and she'd been unable to get the whole rig back into the box. It now lay heaped in the back seat, atop her cello. The cello was not for the wedding. She intended, even that day, to be something more than a wedding slave and had planned an early hour of music with Lila at the Goat Pasture.

Six A.M. was nothing to Lila. In mid-summer, the farm girls were up with the sun. Rose found Lila already waiting at the studio door. The studio, trellised with morning glories, stood on a quiet spot on the river, out past the gazebo and the garden bridge. It was narrow and high, with windows that diffused light downward, and held a table, chairs, and a wood stove that lit quickly and took off the chill. It also had a closet, built-in drawers, and a futon that folded into a cabinet. At any time, Rose could move out and live there. It didn't bear thinking how a day spent at the Goat Pasture—gardening, swimming, or napping in a hammock—contrasted to the wedding day ahead.

The studio acoustics were perfect. Rose's playing was not. She hadn't picked up her cello in weeks and, after several flubbed notes, dropped her bow.

"What was it like when you retired from the world?" she asked Lila.

"Don't you even think of it," said Lila. "You haven't yet hit your stride."

"Haven't I?"

"The Seattle Sinfonietta is not the only orchestra that will ever play a symphony by Rose MacGregor. Stephen Orrick is not the only conductor in the world."

On vacation from a busy concert schedule, Lila was sunburned, bearded, pungent, and full of herself. She went to the table where Rose had dumped the frothy heap of wedding regalia and lifted a corner of hem. "Stephen Orrick," Lila continued, "is a mere wood tick on the coat of a mighty dog. The tick bites on, bloats up with blood, of which the mighty dog has plenty. The tick falls off, goes through its pitiful reproductive cycle, and dies; the mighty dog runs on."

"So I'm a dog?" Rose inquired.

Lila shook the dress out. "Great skirt. Where's the top? Oh, my beating heart. You have *got* to model this for me."

"*Lila*," said Rose, her face hot.

"You can't retire," said Lila. "I rely on you for my repertoire."

"Oh, *right*," said Rose. "Bach is not sufficient."

"Gotta have new stuff. Don't think I don't." Lila picked up her bow. She would not be attending the wedding, nor would the others from the Goat Pasture—Ursula barely knew them, and they were undoubtedly glad not to come. But it was troubling that Ursula had also failed to invite Emma. Hadn't Emma, not many months before, put Ursula up overnight? Hadn't Emma arranged the loan of the neighbor's round barn, farmhouse, and pasture for the wedding? Ursula gave some muttered reason about cost per plate for the reception, but Emma was just across the road and Rose thought she had wanted to come.

Emma, anyway, had graciously chosen Ursula's wedding date to host her summer sing. A great group of singers from across the county would serenade Ursula faintly from across the road, singers in concentric circles on the grass by day, around the fire ring by night. Despite her slurred speech, Emma could sing with a clear tone, and her cherishing friends lost no opportunity to sing with her. If Rose could manage a break or two from the wedding, she'd slip across the road and sing her lungs out; she'd get herself into the innermost singing circle and howl at the moon.

At midmorning, she perched on a ladder at the door of the round barn, arranging strands of grapevine garland into symmetry atop a rented awning. When I get married, she told herself, at *my* wedding, everyone will be invited who could possibly want to come. Rose's wedding? What wedding was that? No wedding at all.

A curl of dried grapevine in Rose's hands, twisted too hard, flaked and splintered, dropping gunk onto the white-draped table below, onto the stacks of gold-rimmed plates. She scurried down the ladder and dusted off the plates.

Out in the pasture below the oak, the bridegroom's brothers were scraping up cow pies and stamping and pounding where they could—a pasture was not a lawn and tree roots could not be flattened—and setting the chairs out in crescent rows, none quite level.

Rose caught sight of the bridegroom hurrying from groom's headquarters in the stable, his chin lifted, his hand pressed to his face, shirt open, cuffs flapping.

A window shrieked upward in the farmhouse and Ursula stuck her head out, hair looped up and bristling with clips.

"Nosebleed," somebody shouted.

Though Ursula had been adamant that nobody see her that day until it was time, she now stepped out onto the farmhouse porch, dragging the hairdresser with her, his hands embedded in her high-piled hair.

The brothers knew what to do—Bruce had had nosebleeds since childhood. Somebody came running with a Styrofoam cooler. Of course they were sitting him up straight, of course applying ice, of course stuffing his nostrils with cotton. Of *course* he had a spare dress shirt—Ursula herself had packed it.

Rose hurried to Ursula and herded her back inside. And then it was no longer possible to put off dressing.

They stood before a pair of full-length mirrors, oval bridal rental mirrors. Rose's body seemed stopped in time: breasts, still high, belly, a blank stretch, and skin, except on the back of her hands, no more creased nor veined than when she was twenty, no surface sagging or fading to match the sinking feeling at her center. She laced up her corset and shoved her breasts down. They popped up again as they were meant to, each breast pushed up into a mound, halfway visible above the sharp top line of the corset.

"Ooh," cried Ursula. "You're perfect!" Over Rose's bosom, Ursula dusted blusher, turning her breasts into rosy apples. Below her waist the crinoline belled out, creating a chilly open chamber around her legs. She dropped the dress over her head and tugged the bodice down past her shoulders and the skirt down over the crinoline—done.

Ursula asked again to check the ring. Rose had charge of the bridegroom's ring: her dress had a small pocket, a ring pocket in easy reach at the waistband. After the vows, she was to hand the ring to Ursula, while taking charge of the bridal bouquet: white roses, small and large, nearly a bale of them wired together within a huge clutch of ivy, now resting on the kitchen floor within its own cooler, which was large as a child's coffin.

At Ursula's behest, Rose opened the cooler and admired and even hefted the bouquet to make sure she could handle the weight of it. Once Ursula had turned it over to her, she was to rest the bound end of it against her hipbone and mind her balance to keep from letting the roses touch the ground. To her relief, her maid-of-honor posy was smaller, and the nosegay Ursula would toss to the unmarried women after the ceremony was smaller yet. Rose would be expected to catch it, as Ursula planned to aim it right at her and when that little nosegay hit the air and landed, then and only then would the team of bride and maid of honor be sundered, Ursula at a quick run in a black silk suit and a hat with a veil, under a shower of rice, Rose loping behind with the rice bag.

Together, they began to arrange Ursula's bridal attire, layer by layer.

Ursula's mother, round and heavy unlike her slim offspring, and with a face as open as a pie, sat quietly on a chair outside the farmhouse door.

She might have enjoyed helping Ursula to dress, but Ursula rolled her eyes at the thought. Her mother was dear but useless. Even Rose was deemed inept—Ursula shooed her from the kitchen so she could finish dressing alone.

The bridegroom's brothers were rolling big, round tables and setting them up beside the barn, whooping and crashing. Rose was surrounded by big men; even the fourteen-year-old loomed over her when he came on a dare to blurt out that they all thought she looked bodacious. The corset, binding her waist to sternum, gave her a bellyache, and at the boy's words she was overtaken by awareness of her posture. Her neck felt hugely long. Her shoulders were freezing. She was all separate parts.

"The guests are here," cried Ursula from the farmhouse doorway and signaled to Rose to go greet, but it was only a single car, disgorging a young fellow with wide cheekbones and high coloring who stepped straight up to Rose.

Small world—he'd been traveling buddies with Bruce on a walking tour of England the previous year and now, by crikey, he was Best Man.

"Victor," said Rose. "Victor Zeiss."

In her scrambled inner files of former students, most of whom held a more vivid image of her than she'd ever had of them, there were the exceptions. She straightened and felt her spine shove upward inside its tight casing. Hadn't he sat next to her at that Composer's Guild concert?

He produced a dazzling smile.

And hadn't he been all shaggy and bearded that night? But here he was, in a dove-gray suit, shorn and clean-shaven as a choirboy.

"A choirboy?" he echoed quizzically.

Victor Zeiss. Say, hadn't she seen his name again on her class lists for the coming school year? He was a little old for matriculating. She'd been a kid herself when she'd taught him way back when. Why, he must be pushing thirty.

He hadn't quite gotten his degree, he admitted. He wondered whether, just for that day, they might forget the school crap?

"Of course," she said.

And what about her? Was she married yet? No, of course not. Too smart for that, wasn't she? Though perhaps she just hadn't met the right chappie. Victor bared his teeth. He produced a camera and peered through the lens, circling her bare shoulders.

"Give me your suit jacket," she said, and slipped her hands through the silky sleeves, did up the buttons, and hugged herself.

Perhaps she had met the right chappie. The piano tuner. Graham Lowe had returned her awkward phone message, and they'd gone to lunch at a place he knew with an outside courtyard framed by locust trees.

The trees were feathery overhead. The table was sticky. He had jumped up to get a washrag from the wait station. As he'd swabbed the table, the power in his shoulders had struck her, and the stringy muscularity of his forearms.

"Where's the old suit coat? Where's the suspenders?" she'd asked. He'd worn jeans and a polo shirt.

"Ah, the work clothes," he'd replied. "For the image, you know—the ancient craftsman. I'm not at work now."

"No, you aren't," she'd agreed.

"So, tell me about yourself," he'd said, and she'd been taken aback by the frank inquiry. But it was the question, wasn't it, that one most wished to be asked? Still, she feared what lament she might launch into. And he already knew more about her than she about him, having been in and out of her place any number of times.

"You tell first," she said.

He'd just gotten back from a week running whitewater in Wisconsin. He was an amateur naturalist—birds. The Midwest was a paradise of herons. Did she know that a heron rookery stood not five miles south of the city? The flashy Great Blue nested there, but also green herons, night herons, and egrets. If she liked, he would take her there after nesting season—no disturbing rookeries during nesting season.

That's what it was upstairs at the Gilpins with the pregnant Frances:

the rookery in nesting season. Gingerly, like probing a sore tooth, she told Graham about the Gilpins and also mentioned Natalie and Meggy, but she didn't tell much. The legs of the chair sat solid beneath her, yet she felt herself losing her balance as she had that night she'd first really looked at him, after slipping and falling with his tuning fork in her hand. What was it about him that put her off balance?

It was plain that they liked each other. After that first lunch, they'd met for coffee. And then he'd cooked supper for her.

He lived deeper in Tangletown in the rented top of a carriage house on an alley that curved in from where three streets met and a fourth dead-ended. The carriage house, though substantial, seemed a toy version of the big house to which it belonged, separated by a garden with benches and a fountain.

Enchanted, Rose had wondered aloud whether he had use of the garden.

He supposed so, but he didn't much care. The grandeur ended at his outside door. A rough staircase inside led to a landing that opened into his rooms, into the kitchen where a network of cracks embedded with grit zigzagged across a porcelain-tiled floor. But the rent was low and, short of digging up and replacing tile floors, he liked being left alone and made his own repairs and renovations. It was home and workshop: one side of the garage below served as his piano hospital, and fragments of old pianos and organs were set on shelves he'd built that also housed a jumble of books, maps, and curious objects: a gray balloon of a paper wasp nest, a badminton birdie made of leather and string and black gull feathers.

He'd confessed himself to be a terrible packrat. This was true, and the place needed cleaning, but the objects exerted a fascination, as did the conversation, which was jumbled and packed and disordered and unending. He'd painted his rooms yellow. A crushed lute hung on the yellow wall above his bed, visible through the doorway at the back. He'd repair the lute one day, he told her, but meanwhile, wasn't it something to look at—the sound chamber splintered inward? His bed was a double, she'd been quick to notice, but she saw no evidence of anyone else, no bed partner. Was something wrong with him that he slept alone? She of course did not ask the question aloud. She slept alone, too, after all.

Once that evening, she heard the muffled creak of big doors opening below and an engine revved. But Graham had sealed his place from exhaust, and she smelled nothing but a spicy dust: his junk mixed with the odors of his excellent cooking. He set her plate before her with a flourish and, reaching for the bottle to refill her glass, brushed the back of her hand with his fingers, leaving the spot on her skin burning.

"Okay," he said. "Who's Sweetheart? Who's this person on the phone you call sweetheart?"

"Oh. It's Ursula. My girlfriend, Ursula." He regarded her. "Girlfriend in the *conventional* sense. Ursula is about to get married. She needs to be soothed. I call her sweetheart. But I am," she'd heard herself say, "entirely heterosexual. And on my own."

He'd given a yip of laughter, nervous and relieved, and took her hand, but she got up and excused herself, blushing, and hurried home, somehow unready.

But if she wasn't ready at thirty-four, when would she ever be? Still, wasn't there something too steady about him, something altogether too self-reliant? If he was so great that he made her nervous, why wasn't he already with someone permanently, already married? Oh, and did she judge herself the same, unmarried and therefore defective? Was she knuckling under, finally, to the great imperative of Wedding?

Ursula, from the farmhouse window, cried to Rose to take the suit jacket off and give it back to Victor. "If people see you covering up, everyone will think they're cold."

Victor pointed his camera at Ursula, who squealed and vanished. Retrieving his jacket from Rose, he ran his thumb across her back. She caught his wrist, but he pulled her toward him, strong for a man so slender.

"We hate weddings, don't we?" he drawled.

"I don't know what you're talking about," she said. A fib, but this was Ursula's day, and Rose would play her part.

The band was tuning up: fiddle, hammered dulcimer, guitar.

Victor, Bruce, Rose, and Ursula stood in final rehearsal at the foot of the oak, Ursula's gown hidden under a trailing rubber poncho, her hair under a shawl. Her hands trembled, and Rose rubbed them for her. Bruce, practicing his vows, muttered under his breath to Victor, his ears reddening. Victor giggled.

"Don't bug him," said Ursula.

"Don't worry, old man," Victor told Bruce.

"Don't call him 'old man,'" said Ursula. "Don't you try anything, Vic. You don't have to be in this, you know. Any of his brothers could stand up with him."

"It's fine, Ursula," said Bruce, making of her name both a caress and a tribute.

She turned to Rose. "Have you got it? The ring? Double-check the ring."

Rose was hardly going to lose the ring. Bruce had enormous hands and his ring was large and heavy. She plucked it out of the little pocket at her waist, slid it over her thumb, and gave Victor a wink. Later, she'd wonder if even a wink was over the line and Victor had taken it as a dare.

"They're here," cried Ursula and rushed off to hide as the first caravan of cars came down the dirt track and onto the grass. The sun seemed to switch its heat on, and the day quite suddenly warmed to perfection. The guests strode up, erect and jaunty, voices bright, a crowd of a hundred childhood pals, aunts, uncles, cousins, and colleagues.

Little Max pranced up, resplendent in a blue striped seersucker suit, matching his father's. Max, who loved ceremony, sported a bow tie in a bright cherry red which matched the cherry-colored suit that Frances, her pregnancy not yet showing, had just managed to zip herself into, and James trailed alongside in pale pants and a floating shirt: the foursome.

With uncharacteristic recklessness, Alan had introduced James to Frances and now brought him around all the time. They touched constantly, Alan and James. Frances, occupied with being pregnant, raised no questions, but instead professed pride in Alan's friend—his *Ethiopian* friend, such an *affectionate* man. Rose agreed, hoping that Frances had fully grasped what she'd observed and was taking a large view. Rose wasn't pointing anything out. No disturbing the rookery in nesting season, Graham had said. Rose hadn't told Frances about Graham, either. Really, there was nothing yet to tell.

The crowd grew. The band struck up. Rose danced a few steps. Victor reached for her, and they revolved in a waltz. It must have been then that he filched the ring, because when they stood in the dappled shade under the tree a bit later, Bruce, Rose, and Victor, in front of the guests leaning higgledy-piggledy on their chairs on the humpy ground, Rose patted her pocket and it was gone.

To the tune of the fiddle and the dulcimer, Ursula approached on her mother's arm, the fine contours of her breasts and hipbones draped in ivy-patterned cambric, her hair piled and pinned with tiny rosebuds. She seemed not so much decorated as disclosed, unearthly, an ideal—she didn't smile—a dream of clarity, of things made eternal. Rose, holding in one hand her maid-of-honor posy, stroked and stroked the little pocket but felt no ring. She tried to search the ground at her feet without bowing her head.

A flicker in the crowd—Frances availing herself of Alan's handkerchief, crying already. On Alan's other side sat James, the two shoulder to shoulder, fingertips entwined, and on Alan's face, a look either of ecstasy or of excruciating strain. Rose was losing her bearings. Unbidden came the thought of Guy and of Stephen Orrick and then of the possibility of Graham, whoever he turned out to be, and it all struck her as accidental, how love went, and none of it eternal. A nausea of the ruined and the hoped-for heaved up in her, mixed with anxiety. She couldn't find the ring.

Bruce began his vows. Ursula glanced over, the slightest lifting of an eyebrow, at Rose's rustling. Let the ring come. The ring would appear if she just let it. Ursula uttered the last of her vows in a whisper, gazing into Bruce's eyes. Then she turned and, as planned, piled upon Rose the enormous bouquet and extended her palm. And as Rose jammed her hand inside her ring pocket one last time and brought it out empty, the bride's gaze went from puzzlement, to alarm, to horror. The time was now and it was unrepeatable. Within the stricture of her corset, Rose felt anew a plummeting sensation, a desperate sense of falling. She dropped to her knees, dumping the bale of roses and ivy back into Ursula's arms, and bent and clawed the grass for the small, heavy circlet of gold. She had an upside-down glimpse of Ursula's mother in the front row, leaning forward and cocking her head, her face like a pie spilling out of its plate. Rose's breasts sprung loose. It was vaudeville.

Low to the ground, Victor opened his hand, revealing both rings. She shoved her breasts back down, reached over and grabbed the larger ring and thrust it at Ursula, and then staggered up into Victor's puckish gaze. The judge cleared his throat, and a chuckle rippled through the congregation. Victor gave a tiny bow. Rose tittered, a high, startled sound. The mishap had been entirely Victor's doing, but Ursula would assume Rose was in league with him.

When the last of the receiving line had moved past bride and maid of honor, and Ursula said "Let's walk," Rose prepared herself to hear that the friendship was over.

They set off as they had so many nights in grad school, though not at their former athletic stride, but at an uncertain saunter. A rosebud dropped from Ursula's hair, and Rose bent to pick it up.

Alan called out to them. Could he borrow Rose's Volvo? He would get her home, he promised, but James needed to go back now. "*Right* now," he said.

Rose tossed him the keys. Max, in his striped suit, danced a circle around his father. Alan nudged him away. Rose called her godson and handed him the fallen rosebud. Max, delighted, crushed it in his hand and careered off.

Ursula led Rose across the dirt track and onward through muck, sand, and anthills, neglectful of their satin shoes. A toad hopped into their path, huge and wart-encrusted; Ursula's white hem closed over him briefly, and Rose exclaimed. Ursula ambled onward, unseeing. A garter snake flashed out of the grass, buckled itself over Ursula's toe, and streaked away. Were these warning signs or signs of luck, of Ursula's luck, of her untouchability? Whereas an hour before Ursula could see and hear everything, now she saw and heard nothing.

"I'm sorry about the ring," said Rose mildly.

"Oh, that's over." Ursula said and gave an easy, absent-minded smile. Waves of grasshoppers crashed around them. It seemed their friendship, however diminished, would go on undisturbed.

A boiling, hissing, droning cloud of insects, nearly head-high, now enclosed them. Ursula waved a hand vaguely in front of her face. Rose reached for her elbow to lead her back and, glancing across the pasture, spotted a pair of figures facing each other beneath the wedding oak in the emptiness where the ceremony had been. There Alan, with slow emphasis, ticked off points on his fingers to Frances, who stood absolutely still, her neck extended, her back rigid, as straight as an arrow shot into the earth.

"Oh god," said Rose.

Now Alan pounded an open palm with his fist, now reached both his hands out toward Frances.

"What is it?" murmured Ursula, safe in her slice of eternity, snug in her vows.

Across the field, vows were coming undone.

As the pop of champagne corks sang out at the barn door and Bruce's brothers unknowingly covered, loudly cheering the return of the bride, Frances cried out beneath the great tree and reared back and struck Alan across the face, not a slap, but an open handed blow.

Rose abruptly left Ursula to find Max, to shield Max.

But Max could not be shielded. Able to pick his mother's voice out in any crowd, he was running full-tilt across the pasture, already halfway to the tree.

Chapter TWENTY-SIX

Alan snatched Max up and strode toward their car as Frances scrambled after them. They jerked to a stop every few paces to shout at each other.

At the barn, a summons rang out: "Maid of Honor to dance with the Best Man!" Rose, uncertain where her duty lay, grabbed up her skirts and rushed after the Gilpins, but the car pulled away before she could reach them. As they sped off, Max could be seen pitching himself into the front seat while Frances flapped her hands and Alan, who was never rough with Max, heaved up and shoved him backward into his booster seat.

The dance floor was little more than rented risers on unlevel ground, and Rose had the extra challenge of keeping her dress on. She could count on the corset to hold things in place only if she held herself upright. Victor danced well—held them in balance and dipped and spun her around—but she left the dance floor as soon as she could and dumped down on a bale of straw. Alan was bound to come racing back for her once he recalled that she'd given James the Volvo. She leaned back a little on her hands on the straw, and the corset held. She instructed herself not to worry. When she closed her eyes, however, the condo building in Tangletown loomed up, the walls buckled and the roof exploded.

She opened her eyes on Victor holding two brimming glasses of champagne. She took a glass and waved him off. "It's a big world of wedding. Go get 'em, Victor."

The cake was cut. Victor, at her side, passed plates. She toasted the health of the bride. He lifted his glass to the groom. The band struck up a polka. Victor reached for Rose again. Their dance was all stomp and no grace, and they went straight on into a Virginia reel. As they joined hands in an arch, he called to her: "Are you seeing anybody?"

"None of your business," she shouted back.

Across the road, Emma's high window flared, glass and gable lit by campfire, and singing could be heard.

Ursula and Bruce appeared in their traveling clothes. Ursula tossed her bridal nosegay to Rose, who caught it and, smiling brightly, allowed herself the small satire of a curtsey, and then fetched her rice bag and split the contents with Victor, who seemed determined to assist her in every detail. They led the guests along the track either side of bride and groom, tossing the rice, or, rather, the bird seed—Emma had warned that wedding rice killed songbirds, swelled their tiny bellies and burst them—so it was parakeet mix they tossed: millet, flax seed, carrot granules, spinach flakes: fine stuff that, as they flung it, penetrated the netting of Ursula's hat and got into her eyes. Squealing, she unpinned her hat and shook it, giving Victor the chance to really get her. She shielded her face as he pelted her. Rose grabbed and held his arm. Ursula fixed them both with a broad smile and a giddy questioning stare.

Rose rolled her eyes and Ursula was gone, folded into the wedding car, the door slammed shut by Victor, gone in a burst of motor and a clatter of rattling cans.

"Rattle bang," said Victor, at Rose's ear. "Noise meant to scare off evil spirits." And before she knew it, he'd pulled her to him and kissed her.

She lurched backward and groaned. "Such a cliché, Victor—Maid of Honor and Best Man. Not gonna happen. Don't waste your time," she said, but the wet heat of his lips left her shaken. She stepped over to ask the groom's youngest brother to the dance floor, the fourteen-year-old.

Alan did not reappear. The Gilpins, it seemed, had forgotten her. But she had to stay anyway; she was sworn to stay, and everywhere she went, Victor went too. He popped up beside her at the buffet without anyone seeing him cut in line. She went to use the port-a-potty, and when she stepped out, he headed the line, and then he didn't need to pee after all; he was walking her back to the dance floor. He was mannerly; she couldn't fault him. Except for the one kiss, he kept his hands to himself and his eyes off her cleavage.

He was probably impressed with her public face, her concerts, her recordings, her stance at the front of the classroom. But how did he know she wasn't seeing anyone? (She couldn't count Graham.) Was there something about her that revealed, beneath the music and the professorship, a battered and lonely private life?

Or was it the dress she was wearing, her boobs pushed into view? The dress was a tease. If she got the thing off, she couldn't appear bodacious. She excused herself to change clothes. No, Victor, she didn't need anyone to walk her to the farmhouse.

In the twilit kitchen, she tore everything off, plopped the skirt over the empty crinoline, and fixed the corset inside the bodice. The rig stood up by itself when she stepped away. In her sweatshirt, she felt her rib cage expand. She spread her toes inside her running shoes. She was just someone in jeans now, a member of the clean-up crew. Victor could find someone else to track, someone more in the wedding spirit. She told him so.

He caught her hand. She'd talk to him, wouldn't she? Or was talk off limits?

Talk was never off limits, she allowed. What was she doing these days? Well, she was writing a symphony.

Relieved of deadlines, she was working again, making her symphony entirely her own. She'd returned to the sound of solo cello, moving from piano to work things out on her old cello and sometimes merely singing what she wrote or perhaps quavering, but the work was going forward. She'd stumbled into a movement that was darkly, vigorously sad, a dance in which melody, at first sprightly and full of itself, got lost in rhythm, so that rhythm alone existed for a time, as day follows day and breath follows breath through good fortune and bad, as the body, eating, sleeping and breathing, leads the bewildered soul onward: Rose in all her variations. Not quite coherently, she described this to Victor.

They sat just inside the barn doors, away from the noise of the band.

"Exposition, elaboration, complication, reiteration, and coda: the movements of the symphony," chanted Victor.

"Bravo! Could this be the young man known for difficulty in retaining concepts?"

They exchanged a look, both seeming to recall that, years before, he'd brought endless questions to her office hours but had rarely listened to the answers.

"Hey," he said, "let's take a look upstairs."

"Up to the hayloft, Victor? You must think I was born yesterday."

"Gotta see what's up there. Come on," he said and sprang up the wooden ladder to the loft and spoke from the dark above. "You really have to see this."

He was leaning back against a wall of hay. She stood on the far side of the loft. Moonlight and starlight leaked through gaps in the walls and misted down from the great wagon wheel of the ceiling. It was unbelievably lovely, she admitted.

And was that a cliché, he asked her? Could she please explain why she wouldn't give him the time of day when he knew she liked him and she wasn't seeing anyone and neither was he?

"I might be seeing someone," she said.

"Are you?"

"Give it up, Vic. It isn't happening."

"But," he said, gazing up at the ceiling, "who's to say what will happen even five minutes from now?"

She needed no reminder that life was unstable. There were always choices, and some were no-brainers. "Don't force me to be rude in the moonlight," she said.

"Oh, I wouldn't force a thing," said Victor and laughed, and she laughed too.

"Okay," she told him. "I have my reasons and now I'm going to bore you to tears. I can't fool around with you, Victor," she said, "because I'm still your professor."

"So?" said Victor. "Big deal."

But it was quite a big deal, sex between professors and students, much in the national press just then: rapacious professors, jilted students attempting suicide in the library stacks. Some of it was true, some false, but it all added up to new campus rules, and she couldn't be flaunting rules or there'd be hell to pay. She was up for tenure, did he know?

The distant sound of singing swelled from Emma's across the road. Rose could see that Alan wasn't coming back to get her, a bad sign, a sign of things flying apart, of hell to be paid. She would go to Emma's across the road—Emma, her friend, her sort of grandmother. Rose thought she'd rather sing than talk. She bid Victor good night.

"Can anyone come?" he wanted to know. As it happened, he liked to sing.

"It'll get you nowhere with me," said Rose, "except across the road and back."

The wedding noise gave way to the crunch of gravel underfoot as they walked toward the singing. In the dark driveway, he took her hand.

She gave it a formal shake and dropped it. "Professor MacGregor," she said.

She was annoyed. This not-so-very-young man, this older student—though she didn't care if he was old as Methuselah or a squalling baby—

would be in her classroom soon. She didn't want to offend him. She wanted to kill him, was the truth. She'd come to the end of her wedding rope. She was thankful that they'd arrived at the sing.

The Larks, as the singers called themselves, liked to sing almost anything —hymns, labor songs, rounds, dancehall tunes. Many were old friends who'd brought daughters and daughters' friends and then granddaughters and granddaughters' friends. The men were few and cherished for contributing the low notes, but otherwise they were cheerfully neglected. Victor would be pounced upon—what was he? a bass? a tenor?—plugged into the circle and forgotten.

At the fire, Emma got up to greet them, rested her palm against Rose's cheek, and then threw her arms around Victor who was at first startled and then hugged back.

Emma was in her glory with the Larks. Though pushing eighty, she'd barely been hindered by the stroke she'd suffered. She sported a pencil behind her ear and, on a string on her belt loop, a spiral notebook in which she wrote out what she had to say. And she could still sing in perfect tune, even if her lyrics were not quite clear.

What the Larks sang wasn't quite music. Strength of voice and spirited delivery were valued, but tempos dragged and voices could be heard going sharp and flat like an out-of-tune orchestra. The trained musician in Rose went to sleep. Voices dawdled and then roared. The fire crackled. Rose sat with her arm around Emma. Victor wandered over, dropped his head beside Rose's and offered a harmony in a clear, light tenor, and then returned to his place across the ring.

Emma raised an eyebrow and scratched something on her pad. "Who is he?"

"A student," Rose told her.

"And what are you teaching him this evening?" scribbled Emma. She lifted the one side of her mouth in her elfin grin.

"Not a damned thing," said Rose.

The singers began "Balm in Gilead." She wondered whether there could be such a thing, a balm to make the wounded whole. The voices slid muddily upward—*who-ole*—and her skin crawled. She was whole already, just as she was. She was suddenly terribly hungry; but if she went to Emma's kitchen, Victor was sure to follow.

She had on her running shoes. She slipped from the circle and back across the road at a run. Beside the round barn, the buffet table was almost empty. From somebody's abandoned plate, she helped herself to a half-eaten roll and a smear of cheese, then dashed out of sight to the farmhouse. A shape loomed up in the dark kitchen. She cried out, but it was no one. She'd spooked herself with the standing shape of her bridesmaid dress.

She fled up the stairs to the room with the straw mattress, shut herself in with her back against the door, and gnawed her roll and cheese.

Bruce's brothers welcomed Victor back in a rowdy chorus. Here he came, calling "Rose?" He called from the buffet table, then from the dance floor, and then from what might be the hayloft—he had to be kidding; the hayloft again—and then he was at the farmhouse, and she pulled her head away from the window, out of view.

The door opened below. A switch clicked, but no light came. The place had no electricity. Go, pioneers, said Rose to herself on her straw mattress. He called from the porch, outside again. "Rose? Rose MacGregor?"

No such person, she said to herself, but still she lived and breathed.

"Professor MacGregor?" he called, laughing to himself unhappily.

She stretched out on the lumpy straw covered with rotten ticking.

Minutes passed. Voices dwindled. Good-byes drifted on the air. "Rose MacGregor?" she heard once again.

The young fellow was determined, and who could fault him? The mating call was strong. But there were other calls, and she was even more determined than he.

Winning by hiding wasn't much to boast about, however. And she could only hide for so long.

Twelve hours and three buses later, she stood in the street in front of the condo, reading a note under the wiper of the Volvo at the curb where

James had parked it. The note informed her that the tank was full and that her keys were upstairs with the Gilpins.

The front door of the building stood ajar. She took a breath, stepped inside, and upheaval broke over her.

Alan slammed into view, a suitcase in each hand. He dumped them on the landing and turned back to Frances, who stood hissing in their doorway, her voice hoarse, poisonous and then piteous, restraining Max, who was trying to get past her, shrieking "Daddy, I want my Daddy!"

"It's the third time she has thrown me out," Alan announced crisply, "and now the third time she has begged me to stay."

"Who are you talking to?" quavered Frances. Glancing over the railing, she saw Rose, and her face went hard. "Give me your keys," she told Alan while glaring at Rose.

"I've got stuff in there," said Alan.

"Take it all right now."

"Furniture—my desk, for instance? I cannot take it all right now."

Frances extended her hand. He sighed, pulled keys off his chain, and gave them to her. She went in and closed the door.

"I've told her the truth, is all," he said, as though to himself. He looked down at Rose, who stared back at him, oafish in her dirty clothes.

"Oh, Christ. I left you out there overnight at that godforsaken farm wedding. I cannot believe it. Frances," he said, raising his voice not at all. Frances opened the door. "Get Rose's keys for her, please. James gave them to you."

"James touched them, and you expect me to?"

"You know where they are. I do not," he said. She went. She returned, dropped Rose's key chain down the stairwell, and was gone again.

"I've told her the truth," Alan repeated, suddenly tearful. He picked up his luggage and went down the stairs.

Rose retrieved her keys, went into her apartment, unplugged her phone, ran a bath, and got in. Frances stalked down the stairs and pounded on her door. Rose heaved up out of the water and pulled on her kimono. Through the doorway, they looked at each other. Then Rose sighed, stepped forward, and put her arms around Frances who first crumpled and then struggled out of the embrace.

"You knew," she said. Rose led her to the big chair. "And you never said a word."

"But I did tell you," said Rose gently, kneeling beside her. "Almost the first thing I ever said to you was that Alan was gay."

"We are not going back there. We are not going back to that point in time."

"Oh, but Frances. They held hands in front of you. You had to know."

"I thought the holding hands was an African thing." Frances looked at her wonderingly, and Rose was appalled at herself. That Frances "knew" had been Alan's excuse, and it wasn't true. Frances had decided not to know, but she'd also been allowed not to know. She looked blasted; her face like crockery shattered and glued back together. The door nudged open, and Max stood snuffling at the threshold. Frances held out her arms. Rose wrapped them both in an afghan and went to the refrigerator. It was the first of the many, many meals she was to make for them.

But Frances had, after all, given Rose years of comfort, of solace. Weary as she was, Rose found it a relief—no, a pleasure—to return the favor. If Rose felt a slight satisfaction that Frances hadn't gotten away with it after all—the perfect life and the lording of it over Rose, kissing her daily on both cheeks, the years of looking down upon her from the heights of married life—Rose was still genuinely sorry. And, really, if Rose was a little false, comforting Frances, this was nothing new and it went both ways.

They'd had days and nights and years together and they'd always held up the mirror, hadn't they, offering each other encouragement in the form of envy or warning in the form of pity? Rose, in comforting Frances and the pity that implied, warned Frances that she was truly in trouble. Frances, in allowing Rose to comfort her, envied Rose for keeping safe and encouraged her to keep even safer.

Yet they were so little alike. What had they ever been but two women brought into relation by happenstance, by circumstances?

Circumstances were just now crashing down. Rose, too, was on the verge of a crash, as Frances was certain to know. In the near future, Rose would need Frances, though how much sway Frances actually held over tenure was impossible to say.

Rose recalled telling Alan not to worry, fatuously lecturing him to ignore Frances, to stand back and let the wheels turn. But one never could exactly gauge the power of a department secretary who might convey or fail to convey the bits and scraps that kept things moving or brought them to a halt, who didn't turn the large wheels but might redirect things by the slightest turn of the smallest wheel.

So what if Rose and Frances had little in common but their history? Frances might still help Rose survive it all safely. Hadn't it been Frances who, in the past, had pointed out Rose's future to her, when she herself couldn't see it? For some seven years, hadn't Frances been the one to light the way?

Chapter TWENTY-SEVEN

I n and out of her rooms and theirs, upstairs and down, Frances and
Alan carried out their furious leave-taking. They seemed to prefer
Rose's apartment for their battles. She understood that: neutral
ground. Willing and curious, at first, she cooked and tidied for them
all and calmed Max, who cried and raged and built teetering block castles under her piano and smashed them down. Late summer, school
not yet in session, Rose and Max and Frances were home at Rose's all
the time. Alan was also present, in person or over the phone to
Frances, a dozen times a day or, lacking keys, over the speaker box
down at the front door.

He could get in if he *wanted* to, said Frances. He knew everyone in the
building; someone would let him in. She demanded that he come upstairs
again and *show his face,* even if he'd been there not an hour before. Telling
him so, she banged Rose's call button and broke it, which was okay by
Rose, who was growing weary of the buzzing.

Between rounds, Frances and Alan rehearsed to Rose what they would say next.

Frances: Alan had responsibilities. He was condo president—he should repair Rose's buzzer at once. He was a father—dishonest and weak, but, even so, she would take him back. Would she deny her children a father—little Max and the babe-to-be? No, but he would keep his vows; he'd admit he had been dishonest and weak; there would be no men.

Whenever Alan saw Rose at home or at school, he clapped his hands to his forehead. He was not afraid to face Frances. He was over every day, was he not?—yes, to caretake the condo. He'd get to Rose's buzzer. (No hurry, Rose told him.) *Frances* was the dishonest one, trying to bully him back into her bed and make him pretend he was someone he wasn't. Was Frances against joy? He loved men; she was not a man.

Between rounds, Frances moved furniture, slammed things, stacked things and rearranged things all over Rose's apartment. Opening her cupboard, Rose found her shelves stuffed with Frances's saltine boxes and had to ask where her plates had gone. And had to wait for an answer, because here was Alan again, in person.

He threw his arms around Max and raised his voice to Frances. Even more than he missed his boy, he seemed to miss his wife and to hold her to him, somehow still his. Otherwise, why try so loudly, so relentlessly, to make her adopt his version of things?

He loved men; she was not a man. Would she never *get it*?

Frances was more than *not a man*—she was a woman, Rose heard herself say, forgetting for the moment that she'd declared herself neutral.

What did that mean, Alan wanted to know.

Frances rolled her eyes and returned to her subject: vows, eternal *promises*.

But Alan had to know what Rose *meant*.

Alan loved men. Frances was a woman. Life moved on, Rose couldn't help saying.

So?

So, however much Alan missed Frances and Max, it was clear that he wasn't coming back—except here he was again.

Alan turned to Frances. He had always and would always admire and respect her, he said, and burst into tears.

"What are you trying to do?" Frances demanded of Rose.

There were many things Rose could say about letting go, she told them. But she herself had always let go with frightening ease. And she would shut up now.

"*Right*," said Frances.

"Right," echoed Rose. At least she could spirit Max away and leave them to their dismantling. She packed up the satchel of blocks and took Max off to school with her, where he built his castles beneath the piano in a practice room while she played. It was loud under the piano, but Max seemed to crave a blanketing of sound.

Rose too. She wanted music. She was back at her symphony. She wanted to get it done, get it out, rush a commitment from some new orchestra, slam a new entry into her tenure portfolio, but all she seemed able to do was to rearrange the parts of it, as Frances rearranged furniture, shoving and slamming and stacking with nonsensical precision, only to unstack again.

Fortunately, Frances wasn't strong enough for every rearrangement she imagined. She wanted to switch Rose's study and bedroom—Rose should sleep behind the kitchen and work on her sun porch. She wanted Rose to help her lug the bed back and the desk forward—better light for work, all those windows, said Frances. But that wasn't it.

After bedtime, after Frances and Max said goodnight and clumped upstairs, after the distant sounds of the bath—tap gushing, faint sloshing, and then a dim tunefulness, Frances managing a lullaby—after the quiet interval during which Max fell asleep, Frances came alone to Alan's study on the sun porch, directly over Rose's bed. There, she wept softly at his maple desk in his swivel chair and talked to herself so quietly that it was clear she didn't want to be overheard.

But Rose, coming to bed below, heard the swivel of the chair and the muttering and weeping. Frances didn't mean to admit anyone into the privacy of her defeat, but Rose couldn't help listening and then making use of what she heard.

The symphony came together: a burst of tears. First movement: *Utterly lost and alone. What must I undergo?* Then the question posed calmly and more emphatically, elaborated with greater dread: *Must I walk through the world alone?*

Second movement, complication: *Could there be something, someone to help me? What is love? Where is it found?*

Rose took to setting paper and pencil by the bedside. Her bed became her desk. She went to bed to work by lamplight and by the sound of Frances's grief—moaning, sobbing, and sighing.

Third movement, argument: *This can't be love, this confusion, this frailty.*

Rose made rapid progress and would have liked to give thanks and once or twice, in the day, nearly did, nearly thanked Frances for grieving so openly, as if for them both. Sometimes in the night Rose wept too, quietly, and imagined that they'd drawn close, she and Frances.

Then, as the nights passed, Frances's grieving lost its labored sound, and then the sighing lessened and Rose could barely hear her. No matter; the symphony was nearly finished. All she needed was a bridge to the end to bring her to what she'd written long before, that final movement of ease, assurance, and peace.

An evening came when Frances and Max went out visiting. Was it to Frances's mother, or had she said friends? It didn't matter; Frances was finally seeking someone else to talk to, and Rose was glad to find herself alone, except for the unnerving quiet. So when she heard a thump on her porch, and then another, a heavier sound than her cat's thud from bed to windowsill, from windowsill to floor, she went to investigate.

Outside her windows, opposite the sunset, a full moon lolled on the horizon, huge, membranous and scarlet. From below, a badminton birdie flew up, thumped her window, fell, spiraled up, and thumped the window again. It wasn't the usual frill of white plastic, but something old, knotted and black, black-feathered—Graham's shuttlecock.

She ran down to open the door. And there he stood, the moon huge behind him.

She pointed and stuttered, "Blood orange."

He asked her, naturally enough, whether she'd been away.

She might as well have been—her phone in constant use and her buzzer broken.

Not that she'd forgotten him. In the practice room or working alone in bed at night, she'd allowed herself to dream about Graham, urgent, embarrassing fantasies.

She felt she shouldn't think of him. After she'd told him she was entirely unattached, how could she explain that a sexual indiscretion might cause her to lose her job? Soon she would have to redraft her portfolio, crossing off the Seattle Sinfonietta. Still, she returned in her mind to Graham's house and his cooking, to the night when, if she hadn't lost her nerve, they would surely have climbed together into his bed beneath the shattered lute. She'd thought of how that lute might appear from beneath and the cracked resonance that might come from the chamber if an arm were to fling against it in the throes of lovemaking. She'd imagined Graham's weight on her, and that made it all the harder to phone him. She knew she ought to phone him. She hadn't properly thanked him for supper, and it was her turn to call. She'd even tried to joke herself into it, scribbling out a phone script—*Hi, Graham, it's Rose, how're you?*

He leaned against her kitchen wall, his hands stuffed in his pockets. The glossy white of the wall made a sort of corona around his dark head with its close-cropped hair. Though slender and no taller than she, he seemed huge, as though the moon had gotten in.

She turned her back to him, putting on the teakettle, gabbling about her music and about how tenure was making her nervous, hoping her hands would stop shaking.

She'd imagined not only lovemaking but fantasies of him running to her rescue. He'd carry her away from all worries about her future. It would be a rising-up on the wings of love. How sentimental of her, how pathetic.

She passed her glance over his head, the bristly hair, the emphatic eyebrows, the wide forehead, the abruptly pointed chin—a face both sharp and kind.

She'd lost a commission she needed for tenure. She could tell him that much without saying how. And, of course, a symphony, however great on paper, did not exist until played, she told him, in a tone so jaded that anyone might think she was not at all aware of this man standing before her in whom she'd put such huge, outlandish hope.

He had crow's feet like she did, and deep laugh lines. At the moment, however, his mouth was still and his face was a mask. She recognized this as a trick of his: his courteous blank look, his "ancient craftsman." She could understand why he'd mask himself to her now. She was rambling on about orchestras in her professional voice, *her* mask, her official stance with its any number of words to keep her out of trouble. Not that she'd succeeded in keeping out of trouble.

"Well," she said. "Why should it be easy? Aren't humans made for difficulty?"

He spoke up suddenly. "Difficulty? What about happiness?" His voice, for all its Midwestern plainness, had a sparkle in it. His face, though wary, had come alive, his eyes so suddenly keen on hers that she dropped her gaze to his hands and the shuttlecock he was turning over and over.

"Happiness," she said. "What's that?"

"You tell me," he demanded.

But all she had to offer was sadness. She fetched the teacups. She asked him to sit down. But he went on standing against her wall, fidgeting with the shuttlecock, longing and apprehension washing across his face.

That morning, she told him, sadness had announced itself again. Out behind the building, very early, she'd heard such a banging that she'd struggled out of bed and gone to the window to see a figure in a tan coat in the alley casting lids off garbage cans, pushing the cans over and strewing the garbage. It was Doris Atkinson, the Alzheimer's-afflicted wife of the Chair of her music department, in her Burberry coat.

"No kidding," said Graham, in a toneless voice.

"No kidding," Rose echoed witlessly, keeping her story going, making strings of sounds just to keep his eyes on hers.

She'd spotted Doris Atkinson that morning and rushed to her closet and wrenched on her jeans in a hurry to go down and help. She didn't admit why to Graham: that she'd recognized the opportunity for a private talk with her Chair to gain assurance that he, at least, was on her side and would fight for her tenure; and what better pretext than by leading his poor, demented wife home to him? But it didn't matter—Frances had saved Rose from her ignoble errand. Frances had got there first.

Frances Gilpin, her upstairs neighbor, was someone Doris recognized, Rose explained. Frances dropped over to the Atkinsons' at least twice a week to help the Chair manage, and so it was better that Frances be the one to take Doris home.

There they went down the alley, Frances in her nightgown and bathrobe, with her little boy, Max, in his pajamas and Doris with garbage down her coat front, going off toward campus and the Atkinsons' duplex as though this were normal: Frances with her head held high, her robe sashed around her swollen belly, coaxing along her little son, who dragged the rubberized treads of his pjs, coaxing along Doris in her expensive, soiled coat—a brave parade that seemed to Rose the very picture of sadness.

Some of this she had put into her symphony, she told Graham. She had no orchestra to play it, but she was finishing it anyway. Perhaps that was how she defined happiness—work? Solitary progress in work? The teakettle whistled, full boil. She turned to fill the teapot. She placed upon the table a plate of saltines.

Graham moved his shoulders away from the wall, leaning upright so that, though he hadn't moved his feet, it seemed he'd taken a step toward her. "Maybe you need a change of scene," he said.

"A change of scene," she echoed agreeably. "Yeah, maybe I need to get outdoors." But she knew otherwise. What she needed was to stay put, to keep a grip, to finish the symphony and find it an orchestra, and, above all, to stay close to Frances right up until tenure was decided.

"I have," said Graham, clearing his throat, "just the place for you."

"The heron rookery?"

"We'll keep that for later. An ocean." A freshwater ocean and an island, he told her, and not far away. The ocean had gulls and breakers. The island had herons, but owls were more the thing. The Great Horned Owl nested there and, in August, other owls were sometimes seen, Barred and Snowy Owls, and there'd be ripe thimbleberries. The island stood so far out in the ocean, they'd have to take an hour-long ferry.

Lake Superior, she guessed. She'd heard of it.

But had she seen it? Would she come with him and camp on Isle Royale? He'd gone up every August for years, usually alone, but his tent could hold two.

Distantly, the outside door opened and Frances, returning from her evening visit, wherever it was she had gone, came up the stairs, her high-flung footsteps trailed by Max's trundling tread.

"You and me in a tent?" Rose asked Graham.

He shrugged and offered a trace of a smile, and when a rap came at the door, told her not to answer it. "I don't care who it is," he said.

But Rose had lost the habit of locking her door. Frances opened it and stepped in.

"Who's this?" she blurted, as though Graham were the intruder.

"Graham Lowe," Rose announced nervously. "Frances Gilpin." Max wandered past them to where his blocks were waiting. "And Max. Her son, Max."

"Rose's godson," Frances added brightly and looked expectantly at Graham as though he should explain himself.

"Rose's piano tuner," he said and gave a nod, masked and formal again.

"My friend!" Rose cried out. "My friend," she said more calmly.

"I see," said Frances and flushed deeply. "Max," she called. "Maxie, put your blocks in the satchel."

Unable to look at Graham, Rose continued to stare stupidly at Frances. "Rose's friend," said Frances. "Imagine. And I've heard nothing about you."

Graham, torturing the shuttlecock, refrained from chat.

"So, we'll be going." Frances, offended, gathered Max and went.

Oh, dear, Frances, Rose thought. And then stopped thinking and grabbed the shuttlecock from Graham and aimed and shot it across to the porch, where it bounced off a window and dropped to the bed, the unmade bed with its mess of pencils and papers.

Closing the door after Frances, Graham turned the lock. Rose laughed, an awkward croaking. His arms closed around her. She reached up and pressed his shoulder blades and felt his fingers slide together and lock at the small of her back and felt his breath on her cheek and his chest rise against hers.

The answering pressure from his mouth, as she kissed him, was firm. His lips had a slight tang, as of vinegar, and a pleasant dryness, as of chalk. She wanted him, but she felt unprepared. She began to tremble. He enclosed her more tightly, shushing her before she could speak. He was leading her to where the shuttlecock flew.

She took his hand and stepped ahead of him—why should she have to be led? As they passed the piano, they both trailed their hands over the keys, making a brief, dissonant glissando. She pulled down the shades and shoved her manuscript off the bed to the floor, scattering pencils. He lifted a hand to her hip and rested it there, a large hand that seemed already on her bare skin, its heat came so strong through her clothing. He reached a caressing hand to her face, a thumb to the hollow of her throat, and then put his lips there. His temple with its pulsing vein running up into the dense, dark hair filled her sight, and the smell of him, chalk and vinegar. If warmth had a smell, his was that, something furry, something damp, a smell that was partly hers as she grew hot and answered him, rising to join her mouth to his while reaching to undo their clothes.

He put his hands over hers, forbidding hurry.

This is Graham, she told herself.

"Graham," she said aloud but couldn't hold still. She needed stillness in which to sink down. Instead, she felt herself going up and up, groping upward in her mind, up past Frances, up past tenure, up, up, groping her way up the face of the moon, no handholds nor footholds, just a dazzling, slippery surface, and an upward urge no one could sustain.

Chapter TWENTY-EIGHT

O ut of the dark she said, "It'll be better next time," not knowing whether there would be a next time, not knowing if he'd heard her, her voice so hushed, so constricted. Not ten minutes after they'd begun, she'd cried out and it was over, she was done, and if he'd come too, she'd missed it. He must have, because he was going off to the bathroom to flush away the condom.

She turned on the bedside lamp and pulled the sheet to her chin. She'd been a long time without sex, despite the night with Stephen, whatever that was. It was as though she'd forgotten how. How could she tell him she wasn't always like this? Maybe she was, now. After so much raw luck and adventure, after so much loneliness, maybe this grabbing and scrabbling was all the lovemaking she had left.

He lifted the covers and slid in beside her. "Next time," he said, "starts now."

"It does?"

He mimicked her, all round eyes, and tugged the sheet from her chin. So he wanted her again, wanted her, too? The way he looked at her had nothing superior in it. In his hands, she rediscovered the thickness of her hair and the weight of her head and how it moved nonetheless lightly on her neck, how her breasts rose and fell with her breathing, and how changeable she was in her feeling—first defeated, but now flaring up bold.

Hurry vanished. She had nowhere to be but in her bed with him, nothing to do but to feel with her hands what he was. She settled again into the smells of vinegar and warm fur. Finding him hard, she hoisted herself astraddle him. He gasped and began to move under her and she settled into the rocking sounds, the gasping and grunting and liquid sounds, the sucking and sliding that had embarrassed her when she was very young but now seemed friendly and familiar. It was good. They were going to be fine.

Going slow was now the thing. It became a game—was she even moving on him?—and he laughed aloud. They'd come to call this glacial slowness though it only made the heat more intense, lowering their melting point together, so that the rush, when it came, made them both one thing.

They slept. From the apartment overhead, if anyone was listening, came the distant sounds of bath and bedtime and, later, of Frances coming to sit at Alan's desk for her now brief and nearly silent vigil. Rose had come to know, moment to moment, ticking, nervous, at the center of her life, where Frances was, what Frances felt and what she would likely say or do next. But now Rose slept all tangled up with her new love.

And what was there to do in the morning but make love again? It was August; they had no reason to put on clothes. Eating, bathing, making love, they wandered her rooms—white paint, dark wood, pale of bare legs against the dark plush of her easy chair.

She'd been alone with her thoughts for a long while. Alone and now not alone, perhaps never alone again. She'd had no one to talk to except

Frances, who only listened for what was pertinent to her, what she'd already heard of, what she could understand. Graham listened for everything, even what was strange, what Rose felt and thought and *was* that he might never have guessed. She was only beginning to feel how essential he would be to her. She found herself blurting out nearly everything that came into her head.

Walking over to his carriage house to "break in" his big bed, they went hand in hand, so giddy and giggly that kids paused in play to watch them. Passing through the gate in the brick wall felt to her like stepping straight out of the world. Here it was again, the loneliness that came with love, the spookiness of being two alone. Suddenly not alone, never alone again—and then, somehow, doubly alone. Shivering, she followed him up the rough wood staircase. It was either loneliness with love or without it, and she would take hers *with*.

Graham laughed, picked her up, and hoisted her over his threshold.

This can't be love, this confusion, this weakness. But it was. In a flash, she saw the end of her symphony and, over several fevered days and nights, got up from bed at her place or his and threw a towel over the chair or piano bench and wrote naked, cum oozing from her as she played and sang for him of loneliness linked to love, then fused, and then the resolution that wove up all the ragged strands.

Just like that, she was done. Finished.

What did he think?

He thought it was great.

Aw, but he was partial. In his music collection, she'd discovered every piece of hers ever recorded. How long had he been collecting her, anyway?

None of her business. He didn't want her getting a swollen head.

"Hah," she said. "Too late!"

She copied the symphony and sent it to London to support an application for a fellowship there with an orchestra that had once performed a piece of hers, and sent another copy to Lila, inscribed "To my teacher, my maestro," and danced it to the mailbox, thrilled as Meggy in her brand-new, starry nightgown, a sight Rose recalled with an ache. It wasn't a swollen head she had, but a swollen heart. She loved Graham and she missed Meggy; she loved Graham and missed Frances and Max. She ran upstairs to see them any number of times, but they were suddenly never at home.

Neither was she. Home was now wherever Graham was, her place or his.

August turned to September. Crossing campus on the first day of classes, a warm day when the few fallen leaves lay live and wet underfoot, she remembered her first view of the college: the ivy-covered walls and great stone steps that had seemed corny to her then. By now, the place was thoroughly peopled for her. Every corner of campus held a memory, and, as she went, she was called by name, by first name, as she'd long insisted, artist's prerogative, the informal, the real. "Rose, hello, Rose, hi, Rose, Rose, Rose," came the voices of professors, staff, and students like the chiming from the clock tower welcoming her back to where she very much hoped she belonged.

"Hello, Rose," said Frances at her desk in the glass front of the music department.

"Frances—how are you?" she blurted—an unfair question. Frances could hardly give a real answer in the midst of the busy office, and Rose was due in the classroom.

There, third hour, Victor came to every class and took a place in the back and participated, his answers proficient and pointed. He alone would not use her first name, but addressed her as *professor. Professor Mac-Gregor,* a personage. She let it stand.

The Rose that ran home and stripped off her clothes for Graham was someone else entirely. When she was in front of her students, she sometimes felt this other self impatiently waiting, and it worried her. She couldn't afford to lose concentration.

It occurred to her that Frances might serve as her model. Frances held the department together, its entire workings, and nothing in her private life ever interfered. Her pregnancy was showing now and she was back and forth to the bathroom often, but her posture radiated poise. However devastated, she looked luminous, her eyes enormous, her features so distinct that they seemed carved.

Passing her desk, Rose developed the unfortunate habit of asking Frances several times a day how she was. And then she'd kicked herself, only to hear herself shortly after asking again. She knew she was asking not about Frances, but about herself—meaning tenure, a reading on her tenure situation that might be gotten from Frances.

Frances would give an eloquent pause and, in a brightly neutral tone, always answered, "Well enough." If Frances knew anything about Rose's tenure, she wasn't saying.

"Rose," said Graham, "Rose, Rose, Rose."

"What?" she asked and he told her how lovely she was and how long he'd waited for her. He had a past—girlfriends who hadn't worked out. He told her only enough so she'd know that she hadn't been the only one, over thirty and still unpartnered, to worry that there might be something wrong, some inner flaw.

"And who's to say there isn't?" she said. "Who's to say it'll work out this time—the confirmed bachelor and the settled spinster?"

And she wasn't even settled—her career still hanging, her fate yet undecided.

Graham didn't see it that way. He claimed she was only in danger if she thought she was. There were ways to earn besides teaching. Not all composers and musicians taught. He was surprisingly stubborn on The Subject, which was how he'd begun to refer to her tenure worry. She did talk about it, but that was understandable—it was *pending*.

She found him sometimes tactless.

He called it being direct. He was thinking of clearing the pianos out of the garage stall below his loft, of finishing repairs and selling them off. He could insulate and soundproof down there, put in heat and a good wood floor. There were decent windows facing the garden, and windows high in the carriage doors. The place could be a studio. A composer's studio was what he meant, a place for her.

When she imagined how it might be to live and work in the carriage house, a longing seized her, followed by vertigo. She had fallen for him and would probably go on falling for some time to come. Yet she had maintained her own household for years. If anything needed to be built or bought for her, she'd built it; she'd bought it.

Deliberately misunderstanding him, pretending that he meant the studio for himself, she asked whether he was planning to take up an instrument, or maybe get serious about his drawing, his bird drawings? They were sitting after supper at his table, which, through a small window, overlooked the wall across the alley where a creeper climbing the brick showed bright red leaves, a possible warning of an early winter. He leaned back, his alert, brown eyes on hers, and dropped his chin.

Also, what was the use, she wanted to know, of putting money and labor into the place when he was only a renter?

Only a renter? Renting was what he believed in, renting and renovating to suit the present, the best way to deal with fleeting time. "*Life* is a rental," he said and got up and grabbed his coat and went out the door.

For the first time, she realized, he was really angry with her. But his anger didn't worry her. Skipping over his offer and its import and the fact that she'd deflected it, she stepped into a new, warm certainty of him and imagined a life within his yellow walls. If she had no mortgage nor condo dues to pay, if the two of them split expenses, it might not matter whether or not she got tenure. A rescue! But she had no intention of letting him know how much the idea appealed to her, to what she thought of as her weakness. And was time really fleeting? She didn't think so. Tenure, in fact, *was* time to her. Tenure was something permanent. Tenure would be her strength, her calm from which she'd plan life afresh and give of herself, of her plenty. She could be the rescuer then. Maybe she could even help him buy his place, though she wouldn't suggest that now, not yet, not till she figured out his pride. And, of course, not until she knew for sure she had it—had tenure.

He came back from his walk and she kissed him hard. His way, free-lancing and renting, was good, she acknowledged, a good way of life. And she could do the same, scrounge a living and write music somehow. But she made real money teaching. Did he think it would be nobler if she made peanuts? Did he see her waiting tables?

"Know how I see you best?" He tugged her to the bed and pulled her shirt off.

Seriously, would he prefer her as a nurse's aide? A secretary, like Frances?

"Status," he said.

"Money," she countered. Money to buy freedom from worry, money to buy the dreaming time she needed to write good music. Okay, so she enjoyed a certain standing. A college job conferred status, but it also opened doors.

She'd earned it, though, hadn't she? She'd applied herself, won artist trophies, won teaching awards—the teaching award by student acclaim her first year back on campus as a member of the faculty, bona fide, that is, on tenure track. If she'd been lucky, she'd made her luck.

"Rose," he said and raised himself over her. "Haven't we said enough on The Subject? Can't we find something better to do?" Readily, she opened her legs to him.

For good measure, she'd dropped a note to her Chair, offering, in addition to her regular load, to take on Alan's committee work. Alan had left town with James. He'd applied for sabbatical the previous spring, as if he'd foreseen the split with Frances, which he probably had, having caused it. This made an opportunity, anyway, for Rose, who offered to take Alan's tutoring responsibilities, as well—anything to demonstrate her worth, her versatility to anyone who might be watching and judging.

She reached up and picked at a string on the broken lute overhead, and Graham paused in his motion. She'd later have to wonder why she'd done that, plucked a dead string in the midst of love? The string made an inert snapping sound. She could make music; she was meant to make music and to get her music *out*. If not tenure here, then at some other college, some other platform from which to launch her music. She could go else-where. She recalled that, when she'd first come there, she'd only thought of it as a stopping place on her way to the rest of the world.

He lifted himself from her. "What?"

Had she really said that aloud? She hadn't meant it. She was just talking.

"You're going. You're already gone," he said and rolled away from her.

She hadn't meant it. She had no other teaching offers. She wanted him; he felt good inside her.

"What am I? A fuck on the way to the rest of the world?"

"No, of course not," she said, horrified.

But he'd had enough of The Subject for a while. His backpack, half-filled for the island, sat in a corner. They'd never managed to go. August over, the berries were gone, but the leaves would be turning. He thought he'd go up for a while.

He understood she couldn't come with him.

She agreed it might be for the best. She didn't dare miss a single class, committee meeting, or campus event. She'd get notice of tenure any time, possibly by the middle of October—at the very least by Christmas.

He didn't plan to stay away on the island till Christmas.

"Of course not—I never meant that," she said.

It got cold up there early. By the end of October, the ferries stopped running and the place iced in for the winter. But he'd stay awhile and air out his brain. He could afford it, as a matter of fact. He made enough money to take a month off whenever he wanted.

She watched him pack his tent, his maps, and his food and hoist his canoe to the roof of his van. She kissed him and stood waving till he drove out of sight.

And then she was bereft. She'd expected to feel released, to move lightly and swiftly to all she had to do. She had not expected to feel dead. His mail would be held at the post office. Why hadn't he asked her to bring in his mail? She did feel lighter, but painfully so, as if a weight she had thought was herself had been wrenched off. She stood at the curb, achy in her skin.

She'd been thinking of nothing but tenure. Now, without Graham, she could think of nothing but love. She couldn't bear to be the sort of woman who thought of nothing but love. She went to the condo, looking for company, but Frances and Max were not at home. She trudged through her days, to her office, to her classroom, to her condo.

Her London proposal came back far earlier than expected. A refusal. She hadn't even made the first cut. Shocked, she read closely and found the reason why: on the list of names of preliminary judges was Stephen Orrick of the Seattle Sinfonietta.

She crept over to the carriage house and let herself in with the hide-a-key. In Graham's big chair, she talked to herself. She'd put her symphony in a fresh envelope and send it out again immediately; she'd hold to her course; she'd hold on. She turned back Graham's bedcovers and lay down to sleep in his bed that night, and the next night did the same. Without his permission, without his knowledge, she tried to sleep with him that way, she in his bed, he in his tent on his island.

They were exchanging postcards: mild jokes, short accounts of life in a tent or in a music department. Love, she signed hers, love, love, love.

Love, Graham, he replied. Love in the singular. It began to seem an injunction: love Graham. She didn't have to be told to love Graham. She loved him, but she must have blown it with him because otherwise how could he stand to be apart from her?

Word came by departmental memo that Alan's tutoring duties would be covered by a temporary hire. She dropped by Chairman Atkinson's office to ask why.

Oh, they could afford it, the Chair said, and reminded her in his genial way that she, their composer, had never been expected to take on extra duties. They all knew the creation of new music required ample time. This was so, but Rose noted that his tone was perhaps a bit distant. She was the department's only woman professor; they'd think twice before dumping her, wouldn't they? she thought, as the Chair went on to tell her that the new hire was Vietnamese, a fresh-faced young man, an expert in computer-generated music. Racial diversity was the new mandate.

Hold on, hold steady, Rose told herself, but she felt her grip slipping. Frances. Time to go to Frances. She'd humble herself and ask Frances what all this meant, what it would mean for Rose vis-à-vis tenure.

But Frances was not at her post.

"She's packing up to move," explained the student answering the phones.

Rose ran over to the condo. On the landing sat a stack of cartons.

"What's all this?" she called out, as if she couldn't see for herself.

"Selling the place, if a buyer can be found," said Frances. And as though there had been no interruption in their life together, she beckoned Rose inside. "The market's flat, so it may stand empty awhile. Either way, it's time for us to go."

The curtains were down. The dining room stood entirely bare. In the living room, a pair of chairs and a small table were set in the place of Alan's great old couch. His rug, also missing, left an expanse of freshly waxed wooden floor across which the light skated, chilly and dazzling. The table appeared to float, and on one side sat Max, his tousled hair shining and blueberries in a white bowl before him like bubbles of ice. Max slid off his chair, took his bowl, and came and climbed into Rose's lap. His cheek against hers burned. She clutched him and recalled his baptism, how she'd held him in her arms and promised in his stead to trust entirely in grace and love. Max was still her godson and Frances her—what? god-sister?

They hadn't had a real conversation in weeks, but it wasn't as though they'd quarreled. They'd simply stepped apart. Rose had stepped first, but she'd done nothing to Frances, really, except to fall in love.

She would ask Frances for news of tenure. She would be direct.

"How are you, Frances?" was what came out of her mouth.

Frances laughed, and Rose laughed with her.

"I'm sorry," said Rose. "I can't seem to quit that."

"Oh, I'm fine, really," said Frances. "I'm sure I'm just fine." Exhaustion showed in her eyes, and her features seemed once again as oddly sharp as they had on Rose's first impression of her, though her hair, growing out from its boy-cut, softened her angles. She wore no makeup and the man's white T-shirt she had on—V-necked and immaculate—over a pair of sweat pants, accentuated her swelling belly. She was simply, strikingly herself.

"You look wonderful," said Rose. It was true.

Frances rolled her eyes. "You look worried."

"Tenure."

"Right," said Frances, but offered nothing more.

"You know, Frances," remarked Rose, "you really do look stunning."

Frances sent Max from the room on some obscure errand—to get a dinosaur book or something of the sort—and when they were alone, she reached across the table, almost but not quite touching Rose. "Why did he say he loved me?" she asked. "Why did he insist over and over that he loved me? Do you know?"

For a moment, Frances let her grief show and wasn't any sort of beauty, but a pregnant mother, burdened with children but otherwise alone.

"Alan did love you," Rose stammered. "You made him a home and a family."

But Frances shook her head, unsatisfied, this new Frances who had torn down the curtains, who seemed intent not on preserving, but on removing illusions. Rose couldn't imagine why Frances would want to punish herself with the why of it. But Rose did know why, and Frances was asking.

She offered up the ancient history, how, back in the spring before Alan was tenured, she and Alan, standing outside the open door of the Chair's office, had overheard Frances speaking against Alan, saying he shouldn't be trusted with students because he lacked a family.

"And so he married me?"

"He thought you were going to put him out of his position."

Frances regarded Rose, and her eyes had never seemed more piercing. "You people," she said, "and your positions." She got to her feet, and Rose struggled up after her. "I suppose you were only ever Alan's friend, not mine."

"Oh, no," said Rose. "Come on, Frances."

"Really," said Frances. "Do you think we were ever true friends, you and I?"

"Of course we were. *Are*. After all we've been through together, of course we're friends. Oh, Frances, why ever not?" Rose begged and realized she had not gotten what she'd come for and would not get it. Frances gave no reply. Frances had controlled the interview, and Frances had the last word, which was no word at all.

At the end of September, having sold the last of the furniture, even the table and chairs and the beds, Frances moved herself and Max and a dozen neatly labeled cartons of clothes and toys, barely filling a college maintenance van.

Not far, was all she would say about where she was going. Rose supposed she didn't want to admit she was going home to her mother's, only a few blocks away.

Back inside her own place, Rose found the ceilings too high, the space vaulting and colder yet with the empty rooms above. She packed Jewels, the cat food and litter box, and carted them over to Graham's. Wrapped up in Graham's blankets, wearing his sweater and his socks in double pairs, she began to cook with his pans and utensils and to eat out of his dishes. But she hadn't moved in—oh, no. Before he returned, she intended to wash every dish, all the sheets and towels, and put it all back the way he'd had it. He was never to know.

On a night in early October, however, a key turned in the lock and there he stood. It was snowing on the island, he said, and dumped down his pack. Even from across the room, he smelled of campfire. Though she had no right to be, she was completely taken by surprise, not frozen, but painfully alive as if thawing too quickly. He was bearded, shaggy, and so bundled up that he seemed bearlike. He took her breath away. She jumped up to fill the kettle and halted. Glancing sidelong, she saw the many signs of her trespass, her failures written in her disarray: her jacket flung on his floor, her underwear in a dirty pile at the foot of his unmade bed. She turned to face him.

His gaze went by slow and exhausted degrees from puzzlement, not to dismay nor disapproval, but to what seemed like relief and then to a sort of merriment and a radiance as though he'd solved the puzzle, coming to the answer he most wanted. He sat down unsteadily and opened his arms to her.

Love, love, love, she'd signed her postcards. And here she was, waiting for him.

"I was only borrowing the place. Only camping out. I know I didn't ask," she blurted and rushed to the nearest pile of her things and began to gather them up.

"Stop that," he said sharply.

If ever the time had come for trusting in grace and love, it might have been then. But she couldn't stop—she was too embarrassed. Why trust, why fall in a heap on someone else when she had something private and far less helpless? She had her luck; she preferred her own if she had any luck left at all.

Chapter TWENTY-NINE

L ila burst into town from the farm harvest, unpacked a box of
apples and potatoes, a pair of pumpkins, a tub of goat cheese, and
an enormous rutabaga with the dirt still clinging to it; pounded
out a fanfare on Rose's piano and halted, mid-chord.

"You don't look like someone who's just smashed home her first
symphony."

"No," said Rose. She wasn't going to cry. Her solitary state was too
much her own doing to think of it as other than her natural condition.
"Love," she muttered.

"Who?" said Lila.

Except for the time Rose had introduced Graham to Frances—when,
really, she'd been unable to avoid it—she had never mentioned Graham
to anyone. She'd done that once too often, talked up this new man or that,
and where were they now? "You know how love goes."

"How?"

Rose shook her head. Missing Graham while he'd been on his island was nothing to how she missed him now, a feeling made worse by his nearness in the neighborhood and the dread of meeting him by chance. She might have walked over and knocked on his door, might have called him, but couldn't bear, not even by phone, to contend with what was behind the terrible look on his face when she'd rushed out his door on the night he'd returned from the island. And it struck her with finality that he hadn't called her, either.

"Okay. Love goes bad," Lila agreed and reached for a box of tissues.

"Most of the time, yes, it does. Remember you and me?"

"Yeah, and now look at us," said Lila, dabbing at her friend's eyes.

"Don't laugh," said Rose.

"You'll laugh, too," said Lila. "Listen up."

Rose had in the past written some exceptional pieces, but the symphony was, in Lila's opinion, the best thing yet. She'd copied the manuscript—*without permission,* given Rose's recent threat to retire from the world—and had located a terrific conductor, a woman and so, predictably, a freelancer, which was, in this case, a stroke of luck. Lila's eyes sparkled; her cheeks shone ruddy through her tan and a fresh, luxuriant growth of beard—the very face of luck.

Rose bit. "Because?"

The conductor had an open slot to fill, last-minute, in the Santa Fe Music Festival.

"It's a chamber music festival," said Rose. "I need an orchestra."

"Will you *please*? They will hire the Santa Fe Orchestra and just about any soloist you'd care to summon. I, myself, very much hope to be considered."

Rose did laugh then, or rather, let out a tortured coughing.

"It's gonna be a triumph," said Lila. Then she took herself back to the farm.

The day before Halloween, the confirming call came from the new conductor, who was ready to talk terms. Rose's hands shook, holding the receiver, but she answered calmly about timing, fee, and travel. The thing was real and would likely make all the difference for tenure. Was it possible that a single phone call could set her life on track again?

Hanging up, she got out a knife and Lila's pair of pumpkins and carved one with a careless, silly smile and the other tense and slit-eyed. Then she phoned the guest house in San Francisco where Alan was doing sabbatical "research" on "West Coast jazz influences"—running all over the city with James. He'd begun life over, *living with a vengeance.* He was giving Frances *total* proceeds from the sale of the condo. And Frances was letting him see Max. He was going to get to show Max California. It was early morning in San Francisco, and Alan and James, just going to bed, were dizzy with hilarity and alcohol.

Rose told him about her Santa Fe premiere.

"Wow," he said. "*Wow.* James, listen to this. I'm putting James on."

"Wait," she said. "Alan, I need you. How should I spread the word at school?"

"Oh, *right.* You're all hung up on that tenure crap."

"Look who's talking. And I don't see you throwing over *your* teaching job," she said, though who knew?—that might be next.

"Rose," he said, "sweet Rose Marie. Of *course* I will ferret out the names on your tenure committee and I will talk to every one of them."

"You can do that?"

"I have my methods. I will *immediately* spread your news."

"You're pleased for me?"

"Thrilled."

She thanked him for that, very much; thanked him for being so ready to help her.

She was entirely welcome and she could stop thanking him now.

No, really, she was grateful that he was happy for her because, the truth was, she didn't feel anything.

"It'll come," he said. And if she'd get off the phone, he'd start tracking down her committee, all but Chairman Atkinson, whom she should tell the news herself, in the boldest of terms, in *superlatives,* and in person before he heard it from someone else. "Run, run, run to him," said Alan. "He'll love it."

She put down the phone and tidied her hair. Since her sloppy days squatting at Graham's, her days of falling apart alone, she'd pulled herself together and now dressed correctly in public and private—was there any difference in her life any more?—and if she felt cold, that void at her center, that ice in her bones, she shivered through it. She put on a light jacket over a pressed white shirt and trousers and stepped out the back door. Some eight years had passed since she'd first set foot in Minnesota, years of good luck and bad, of finding and losing. And now, it seemed, her best luck might hold.

At the back door, however, she was halted by a wave of chill: not the cold in her bones, but in the air. The frigid Canadian weather that had chased Graham from his island had made its way southward, and white stuff was falling, a sight so startling for October, she had to step out in it to prove this wasn't some eerie downflux of rice, but cold, hard, wet grains of snow. She went back inside to dig out her overcoat. It occurred to her to call ahead to Frances for a formal appointment with the Chair, but nobody answered at the music department. The switchboard confirmed what she saw out the window: snow heavy enough to close school. The sky was a mattress shredding downward. They were in for an actual blizzard. Up and down the street, small vampires and princesses and super-heroes would be in despair—*could Halloween be cancelled?*

Here was the fabled snow of October, foretold to her as a warning back East, a reason never to come to Minnesota. Flaming leaves still clung to branches, while leaves on the ground, unraked or in piles, lay whitening. Her mulberries had turned to plaster; the houses across the way were vague white shapes; the tower of Old Main, a vertical smudge. Still, a blizzard was something. Its power to nullify schedules, to send people home and keep them home, created unplanned hours, the great freedom of a snow day. She'd use hers to meditate upon her future. She was going to have a future, after all.

She told Jewels all about it as the cat paced back and forth on the summer quilt, jazzed by the change in air pressure. Dragging out her comforter, Rose wrapped herself and the cat up in it. Storm windows not yet in place, the screens were clogging up, whiting out the view. She whispered into purring fur and down feathers. A concert hall in Santa Fe, wild applause, herself ascending the stage in new clothes: she tried to see it but only got a blur. All she could see was this: herself crossing campus once the blizzard was over, *not* run-run-running but, with quiet purpose, walking past Frances in her glass guardhouse, past her own office, soon to be hers permanently, to the inner sanctum, the Chair's office—*Harold,* rather; Harold's office. As they were to be permanent colleagues— peers—she must learn to call him Harold.

She could see all this, but couldn't hold it in mind. She closed her eyes, and a figure appeared—not quite a person, but an empty dress, a silly bridesmaid dress, peony skirt and décolletage inflating with snow and wind. A man with salt-and-pepper hair turned in a movie theater seat and was swallowed up in snow. A little girl in a raggedy coat with blue-blue eyes, her own eyes, rushed toward her, blew through her. A shuttlecock flew upward. She leaned her forehead against the window toward the pounding storm and tasted the longed-for tang of vinegar. Then she got up out of her warm nest and went to the phone to dial.

"Hello," said Graham. "Hello," his actual, living voice said to her before the line went dead, the phone service knocked out by the storm. She switched on the radio to road and airport closings, dangerous wind chills and predictions of record snowfall. Out the window, a fog gone solid beat against the porch, came straight on, then battered from the sides, and beneath the racket outdoors, an interior creaking could be heard, an echoing in the empty rooms above, a wandering in rooms occupied, the entire building settling in for the siege.

It was afternoon, but it could have been the middle of the night. Avoiding a too-early bedtime, she scrubbed and pared the rutabaga and tossed it into the oven. An hour later, though it could have been a week or a year in her pocket of warmth within the roaring storm, she wiped her mouth and leaned down from her plate with a lump of goat cheese for Jewels, who took it and worked it unhurriedly in her jaws.

Curled up in bed again, she and her cat slept.

Morning, calm and silent, showed, under a brilliant sun, sidewalks indiscernible from lawns, fences merged with garbage cans, and the unplowed street, little more than an indentation in a snowfield. Phones still dead and college closed, she might take her news across campus to Atkinson at home, but how far could she get in snow up to her thighs? Bedazzled by the glare pouring in from the windows, she was snowbound.

Soon enough, snow shovels began to flash silver, blue, and orange up and down the street. Snow blowers whined. In the past, Alan had hired neighborhood boys to shovel, but, given the nearly four feet of snow now, there would be no boys to spare. Someone would have to clear the snow from the condo sidewalks and the driveways behind the garages.

Rose would do it. She was a Minnesotan, was she not—and intended ever more to be? She pulled on two pairs of jeans and a woolen stocking cap and, in the basement, found mukluks, an old feather-filled vest, leather mittens, and assorted brooms, shovels, and ice choppers. She'd make quick work of shoveling and then march over to the Atkinsons' duplex and give the news of her symphony premiere.

Other tenants called out to offer help, but she turned them down cheerily. She'd do it herself. She wanted to. To prove what? She had nothing to prove any more.

The snow was heavier than it looked. The wind had compacted it into dunes, undulating over where the sidewalk had been. She dug in. Growing hot quickly, she shed hat, then jacket and then prickly vest, and worked in her shirtsleeves.

Snow slid from roofs and branches under the steady sun, dumping small avalanches onto pathways she'd cleared. It was noon before the sidewalks were done. At lunch, she drank what seemed a gallon of water and, girding herself with the memory of long days of labor at the farm, went out again only to find that the city plow had been down the alley, leaving a ridge in front of the driveways to the garages.

Nothing to do but keep shoveling, to pile this new, even heavier stuff onto banks already heaped high, banks she herself had heaped high as her head, and now higher. To think she could move so much snow, so much anything, had at first amused her, but then she grew tired. In the rhythmic pitch of her shovel, thoughts came flooding, foolish thoughts and girlish wishes. She was not a woman pitching snow, but a shy girl pounding a piano all alone. And then not alone. She glanced up from her shovel and no one was there. Yet she felt observed and mocked, as though her sister sat on a snow bank and mocked her—Natalie, who was so wrong about practically everything, was right at least about this one thing: that in all Rose's striving was something ridiculous. Or could it be Graham watching blankly as she wore herself out, filling her shovel and slinging it?

She worked on, finishing the job she'd started. At sunset, the temperature dropped. She plunged her shovel into the bank by the back door but did not go inside. Instead, she stepped again into the alley and turned not toward campus and the Atkinsons' duplex, but another way. Pulling the woolen cap over her snarled, sweaty hair, she went with a purpose but without a plan, slowed only by the few derelict sidewalks where the snow had not been shoveled but tramped to a furrow.

Around her, porch lights were coming on, jack-o'-lanterns being set on snow banks. Halloween was back—bright orange rind and candle fire. Tiny electrified strings of plastic pumpkins and bats and skulls multiplied the sparkles in the air.

Turning into Graham's alley, she saw no lights at all. She'd heard his voice on the phone line just the night before—his actual, living voice. Could he have filled his backpack and gone off again in the midst of a blizzard? Graham's rooms at the top of the carriage house seemed entirely dark, but, above the snow bank, from a window in the garage where he stored his broken pianos, a faint glow came and a grinding hum could be heard. Boosting herself up onto the bank there and scraping snow from the window, she looked down into a bright, empty room.

All traces of pianos and piano parts were gone. Narrow, interlocking hardwood boards lay over what had been a cement floor. Graham stood at the far end, guiding a floor sander. A studio. Her studio. She pulled off her mittens and tapped the glass.

He looked up, frowned, and shut off the sander. He seemed not to recognize her and she quailed. Still, what could he see up in the window but a dark head, backlit by sunset?

"It's me, Rose," she said, when he appeared at the gate.

"Hi," he said faintly. "Want to come in?"

She shook her head. "I've got something to say." She didn't dare accept his hospitality—not yet. "Maybe the snow will improve my acoustics," she added. Though the joke was feeble or just peculiar, the thought of the night they'd first met gave her courage: the night before her Guild concert, she the only one in the seats, he on stage tuning her piano and possessing the courtesy and the boldness to speak to her for the first time. She felt again the confusing pleasure of his alert eyes upon her. This time, she would speak first.

She cleared her throat. There came a rustle at the entrance to the alley. Beneath the streetlight, a large overcoat herded several smaller overcoats, hung with sacks for candy. A skeleton followed, jittering Day-Glo bones.

"Hold on a minute," Graham said and went back inside. She felt vaguely alarmed to see him go. But he always had, in their short past, come back when he said he would.

Here he came with his thermos and a bowl of candy—Heath Bars— and a jack-o'-lantern with a small, amazed face. He boosted himself up beside her, sculpted a ledge for his pumpkin, and lit the candle inside it. She might have taken from all the nervous busyness that he was excited to see her. But, distracted by his nearness and, lacking permission to touch him, distracted by the sight of his hands pulling on gloves, pulling up over his head the hood of his sweatshirt, leaving all but his face hidden, she shivered, stunned, loving him as strongly as when they'd been naked, chest to chest.

The evening air was mild enough, though cold radiated from the snow bank and dampness seeped upward through her pairs of jeans. He filled the thermos cup for her. Lifting the cup, she inhaled her own sweat smell. Whatever she had to say sat in her throat, a painful welling. She glanced down into the empty garage bay.

"You did it. You built the studio."

"Yup. Almost done."

"It's great. It's going to be lovely," she said. "I'm so stupid."

"You don't need to think I built it for you. That would be pretty pathetic."

A chirping at the streetlight—a tiny queen hopped impatiently while her green-caped sister adjusted a warty mask.

"Hey, trick or treat," called Graham and scrambled down the bank with his bowl. Queen and witch froze, and then reached for the candy, doing him a favor.

"It's too dark back here," he said, resuming his seat on the snow bank. "Nobody wants to come down my alley."

"I do," she said. *I do*—the wedding words, but out of place, out of kilter and too dramatic. Who did she think she was—a bride? A queen commanding a suitor?

"I miss you," she said. This was so, and in no way exaggerated. Even sitting beside him on a snow bank was a relief, a break in the relentless missing of him.

He nodded, not looking at her.

"We didn't even break up properly," she added. "Nothing was said."

He sighed, puffing out his breath.

"So. First, I want to say I'm sorry."

"Don't. I don't want you to be sorry. Just go ahead and do whatever you have to do." He laughed painfully. "Okay. That was bullshit. I admit that's bullshit. It's not what I want. But it's what I wish I wanted."

"I have news," she said quickly, not daring to know what he wanted. Quickly she told of the symphony premiere and her near-certainty that tenure would be granted.

"Well," he said. "Good for you."

But that wasn't it—tenure wasn't it. Tenure was beside the point. "I expect to be myself again," she ventured and opened her hand to him.

He took it, squeezed it, and let it go. Half a dozen teenagers trooped beneath the streetlight in thrift-shop coats and ruined hats, on their way to some party. He shook his bowl of Heath Bars, but the teenagers weren't interested in candy. He unwrapped a bar and broke off half, put it in her cup, and poured in more coffee. A straggling girl, hatless, appeared in the streetlight, hurrying to catch up.

"What I mean is," she said, "if I made up one sort of self, it seems to me I can make up another." It was the sort of thing a teenager would say, and she did have that awkwardness, though less of the stiff dignity, thank god, and perhaps no dignity at all, leaning back against the hardening snow, bracing herself for his answer. Her jeans stuck to the bank beneath her. The night was growing dark. The cold was beginning to insist.

"Rose," he said, "why should you have to be anything else than what you are?"

"Because I was nothing to start with," she said, inviting argument of the wrong kind—he'd feel obliged to tell her that she was not nothing but someone very special, a gifted composer, and blah blah blah. It wasn't *what* she was that was in dispute, but *how* she was. Had been.

She thought she was already different, speaking up like this. Wasn't she already the new Rose?

Chapter THIRTY

S o, what do you say?" she asked Graham.

He owed her an answer and he hadn't said anything. Hadn't she been direct?

"I want another chance with you," she said, and noticed that her voice had grown mournful.

The straggler reappeared under the streetlight and looked about her.

Rose pulled herself together. "That way," she called briskly and pointed. "Your friends went that way." But the girl seemed bewildered and turned instead toward them, stepping high over the rubble. Bare-legged, wearing what seemed to be bedroom slippers, she slid and fell. They staggered down the bank to her.

Rose looked into the girl's face—an aging, freckled girl. Doris Atkinson. "Doris, what are you doing out here? Where are you going?"

"Someplace," Doris replied blandly.

"Graham, this is Doris. She's married to my department Chair.

Remember, I told you about Doris?" *Alzheimer's*, Rose mouthed, and took Doris by the shoulders.

Rose hadn't seen Doris up close in years. She looked very much the same, pert and trim. She wore a wool suit, well fitted to her small shape, and though her legs were bare, she looked well tended: the milky, freckled skin moist; the eyes bright.

"Aren't you freezing?" Rose asked her.

"Of course," said Doris. "That's the price for going someplace." Her fingers agitated, trying to pry Rose's hands from her shoulders.

Rose gave a short laugh. "I know what you mean."

She turned to Graham. "I'll take Doris home," she said. "I've got to see the Chair anyway." She was going to have to walk away from Graham, back into her grief at missing him.

Doris let her feet slide out from under her and Rose lost her balance.

"I'd better come," said Graham.

"I can manage," Rose told him and, squatting, brushed snow from Doris's legs.

"You need help," said Graham.

"Please get up," Rose told Doris. Suddenly furious, she swung around to Graham. If they were done, he should say so. "Just tell me," she blurted. "Just say there's no chance, if that's your answer."

He glared back at her. She wrestled Doris to her feet and took one arm. Graham took the other, and the three set off.

"I can't just come when you beckon and go when you change your mind," he said.

"Not fair," said Rose. "I have never—not once—changed my mind about you."

"Slow down," said Doris. They slowed, Rose unwillingly. The streets were far from empty. A tall shape raised bat wings. A small shape dropped a wand.

"You disappeared for weeks," he said. "Or you were only technically present."

"True. But you've forbidden me to say I'm sorry." She turned them down an alley, the shortest way to the duplex, and then they were climbing the back stairs, Rose tugging Doris up each step while Graham blocked her exit from below.

Chairman Atkinson swung the door open. "Good god, Doris," he cried. "Here she is. Rose found her. Rose MacGregor," he called over his shoulder. "Come in, one and all. The police are out looking. Call off the police. Pardon our disarray."

The Atkinsons' apartment, though changed in ways that Rose did not at first identify, was in no way disarrayed. Lamps glowed; cleanliness and order prevailed; and the smell of fresh baking hung in the air. Now that Doris was home, she seemed pleased to be there and seated herself in a kitchen chair and folded her hands expectantly.

Then the force behind the cleanliness and order walked in—Frances Gilpin. This was natural enough: Frances was the one who lent an extra hand; the Chair would call Frances in an emergency. Despite her enormous belly, Frances knelt easily before Doris and tugged off the snow-caked slippers.

"Rose, thank you," she said and bid Graham hello.

Rose stood with her back to Graham, waiting for him to excuse himself and go.

At the sink, Frances filled a basin with warm water. The Chair muttered into the phone. The doorbell chimed, and Max stepped into the room and picked up a basket of candy.

"Don't let Mrs. Atkinson loose," he advised and went off to answer the door.

Of her own dishevelment—jeans soaked, hair matted—of her need of a bath, Rose was dimly aware. She heard the hollow clunk of an empty boot and turned to see Graham pulling off his other boot. He pulled off his hood and there was his dear face, entirely revealed to her, his eyes on hers. They were not done.

"Have you two met?" Frances asked, and Rose, for a startled moment, prepared to have Frances introduce her to Graham.

"This is Graham, Rose's boyfriend," Frances told the Chair.

"Graham Lowe," said the Chair. "The piano tuner, I believe?"

"Yes," said Rose, fiercely proud of Graham. The men shook hands.

Frances lifted Doris's feet, one by one, and lowered them into the basin.

"And how are you, Rose?" asked Frances.

Rose registered the trick question—how are you?—the sign that all was not well with whomever was asked how.

"I'm fine," she replied. "Actually, I'm terrific."

"You'll tell us all about it?" said Frances. "We'll have cocoa? Apple-sauce cake?"

"Applesauce cake," agreed Doris and lifted her feet for Frances to dry. "Rose MacGregor," said Doris. "We sublet our apartment to her once."

"Why, that's right," said Frances. "Absolutely correct. Good, Doris."

"This is Frances Gilpin," said Doris blithely. "She took my husband away."

"No, no," murmured Frances. "He's right here beside you." Harold leaned and planted a kiss on his wife's forehead.

The doorbell chimed and chimed. They were running out of candy. Max gave away the last of it, and Frances turned off the porch light.

Around the old mahogany dining-room table that, when she had lived there, Rose had shoved out of sight, they all sat down for cocoa and applesauce cake. The table now stood in the living room, however, where the couch was pushed to the wall and a folding screen hid what had been the dining room. Behind the screen, Rose glimpsed a small cot and a familiar satchel of wooden blocks.

Into the middle of the table, upon a tablecloth as snowy as all out-of-doors, Frances placed the cake—an old recipe of Alan's via his chef boyfriend. Doris crowed at the sight—the crusty, cinnamon-speckled square—and, given the first piece, picked it up in her hands and bit down, squirting applesauce. Frances made quick work of Doris's face and hands with a napkin. Max nudged a spoon into Doris's hand. And Rose finished what she'd begun, telling her news about Santa Fe. In the boldest of possible terms, in superlatives, Alan had coached her—as she remembered only after she was done. She forgot to put it in superlatives, and it hadn't taken long to tell.

Graham, seated next to her, sent her a nod of encouragement. Here he was, her love. She might have known he wouldn't say yes all at once. But if she had—ahead of time—stopped to think how long he might take to answer, she might have lost her nerve and not come to get him, and then what?

"A symphony premiere. Congratulations are in order." The Chair hoisted his cocoa mug. "That should fetch a pretty penny," he added.

"Not really," said Rose. Large sums rarely came to living composers, unless they wrote for the movies. The Chair would know that. Why mention money?

"You should be very proud," said Frances, with a show of warmth. She picked up the spoon Doris had chucked aside and began feeding her. As the spoon lifted to Doris's mouth, Rose felt an odd shiver, half longing, half repugnance, recalling how, with Alan and Frances, she had sometimes felt herself to be the child. Still, it had gone both ways, hadn't it? What of the weeks she'd spent mothering them through their disaster? Was there anything really so wrong with that, with mutual dependence? People seemed to lean on one another if they grew at all close. Trusting entirely in grace and love might not, after all, be servitude, but, instead, how things had to be. She knew she had leaned on Graham. She might be leaning on him now. But she'd give him his turn to lean on her if he let her.

Across the table, Doris dribbled applesauce, and Frances cleaned her up again. Frances seemed to have gone from the worst of luck to peace, and Max was peaceful too. The Chair, at the far end of the table, tousled the boy's hair.

It struck Rose that this was her world: Frances and Max, old friend and godson; the Chairman and Doris—Harold, rather—colleague and his wife; and Graham, her true love. Some were missing—Alan, though he seemed present in the applesauce cake, in the advice that had brought

Rose here, in his twisted example, the damage he'd done in the name of tenure, and also the freedom he'd lately claimed. But it also seemed free there around the table, and she couldn't help wishing Alan present, and Lila and Emma, and everyone else she could think of, past and present, all sitting together at some great table where her tenure insanity was forgiven, with all the insanities of the past.

Rose had learned to trust in music, but perhaps she might also trust these people, to whom her luck had carried her? Even incomplete, it was still a world there around the Atkinsons' table, all leaned together, one depending on another like the music of a fugue, which, once you heard it and if you loved it, became part of the shelter in your mind.

Max, done with cake, got up. "Would you like to see my room?"

"Not till she's finished eating, honey," said Frances.

"It's only right here," said Max. Folding back the screen, he revealed the cot made up with his blanket, his toys stowed and his drawings nicely hung.

"Great," said Rose, beginning to see. If Max lived here, so must Frances. "It's just wonderful," Rose told her godson.

"Isn't it?" said Harold Atkinson. Frances was making the rounds with cocoa, and Harold caught her hand and pressed it. "Isn't she marvelous?"

Doris piped up, calling for milk, cold milk to cool her cocoa, and Rose got to her feet. Outlandish. In that same room, years before, Doris Atkinson had pronounced Frances outlandish. But Frances had gone from outlandish to marvelous. Rose, having lived in those rooms, stepped to the fridge like a sleepwalker and saw, through an open doorway, in what had been Doris's study, a new bed, sized for a lone adult, a bed with a railing, where Doris must sleep. While Frances, of course, slept with Harold. There was no other place for her to sleep. The shelter in Rose's mind quaked a little.

Frances, Rose had always thought, had stuck it out with Alan for pride's sake, for respectability. In her new situation, however marvelous, she couldn't marry Harold. She might share his bed but, as long as Doris lived—and Doris was still young—Frances would have to go on this way, mother to Max, to the new baby, and, of course, to Doris, while to Harold she would be not the acknowledged wife, but the secretary about whom things were said, as they'd always been said about Frances, but now this would be even more the case. Frances was outlandish, but now she must know it. Rose was proud of her, and amazed.

Rose poured milk into Doris's mug. Graham caught her gaze and held it, waiting, glancing from her to Harold. She'd said what she'd come to say? They could go now?

"In regard to tenure, Harold," she said, the name leaving her lips easily, "I'd like my committee to know of my premiere."

"Your committee. You haven't heard yet?"

She shook her head. Should she have?

"The letter must be in your mailbox at school. Isn't that so, Frances?"

Frances said nothing.

"Tell me," said Rose.

His eyes, casting down and away, told her. The shelter in her mind collapsed.

"Why, it's past suppertime," said Frances, getting up. "How silly—giving you cocoa and cake when it's time for supper. Sit down, Rose. I'll get cooking."

Rose's godson—her Max—came and tugged at her to sit down. She could see he was alarmed. Something in her face was alarming people. She sat down.

"It's a crapshoot, really—tenure," murmured Harold.

They had turned her down. It was too late for any symphony news. Harold rambled on about criteria, about balance on a faculty, about racial diversity.

It was over. Rose knew she could appeal to the college president. She could rally the students. She could muster her friends on the faculty—even now, Alan would be on the phone to the various members of her tenure committee and, startled to find them cool and shifty, would be growing outraged on her behalf. But that sort of thing rarely changed the outcome. Any protest would be too late and would only increase her humiliation, painful especially in front of Graham: she with her big news and her big future and her new self.

What—who had done this to her? Stephen? Certainly Stephen. But had anyone defended her? She doubted Harold had, rambling on so placidly. Who was Rose to him but a résumé that had once come over the transom?

"And, of course, the college is suddenly short of money," Frances said sharply, looking in from the kitchen. Her eyes flickered in Rose's direction. Frances was possibly laughing at her.

Ah, but Rose had laughed at Frances at the start, hadn't she?—those years ago, judging Frances deluded in her passions, willing herself into beauty, into love? And in laughing at Frances, Rose had launched the contest, the long race they'd run to its surprise conclusion: Frances, first at the finish line, settled and beautiful, beloved and secure, no matter how outlandish the arrangement. Hadn't Rose always underestimated Frances? Frances had been both lucky and crafty and likely deserved her turn to laugh. Hadn't Rose all along been the one more severely deluded, imagining herself a professor when she'd never been more than that oddity, the Girl Composer?

Frances. Of course it was Frances who had done this to her, by whatever she'd said from her glass box, whatever damning or belittling thing Frances had said, whatever silence she had let fall, in the recent days when Rose's fate was being settled.

But the flicker in Frances's eyes flared. The tone of her voice was angry. "The new mandate on race," she repeated, glaring at Harold, "and the sudden shortage of money so we can't have both a woman and a Vietnamese. Isn't that what you all say?" said Frances and smoothed her tunic over her belly and went back to the kitchen.

It seemed Rose had had a defender after all: Frances. That was astounding. What could it possibly mean? Frances and Rose were not even friends, as Frances had said herself, and yet Frances was her defender. In practical terms, it meant nothing: Frances was, after all, merely the secretary: her opinion, her unofficial vote, could change nothing.

Rose sat trapped in her chair, stupefied in the smell of her own sweat. It would be quite some time before it would occur to her that she and Frances had much else to say to each other. Just then, all she could see was failure. She had undergone a test and failed. Just then, she felt only chagrin to be possessed of a self, a mind and body so capable and so susceptible—she with her delusions of tenure, her applesauce cake-induced fantasies of togetherness.

"Let's get out of here," said Graham.

Rose kissed Max and nodded to Frances.

On the back porch, she stopped to catch her breath in the fresh cold while Graham pulled on his boots. She'd wanted the world, and for a moment she'd had it. She'd risen in the world and, given Santa Fe, she might rise again. But now she was falling. Could falling, of its own accord, make her a new self? She didn't think so. She'd sell her condo as soon as she could. She'd be offered, before severance, a final year of teaching, a one-year contract to give her time to search for a position elsewhere.

She felt her way down the stairs. She'd left the leather mittens behind, just a few steps up and through a doorway. But she couldn't bring herself to go back for them. Graham pulled up his hood but stuffed his gloves into his pockets. Stepping into stride beside her, his bare hand brushed hers. Overhead, the stars sizzled and the snow seemed to soak up the light from Atkinson's back windows and from the alley lights and the streetlights, shining brightly into Tangletown, as far as any street could be seen.

She took the hand so discreetly offered and for a time attended to nothing but the warmth of their fingers and the sinking and lifting of her heart as they walked along.

She didn't want to go anywhere else.